MAIDEN POINT

J. T. CROFT

First published by Elmfire Press 2022

Copyright ©2022 by J. T. Croft

First edition

ISBN 978-1-8381089-7-7

Cover design by Fay Lane:

www.faylane.com

Elmfire Press

Unit 35590,

PO Box 15113,

Birmingham, B2 2NJ

United Kingdom

www.jtcroft.com

"Grace meets you where you are, but does not leave you where it found you."

Anne Lamott

PREFACE

Maiden Point contains subject matter relating to personality disorder, mental health, and suicide. I make no causal link and the latter is written implicitly, addressing primarily the grief and sensitivity of loss in those that are left behind.

I am grateful for the sensitivity, support, and advice on the topic, from a mental health worker and advance reader who wishes to remain anonymous, but by her and the actions of others, is the world, and the mind, made a better place. I speak from experience, and I dedicate this book to all such people.

Timelines for action and mental health provision in the story have been condensed to create a narrative that hopefully engages whilst reflecting that, in the UK, such pressures on the 'fourth' emergency service are often stretched, but no less undervalued.

Maiden Point is a work of fiction, though no less real or honest in its sentiments, sympathies, and admiration towards those that remain behind, those that are lost, and those that go on to new futures, finding new ways to gain control and live life on their terms.

J. T. Croft
  March 2022

ACKNOWLEDGMENTS

For those health care professionals who continue to be anonymous...angels are not always found in the alcoves of churches.

To my Advance Reader Team, *The Muses*:

Audrey Adamson
Siobhan Allen
Richard Brulotte
Tracey Bryant
Ali Christie
Laura Coveney
Matthew Coxall
Scott Dauman
Karen Furness
Lana Kamennof-Sine
Daniel Nobles
Christine Ruiz Noriega-Hollnbuchner
Jackie Tansky

CONTENTS

CHAPTER 1

She strode from the cool green of the wood into the seaside sun, sweating with the exertion across the tussock and gorse of the headland heath. A salty tear streaked down her cheek, kissing her lipstick-smudged mouth as her senses took stock and savoured the final half mile to the cliff top. The squawk of the circling gulls, rejoicing in the thermals from the radiating granite, beckoned her towards the source of the breaking surf on Maiden's beach far below.

She flicked away a dark lock of damp hair and caught her breath in the centre of a grassy, stone-lined ring. Her heart thumped with the effort, but the long south-west odyssey would soon be over. A final hesitation and attempt by her wandering mind to return to the safety of the wood, and her former life, resurfaced. A glance towards the ocean horizon steadied her nerves and calm purpose descended once more.

No one would ever find her here; she was safe from everyone and everything.

Even *him*; after all he had done.

There would be no more pain or suffering at his hands, only peace and tranquillity with every step taken in this beautiful, isolated spot. It was the perfect place to erase those unhappy moments.

She scanned the empty, early-morning moorland behind and undressed, focussing upon a solitary sea bird, twenty yards away, perched upon a lichen-crusted field post. It raised its beak to the blue sky and gabbled its gull-like grace in anticipation of tasty tourist treasures that might arise from the disrobed woman's clothing. She left the hungry creature's gaze and pulled her long-sleeved T-shirt over her head, brushing the blue-black bruises bleeding into the tattoo on her forearm. Given time, they would heal and disappear.

Just like her.

The sea bird chattered and flew off in empty-bellied annoyance as she removed her sandals and jeans, revealing the pockmarked scalds of cigarette ends upon her inner thigh. Her white skin pricked with the suddenness of comforting heat, now uncovered and visible for the world to witness; no longer hidden in shame or fear of interference from those meaning well. She rolled down the age-stretched elastic, and the underwear slid from her thighs. After unhooking her bra, she raised her arms above her nakedness, and it fell like a fallen standard from a defeated banner-bearer. Her chipped painted toes clenched into the springy moss-green turf, revelling in the sensuous softness as though for the first time, while her clothing lay scattered, cast aside in preference for a future without need or reminder. She left the sanctuary and crunched her way across the encircling bracken and heather.

Her feet protested against the loss of protective leather between soft skin and rough ground until the approach of a turf-lined path gave some respite and made progress a gentler affair.

'Not much farther, now,' she whispered into the air, laden with sea spray and salt, signalling the approach of the headland's end. Nearby, the crooked, wind-worn sign greeted its first visitor of the day:

Danger – Cliff edge liable to subsidence. Stay back.

Approaching the edge, she looked over to the perilous outcropped islands of granite encircled by glittering sand and the low tide of seaweed-strewn saltwater.

It would happen on the seventh wave.

A distant dog barked along the broad miles of beach, demanding another throw of the driftwood from its phone-occupied owner. The first wave rose and sighed into the sheltered sand, disappearing within the tide line as it retreated for another rhythmic pulse.

Further along the coast, the pretty seaside town glinted with promenade-parked cars and the east-facing windows of houses, hotels and holiday lets. Her drive through had been unmarked by the early September slumber of holidaymakers, resting from their migration to the north Cornish coast with all the optimism of a guaranteed Indian summer.

The sea poured back onto the beach for a second time.

Many moulded footprints meandered far along the beach to the foot of the cliff, and she gazed down upon the miniature of a man intent on the detector he held. He swept side to side, searching the higher regions of the rocky shore, head down and oblivious to the outside world in his quest for Roman hoards, ring-pulls, and wedding rings cast from the cliff top.

A large wave rippled to its breaking height and flooded the foreshore, lining the edge of its travel with spent jellyfish, far-travelled flotsam, and foam.

She crept forwards to the very edge, testing the ground for firmness, and returned her gaze to the near-vertical cliff face below. Several narrow ledges existed in the igneous buttress, occupied in part by spent flowering grasses, moss, and the untidy nests of seabirds. The twisted, gnarled jutting of a thickly stemmed and stunted rowan tree lay wedged and melded within a deep crack overlooking the sea like a solitary, forlorn figurehead.

The thin soil surrounding her toes settled, causing a rush of adrenalin to course through her body, and she gripped the edge of the land beneath with her folded toes like a high diver clinging to a board. The stony soil cascaded down, unceremoniously dislodging a preening gull, to shower the next encroaching wave some eighty feet below.

She bit down on her lip, and it bled into her mouth with an overwhelming rust-tasting rawness, as she witnessed the most emotionally unencumbered moments she could recall. Goosebumps, on her girlish skin, raised and rejoiced with the competing sun on her back and the fresh breeze at her belly, adding to her euphoria. She had conquered her fears, and all was set.

She would stay and welcome the penultimate wave.

A distant boat crew waved from far out in the bay, and she replied, steadying herself from the shifting and softening edge at her feet.

The thought of a beautiful face and the moments of hope they had snatched came into her mind. Perhaps now they could finally be together, far removed from the controlling, abusive and vile reach of *him*. She stroked her smooth stomach as the seventh wave bulged out in the bay, giving birth to the largest break of water thus far.

She raised her arms and heard the cry of alarm from the distant walker. Turning to call for his dog, he stood, waving his arms frantically at the woman, warning of the perilous closeness of the edge of the towering cliff. The terrier barked and raced on ahead, impotent to outrun and prohibit the approach of the final wave like a canine King Canute. The detectorist below looked over at the approaching animal, before looking up with sudden realisation. She peered down into his stricken face and then beyond as the seventh wave rose and fell.

Her breath slowed and deepened, becoming the dominant focus within her consciousness. All other noise receded to be replaced solely by the intake and exhalation of air within her chest, the tinnitus of internal stillness, and the faint and intangible murmur of a woman's voice. It hummed a gentle lullaby, broken with whispers of comfort and encouragement. The inexplicable and transient sound continued to baffle her senses as the wave broke higher up the beach, reaching out its spreading foam-tipped fingers to greet and claim her. She balanced and glanced back across the empty headland, searching for the source of the beautiful voice, hearing only the melancholic piping of a hen harrier, high above the heather. Her curiosity and imagination receded, along with all thoughts, as she returned to view the horizon for the final time and lifted a foot over the edge.

'*Do not be afraid,*' it had whispered deep within. '*Let go.*'

She leaned forwards, eyes closed, seduced by the soothing words sent by the sea, and embraced the welcoming suddenness of sun-soaked silence and forgetfulness.

CHAPTER 2

J ames adjusted his tie for the third time and glanced at his watch. The sterile waiting room of the county hospital boardroom was an unwelcoming place to await his fate.

The furious typing of the personal assistant ceased, and she pushed down her glasses, turning to raise an eyebrow at his tapping foot, the unspoken insistence he refrain from the annoying nervousness during her transcription of medical files and appointments.

He clasped a sweaty hand on his knee to dampen the involuntary movement, offering her an apologetic smile.

Normally, the quiet reflective periods of stillness between doctor and patient offered a gentle, non-judgemental space for thoughts and self-reflection to emerge. As he waited for admittance to the fates beyond, the silence in the room offered no such therapeutic value – quite the opposite. James sought for an opening trigger line to engage the stoic and impersonal assistant.

'You have a nice view from your office,' he said, desperate

to take his mind from the closed double doors to the meeting room.

The assistant remained studiously focussed on the screen in front. 'Not much time to look out of it. On a clear day you can see Bodmin Moor.'

'That's a fair way from Truro,' he said.

She hit the delete key sharply and glanced over the top of her spectacles. 'You used to consult at St Jude and Penzance – psychiatry department, wasn't it?'

James detected the past tense, unsure if she was aware of his dismissal or recalling his face from a previous encounter.

'I do,' he said, restoring the present tense. 'I'm based here now but Dr Lewisham has me running around as far as Penzance and the Scillies.'

A notification sounded from the desktop and the secretary adjusted her headset, smiling into the screen like a customer service handler taking a monitored call.

James shot up from the chair, brushed down his trousers, and fiddled with his collar.

'Yes, of course, Dr Fellows. I'll send him straight in.'

James strode to the door, hopeful for any last-minute sign of encouragement from behind the desk. The smile evaporated from her face as quickly as it had appeared.

'You can go in, now.'

He gripped the handle of the door and entered the boardroom beyond.

The bright, long room stretched out, bathed in early-morning sunshine filtered by the row of vertical blinds. They clinked gently like a tuneless wind chime, brushing past each other in the breeze from the open window on the third floor of the hospital. He approached the solitary chair provided in front of the three members tasked by the Trust's board to deliver a verdict. He knew them all: the prim, tiny and ambitious Ms Gayle, Director of Performance Management, and the familiar ponytail and poker-face of his line manager and senior psychiatric lead, Dr Caroline Lewisham. The hospital's director sat centrally, arms resting on the table, his wrinkled hands turning over a ballpoint pen in his manicured fingers. James nodded to his old mentor, who glanced away, avoiding any hint of personal connection or recognition to study the document beneath him. James lowered his eyes with the rebuttal and readied his hands tightly in his lap for proceedings to begin.

'Dr Marshall,' began the director. 'The hospital board convened earlier to review and conclude our response to the complaint raised by the family of Isobel Lee. Your involvement as lead consultant and critical care leader in this case has led to serious implications and consequences for the Trust.'

James raised his eyes from his white fingers. 'My failure led to even greater consequences for her, Dr Fellows.'

'Your extreme contrition has been taken into consideration,' said Fellows, spreading his hands on the desk and reading from the top page before him.

'The warning given by the General Medical Council on your recent conduct does not restrict your practice as a doctor. It is their view that your fitness as a consultant in general psychiatry, as well as your ability to hold a medical licence, is not impaired.' He flicked through several sheets with his shaking hands. 'However, given the seriousness of the incident in question, the Trust is indicating that your conduct, practice and behaviour represents a departure from the standards expected of members of the profession and should not be repeated.'

James shuffled in his seat, trying to gauge the meaning behind the response in the lined face and tired grey eyes.

You haven't decided what to do with me yet, have you?

Fellows continued. 'The hospital has investigated the level of insight into the failings, ascertained a genuine and sincere expression of regret from Dr Marshall, and considered the full apology to the family, the Board, as well as the Royal College of Psychiatrists following their own investigation.'

James raised his clenched fist to stifle an emerging and thoroughly unconvincing cough. Fellows paused and looked up, taking his glasses off and rubbing the arch of his nose. 'You wished to add something?'

'The hospital has ascertained my expression of regret,' said James, turning to fix his gaze firmly on the performance director's rapidly widening eyes, 'but not its own in allowing an understaffed, overstretched and under-resourced critical care team to continue despite repeated attempts—'

Ms Gayle adjusted her glasses with a shaking hand. 'Dr Marshall, your comments are well documented, but the independent panel reviewed the case and progress at the time; Isobel Lee did not require round-the-clock supervision.'

'Close monitoring would have highlighted that she stopped taking the anti-psychotic medication,' he said. 'I asked she be monitored on three separate occasions when the spasms and other side effects she suffered from disappeared; I stepped in to keep her together.'

'And in doing so,' said Ms Gayle, 'you ended up creating a prop she could not live—' She paused, correcting herself in the sharp glance of the director. 'Could not do without.'

James closed his eyes, trying to shut out the room, and the memories begging to be let into his mind like a clawing dog at a closed door.

'You overstepped your authority and took matters into your own hands without consulting your care team or with regard for your welfare, resulting in a medical leave of absence from which you have only recently returned.'

'Yes, but—'

Fellows replaced his spectacles, ignoring the interruption. 'I agree with the conclusion of the investigation that over-work, exhaustion, and your mental state at the time may have significantly contributed to mistakes being made. It also blurred the boundaries of the patient–doctor relationship.' He held up a hand to stifle further discussion and returned to his sheet.

'Your previous good history and the isolated nature of the incident, as well as relevant and appropriate references and testimonials, have been recorded.' He paused, curiously scan-ning the adjoining list and dragging his fingers down the page, pausing momentarily at a line hidden from view. James caught the fleeting sideways glance towards his psychiatric lead, who responded with a conscious urge to peer out of the window through the shifting blinds. James caught the broken reflec-tion of her anxious face peering back as Fellows coughed to attract his attention.

'I also recognise the situation with your wife, leading up to the incident, which you have voluntarily identified may have been a factor in your lack of judgement.'

James shot a glance to the polished panelled pine to his side, forcing the painful memories back to the locked room in his mind.

'If I may, Director?' said Ms Gayle, taking the lengthening silence as an opportunity to interject once again. Fellows folded his arms and sat back in his chair, nodding for her to proceed.

'I'm interested in your readiness to return to the demands and challenges of general psychiatry, especially those more serious cases that you are called upon to oversee.'

'I've concluded a return-to-work consultation—'

'That's not what I mean, Dr Marshall,' she continued, rubbing the ends of her fingers together. 'Are you able to express how this might affect you and those around you, given your recent period of poor mental health?'

'With the greatest of respect, Ms Gayle,' said James, adjusting his collar, 'I've been cleared by my care co-ordinator to return to work, and I don't see why my current mental health is now relevant.'

Fellows held up his hand to interrupt. 'I do, if you are looking to get my approval to practise in this hospital, Dr Marshall.'

James stared at the pen in the director's hand, weaving once more in and out of his fingers. 'How I feel is not contingent on my ability to perform psychiatry.'

The pen halted, poised between the mid and third finger of the director's hand. James glanced over at Dr Lewisham for a way out. She threw him a lifeline.

'James, if I understand Ms Gayle's original question, and the director's more than reasonable follow-up – have you fully come to terms with the events that led to Ms Lee taking her own life as well as your own, thankfully brief, period of ill health?'

James shuffled uncomfortably with the reminder and rotated the band of gold on the third finger of his outstretched left hand.

'I accept I made mistakes and overstepped boundaries, but I stand by my diagnosis – mental exhaustion, or no.'

'Whether the diagnosis was correct is now immaterial, Dr Marshall,' said Ms Gayle. 'One cannot re-examine the mental state of a suicide.'

Dr Lewisham turned sharply. 'I protest!'

Fellows held up his hands to calm the ensuing exchange, but it was James that silenced them in one stroke.

'One cannot say sorry to one either.'

Fellows and Lewisham widened their eyes as Ms Gayle

continued, flushed but unmoved by the previous challenge and subsequent response.

'What we are seeking is reassurance relating to your fitness and judgement, and if I may—' She turned a page and quoted a section of text. '"Reflect on a possessive and over-attachment to cases where life and death are at stake or reputation is challenged".'

James winced with the assertion and clenched his hands on the ends of the armrests. 'I prefer the term "dedication" and my intentions, with or without my crisis care team's consent, were not influenced by any externally influenced pressures, let alone thoughts of my reputation.'

'You are a third-generation psychiatrist whose father was eminent in personality disorder—'

'*Is* eminent,' corrected James. 'He isn't dead yet.'

Ms Gayle twitched with the correction and folded over the document. 'Nevertheless, certain historic grievances raised by previous colleagues, and your return-to-work assessment, note a strong propensity to single-mindedness and inflexibility, possibly related to a drive for recognition and assurance amongst your peers and superiors.'

'You are accusing me of having an inferiority complex?' said James, conscious of being a passive observer. 'My personality flaws are not on trial here.'

'And neither are you,' said Dr Lewisham, glancing at James, and then sternly across at the small figure on the other side.

Fellows leaned forwards to block the two women, worlds apart but separated by mere metres. 'Final question on the subject if you please, Ms Gayle.'

She poured herself a glass of water. James saw her hand steadying a small shake as she brought it to her mouth.

You enjoy creating conflict but can't cope being in the thick of it, he thought. *What won't you do to see me gone?*

She put down the drink. 'Can you remain detached, open-minded, and objective to other diagnoses that conflict with your own when your authority is challenged? Yes or no.'

Fellows repeatedly clicked and re-clicked the end of his pen, hovering over the document below, waiting for a response. James's leg trembled, and he clasped the thigh, eager to prevent the wayward limb from silently but honestly answering on his behalf.

He became aware of the lengthening silence and the widening eyes of Caroline Lewisham, urging him for the right response, truthful or otherwise.

'The question is hypothetical, but the answer you are seeking from me, as a medical doctor, is yes.' James released the grip on his leg and released his shoulders against the hard wooden seat rest. Dr Lewisham relaxed back into her chair, prematurely, as James continued.

'But, if you are asking me, as a human being, if I can walk away when someone is falling apart, then the answer is no.'

Ms Gayle shook her head with the unlooked-for amendment to her question but was curtly cut off in her response.

'You have undertaken the additional training prescribed by the hospital willingly, and voluntarily,' said Dr Lewisham, rising to her full seated height, 'and I accept you have made strides that the situation will not arise again.'

'It will not,' replied James, drawing in and releasing a long, drawn-out breath.

She took out a pen and signed the document before her. 'You will be issued with a letter of advice, outlining the mechanism to provide helpful guidance to you on the protocols surrounding your own obligations to care for your mental health, and another to provide a refresher on patient–doctor relationships.'

James leaned forwards, gripping the ends of the chair. 'There was no relationship.'

'Unfortunately,' interjected Fellows, 'that is not how Isobel Lee saw things, not until it was painfully clear and too late.'

'Don't you think I know that?' said James, raising his voice. 'All the facts led me to a conclusion of Ganser syndrome – the mimicking of schizophrenia to gain attention, her previous physiological dependency on alcohol, the visual pseudo-hallucinations, and—'

Fellows slapped his pen on the table. 'Our questioning relates to your inability to consider all other possibilities despite them staring you in the face or being raised by your care team. We are also well aware of the symptoms, Dr Marshall, along with your misdiagnosis.'

'Misdiagnosis?' exclaimed James, rising to his feet. 'With respect, my report and findings are open to review, but I stand by them. What is unexplained is why she committed suicide – Ganser doesn't lead to—'

'Then it can't have been Ganser then, can it!' barked Fellows, rising and slamming his fist down on the table. 'Your cognitive dissonance or professional arrogance is still refusing to accept the facts – there hasn't been a single suicide-attributed case in your professional lifetime.'

James sat, face flushed from the dramatic dressing down, conscious of the performance director tapping a forefinger against her lips with the merest hint of cat-like contentment. Fellows continued unabated and unchallenged.

'Your failure to recognise your own temporary impairment and blinkered adherence to putting patients into your father's famous pigeonholes, not to mention the misguided allure of working on an extremely rare and often misunderstood disorder, has indeterminably contributed to a young woman losing her life. She formed an attachment that you were too naive and late to realise while you ignored all the other symptoms not conforming to your initial diagnosis. The mood swings, the dramatic need for attention, the intense, unstable emotions. She wasn't faking it like you see with Ganser, Dr Marshall, she was suffering from mild schizophrenia with a complex "cluster b" histrionic personality disorder; you played right into her condition by forming a bond she believed to be something more.'

Doubt suddenly overwhelmed him, and James reeled from the implications of the counter-diagnosis. 'Right until the moment I told her it wasn't,' he whispered, burying his head in his hands, 'and she poisoned herself.'

'Exactly.' Fellows lifted the pen and looked across at Ms Gayle for her opinion. She curtly shook her head. Dr Lewisham witnessed the deteriorating end game and coughed to attract Fellows' attention.

'While this may be an irregular suggestion,' she said, 'subject to your approval, I propose that a period of reflective and monitored probation be prescribed in cases that Dr Marshall would be assigned to relating to personality disorder and suicidal tendency. I would ensure he adheres to the work time directive, and our well-being policy, to prevent future over-working or obsessive behaviour in the role.'

Fellows turned sharply, studying the lead psychiatrist.

'I understand there is a historical precedent for this...' she said, staring poker-faced in reply. James glanced over, face flushed, as his advocate remained calm and continued to hold the gaze of her superior, challenging him to overrule the suggestion. It was Fellows who turned away first, and James saw the strained look on his face, portraying some conflict at play. Dr Lewisham relaxed her eyes and continued.

'As the head of department, I propose a one month—'

Ms Gayle interrupted. 'I propose we demonstrate that there are consequences and allow some closure for the Lee family. We need to show we understand everything they spoke so passionately about to the Board has been listened to. They insist on some consequence in the matter – as do I.'

'Meaning?' said Fellows, turning to his right.

She wiggled her fingers like a spider weaving a web. 'I am not convinced of Dr Marshall's readiness to return to front-line psychiatry, not in his current role.'

Fellows stared at the empty signature line on the release form and turned to the doctor on his left. 'The Board has decreed that our decision needs to be unanimous.'

'I disagree,' said Dr Lewisham. 'James is our most highly qualified consultation-liaison psychiatrist and counselling psychologist. He is our specialist in the diagnosis and management of personality disorders that are co-morbid with general medical and surgical illness. A departure of this magnitude would create extreme caseload reallocation and loss of expertise at this hospital when we can least afford to do so. I will provide the assurance that Dr Marshall's conduct will exceed the expectations of his profession and the stan-dards of this hospital while safeguarding the hospital's obliga-tions towards the mental health of its staff.'

Ms Gayle smoothed the front of her skirt and pursed a faint and victorious smile. 'A reassignment to St Jude might be worth considering to protect the reputation of the Trust and this hospital, to allow confidence and competence to be demonstrated, and allow an appropriate level of reflection for Dr Marshall and all concerned.' She pivoted towards him, and James realised a well-constructed backup position was revealing itself. 'The good doctor, himself, has informed us of the current mental health staffing crisis there...'

'That's harsh, Deborah,' said Dr Lewisham. 'I need him here—'

'Is it, Caroline?' said Ms Gayle, triumphant. 'We all worked remotely for much of last year.'

She took out her pen, flicked to her release page, and glared at the woman opposite.

'Well?' said Fellows, turning to hear her defeated whisper.

'Agreed.'

James sat impotently, watching his immediate fate being sealed as the director lifted his pen and clicked the ballpoint into action.

'It's both your hinds I'll be after, Caroline, if he screws up again.'

CHAPTER 3

The warm, red brick partition wall of the hospital garden at St Jude glowed against the late-summer salvia in the midmorning sun. James sat on the silvered, time-worn bench and looked past the memorial plaques, penstemons and play equipment overlooking the seagull-crowded rooftops below, to the bobbing boats in the bay. He picked at a pastry, scattering crumbs to the watchful and hungry sparrows.

'I heard you were back,' said an approaching voice from the closing staff door behind him.

'If only everything ran as efficiently as a hospital grapevine, Mike,' said James, extending his right hand. 'How've you been?'

The smartly dressed doctor shook it warmly. 'Good, but more importantly how are you?'

'I'm fine.'

'As bad as that?' said Mike. He shuffled his feet and stretched his arms over his shoulder, breathing in the fresh outside air. 'Have the antidepressants I prescribed helped?'

'I've stopped taking them, though in hindsight following yesterday's debacle, I wish I hadn't.'

'Considering your reticence a few months ago to take anything at all,' said Mike, sitting down beside him, 'I'd still say that was progress.' The genial face of his friend turned to avoid his own. 'Caroline's here.'

James caught sight of the returning tourist boat as it meandered across the glistening waters to the narrow quay. 'I know. I'm seeing her in thirty minutes. She fought tooth and nail for me, but a major talking-to is on the cards. She pulled out a historical precedent which threw Fellows a curveball; I think that's the only thing that saved me from being dismissed.'

'She should have been a lawyer,' said Mike. 'She always had a soft spot for you.'

James shifted uncomfortably. 'I let her down and screwed up yesterday, making a right fool of myself in front of Gayle and Fellows; I should just have told them what they wanted to hear, but my pride and mouth wouldn't let me.'

'Want to talk about it?' said Mike, twisting round to look into his eyes. He removed his lanyard and name tag to a top shirt pocket. 'Grapevine mode is now off.'

James nudged into the doctor's side. 'Not really. Baring my soul seems to expose further inadequacies and self-doubt.'

'Isn't that the whole point?' said Mike, nudging back.

James shrugged. 'I'm going to be on a very short leash for the time being. It could be better, but I deserve worse.'

'If you don't want to talk to me, then I can recommend the new counsellor, Harriet Swanson; she's extremely competent.'

James shook his head. 'I'd talk to you if I could. I know you can be trusted, Mike, especially after what happened between Karen and me.'

Mike sat back and crossed his legs. 'The four of us – you, me, Jory, and Karen – have been friends for thirty-odd years since school. When she told me, I was a complete wreck; God knows what it must have been like for you.'

'I think in some ways you had it harder, keeping her secret from me, and I don't blame you for that,' said James, rotating a golden ring on the third finger of his left hand. 'It was what she wanted, and she put you between a rock and a hard place – I never properly thanked you for being there for her when I wasn't.'

'You had a lot on your plate, James. Don't beat yourself up.'

'You were always fond of her when we were growing up. Do you remember running around after her in caves and crevices over at those cliffs, searching for treasure none of us ever truly believed was there?' James looked along the miles of beach to the hazy mist of the distant headland. 'Karen was always fascinated by that old story, and I promised her I'd find her that jewel one day if she'd kiss me as a deposit. I never fulfilled my end of the bargain, though she kept hers.'

Mike followed his gaze and chuckled. 'Sorry to burst your bubble but she hedged her bets with Jory and me; she was the first girl either of us had kissed, and in Jory's case, probably the last.'

James felt the tension momentarily recede as he let out a long sought for and much-needed laugh. 'You are a tonic, Mike; you really are.'

The GP wiped the comic tears from his eyes. 'We clambered over those boulders every long, low tide before we gave up and buried ball-bearings to annoy the metal detectorists from out of town.' He held out his empty hands. 'We didn't find any legendary treasure either. It's a bit like love – you can't find what doesn't exist in the right location, at the right time, no matter how much you look for it.'

James slapped him on the knee. 'Perhaps she should have married a poet or philosopher, like you?'

Mike stretched out his legs and squinted into the bright September sun. 'To go off with the brilliant and handsome Dr Marshall at any moment? No thanks.'

'You forgot flawed, obsessive, stubborn and lacking in confidence,' said James, casting aside the remnants of the uneaten pastry. The birds fluttered away before returning to peck furiously at the unexpected feast.

'I'd add honest and loyal to my original description to balance out those other traits.'

'I appreciate it, Mike, even if I can't see it. You still have my back, and that of my father.' James turned to point at the polished brass plaque on the bench.

Dr Joanne Marshall, St Jude.
1947 – 1982

'You've been keeping Mum's memorial tidy since the old man went into care. Thank you.'

'It's part of our arrangement,' said Mike. 'He agrees not to argue with me, as his general practitioner, or suggest I don't know what the hell I'm doing, and I look after the bench.'

'How is he?'

'Okay, all things considered,' said Mike, bridging his hands and resting them on his chin as he leaned forwards to study the sparrows. 'He's busy with his jigsaws and genealogy when he's not critiquing you and your personality faults.'

James smiled. 'The latter must keep him busy.'

'You read the latest prognosis I sent last week?' said Mike, glancing away at a bumblebee crawling through the hood of a scarlet salvia.

'Six to eight weeks,' replied James, checking his watch. He observed the valuable and finite passage of time ticking away. 'How did he take it?'

Mike pursed his lips and folded his arms. 'He insisted on checking the medical file for typos and inconsistencies.'

James snorted. 'He's still the Professor Edward Marshall we all know, then.'

A ice cream van zoomed past, chased by several children on mountain bikes and e-scooters.

'Shouldn't they be in school?' said James.

'That's rich,' said Mike. 'Considering we bunked off whenever we heard the chimes. Those months of school holidays never seemed to end.'

'Months ago, all our lives were different. What I wouldn't give to go back and crack heads with myself.'

'Regret is a powerful teacher,' said Mike, leaning forwards and rubbing his hands. 'It's probably none of my business, but now is the time to put things right between you and the old man. He seems open to the idea, providing his sense of superiority was maintained and he felt as though he had the upper hand.'

'Nothing like going to war knowing you've already lost, Mike.'

'Even a truce is better than conflict, James.'

'I guess I'll have plenty of time on my hands to think about it.'

'Well, don't take too long. Are you staying over at the old house?'

James nodded. 'Unless the locks were changed when he moved out. I'll need to bring some stuff back from Truro if I'm spending the rest of the year here.'

Mike got up and retrieved a small plastic object from his back pocket. 'I hoped I might bump into the final member to make it into the middle-aged club.' He extended the worn, moulded figure to James. 'Happy fortieth birthday for last week. Hopefully, life begins again for you and all that.'

'It's your Chewbacca,' said James. 'My goodness, you're giving me your most prized possession as a kid.'

'Do you remember when the four of us used to bunk off to that old ruin in the plantation on the down and play Star Wars or knights of the round table?'

James nodded and looked into his friend's face, raised to the horizon, reliving halcyon summer days out of school.

'I haven't been up to that place in donkey's years,' he said, rubbing his finger over the grooves in the alien's moulded plastic fur. 'I doubt I could remember where it was.'

A police car pulled up in the lay-by beyond the low brick of the roadside wall.

'Speaking of truancy...' said Mike.

A stocky, middle-aged officer clambered ungracefully out of the driver's seat. He adjusted his tightly fitting tabard vest, hoisted his trousers up, and strode across the road with an exaggerated swagger.

'Here comes Dirty Harry,' murmured James.

'The only magnum Jory will be dealing with today is a chocolate-coated ice cream on a stick,' whispered Mike, stifling a grin as the policeman approached.

'Morning, ladies,' said the sergeant, leaning on the wall and nodding towards his old friends. 'Heard you were back, Jimbo.'

James rose from the bench and wandered over to clasp the officer's extended hand. 'Good to see you, Jory. How's Gotham this morning?'

'Don't ask,' he said, placing his fingers through the loops on his vest. 'I sharpened some pencils down at the station earlier, issued a ticket to a littering tourist, and evicted a van-lifer parked up at the old telegraph pole on Maiden Moor; it's a dangerous world out there.'

'Are you still going up there most mornings to spy on the pot-smoking nudists minding their own business?' said Mike.

'Indecency and drug taking are criminal offences, Dr Trebarr, and besides,' he said, scratching his stubbled chin, 'it's the quickest way over here in the morning from Cennen Bridge. By the way, I've just had to deal with one of your patients.'

'Oh?' said Mike.

'I had to sort out old Tom again, loitering outside the off-licence on Clipper Street.'

'Did you take him back to the hostel?'

'What's the point? He'll only walk back to the shop. I dropped him off at the lifeboat slipway bench with a can of orange and a sausage sandwich to keep him quiet from his talk of secrets and such. It'll take him a good half an hour to find anyone else to bother.'

'Tom Cotter?' asked James. 'He's still alive?'

'He was only in his forties when he pulled you from that deflating dinghy out there.' Mike turned to look out into the bay.

'Well, I'm not picking him up every other hour and having him stink out the car any more than is necessary,' said Jory, folding his arms and scowling at a seagull perched on the dormant blue light on the roof of his police car.

'Which alter was he showing?' said Mike.

'Alter?' said Jory. 'What do you mean?'

'Which alternate personality,' said James. 'Which version of Tom is fronting today?'

Jory plucked at his lips until the penny dropped. 'Smelly, sweary, thirsty Tom.'

'I'll check on him and his meds first thing in the morning,' said Mike, 'though he might fall under James's wing now.'

Jory wrinkled his face in delight. 'So, it's true, you're coming back for good?'

James shrugged. 'Just for the time being, while I work

some things out. You might as well hear it from me as anyone else.'

'We'll have to meet up, just like old times.' He glanced at the toy figure in James's hand and back to Mike's look of mock innocence. 'You told me you lost that thirty years ago.'

Mike shrugged. 'James joined the forty club last week, and now I wish the force was somewhere else and not dawdling about here.'

'I'm jealous,' said Jory. 'You can officially have a mid-life crisis now—'

The words died on his lips and James momentarily caught the gritted teeth and clenched eyes of the GP before he turned away.

Jory look puzzled and then covered his eyes in embarrassment. 'Sorry, mate. Foot in mouth; I didn't mean—'

James pulled down the policeman's cap to shield the rising colour in the round, kindly face. 'It's okay; I'm doing fine.'

Jory recovered his blushes and removed his cap, wiping his sleeve against the receding bristles on his head. 'Anyway, I'm not dawdling. You ladies will be interested to know that I am on my way to investigate what will probably end up being local front-page news.'

'How so?' said Mike.

'Some report of a naked woman, off her head on pot or mushrooms probably, roaming the outskirts of town.' He slapped his hands together, rubbing them vigorously with a grin. 'It's a tough job but someone's got to do it.'

They watched as the policeman strode back to his car and got in awkwardly. Raising a reversed middle finger in offensive, well-rehearsed and inappropriate farewell, he raced off towards the suburbs of the sleepy seaside town with a beep of his horn.

'I still can't believe the person in charge of our civic security is Jory Richards,' said James.

'You mean the boy who wrote out his hundred lines in indelible ink on the bonnet of the geography teacher's yellow Triumph Spitfire?' said Mike. 'That was a detention to remember.'

'God help him, and us all, if he finds himself in any serious trouble.' James stared down at the toy. 'I was planning on going to see Karen later; perhaps I should give this to her? She always had a thing for Wookiees.'

Mike smiled. 'It seems right that it stays with one of us four.' He shuffled, avoiding eye contact. 'Just thought you should know that the Lee family put up the permanent memorial to their daughter last week. It's pretty close to—'

James wiped his hands down his face. 'It's been nearly five months, Mike. I'll need to deal with it at some point once I've got my head straight and I've built up some resilience.'

'You want some company – Dutch courage and all that?'

'No, thanks. I'll maybe spend some time reflecting on things; it's going to be an eventful day,' he said, glancing down at the buzzing hospital pager on his belt.

'I have to go – it's Caroline, and I'm gearing up to make amends to one person at a time.'

CHAPTER 4

'What the hell did you think you were playing at?' said Caroline Lewisham, scattering sheets and unsecured stationery across the table. She leaned towards James, who sat downcast and motionless like a scolded schoolboy. 'And arguing with Cameron Fellows and Deborah Gayle, for heaven's sake. Even I don't have the balls to do that, so you had no chance, famous father or no.'

James raised his hand and began to speak.

'I'm not finished yet,' she interrupted. 'You realise he was all set to sign off on your release back into practice with us, but no, you had to go act all "I'm still convinced I didn't get it all wrong". Good grief, James, we gave you three chances to say what you still can't admit to yourself. You only had to say what they wanted to hear.'

'I admitted I made mistakes,' he said. 'What you wanted to hear was that I got it wrong because I was ill and made the wrong diagnosis, and I'm sorry, Caroline, I can't.'

'An expression of regret is nothing without the ability to grow and learn from it. All you had to do was admit you took too much on and went too deep with Isobel Lee to resolve her many issues.'

'Isn't that what the ultimate objective is?'

'No. People cannot be helped by obsessive psychiatrists who cannot disassociate themselves from their work, no matter what other issues are in play with their life. Not everyone has a solution, despite what your father preached at Oxford.'

'He and his cronies were on the list of advocates, weren't they?' said James. 'Don't deny it – he saved me from an embarrassing dismissal and now I have to kiss his arse—'

'It's my backside you should be kissing,' said Caroline, stabbing a finger towards him. 'I oversaw every name on that list, all genuine in their desires to see a brilliant man saved from his own blinkered arrogance or ignorance – you choose.'

'Where did you dig up that historical precedent? Fellows turned pale when you mentioned it.'

'Your father mentioned it to me,' she said, raising her hands upright and looking to the ceiling as though seeking divine help. 'To be used as a once-only "get out of jail free card", and guess what – you landed right on that Monopoly square, that's for sure.'

James pursed his lips. 'Even when I fail, he has to catch me to make sure the reputation and legacy of the Marshall name are preserved.'

Caroline sat down, dragging the noisy chair across the tiled floor. Her hands quivered with the confrontation, and she threw open the leather-bound file.

'This is how it's going to be. You will base yourself here, while I re-assign your Truro cases to Roscoe.'

'Roscoe?' exclaimed James. 'He's not qualified to manage all of those.'

'He's ready to take on more challenging patients, and he's proven to be quite useful during your absence.'

'I bet he has.' James kicked at the table leg like a petulant child.

Caroline forced a smile and returned to the document in her quivering hand. 'You will report to me on the outstanding cases you have in priority order, including those local enough that need attending to here. We can discuss which patients can be dealt with remotely, but you are staying out of the way for the time stipulated to keep Miss Prissy Pants and the Lee family happy; do I make myself clear?'

'They are demoting me, in all but name.'

'Deborah Gayle has had her full and bitter entitlement, and I don't like it any more than you do.'

'She hates men – that's well known, if impossible to prove.'

Caroline crossed her arms and cleared her throat. 'That's another misdiagnosis on your part. She hates anyone *close* to men in authority, me included if you hadn't noticed.'

'What have you or I done to upset her, anyway?'

She slammed her hands on the table. 'If you had been paying attention, you would have heard that Fellows is planning to retire now that the fallout from this case has been dealt with. The fight for succession is materialising, pieces are being placed on the board. It's politics, James, not medicine, that is at play.'

'She wants the job and so do you?'

Caroline shrugged and distracted herself by collecting the dispersed and wayward pens and paper from the floor. 'Considering this new situation, and the prospect of not having to deal with rogue psychiatrists who should be at home recovering from nervous exhaustion, I'm damn well thinking about it.' She breathed out, releasing a pressure-valve of pent up emotion, flicking her eyes across to his own. 'Either way, she's sorting the wheat from the chaff, James, dividing and conquering. Now stay out of it, shut up and listen.'

James folded his arms and lowered his chin to his chest.

'The hospital concludes there has been a significant but isolated departure from good medical practice, and there is no significant cause for concern based on our assessment of your recent performance and your recent return from mental health leave.'

'But?'

Caroline frowned and continued. 'However, it has been decided that a minimum period of three months' supervision at St Jude Hospital would benefit you and raise confidence among the Trust in your readiness to return to full, frontline duties.'

'I'm going to appeal.'

'Well, you can do so without my backing,' said Caroline.

'You won't support me?'

'After yesterday's performance,' she said, stabbing the document before her, 'I pretty well agree with most of what is written. You came back too early, James; I still think you should have taken more time to come to terms with—'

He exhaled and stretched his fingers. 'I'm worse when I'm moping about, not at work. Look, I screwed up yesterday, but you misunderstand me. I want to appeal because of what you are putting on the line, especially considering your possible application for the top job – you heard what Fellows said about taking your hide. He's bound to have a big say in who follows in his majestic wake.'

Caroline shook her head and put her head in her hands. 'If I hadn't stretched out my neck, he would have had no alternative but to remove you. Either way, it weakens me and does you no favours. He might favour me for the role and be soon out of the way playing golf and tending his gerberas, but he won't overrule his performance director, not in front of me or you; he came up through the ranks in the same way via your father, remember?'

A flush crept across his cheeks and he glanced with sudden interest at the lines of diminishing letters on the wall-mounted medical eye test chart. 'I don't know what to say.'

'Then just listen,' she said. 'Deal with this, and what has happened. Come to terms with it, I mean fully come to terms with it, in familiar surroundings with friends and support around you. I need you—'

James looked up as she corrected herself. 'This hospital needs you. You are a brilliant man, the most highly qualified guy we have in mental health support services.' She hesitated and glanced out of the window. 'You need to stop striving to be perfect and trying so hard to please everyone but yourself.'

'Well, we both know who to blame for that.'

'Your father was one of the best teachers I ever had,' said Caroline, turning back and rubbing her eyes. 'I learned from him, just as you did, but the difference is – I never wanted to be him, or, dare I say it, better than him. You know what they say about moths being drawn to a bright flame, right?'

'You're lucky. I had my father morning, noon, and night, as well as Fellows, taking it out on me at Oxford for whatever caused the rift between them.'

'I thought Fellows was your father's star pupil?'

'He was. "Uncle Cameron" used to come round and drop off some jigsaw or other to occupy me while they locked themselves away for hours.'

Caroline sniffed and rolled her eyes. 'Parenting by proxy; that explains a lot...'

'I was around six when he stopped coming and didn't see him again until my final year – I had to work twice as hard as everyone else for being my father's son; he's just trying to get back at my father by kicking me instead.'

'I disagree and he was ready to sign off before you opened your mouth. I do agree that the acrimony is still mutual if your father gave me that curveball to use; it saved you from the boot this time though, didn't it?'

'Did he say what or who the precedent relates to?'

'No. Even if he had told me, I couldn't reveal it, even to you despite our *fluid* confidential exchanges of information on occasion.'

James weaved his hand through his hair, tugging on the dark lengths as though to anchor his emotions. 'And here was I thinking my father would do something for me as an act of altruism. I'm really grateful now; thanks for putting this in perspective for me, Caroline.' He stamped his feet on the floor like a sulking child.

Caroline sniggered at his moody, finely lined face, blue-eyed beneath his now messy dark curls, flecked with the first signs of grey. 'I'm glad you appear to be returning to your petulant self again; it's a good sign.' She cleared her throat and softened her voice. 'It's okay to step out of his shadow and be yourself, now more than ever. Settle for less than being the eminent Edward Marshall, but more than everyone else if that's what drives you. God knows you should have had my job long before it became available.'

'I wasn't ready for it,' said James. 'You were.'

'Rubbish,' said Caroline. 'You felt obliged to leave the way open after—'

'Go on, say it.'

Caroline shook her head and bit her cheek.

'After we slept together, isn't that what you were going to say?' he said, cocking his head to one side.

'I can't believe you are bringing this up now.'

'I'm not,' he said. 'You are.'

James rose and headed across the room to stoop in front of her chair like a knight begging a boon from a queen. 'I'm sorry for all this mess I've dropped you in now, and if I screwed with your head back then. I'm also sorry it took me this long to apologise and say thank you for your discretion following that night two years ago.'

Caroline lifted her bag and busied herself with something unimportant within. 'I could see you regretted it, so I didn't make things awkward for you and Karen.'

'Did *you* regret it?' asked James.

Caroline fixed him with an astonished look. Her mobile phone buzzed, and she looked down despondently at the screen with a mixed sigh of relief at the distraction. 'I need to take this.'

'Fellows?' said James, rising to his feet.

She shook her head. 'Get back to work, stay out of trouble, and be ready to be our representative on the Q&A panel at the college halls in London in a fortnight – I've just nominated you for it.'

James rolled his eyes and hung his shoulders in mock teenage angst. 'Thanks, awfully.'

Caroline rotated the screen.

Edward Marshall calling.

'As payment for being your bloody go-between...' she said, flicking him away with a rapid hand gesture to leave the room. 'Here we have a dying man calling me to find out about the events yesterday because he can't talk to his own son about it.'

'I'll sort it soon, I promise,' said James unconvincingly.

'I hope so, for both your sakes,' she said, pointing to the door. 'Before it's too late, and you can't change things; just like with Karen.'

CHAPTER 5

The church bell of St Jude chimed for four o'clock. James left the broken sunbeams and recent rain puddles of the steep, hedged lane and lifted the smooth, salt-rusted latch to enter the quiet country churchyard. The old stone sanctuary was perched high above the town, a Saxon sentinel set above the sea for the sufferance and salvation of the settlement below. The base of the squat tower secured an old, galvanised tap, dripping as it had done for as long as James could remember. Each droplet resonated into a rusted and leaking metal watering can, joining the echoes of the church bell on the breeze. A mossy stain streaked down the glistening granite foundation stone like an emerald tear, weeping for the souls whose floral tributes it watered every Sunday morning. High above, the stones changed to newer blocks of stone, a parochial patchwork from long-forgotten repairs against the elements of the past five hundred years.

Stepping off the weed-compacted gravel path, he descended the strimmer-strewn grass between the more recent memorials and mounds of the newer plots. There were several fresh graves, and he paused at a temporary wooden cross commemorating a distant acquaintance to glance over at the glistening black marble, the sunlight setting off the sparkling mica and gold lettering of the grave. He approached to see the once irregular stone-filled spoil surrounding the base of the new installation now lying smooth, grassing over in the final act of accepting the body of a woman before her time as part of the natural cycle of life and death.

Karen Marshall nee Jackson
Beloved wife
Died April 21st, 2021, aged 38
"Where there is great love there are always miracles."

James stood in front of the stone, gazing at the recently placed flowers in the urn, wondering who had visited without leaving a note or tribute. He had brought her flowers in life and now chastised himself for not bringing them regularly in death. Leaning against the drying stalks was the small woven figure of a corn dolly, a small, polished sea glass bead bulging like an unborn where its stubby belly would be. The curiously crafted thing, with its tufted hair made from shortened ears of corn, seemed an odd thing to leave behind, but it reminded him of his own offering. He reached into his back pocket and withdrew a water bottle along with the toy figure, bending its stiff legs to sit alongside and beneath the seed heads of crackled corncockle and chamomile at the headstone's base.

'I'm back in St Jude, Karen, and I don't know what to do,' he murmured. 'I feel like a pinball, bouncing into mistakes one after another, and I feel so guilty all the time. If I could just begin to put things right...'

Stooping to touch the laser-etched cameo of her smiling face, he pinched his eyes to stem the flow of tears.

'Why didn't you and Mike both tell me sooner?'

A solitary rook stirred from an overhanging windswept oak, landing some distance away on a new and unfamiliar daisy-white slab of Cornish dalmatian granite. The bird squawked and hopped among the fresh flowers and soft toys, pecking at the metallic ribbon of a flaccid, foiled helium balloon. The name could not be discerned, but James knew his guilt and shame lay buried there along with the body of Isobel Lee.

The lactic acid burned in his thighs, but he punished himself by remaining stooped on his haunches, hand resting against the eternally engraved portrait of his wife.

'I can't say sorry to her yet, Karen. One step at a time.'

A prowling cat put flight to the bird, and it hopped into a venerable yew that stood beyond a great mass of untended hedge separating the older gravestones of St Jude's churchyard. James rose, shaking his legs free from pins and needles, and rejoined the path leading to the opening in the shrubby pittosporum. He glanced back at the pale gravestone for a heartbeat before plunging into the enclosed wilderness of wind- and weather-flattened wildflowers bisected by roughly mown grass paths.

His shoes became damp with dew in the older quadrant as he stooped beneath the gnarled, overgrown orchard trees to reach his mother's memorial.

The carved open marble book lay among the long grass. He glanced past the recent gold re-lettering of her name to the blank stone page on the right, awaiting its final chapter and his father's name for nigh on forty years. The recent and short-lived shower had washed the fine, dusty sand from the smooth surface and James caught his haggard reflection as he fought against the idea of losing the only parent he had known. He stared back, wondering how long it would be before the reflective qualities were chiselled away to leave only words and not mirrored expressions of future remorse. Their petty arguments and fallouts suddenly seemed of little worth or lasting consequence. He thought on Caroline's blunt but well-chosen parting words as she hurried him from the room to talk to the man who would soon lie here.

He took out his phone and scanned his empty call log. Even the missed calls from his father had now stopped – a once constant reminder of his fortnightly obligations to visit.

He raised the water bottle to his mouth and swigged several mouthfuls.

A fleeting movement through the opposite hedge caught his attention, and the rook launched itself raucously into the sky with the disturbance. Someone was beyond, out of sight and heavily out of breath.

'Hello?' he called, weaving through the tall, damp grass to the slim, leafy opening. The oldest part of the churchyard lay sheltered within, like a private outdoor room reserved for the leaning crosses and time-worn memento mori of long-forgotten generations. A loud precursory clunk from the tower signalled the quarter-hour chime as James scanned the overgrown hemlock, teasel and bramble searching for the source of the scurrying and panting.

Conscious of the possibility of some sudden childish prank, he parted the brittle milk thistles and flattened the tall nettles to force a path. Lifting his arms to pass, he listened to the great gulps of air drawn in somewhere among the dense, waist-high grass beyond. He stubbed a toe against a fallen, nameless stone, making for the remnants of a taller memorial bearing the slaking skin of a circled sandstone cross. The chime lingered within the enclosure as the rapid breathing slowed, becoming replaced with broken snatches of humming, attuning the key to that of the fading bell. With every step forward, the song-like sound grew more confident and replaced the gasping entirely, realising its full haunting melody.

The broken cross drew closer, shielded from the worst of the elements by a wide, dark perimeter of dense hawthorn and briar that formed the churchyard boundary. Even as children, the four of them had dared only brief, terrified incursions into the gloomy space. Compelled by some forfeit to rush in, touch the cross, and return to the safety and relieved faces of the other three, they had never lingered. James turned to look back at the narrow opening, confirming the direct route back to safety should the spriggan, witch or other child-eating creature of their childhood fears prove to exist after all.

The thinning grass ahead stirred, and he stepped above the broken remains of another grave, listening to the lullaby, lured onwards to outstretch his hand to touch the cross. His urge to flee back to the safety of the hedge materialised as he peered down at the back of the cross, marked centrally with a diamond cut into eight faint segments. Something fleshy slithered at his feet and he jumped back to see a pair of grubby, pale, deeply scratched arms clasped around the stone base, locked in a desperate embrace. The painted nails dug deeply into the heavily soiled palms, pulsing, like the kneading of a kitten against its mother's belly even as the gentle tune began again. For a moment, the childish fears of monsters and malevolence consumed his rationale.

His medical training kicked in and he twisted around the grave to look upon something altogether more surprising.

A naked woman lay on her side, grimy, unclean, and severely dehydrated. Her tucked legs burned and bled with countless scouring rakes, the soles of her heavily blistered feet were blackened and peppered with thorn, and her long, dark hair streaked in mascara-like strands over her sunburned face and neck. Noticing James for the first time, she writhed closer to the cross, clinging to the stony base, and looked up with desperate blue, bloodshot eyes. The flawed sapphires flitted about wildly as James hurriedly removed his jacket to cover her feral nakedness.

'I'm a doctor,' he said, rescuing his phone and fumbling with the keypad. 'I will not harm you. Can you understand me?'

The woman nodded, rubbing her matted head against the inside of her grubby upper arm. She withdrew in shock as the device connected to the call centre.

'Emergency services,' said the handler. 'What service do you require?'

'Ambulance and police,' replied James, performing a cursory examination to ascertain whether the woman was critically injured. 'This is the acting psychiatric lead at St Jude Hospital, NHS 1267895, and I'm at the far end of the local churchyard at the top of Tinkers Lane.'

'Can you state the nature of the emergency?'

The woman relaxed but clung on, as James lifted her feet to discover the skin was cracked and bleeding.

'Female; Caucasian; dark, long hair; early thirties; severely dehydrated, with subcutaneous lacerations to skin and feet; she's confused, suffering from shock or some degree of mental impairment.'

'Just bear with me and I'll connect you straight through to St Austell—'

'That's too far,' he said. 'I need the ambulance from Truro, right now!'

The handler paused. 'ETA thirty-three minutes – it's en route back from—'

James hung up and pressed the speed dial. 'Come on, come on!' he said as the call connected.

'Not you again,' said the jovial voice of the policeman. 'I'm still annoyed about Chewbacca—'

'Shut the hell up, Jory, and get yourself up to St Jude Church, near the back where we used to play at prodding the witch's stone. I need you to fetch Mike and the full emergency treatment kit. Pull some strings and call for the community ambulance from Newquay to meet us at the hospital just in case the Truro one—'

'Whoa, slow down, mate,' he replied. 'You been taking too many pills or something?'

James looked into the wide eyes of the woman. She stared back like a newborn doe, oblivious to the pain and distress of her situation, curiously listening to the conversation as one recognising the language but not the meaning of the words. She ceased humming and licked at her cracked lips.

'M...Marshall?' she croaked, coughing from the dryness in her throat.

James nodded, pinning the phone between his cheek and left shoulder and carefully removing the buckshot of thorns and burrs from her legs, protruding from the jacket covering her sun-reddened torso.

'No,' she murmured, 'but you are like to him...'

'What is it?' said Jory, his response barely audible over the wail of his car's siren. 'Are you all right?'

'I found your wandering woman,' said James. 'The naked one. Now hurry and grab whoever is on call from the hospital on the way up.'

'If you are winding me up, I'll—'

James cast his phone aside and reached out to his water bottle, twisted off its cap, and pressed it into the woman's mouth. She gagged and spat out the water before James tilted back the bottle, allowing her to sip at the remaining liquid dribbling from the bottle.

'Steady,' he said. 'Can you tell me your name?'

He watched her eyes fix upon the only remaining word on the inscription.

'Dene,' she mouthed, as though unsure. She relaxed one hand and traced a grubby finger across the worn four-lettered word. 'Everything is changed. What year is this?'

'It's 2021,' replied James instinctively, watching as she clenched her eyes, and tightened into a foetal ball. Her battered body shivered in a sudden and recognisable response to shock, though whether this was in delayed response to her ordeal, or the revelation of his reply, he could not tell. She hummed soft, broken and quivering snatches of the lullaby accompanied by the first faint falsettos of the distant police car siren.

'Do not be afraid,' he whispered, trying to remove her other hand from the base of the cross. 'Let go.'

CHAPTER 6

'How do you feel about the progress you have made?' said James, leaning forwards into the camera on the open laptop on his desk in the consultants' room at St Jude Community Hospital. 'It's remarkable.'

The patient on the screen dabbed at her eyes to stem the mascara from bleeding down her blusher-bronzed cheeks. 'I feel like me, like I don't need to pretend anymore or punish myself. I couldn't have done it without you and the team's help.'

'We only helped you find your way. It's a process, Florence, and there will be challenges still to overcome, but I'm confident you have the tool set to deal with them. If not, I need you to understand that we are here for you, if you feel you have to act on those negative thoughts, okay?'

She nodded, fidgeting with her beautiful, scarlet-painted nails. 'I'm meeting my father this afternoon, for the first time since...'

'Since you became you?'

Florence averted her face. 'Something like that.' She turned back and wiped her nose with the back of her hand.

'I'm just sad I won't get to see you before I move back to Bristol.'

Sunlight streamed through the vertical blinds, and he adjusted them to filter the light away from the screen, giving them both a moment to compose themselves. 'I'll be keeping tabs on you, even though the care team at the Avon Trust are taking over.'

She waved, blew a kiss to the camera and burst into tears as the screen darkened and a disconnect tone signalled the end of the consultation. James crossed his legs and sank back into his chair.

'She's gone, and that is the correct personal pronoun to use from now on.'

The windowed figure in the top corner of his screen mouthed in response.

'You're still on mute, Caroline.'

Dr Lewisham frowned and adjusted her settings. 'That better?'

James nodded. 'I know I'm on probation, but do you have to eavesdrop on every patient?'

Caroline continued to tap at her keyboard. 'Yes. I can multitask as well as be discreet, and it was fortuitous; Fellows came in while you were full screen just now to ask me a few things and confirm I was doing my job, by checking that you were doing yours.'

'I'm glad I wasn't aware; that would have made me incredibly nervous all things considered.'

Caroline fixed the camera with her full attention. 'Well, don't worry – he left quickly. That was nicely done, by the way.'

'I'll take that as a compliment?'

'Take it as reassurance. How are you settling back into St Jude?'

James's thoughts raced through the events in the churchyard seven days prior. 'Eventful, and everyone has been very tactful but genuine in their welcome. Being a local boy returning home has made things less awkward.'

'What about the house?' said Caroline, pausing from her typing to look into the webcam. 'And your father?'

'The house is clean and tidy, though being on my own with most of his things on the walls has given me time to reflect on our catch-up tomorrow afternoon.'

'You're meeting him up at Fairhaven Grange?'

'Yes, but only so you can stop moaning to me about accepting his calls.'

Caroline stifled a laugh and looked away.

'What's so funny?' he said. 'I thought you wanted me to reconcile with the old devil, or are you secretly hoping your little clique can continue without me?'

She shook her head and began to type once more. 'Do I detect a hint of jealousy? I'm just glad you are taking the same advice you gave to Florence Thompson.'

James frowned, confused by the comparison.

Caroline rolled her eyes. 'You'll be seeing him for the first time since you became you, if your little speech the other day hasn't slipped your mind – "I'm going to be myself and not who I think he wants me to be", or you are backtracking already?'

'I didn't say that exactly.'

'I was paraphrasing, but the sentiment was clear, at least to me.'

'It's a waste of time, and besides, that's not a path to any absolution with him.'

'How do you know until you try?' she said. 'Consider it a marker, put down to start the journey, even if where you end up is down to him.'

'That sounds like an incredible counsellor I used to know before she became my probation officer.'

Caroline gave him a withering look.

'Speaking of counsellors,' he said, 'I met Harriet Swanson this morning.'

'The bright young transfer from St Guy's in London?'

James nodded. 'Stepping up from social work and coun-selling; wants to move into specialist psychotherapy and maybe beyond, now she's moved down to Cornwall. She seems very capable, by the book, eager to please, and at that stage in her career where every day begins with a ray of sunshine, and anything is possible.'

Caroline breathed in through pursed lips. 'I remember those days. How do you feel about working with her and Mike with a new patient?'

'Why are you even asking?'

'Because I'm interested in your welfare and professional well-being. Swanson has the experience to be part of your critical care team as well as keeping you and the social worker team in line.' Caroline folded her arms and avoided the camera, waiting for a response.

'You're pulling me from those duties as well?'

'I'd prefer you concentrate on a smaller number of cases, and have you improve on your delegation skill-set.' She fixed the camera with a stern look of exaggerated authority. 'Doc-tor's orders.'

'What about the backlog of non-critical cases to bring down Gayle's precious waiting times and remotely dealing with the patients I have at Truro?'

'Gayle has found herself with few allies following a wider review into standards, and Roscoe's taking on your existing critical face-to-face cases; I'm figuring out the rest. Don't freak out but I've had to give him your office, temporarily, as a sweetener to get him to take on a whole load more work.'

'Crikey, Caroline, I've only been gone a week!'

'Needs must,' she replied, pinching her lips and staring

down at her fidgeting, clasped hands upon the table. 'I'm sending the woman you found, last week, back to St Jude and I want you to take the lead in the assessment and development of a care plan.'

James stiffened with the memory of the churchyard and the shocking condition of the woman he had rescued. His heart thumped loudly in his chest, reliving the adrenalin rush of his initial triage.

Caroline opened a file at her side. 'She's recovering from trauma-induced amnesia, but there may be multiple personalities involved because she uses multiple pronouns to describe how she is feeling – mostly "we" and "us", though occasionally "her". There is some psychosis at play and some divergence from reality. You are the expert and she's asking for "Marshall".'

'I don't recall ever giving her my name, and I found it rather odd when she did, but I was too rattled at the time to process it.'

'Well, I think having her in familiar surroundings might open up what's at play.'

'She's local?'

'From the interactions we've been able to have around her memory loss, it would appear so, though it's sketchy, out of date and frankly nonsensical, which is to be expected. The accent fades in and out but we're unsure if it's rehearsed. One of the accident & emergency doctors reckons she was exposed for over twenty-four hours from the congealed nature of some of the scratches. God knows where we'd be if she'd remained at the church for very much longer. Physiologically, she's recovered and off her sticks – A&E did a good job of patching her up.'

'Does she have a name?'

'She has a tattoo on her right arm with the name "Emily" which she responds to on certain occasions but other times not. The surname she gave to you is extant in your area and hasn't proven of any use finding her.'

'Who told you that?'

Caroline gritted her teeth and looked away, distracting and composing herself with something unimportant on her phone.

'Not my father, surely?'

Caroline raised an eyebrow. 'He is the genealogical guru of the area.'

'He's also your bus ride back to Bodmin and bedlam if Fellows finds out you've been discussing confidential information with the enemy.'

'It was an innocent exchange. I asked if he'd encountered the surname and he said the Denes were wealthy merchants a few hundred years ago, but some calamity affected the family and the line died out. It was fresh in his mind, and I think he mentioned a connection on your mother's side before I switched off.' She screwed her face tightly. 'Sorry, someone else's family history is not my cup of tea.'

James held up a hand. 'Totally understandable. He can talk a box of glass eyes to sleep given an attentive or polite enough audience. The woman may have picked that up from the gravestone I found her clinging to, but one thing is for certain, she's all over the local news, so hopefully someone will contact us.'

'I heard something on the radio as I was driving in this morning,' said Caroline. 'Looks like sleepy St Jude is buzzing.'

'Some are calling her the "Cornish Lady Godiva"; it's all over social media.'

James opened the drawer in his desk and removed a local newspaper. Turning it to face the camera, he flicked through the blurry censored images of a woman in various locations around the town sent in by holidaymakers and residents.

Caroline grimaced in disgust. 'Typical of our time. They'd

rather take images than call the emergency services. Does it shed any light on where she may have wandered from, a nudist campsite or something?'

James scanned the following pages. 'From the timing and locations of the phone images and the type of burrs and thistle found in her cuts, the consensus is that she visited the moorland near the cliffs, which was confirmed by a metal detectorist who, quote, "got an eyeful" from the beach that morning. It's rough and mostly pathless heather and gorse and it's incredible she made it barefoot to the town from over six miles away.'

Caroline took out a nailfile and began to work on a stubborn cuticle. 'She's been unresponsive to anything related to how she got there, with the exception that she says she feels disconnected and someone in her head is trying to keep her safe.'

'I wouldn't call walking naked around the neighbourhood of St Jude and the rough moorland much of a protective influence.'

'Precisely. Which leads me to suspect it may have been a critical event that triggered the memory loss and personality disorder.'

'Any of the secure hospitals in the south-west report any missing persons?' he said, jotting down thoughts on a pad of paper.

'None. She's stable for now but was in a highly anxious state for several days and refers frequently to a feeling of detachment. I want your input, face to face; you've extensive experience with alternate personalities, and until we know what sort of trauma triggered it or whether it was latent before, we can't accurately prescribe a therapeutic course of action.'

'Dissociative personality disorder is my father's specialty, or is this some cynical ploy for me to open up a line of dialogue with him?'

Caroline fiddled with her desktop calendar. 'The thought never crossed my mind – consider it an icebreaker.' She withdrew several finely drawn portraits from the file at her side. She collated the sheets and reversed them to face the camera. 'She remembers someone or something she's seen before.'

James saw the uppermost sketch on lined A4 paper, deftly outlining the downward-turned face of a young woman, long hair centre parted and tied back with curls coaxed out to frame the face. The vintage hairstyle was complemented by the broad open neckline displaying a necklace of exquisite beauty. A linked series of three precious stones hung delicately in a filigree of finely worked precious metal around her graceful neck.

'She has talent – a local artist perhaps? There was a film crew here last year doing period stuff.'

Caroline nodded. 'Art therapy seems as good a place as any to begin if she can't remember beyond the point of trauma. She drew that first, after freaking out from glancing at her reflection in a ward mirror, almost as a response to gaining control of her identity.'

'She looked barely human when I found her, I can understand why she'd be in shock about her injuries. How long did she take to draw something like that?'

'Not long, maybe ten minutes, which is remarkable, but she wasted an hour beforehand trying to work out where the ink in the pen was coming from, like she had never seen a ballpoint before. She murmurs when put under stress and comes out with all sorts of confused babble.'

'A humming, like a lullaby?' said James. 'She made those sounds when I found her.'

She nodded. 'It's some form of audible comfort blanket that heralds a protective influence until things calm down.

She's not violent, just erratic and unpredictable when triggered.'

James raised his pen to his cheek. 'Anything else we should know?'

'She talks as though conversant with different periods, though with the same mix of modern and old-fashioned vernacular. I'm just glad I specialise in addiction psychiatry because all this makes my head spin. She sometimes seems curious about stuff we take for granted, even the smallest things. She spent ten minutes emptying the electronic soap dispenser this morning until the nurse put an end to her play.'

'She has child-like tendencies?'

'Possibly,' said Caroline. 'Though without prejudicing your report, my opinion is that it's ignorance derived from the amnesia, or some other influence, that's driving the innocent and naive behaviour.'

Caroline switched the sheet to display the image of a man clad in a military uniform on horseback.

James came closer to the screen to examine the rider. 'Who's this?'

'No idea, but I showed it to Roscoe; he's a military history nerd. The soldier is from the turn of the nineteenth century, apparently. I've arranged a monitored ward room with the regional team. We'll be dropping her back to you later today with the physical report. The neurological scan came back clean, so it's not physiological, and there's no special needs provision required, so far as we can tell.'

James nodded. 'Mike's on tomorrow, and the new coun-sellor should still be here if you want me to go through the procedures with her.'

'Do it but be careful. She has trust issues, especially around men, but maybe she'll open up to you or Harriet. Just promise me you won't overdo things now you are back.'

'I understand,' he said. 'I'm not aiming to be the same person I was six months ago.'

'Pity you didn't say that last week, it could have saved us both a lot of bother.'

James fiddled with his shirt sleeves and avoided the camera. 'I should have kept my mouth shut the other day – about us, I mean. I'm embarrassed to have pulled it out of the blue; it was an inappropriate time and place to bring it up and I wanted to say sorry.'

'You are apologising a lot now you are back.'

'Though not always to the right people about the right things,' he said.

Caroline pursed her lips. 'Or at the right time.' A smile appeared on her face. 'I think I could get used to this new you.'

James glanced away, waiting for her to break the silence.

She relieved him after a few moments with a similar wayward glance to something out of view on her office wall. 'I owe you an apology, too. You deserved a response last week, and I didn't give you one. It was an inopportune moment, and I was caught off guard – you know how I hate that.'

'Oh?'

'About what you asked me – the night two years ago – I didn't regret it; I just got over it.'

CHAPTER 7

J ames folded and pressed down on the sheets in the hand-over file to avoid them flapping in the breeze.

'Any news on who she is?' said the new counsellor, sitting attentively beside him.

'No one who has witnessed the media circus has come forward yet, Harriet.'

She brushed back a strand of golden hair and removed the end of the pen from her lips. 'You think the surname she gave was influenced by the name on the gravestone?'

'Almost certainly,' said James. 'Patients suffering from temporary amnesia often have a very short-term photographic and retentive memory.'

'Like a hard drive cleared of old files?'

'Yes. I like that analogy,' said James. 'Is it one of your own?'

'No, I updated it,' she said, fishing out a worn copy of a medical textbook. 'Your father used the same analogy in here – *Psychiatry for the Practising Counsellor* – only he used magnetic tape storage as the medium.'

James took the book and flipped through the pages. 'You know, this is a better cure for insomnia than for amnesia.'

He offered it back to her, and she clasped the end of the bench, distracting herself with a casual look at the distant glittering waves.

James broke the silence, suddenly conscious of the unasked request. 'I could get him to sign—'

'Oh, could you?' she said, flipping to the aged cover sheet showing the younger face of his father, moodily resting his fingers beneath his black-bearded chin flecked with the first hints of middle-aged grey.

He can't have been much older than I am now, thought James.

The page showed age-deteriorated foxing, and the tanned spotting speckled the black-and-white photograph. His father's face came to mind, now age worn and liver-spotted in the flesh.

'One way to live forever I suppose...' he whispered.

'Excuse me?' said Harriet.

'Immortalise yourself in print.' James cleared his mind and returned to the subject.

'What we know is Emily's innate personality appears to be subdued when she feels threatened and an innate function of the brain potentially manifesting as a protective personality arises to calm the situation.'

Harriet folded her arms across the pad on her lap, brushing away a wasp buzzing around the hospital garden border. 'This could be transient global amnesia,' she said, 'considering the wandering nature and inability to recall simple day-to-day objects or tasks.'

James studied the fresh-faced and eager member of his team. 'I see you've been doing your homework, but it's important to remain open-minded at this stage. Always be aware of your own bias; pigeon-holing can get you into all sorts of bother.' He shot her a glance, and she pursed a knowing smile. 'Allow yourself to be wrong, just not too decisive or judgemental; diagnoses can be incremental. That's where the team comes in, to keep you, and me, on the straight and narrow. We are here to create a calming environment where talking therapy allows pertinent emotions to bubble up to the surface in their own good time. No good comes of rushing a patient.'

She hurriedly scribbled down the comments.

'I'm very grateful for the opportunity to be part of the care team. You may not recall but you gave a lecture at the College I attended...' She dug out a battered, stapled series of sheets fronted by a title page below which, in his hand, lay a signature and a few words of advice: *Good luck with your studies. Trust yourself, J.M.*

'*Overcoming self-doubt in diagnoses*,' he said, smiling at the subject matter and tapping the cover of his father's book. 'I do remember. You know, if you ever write something, promise me you'll re-read your own work from time to time; the best teacher is often someone you once were, but have forgotten.'

'I will, and I'm really very grateful for the opportunity to be working with you.'

'You can thank Dr Trebarr, here, and Dr Lewisham up at Truro. They have the utmost regard for your work, as do I.' James stood up and half pocketed the large book into his jacket. 'I'm pretty bad at delegating and know you are keen to get stuck in. I've looked over some of the more challenging patients you assisted with at St Guy's, but it would be remiss of me not to mention that acute personality disorders, often connected with intense personal trauma or dependence on drugs or alcohol, require a heightened level of defensive emotional resilience.'

Harriet nodded. 'I understand. How long do you think you'll need to diagnose or prescribe a route to recovery?'

'It depends, but at least two or three weeks with input from the care team though we refine our diagnosis based on new information or revelations from the patient. Often we need to build trust first, and that can take time.' James glanced over to the other side of the road at an elderly man, talking to himself, as he made his way down the sea wall. 'Sometimes, even after decades, we never really know, like Old Tom Cotter, over there, for instance.'

Harriet frowned, then relaxed into recognition. 'The pensioner who suffers from alcoholism and schizophrenia? Dr Trebarr reviewed his medication and introduced us on my second day.'

'That's the one,' said James, watching as the man shuffled out of sight towards the harbour. 'We've never really understood his case and part of me always feels guilty around him, like my father and I should have done more to help. He's an enigma, like a locked box, and we can only peep through the keyhole at what treasures may lie behind.'

'I'm sure you both must have tried your best over the years?' she said, rubbing her bare knees.

James shuffled his feet and stared out into the bay.

'It wasn't so much that, it was that we teased him mercilessly as kids for his condition.'

'There's nothing so cruel as kids,' said Harriet, clasping her hands in her lap. 'I wasn't ready to tie my hair back for years after I left school.' She bit her lip and brushed her fingers past a wine-stain birthmark at the side of her neck.

James looked across sympathetically but did not intrude by asking questions. 'Tom saved me from drowning, out there in the bay when I was young. He dived in off the harbour wall and swam out to my small deflating dinghy while folk were still scrambling to get a boat unhitched from a tangle of mooring lines.'

'Brave fellow,' said Harriet.

'Yes, and I was a stupid boy going out alone in defiance of my father,' said James, standing and stuffing his hands into his pockets. 'The oddest thing is, he swears to this day he can't swim. There used to be times, even years later, when he would fall, drunk, into a few feet of water and flap about or try to do something equally daft, whether to attract attention or revive the goodwill that lasted in the pubs for some considerable time. I remember a colleague of my father's saying Tom admitted it was as though someone else was guiding him.'

'One of his personalities?'

James puckered his lips. 'We assumed so, but it's bizarre that being able to swim is confined to one alter; it doesn't work that way.'

'But he risked his life all the same?'

'Yes, and nearly drowned himself after he dragged me to the boat crew. They said he stopped swimming once I was safe, and just became motionless as though all knowledge of even how to float had left him.'

'So you think he switched to himself, back from whatever personality took charge?'

'The mind does strange things when under stress to protect the body and those around,' he said.

'Maybe you would feel better if you apologised to him for being mean as a child?'

James tugged at his chin and whispered to himself, 'One more for the list.'

A pair of raucous gulls squabbled over a broken biscuit beneath a child's swing. Harriet glanced over. 'They make a noisy change from London pigeons.'

'You get used to them,' said James, holding a forefinger to his lips. 'They are supposed to be the souls of drowned fishermen, but that's a local secret.'

Harriet smiled. 'I like that. The first thing Tom Cotter

said to me was that he had a secret, and he would tell no one about it. Is that it or just another delusion?'

James puckered his lips. 'Maybe. He's been saying that for as long as I can remember. He's told everyone about this secret, so I guess, technically, I'm not breaching any moral code. Tom is waiting for someone he calls "Sweet Nightingale" to come back.'

'A former girlfriend?'

'Not exactly, or at least I don't think so. My father handled him for a brief time and believed that a transient personality arose briefly within him during my rescue or shortly after. It hasn't fronted again, much to his great sadness, though there are plenty others in his head keeping him company, the townsfolk amused, and the local constabulary busy. It's almost as though he misses someone that doesn't exist, at least not to anyone but himself.'

'I sympathise,' said Harriet. 'Like most kids, I once had an imaginary friend, that used to protect me from those who bullied me. "Jemima" left when I could take care of myself, but now and then, I still think of her. I guess we should be grateful, and not try to over-rationalise what our brain is doing to protect us and others?'

James tilted his head slightly to one side. 'Agreed, though I guess that would put most of us out of work. Tom will often be found at the harbour, when he's not bothering people outside the off-licence, as though hoping she'll return, or on some self-imposed sentry duty lest some other child needs help. The lifeboat station manager keeps an eye out to make sure he does nothing stupid.' James bit against the inside of his cheek.

'I used to wonder if his self-sacrifice and what happened out in the bay didn't contribute or cause him to go beyond a breaking point from which recovery to some aspect of a previous life is impossible. I've lived with the possibility that he gave me the best years of his life to save my own.'

Harriet rose and stretched her arms towards the sunlight glinting off the rippling surf. 'You think our Emily Dene might have a similar story?'

'I hope not but recovery doesn't mean going back to how a life was before but learning new ways to live that life the way the person wants to and gaining control over areas of their life that might have felt out of control before.'

'You sound like your father,' she said, smiling.

James savoured the honest and heartfelt compliment.

'Thank you, I guess. Recovery is rarely straightforward, and it's more helpful to focus on learning more about yourself and developing ways to cope, rather than trying to get rid of every symptom of the mental health problem. What recovery means will be personal, but for most people, the most important thing is to find ways to live the life you want.'

'I should be writing this down,' she said, fetching the pad. 'It's helpful. How will we proceed in this case if there are multiple personalities in play?'

James glanced at her notebook as she flipped over to a new sheet. He checked his watch and looked over at the closed glass door to the hospital before inviting her to sit alongside him on the bench.

'With an open mind and a blank page. We are here to listen, observe, and understand, not to judge or form conclusions where there are none. We make incremental and holistic steps. There may be bizarre, nonsensical revelations, some very sad or upsetting memories, but we never bargain with or deny the existence of any presenting or dominating personalities. No matter how delusional the patient may be, we deal with the emotions behind their revelations and reason for existence, rather than correct them on facts that oppose their perceived reality.'

'To avoid pushing them into a state of cognitive dissonance?' she said, joining him. 'Rejecting new information that conflicts with their existing beliefs?'

'In part. We want to reinforce a sense that any alter, not just the protective ones, can trust us and the outside world to take on these tasks providing the emotional and physical hierarchy of needs are met. If a self-generated personality exists, then the mind has a very good reason for creating one.'

'Which is?'

James tapped at the book in his pocket.

'Chapter eleven,' he said. 'Survival.'

'You seem to know the text inside out?' She twisted to shield her eyes from the sun.

'More than I know the man who wrote it, sometimes,' said James, following her gaze and pivoting around; she'd caught sight of the engraved brass plaque, blazing like a golden letterbox cover. 'It's where my father wooed my mother, allegedly, when she was a GP here. Hardly Paris or Rome, is it?'

She spun back to overlook the sea. 'I think it's quite a romantic spot, and I don't mind you telling him, but I would say that his passion and humanity comes across in his writing.'

James leaned forwards, bridging his hands and shaking his head in disbelief. 'I'll tell him, but he'll be incorrigible for the rest of the day.'

They turned around, startled by the opening hospital door, and walked across the lawn-laid stepping stones to meet the GP emerging from the hospital wing.

'All ready for you both,' called Mike, ushering them into the air-conditioned cool of the corridor. 'I've checked her over, and the nurse is just with her performing the hand-over tests and paperwork. She needed some help to change her into some other clothes we had lying around because she's been sick in the ambulance.'

'Travel sickness?' said James. 'Which crew was it?'

'The rollercoaster brothers – Billy and Marcus.'

'The fastest response team in the west,' said James to Harriet as they followed the long strides of the doctor down the hall. 'With all the fun of the fair.'

James buttoned his collar as he walked side by side with the new counsellor. 'Have you gone through the report?'

Mike turned and nodded as the carpeted corridor of St Jude Hospital ran on, labyrinthine in its route to his consulting room and office.

'No obvious signs of neurological trauma, and we can rule out any degenerative possibilities for the amnesia.'

'What else?' said James, striding alongside.

'Early to mid-thirties, average height and weight. Bloods have come back negative for anything relating to narcotic or medicative influence. There are some signs of cigarette end scar tissue on her inner thigh—'

'Self-harm?'

'Or abuse,' said Mike. 'She's—'

'What?'

'Nervy with men, so we've assigned Leigh Anderson as the chaperone. Her memory appears to be returning, but it's confused and any attempts to discover anything pertinent about who she is or how she came to be with us results in some protective element overruling.'

'A caretaking alternate personality?' said Harriet, piping in and trying to keep up with the eager pace of the two doctors.

Mike nodded. 'James is the expert, but there's no denying there appear to be things that Emily is self-realising on a "need to know basis". Did Caroline mention to you about the odd patterns of speech?'

'Queen's English?' said Harriet. 'All indications are that her dialect is local but London or south-east in accent.'

'Sometimes it's modern slang, other times it's like she's swallowed a thesaurus or watched too much Downton; often it's an eclectic mix of the two. Truro General has recommended she stay here under supervision until your assessment is complete. She doesn't require a full-time caregiver, but I'd like you to consider keeping Leigh on as an essential companion or chaperone, just for the short term.'

'On what grounds?' said James as they reached the door.

'There are times, usually when under stress, when she's confused by modernity, unable to do day-to-day things we take for granted,' said Mike, stuffing his hands in his pockets. 'She bit into an unpeeled banana before we stopped her and couldn't understand how to open a bottle of water. An orderly offered her a handful of those old-fashioned American bubblegums in the lift after she drew his portrait. She swore she'd never had it and kept swallowing them till we explained that you had to spit it out; been bonkers for it ever since, like a comfort blanket.'

'Like the humming?' said James.

'Exactly,' said Mike.

'I'll keep it in mind,' said James. 'Is host or alter present at the moment?'

Mike tapped his cheek. 'She's calming down after her trip, but I'd say the latter given her posture and quirks.'

'This should be interesting,' said Harriet, misconstruing the developing frown on his face. 'I've never met a historical alter before.'

James lowered his brow and hardened his voice. 'This is a traumatised human being we are talking about. Just remember, a person experiencing delusions will not change their beliefs when confronted with evidence that the belief is false, but I don't want it encouraged either.'

Harriet blushed and looked away. 'I apologise, Dr Marshall.'

James nodded and let out a long breath. 'It's okay. I'm a little apprehensive about seeing her again, after the last time.'

Mike squeezed his upper arm comfortingly. 'There's nothing to be concerned about. You saved her and now you get to help her find her way back.' James smiled as the GP gently punched him on the shoulder, winked at Harriet, and made his way down the corridor to the surgery.

Harriet looked after him and clutched her notepad against her chest. 'He should have been a counsellor; he seems to know exactly what to say at precisely the right time.'

'He's the best man I know,' said James, watching as he turned a corner and disappeared. 'In fact, he was my best man.'

James shook free the temptation to say more as Harriet turned, listening with both arms crossed against her chest. He knocked on the consulting room door, glancing back momentarily down the empty corridor.

James coughed to attract her attention. 'If you're ready, let's help her find her way back, then.'

CHAPTER 8

Afriendly middle-aged nurse greeted them. Harriet entered with her notepad open, and James closed the door as the two women sat down against the wheeled examination bed.

The woman seated next to his desk was a complete transformation to his discovery in the churchyard. She was clean and dressed in mismatched, donated clothing. Faint freckles speckled beneath intensely blue eyes, furtive and watchful like a cat unsure of its surroundings and the strangers in the room. James logged in to his computer before returning to the curious woman studying him in equal measure.

She followed his gaze to her bandaged feet, visible through the coarse plastic medical sandals protecting them until the swelling subsided. A burgundy hooded sweat top, zipped to her neck, overlay a faded pair of grey tracksuit bottoms. She sat upright, formal, as though the street urchin look was now the required uniform at a Swiss finishing school.

Her brushed brown hair, washed, and wayward, gave some nod to the style in the drawings in the file that James placed upon the table, spilling the contents. He leaned over and the heavy book slipped from his jacket pocket, opening on the author's page. He bent down to retrieve the tome.

'Marshall,' said the woman, pointing at the open, foxed page holding the timeless picture of his father.

James looked up. 'Yes, we are related. I'm the current Dr Marshall, responsible for psychiatric care here.' James closed the book and placed the sheets on his desk before sitting down. The portrait of the Regency-era lady stared gently and sadly towards him as he glanced up to see the crude and hastily arranged similarity in the hair of the wide-eyed woman opposite. Her recently trimmed, shoulder-length hair was too short to arrange in such a fashion, and the woman brushed and tucked the tumbled locks back into position with subconscious regularity.

'This is Harriet Swanson,' said James, indicating the sitting counsellor, 'who will observe during our consultation. You know Nurse Anderson, I understand?'

The woman nodded. 'You are a medical doctor?'

'In part, yes. I specialise in helping those with temporary or long-term mental health issues.' He studied the confusion on her face and pointed to his chest. 'Dr Trebarr, who you met earlier, deals with the body, and I deal with what goes on up here.' James raised a finger and tapped the side of his head.

'You treat the maladies of the mind?' she said.

James nodded, noting the curious description spoken with a recognisable, though gentle Cornish accent. 'Are you comfortable at the moment with us being here and sharing this space with you?'

She inclined her head, pivoting to meet the warm smiles of the women opposite. 'Yes. I am much in your debt for the unpleasantness of dealing with my sickness earlier. Please apologise to the laundress on my behalf.'

Leigh flitted an amused glance at Harriet. 'That's all right, dear; the washing machine knows you have had quite an exciting time of things lately.'

The woman glanced around the room, searching for answers. 'We are only just beginning to comprehend our present condition. Am I here because you believe she is afflicted with madness? I intend to help her, not drive her into a sanatorium to be studied like a botanical curio.'

'No,' said James, glancing across to see Harriet's puckered, pen-topped lips, struggling with the interchangeable use of pronouns. 'You are or were suffering from temporary memory loss, and some disassociation. You say "we", "she" and "our", to describe more than one person with you, sharing space in the mind. Dissociation is one way the mind copes with too much stress, such as during a traumatic event, but I want you to know that whatever may have caused it, you are safe here.'

'The woman, Emily, whose face looks back from the mirror, sought to harm herself, and I intervened though she quarrels incessantly and uses language not befitting for one of our sex.' The woman shook her head, loosening a long strand of hair.

'You both hear voices?' said James, gently tapping into the keyboard. The nuances and lexicon of her speech were unusual, he thought, but not unique, and he listened intently without reaction as though she were describing a mild cold and not the feelings of an alternate personality. His hand brushed across his father's book as he reached for the caps lock key.

She rubbed absently at her arms. 'Not as sound; more akin to thoughts that arise unbidden in our minds. I share her feelings, especially her anguish and despair, and she feels the same as I do when such circumstances are reversed. It has ever been thus.'

'You have been with Emily for a long time?'

'You misunderstand,' she said. 'I have known her for many

days, others for far less, while some for barely a fleeting moment. We part in joy or sorrow either way.'

Harriet glanced across, eager to interject, but he held up a hand and shook his head. The time for listening was now; the time for questions would be later.

She tilted her head to one side and gripped at the arms of the chair. 'Your speech is strange but somehow familiar as though I were living through the other's memory and vocabulary – I must sound archaic to you.'

'It is refreshing to speak with someone with such a generous grasp of vocabulary,' he said watching her white hands bleed back to a relaxed pink as they released their grip on the arm rests. 'I understand, and help people deal with this kind of experience,' said James. 'You may be experiencing co-consciousness with the host—'

Her eyes widened, and she pushed herself into a cradled position within the chair.

'I only hoped to save her from my fate. I am no parasite.'

James retreated to give her space. 'What fate?'

'The fate of one forced into a life of despair, ending with —' She lowered her eyes and became silent, as James reacted defensively to calm her anxiety.

'I don't want you to be frightened. The team and I are here to help you back to health. You are at St Jude Hospital.'

She swung back, gazing at James with sudden focus. 'St Jude has a hospital?'

'Yes,' said James unable to contain his quizzical frown. 'Have you been in hospital before?'

She opened her mouth as though to speak, unconsciously tapping the nylon moccasins against the chair's legs.

'I understand you may live in or know the area?' said Harriet, cutting off his next question with cross-examination of her own. James threw her an annoyed sideways glance, but she remained fixed upon the woman.

'I do—' she said, twisting in the counsellor's direction. 'Or did – all is changed; I don't know where to begin.'

'Then trust us,' said Harriet, peering over at James for forgiveness. He nodded for her to continue and she leaned forward to extend her hand. 'I'm very pleased to meet you—?'

The woman hesitantly offered her own in mirrored response. 'Do ladies now shake ungloved hands as men do, as well as wear their clothes?' She plucked at the hooded top and cotton bottoms.

'We do much more besides,' said Harriet, taking the hand and gently shaking it. 'I'm Harriet, and I'm new here, like you.'

'Mary-Anne,' came the confident reply, 'but Father calls me May.'

'Then I am pleased to meet you, May. I forgot your surname—'

'Dene,' she replied swiftly, folding her arms about herself and turning back to see James watchful and calm. 'You can cure what ails Emily, Dr Marshall, remove the threat that compels her to harm her flesh and her very existence, and allow her the grace to live a long and happy life?'

'We will do everything to help her, or you both, recover from whatever trauma or event may have triggered the amnesia, and any delusions you may be experiencing—'

'You believe I am not real,' she said, rubbing at her wrists, 'that I pretend to be an imaginary fantasy such as children conjure to infuriate their governesses, or that I am lying?'

'No,' said James, much to her surprise, and those in the room. 'You are very real. I am talking to you right now, and I accept you believe who you say you are.'

'That is not the same thing as my existence being true,' she said. 'My assertion that I am not the woman whose body you see before you, does not surprise you? It did on the last occasion.'

'No,' said James multi-tasking and distracted by Harriet's furious scribbling. The nurse looked down at the pad, hidden from view, and stuck out her lips with interest. 'The "why" you are here is more important to you both and your recovery than the "how".'

'Seeking my dissolution would not be a recovery,' she said. 'Even now she struggles to return to the place where I found her at the precipice. She will suffer a terrible fate at her own hand, or his, if I remove myself before provisions for her welfare are made.'

James caught the potential trigger, the mention of a man, and held the gaze of the counsellor. Harriet understood the significance and hid the sudden blush-response with an adjustment of her round-rimmed spectacles.

James probed, considering the presence of a harmful personality within. 'Is he also with you, like the other woman you share thoughts with?'

The woman wrung her hands and tensed, burying her head into her chest. She shook her head and pulled open the top and rolled up her T-shirt to reveal a scrolling tattoo with a name emblazoned in blue ink – Emily.

'There is only the one whose name adorns our pricked and stained skin, and my own. We are alone, unlike others I have encountered. The man who seeks to command and constrain her is outside of us and not in. She will not countenance or further any report, but I have caught remembrances of him, and he is a monster.'

James sorted through the drawings, raising the sketch of the cavalry officer. 'Not this handsome gentleman, then?'

Her eyes sank to her lap, and she lightly brushed a finger across her lips. 'No, that is not he, but someone long dead that was once dear to me; his name was Richard Avery.' She studied her bobbled cotton-clad thighs, squeezing her hands between them. 'He died before I could tell him—'

She became silent, and James was certain that the memory was dear, though not so recent as to be so all-consuming in its grief. He knew well the sharpness of his first year alone and reached out in sympathy with the drawing in hand. 'I'm sorry for your loss.'

'It was something that may have altered both our lives,' she added, taking the portrait and rubbing her thumb across the figure's windblown hair. 'May I keep this and the rest once we have concluded? It is not yet finished.'

James collated the drawings and handed them across. 'They belong to you, and may I say, they are quite remarkable.'

She flicked through them, pausing at the sketch of a fine low cut stone house sitting on pillows of older dressed granite foundations. Roses peeped in around the shuttered sash windows from a foreground of foxgloves and phlox. Outbuildings and a stabled arch were outlined, and several gulls perched upon the hand-cut tiled roof overlooking a backdrop of sea-bent trees. Foreground figures walked alongside powerful horses, many hands high, while others more distant and mere specks of ink raced across the page towards the hint of a distant church steeple that receded into the blank part of the page.

She passed the sheet with a quivering hand, colour rising in her cheeks. 'This one is for you, for your kindness and gentleness at our first meeting. I was at a disadvantage...'

James retrieved it and distracted her from any embarrassment.

'Thank you. It's a grand house, somewhere nearby?' he said, hoping for some clue or background to build upon.

'It is Carmalt,' she replied. 'I live—lived there once; it is now all but a ruinous foundation. Upon my remarkable return, I watched the stones being taken long after our family was forgotten, and the house decayed. They make up the walls of a distant grange now, and children played there, long ago.'

'You came back to the area?' asked Harriet, 'Can you remember from where—London, perhaps?'

She turned, shaking her head. 'You misunderstand and would not comprehend unless you truly believed who I say I am.'

James ignored the interruption, absorbed by the image, grasping at some fleeting memory of the location and arrangement of the buildings. The distant, crooked church steeple caught his attention. 'You say you lived here, but what is the church in the background, peeping out from behind the far plantation of trees? It might help us—'

'It's the church at St Jude,' she said. 'Isn't that clear?'

'St Jude doesn't have a steeple,' he said. 'Could you be mistaken?'

'No. It was drawn from memory, before the storm.'

James studied her face, sincere and with no sign of any intent to mislead. It was the voice of the nurse that broke the silence.

'Well, I'm older than the both of you, begging your pardon, and I've never known St Jude Church look like anything other than what it does.'

'Thank you, nurse,' said James, stiffening the tone of his voice to ensure no further interruptions. Meeting the wide and unblinking eyes of his patient, he noticed for the first time how dilated they were. He removed a small pen light from his pocket and brushed the beam back and forth, causing her to blink. The black empty discs remained steady in the brightness, even as she sucked in a quick breath with wonder at the tiny torch. He handed it to her, checking the screen for any prescribed medication that would account for the permanency. Perhaps a side effect of the anti-sickness pill she had taken, shortly upon arrival?

'Can you recall suffering from any illness before the events of last week?' he said, distracting her from the excitement of pointing the torch into her mouth and biting at the beam like a dog snapping at the wind from a moving car window. 'Or perhaps anything you remember about your family that might shed light...'

She lowered the narrow beam upon the portrait of the handsome soldier before her. 'Father said I should not pursue my ambitions, or his affections, remembering my station and duty to be a good wife when the time came to marry that ogre, Henry Fallon. Richard and I made other plans, but it led to ruin for us all.'

Harriet slammed down her pen, and James spun his chair to prevent her from another unscheduled line of enquiry. However, it was the nurse that spoke out of turn.

'I'll give him a piece of my mind, and every other woman's in this blessed place.' She folded her arms and avoided James's disdainful look at the interruption, but not the sentiment. Harriet bit down on her bottom lip to stifle any snort of spontaneous laughter, avoiding James's growing disapproval.

The sound of light, rippling laughter caught them all by surprise as the woman shuddered with amusement. 'I wish I could have witnessed such an encounter; he would have been apoplectic.'

James relaxed, sensing the improvement in mood and temperament. He pinched his brow and folded his arms, retrieving the penlight and hiding it from view.

'Perhaps there is still time?' said Harriet, out of turn and enjoying the lightness of the moment.

The woman slumped in her chair, head lolling, and became suddenly silent. She looked up and rubbed at her eyes. Her tone deepened and the soft Cornish lilt faded.

'He is long dead.'

James searched the eyes and face for confirmation that

something significant had taken place. The pupils sharpened to a pinhead and rebounded, no longer dilated as though the bright flashlight had been passed across the blue-rimmed glass once more. Her lids hung tired, and she stared at the sheets on her lap as though scanning the unfamiliar drawings.

'Mary-Anne?' he whispered.

'She's gone,' the woman replied in a deeper, neutral voice, devoid of the bright and familiar lilt of the local accent. 'I keep telling everyone and her that my name is Emily; it's on my bloody arm isn't it?' She clutched at her mouth. 'I feel woozy and sick.'

The nurse rushed forwards with a cardboard spittoon as James reached for a cup and poured out some water. She retched into the makeshift bowl and took a sip of the liquid, almost spilling it with the shaking of her hand.

'What is happening to me?' asked Emily, putting down the cup on the floor. She wiped the spittle from her chin with the back of her sleeve and zipped up the hooded top with a shiver.

'The sickness may be because of the travel, or some side effects of the medication to treat your pain. Perhaps some Cornish sea air will make you feel better?' Harriet stared, mouth open, unused to the suddenness of the transition in personality, speech, and posture. James nodded towards the jug as she collected herself and refilled the cup of water, returning it to the side of her foot.

James calmly rose, and she backed away into the recess of the chair as he wound open the blinds to reveal the seaside rooftops and gardens and the sea beyond. She relaxed as he returned to his seat.

Emily tore out the remaining tresses and drew her fingers across her scalp, obliterating the messy formality of the previous style for shaggy, shoulder-length freedom. 'I want to know what's going on,' she said. 'Why I can't remember much of who I am, and why this other person is making me say and do stuff; I want it to stop, right now.'

'Do you remember where you are or recollect our names?'

She nodded. 'I can hear you, even when she is out. It's like I'm watching myself in a film or looking in from the outside, detached, but sharing with—'

'Mary-Anne Dene?'

'Father calls her May,' said the woman, adjusting herself and wiping her hands down her tracksuit bottoms. She placed the bowl on the floor and plucked at the hooded sweatshirt. 'Where are my proper clothes?'

James coughed nervously. 'Do you remember where you left them?'

She shook her head.

'Wait—' she said sharply. 'I know your face – you told me not to be afraid. I was starkers.'

James smiled reassuringly. 'And in need of help. How do you feel now?'

'Hazy, detached, like my body doesn't fully belong to me.'

'You may be suffering from something we call dissociative amnesia. You have gaps in your memory where you can't remember anything that happened or you might not remember information about yourself or about things that occurred before.'

She held out her hand. 'Why does it feel as though there is someone in my head?'

'That is what we will endeavour to find out, but I want you to know this is not uncommon. You appear to be sharing experiences with someone, but there are things Mary-Anne—'

'It's May,' corrected Emily, 'and she's very particular about it.'

'There are things that May,' continued James, 'is keeping from you. Under times of stress or trauma—' He glanced at her tracksuit bottoms and at the hidden burn marks he knew to be on her thigh. She snapped her legs shut as though reading his thoughts. 'It is perfectly normal for the mind to create delusions to protect itself.'

'I've made someone up to look after myself?' The woman winced as she adjusted in her chair, shuffling her clunky feet and testing her weight on one leg at a time. 'That is nuts.'

James clasped his hands and extended them towards her. 'Whatever you were or are going through, you are safe, and we will help you. Can you remember if May or any other personality was with you before, maybe as a child?'

James caught Harriet's eye as her pen hovered above the pad.

'No. I've been on my own all my life, at least I think so.'

'No brothers or sisters, no family members you can recall?' James leaned forwards as she spoke again.

Emily pursed her lips. 'It's all confused with her memories, but I'm pretty sure.' She flicked through the pile of drawings.

'How is it I can sketch these when I can't even draw?' she said. 'I can paint a little, I remember that, but not like this. These are her doing, not mine.'

'Perhaps you can, and you just didn't know it? It's a positive sign, and I would like to see some more if either of you feel like sharing.'

'Are you going to lock me up?' she said. 'Put me in the nut house or something?'

'No,' said James, sensing her rising anxiety. 'You aren't a prisoner, and this is an open hospital. With your permission, we would like you to stay here for a few days until you feel able to cope; we can move you to more comfortable and independent lodgings when you are ready to move on.' He nodded towards the counsellor. 'Harriet will be here to listen throughout your recovery. I'll be overseeing a support team that includes her, a social worker, the doctor whom you met earlier, and a chaperone when you feel the need. We'll develop a care plan together that evolves to meet your needs.'

'What's the alternative?'

Harriet put away her pad and dragged her chair a little closer. 'We will just talk on your terms, about your feelings, and try to unravel what is happening or has happened; but we need to do it somewhere you are in control and safe.'

'No drugs or anything?'

Harriet glanced across for guidance, and James took the lead.

'We only medicate to help people cope, and not without their permission. I promise we will get you through this, if you will trust us, and allow yourself the time and space to heal.'

'Can you make her go away, the woman in my head?'

'That may not be down to us; it will be down to you, and your recovery,' he said evasively. 'If she is here because of what happened to you last week, then there's a good chance your mind is actually trying to help you, or at least keep you from harm by not allowing you to relive painful or traumatic experiences. That is the sense we get when she presents herself.'

Emily shuffled the sheets and held aloft the face of the early nineteenth century woman. 'How can this made-up historical person be helping me when she is stopping me from remembering things?'

'That,' said James, glancing at the evident self-portrait of May Dene, 'is what we intend to help you find out.'

CHAPTER 9

'Can you recall your surname, Emily?' said James, reaching out to tilt the display screen from the brightness of the sun.

She bit on a nail and studied the floor. 'It's like it's on the tip of my tongue but all I keep coming back to is Dene, or something close to it.'

'It will come back, but for now, can you remember anything that might help us contact those that might be worried or looking for you?'

Emily pushed backwards abruptly to the far wall, scattering the spittoon, cup, and drawings, desperately clawing at the window and fiddling with the latch to escape. James shot up, followed by the nurse, and wrestled her writhing arms to her sides as she sought to beat against the glass with her head. 'No! She says not yet, he'll find me. Get out of my head!'

'No one will hurt you, I promise,' said James, narrowly avoiding a finger to his eye. 'But you need to be calm and talk to us so we can help you.'

'I'll call for help,' said Harriet, rushing over to press the emergency call button. An alarm bell went off in the corridor outside and several hurried footsteps approached from beyond the door.

'No,' said James with frustration, but too late, hearing the lullaby hum from the woman's closed mouth over the sound of the alarm. Her body relaxed and slumped back limply, guided by him and the nurse into the chair. The melody became steadier, and her rapid breathing subsided to a calm purr. He knelt, heart racing, as several people burst into the room. The woman rubbed at her temple and shivered as though shaking off an unpleasant dream.

The responding onlookers milled and mumbled at the open door, and James held up a hand to signal for calm and quiet.

'Tell her it is all right, and that I understand,' said James, glancing to follow the woman's gaze towards the crowd of junior doctors and orderlies. 'I'm sorry for upsetting either of you.'

The woman lifted her head, and he saw the increasing dilation in her pupils, sensing that a switch had taken place. 'I'll send them away, I promise. Will you trust me?'

The woman relaxed and nodded, sitting upright and brushing aside a lock of wayward hair.

'I'm very pleased to see you again, May,' said James, waving his arm behind himself for the crowd to disperse. Her eyes followed them out, and Harriet quietly closed the door and reset the alarm.

'You are a man of your word, and did what you promised,' she whispered. 'You didn't hurt or restrain us as others have done cruelly before. Do not permit anyone to speak of this, for I fear he will come.'

He nodded. 'Are you, or is Emily, in danger at the moment?'

She shook her head. 'That is why she came here, to be far

away. Were he to find us, it would be worse than death, but I could not let her die.'

'You saved her from the man she is hiding from?'

'No, only from what she planned to do at the cliffs.'

James held tight his emotions with the mention of Maiden Point. 'You or Emily had negative thoughts?'

It was a long pause and James wondered if he had over-reached. He was about to try a less invasive line of questioning when she spoke again.

'She came to the cliff, naked and alone, and I perceived her intentions.'

'You both became conscious of each other at that moment?' said Harriet.

'As have few others that have opened their hearts and minds to me over the years. My place is at the cliffs and in the bay – rarely the town.'

'You saved her from falling?' said James hopefully. 'She got too close to the edge?'

She shook her head, and James reeled with the confirmation that it was no accident but a deliberate act.

'From self-murder,' she whispered. 'I do not understand why so few listen, but she surrendered to me, and I felt a sudden closeness and connection with her predicament.' She fidgeted with the tied bow at her waist and folded her fingers around her belly. 'Emily heard me, even as she prepared to leap from the high place, and I suddenly knew her and looked through her eyes. She perceived me and we struggled, but I held on, desperate to save one life in exchange for my own folly.' Her face turned to the window, and she closed her eyes, basking in a ray of sunlight. 'Just to comprehend warmth once more is a marvel after so long.'

James returned to his monitor. 'Do you know the name of your doctor or someone that Emily sees for any medical issues? They may have insights and information that would help us.'

'Grayson,' she said, quickly returning to sit up straight. 'I remember Grayson and his revolting, efficacious powders.' Her hands fidgeted; her face was contorted, and she looked confused. 'He treats the milkmaids for cowpox.'

James glanced over at the nurse. Leigh Anderson shook her head, mouthing the same word in a confused reply.

'I don't believe I know a Dr Grayson,' said James, searching in the south-west regional database. 'You are sure he practices in the St Jude area?'

She nodded. 'He aids the parson with his gout. Father rides to fetch him—'

James ceased in the line of enquiry.

'Tell me about this house,' he said, holding up the picture of the fine house and seeking to gain further personal insight. 'Is it somewhere nearby?'

'Carmalt,' she said. 'It was where I grew up, where Mother died, and where Father worried about our future. He was sound in body though he took to drinking with the strain of the impact on the business from the war with France. Tariffs were high, and the county suffered under the heavy yoke of unyielding taxation.' She plucked at the burgundy tracksuit top. 'Even our contract to supply the militia with cloth was in doubt; they said the war went well, but it was at home that necessity was felt the most. I was there the day we sold our beautiful racing horses, and it broke his heart.'

The room fell silent once more, and she snuffled. The nurse took away the cardboard bowl and handed her a box of disposable medical tissues.

'Handkerchiefs you can throw away,' said Harriet, watching her look down in confusion. The counsellor leaned across and pulled out a single pinched tuft like a coarse white flame. The woman tugged at the absorbent sheet and dabbed her eyes.

'Father sought a union between our family and the wealthier Fallons to stem our rising debt, but I would not consent.' She paused and looked down at the hands in her lap. 'I would dearly like to see it once more through these eyes, but the woods, roads and town are changed, though I would know in which direction to go from the church.'

'What about Emily?' said James, pointing to his head. 'Would she know where?'

'She is from faraway,' she said, focussing on a knock at the door, 'but she left something of importance there; a horseless carriage.'

James rose to the sound of portable radio chatter from the other side of the door before opening it to reveal the broad frame of a policeman.

'This had better be urgent, Jory?' said James. 'I'm with—'

'I'm sorry, James – it is,' he said, peering over James's shoulder in amazement at the woman seated near the window. 'Crikey; I would never have recognised her.'

On seeing the officer, the woman skidded back the chair, folding her arms around her sides as though comforting herself. James indicated for Harriet to intervene.

'It's all right,' said the counsellor, drawing her chair closer and shielding her view of the figures at the door. 'He's a policeman; he keeps everyone safe.'

Jory lowered his voice to a whisper. 'I got a call from someone who found something while out walking their dog over at Maiden Point – they thought it might relate to the appeal for info on the naked woman we've been circulating.' He flashed his eyes. 'They were right.'

'What was it?' said James, trying to drown out the gentle chatter between Harriet and the woman.

'Fergus and I found clothing discarded up near that old, burnt, grassy sheep enclosure or whatever it is.'

James looked at him blankly.

'That ring of turf that stands out from the surrounding heather where the women have their blessed bonfire around the time of the fair.' He leaned into James's ear. 'Close to the point where folk jump off.'

'Something you think belongs to her?' he asked, conscious of the implication of the location. 'Women's clothing?'

Jory nodded. 'Clothing size would seem to fit her build and it's been out in the elements for at least a week.' The policeman shuffled his feet and tightened his jaw. 'I'm sorry to have to ask this, James, but I'll be needing a word with her. I had to call your boss first as she is still registered as the primary care lead.'

'But not now surely?' said James, stabbing a finger behind him as though to drive home the point. 'Can't you see she's just emerging from a significant traumatic event – what's the urgency?'

Jory pursed his lips. 'In the back pocket of a pair of jeans was the picture of her with a fella, along with several stolen credit cards belonging to at least four people.'

'That doesn't prove they belong to her—'

Jory held up a hand and retrieved a photocopied sheet of paper from inside his outer vest. 'The banks have come back positive on two of the cards, which were already on stop. Wiltshire police have looked at the time stamps and have her snapped on CCTV at a petrol station on the M3 motorway, and again just outside Salisbury when she tried to buy a bottle of water. While most cards were declined, she bought the fuel with one of them and it's still theft.' He unfolded the paper and James saw a series of blurry digital images looking down on the same woman that now sat, quiet and watchful, in the room, being soothed by the calming assurances of the counsellor.

Despite the shock of seeing the images and the relevance, what struck him first was the time stamp.

4 am

He stared at the static image of the woman entering the station forecourt and wondered what must have been going through her mind, certainly not fear of stolen credit cards if she was on her way to do the unthinkable.

'She drove a car up to Maiden Point. You've got the registration?'

'There's no car up there now, but we'll be doing a sweep later today of the wider area. With all these tracks and lanes we have to cover, it could take some time. If she'll voluntarily agree to being questioned along with your designated approved mental health professional, I can use Section 136 to keep her here as the nominated place of safety and not have to take her down to the station; it's the best I can do.'

James hung his head. 'She's already agreed to remain here until a full assessment is completed. If I call on the new counsellor to be there and get Mike to act as the approved medical practitioner, then you'll still need a duty solicitor.'

Jory nodded and folded the sheet back into his vest. 'Agreed.'

'I don't know how much you are going to get from her. Between an amnesiac and a historical personality, you will need to be guided by us. No bad cop routine if you want my sign-off on this; I know the law as well as you do. No discussion of events around the moment of trauma, and I don't want her reliving a near-death experience. She was going to jump before her mind switched to autopilot and she's running or hiding from someone, possibly an abusive partner. This will not make things easier.'

'I'm interested in the car's location over the cards.' Jory

shuffled his feet and stuck his hands into his vest. 'It's not my call, James. The City of London Police have requested we interview her under caution.'

'She's definitely from London, then?' said James.

'They can't be sure because we only have a first name. Even Emily Dene only crops up a dozen times and she doesn't cross-reference with any of them.'

'Emily's accent is from the south-east, but it's not strong.'

'The car belongs to a known and wanted criminal,' said Jory. 'One nasty piece of work by all accounts, who has dropped off their radar.' He held up the picture of the smiling blonde-haired man, nestling into the sunglasses and suntanned cheek of Emily's smiling face; a photo that might have been taken fairly recently during the hot, end-of-season holidays. 'I need to ask her if she knows where this bloke is so he can help with their enquiries.'

'Him,' James whispered, turning to see the woman staring back, oblivious to the soothing words from the counsellor between them. 'Is there a name?'

'Ryan Williams,' said Jory, over-loud, and joining him to look upon the woman's previously innocent face watching them intently and violated by a sudden look of sheer terror.

CHAPTER 10

J ames paced along the short seafront, biting the nails of his right hand and hoping that Caroline Lewisham was suddenly and unavoidably unavailable. The afternoon warmed the pine-boxed petunia planters and deck-chair-fronted promenade as he fidgeted with the phone's address book and the uncomfortable thought of giving her an eventful update along with his well-rehearsed speech. There was also the meeting with his father to deal with, and he checked for texts from the old man, and the residential hospice, that might mercifully prevent him from visiting later that day. He glanced down the beach towards the cliffs and hazy headland of Maiden Point until he shook off the procrastinating inhibition and tapped on the contact number.

'Talk to me,' said Caroline, brisk and efficient, as the call connected. 'I've just got off the phone to your sergeant, so you can skip the details. You don't need my permission to grant the local police access to a patient under the correct protocols you have in place.'

James bit his top lip and sat down on the metal bench overlooking the breakwater. 'You were on the right track about the mystery woman you sent over,' he said, leaning forward onto his thighs and rubbing a hand past his damp brow and into his hair. 'Emily is suffering from dissociation and delusions of one other personality but she's adamant the woman in her head, as she put it, was not present before we found her.'

'What kind of personality?'

'A historical caretaking alter – the drawing of the woman from the early nineteenth century was a self-portrait drawn from memory when it was fronting. It's very rare to see a splintering like this after someone's late teens. In fact, I've never seen it. If they occur, then it's usually in childhood, sometimes because of sudden or prolonged trauma, and before the mind has formed its unique and singular perspective. What's unique is that the alter has an existential understanding that it is a visitor, fulfilling the caretaker role until the host is out of danger.'

'Understood, but historical alters aren't uncommon, are they?'

'No. This delusion is remarkably convincing; the host has clearly immersed herself in the historical period as well as the local area, though there is some dichotomy...'

'What do you mean?'

'Her accent is more south-east than south-west, but the accent is Cornish, though archaic. It seems the critical need has triggered an attempt at the dialect as well as the disassociation.'

'You've determined what that critical need was?'

James drew in a long breath. 'The alter is in control of long-term memory and has described that Emily attempted to jump from Maiden Point, which is why it suddenly appeared and took control. That's been corroborated by the finding of her clothes near to the edge and several eyewitness testimonies, including a boat crew that was taking a diving team out beyond the headland. The caretaker believes it has done so before with other people. This type of guardian angel personality does crop up, though it is less common.' James paced around the bench, unable to settle his nerves. 'It's an attempted suicide, Caroline, though the alter described it by its older name: "self-murder". It might explain why she removed all her clothing.'

'Exiting this life with the same unencumbered innocence as she entered it?'

'It's consistent with many that jump from bridges and high places,' he said, turning from the headland to locate the church tower peeping from the hawthorn and peppered stands of pine, half a mile from the sands. The distance over rough ground was challenging to most intrepid walkers hardy enough to sweat and toil through bog, briar and the pathless maze of intricate sheep tracks. Under the influence of the other personality, Emily had done it naked and barefooted.

'Any flashbacks?'

James squeezed his eyes shut with the remembrance of her pale, scratched arms clasping for dear life around the memorial to the dead and shook off the question, realising it was not directed at his well-being, but Emily's. He turned and glanced over to a frisbee-catching fox-terrier on the beach, grounding himself for the reply even as the dog hit the sand.

'No, but she's triggered into disassociation with any mention of a particular man that may be trying to get at her or find her. I think it's the guy the police are after.'

'An abuser?'

James switched the phone to his other ear. 'It's a possibility and may explain why she may have travelled about as far as you can get from London and remain in England. We've witnessed several switches, before and after her interview with the local police sergeant this morning. It's quick, sometimes preceded by the humming and followed by a physiological blush response and dilation of the pupil. The personality in charge calls herself May Dene and fronts when the host, Emily, feels threatened or tries to recall memories that might cause her to become anxious or overwhelmed.'

A sound of movement from the distant office, like the sudden skid of a chair being drawn closer to the receiver on hands-free, broke his train of thought.

'Is someone else with you, Caroline?'

There was a short silence before she stammered in reply.

'N...No. May Dene, you say? You discovered the name she has assigned to the alternate personality? Good job, James.'

He sat down listening for any further unexplained interruptions, eager to get to the point and release his anxiety and responsibility back to his superior now that suicide had cropped up as a prime mover. 'I've never seen an adult case of sudden disassociation not related to injury, drug or alcohol misuse in this age group that hasn't been part of the host's previous life experiences before. Have you?'

'No,' said Caroline, unable or unwilling to see his intention to wriggle from the case, 'but I'm glad she's in the best possible hands.'

James tried again. 'Emily claims she has no skill in sketching something as accomplished as the self-portrait or any of the other works. Harriet calmed her down with paper and pen once the police left and watched her at work; it's the alter fronting when the drawing is going on. She switched halfway through a sketch of a sailing ship, incredibly detailed, and Emily's attempts at completing the scene were no better than my own, and the only thing I can draw is a flowchart.'

Caroline clarified the statement. 'You mean she has no memory of such skill; an alternate personality can't possess abilities that the host doesn't innately have, right?'

'Correct. They are co-conscious and she recalls drawing them in Truro, but just not why or how. The caretaker fronts and takes charge when the host is under stress but every time they switch, there appears to be a brief exchange of memory before May Dene gains control and the door slams shut again. Whatever trauma led up to the manifestation of the alter is being concealed, though Emily suspects she wasn't up at Maiden Point sightseeing. Now we all know what she was planning to do, it might be better to reveal this carefully rather than it suddenly materialising outside of a controlled setting; it could cause a relapse.'

'Agreed. You need to gain the trust of May Dene first, by the sounds of things.'

James gripped his leg to avoid the nervous juddering and waited for a skateboarder to pass by, summoning the courage to broach the subject that had consumed him all afternoon.

'I'm just here to do the initial assessment, that's what you agreed,' he said. 'It's what I need to talk to you about,' he said, closing his eyes, trying to recall fragments of a pre-prepared speech. 'You suspected this was an attempted suicide, didn't you? It's why you asked for a second opinion.'

A silence caused him to remove the phone from his ear and check that the call was still connected. 'Are you there?'

'Sorry, James. Can I put you on hold for a moment?'

James waited several long minutes, controlling his increasing heart rate with long in and out breaths.

'Suicide was always a possibility,' said Caroline returning from the silence with no explanation. 'St Jude has a distinct statistical skew in the number of cases because of that beauty spot up at the cliffs. I still think it's macabre those metal detectorists scour the base looking for cast wedding rings; it should be renamed "Divorce Point".'

'They aren't just after rings,' said James, suddenly defensively proud of the quiet seaside village. 'They are after jewellery said to have gone over the cliff years ago with some unfortunate heiress. The locals commemorate every harvest by throwing a willow effigy into the sea and lighting a bonfire; it's why it's called Maiden Point.'

'How very "Wicker Man" of you all, down there in St Jude. Make sure you tell that policeman to be careful...'

'It's not funny, and you aren't listening to me. You wanted my opinion and I'm happy to write the assessment, but I don't want to get involved. It feels too personal, too close to home.' James stumbled in his rapid speech. 'Too close to what happened before with Isobel Lee.'

'It had to happen eventually this year, James. I've reduced your caseload so you can prove you are ready to get back to work on a serious case,' said Caroline, her tone now changed from the familiar to the formal. 'I'm happy with everything I have seen up to now with your other patients and we—I mean, I, want you to see this one through.'

'You want me to take this attempted suicide so I can prove I'm no longer a liability to the Trust and we all get to go on as before?' he said, shaking his head. 'No. Besides, we don't have any sheltered accommodation in the area, not to mention only a single social worker we are still hoping will stay on until the two new positions are recruited; it could take months.'

'That sounds like avoidance and excuses,' she said. 'You were keen enough until the possibility of trauma-induced attempted suicide appeared. You need to calm down and gain some perspective – she's not Isobel Lee, James, and I'm looking to get you back not for my benefit, but yours. I'm ready to see you succeed again.'

'It's more complicated than that,' he said. 'My friend, the sergeant, is sympathetic, but he has another force breathing down his neck for answers on a wanted criminal connected to the missing car she drove to get here, so he has a right to be cynical. He was unimpressed to be interviewing a woman claiming to be from the nineteenth century and convinced her behaviour was being staged to avoid prosecution or avoid answering questions relating to the man they are after.'

'Why does he think that? You suggested the personality is passive, protective and consistent?'

'Emily believes the delusion, I can attest to that, and I've seen enough fakers in my time, but he thinks the archaic Cornish accent is put on, especially considering the name of the protective personality – Mary-Anne Dene; do you want me to spell out the initials for you?'

Caroline huffed. 'Coincidence. Your policeman can play at being cynical, but we have to remain professional and open-minded. You don't honestly think she spent £8.34 on a stolen credit card in part payment for fuel using her own cash, before fabricating an attempted suicide, and near-death, attention-seeking jaunt in her birthday suit, so she could take a freeloading holiday to the back of beyond?'

James threw his head back and stared into the gull-filled sky. 'I didn't know that about the credit card; he gave me the impression she'd gone on a mini spending spree.'

'At a service station?' said Caroline with amusement. 'No, and as I've just revealed confidential information that your friend revealed to get me to agree to his interview without extra paperwork, I haven't told you either. How did the new counsellor perform?'

'She's competent but over eager. I had to clip her wings following the initial meeting to avoid any repeat interjections that could jeopardise the building of trust.'

'You are sure it wasn't just providing some much-needed perspective or a new line of enquiry?'

James waited for the screech of a nearby gull to cease. 'She was there to observe, not to interfere.'

'Just what she said herself when she called me to apologise.'

'Harriet called you?'

'Yes, and from the sounds of things you over-reacted though I didn't share that thought with her. I am an advocate for the chain of command. For the record, I thanked her but reminded her that things of this nature should remain within the care team unless there is a critical cause for concern or an undisclosed conflict of interest.'

'I know the rules, Caroline. Anyway, Harriet said Emily recognised the guy in the photo, though not by name, but it's not the man they are after.'

'Who is it? A brother, lover or some friend of hers?'

'We think some combination of the last two, though she can't remember except for being incredibly upset on seeing it.'

'I thought you said it wasn't the criminal they were after, the potential abuser?'

'She was upset, but like it was someone she cared deeply for. She believes he is missing or worse, which might explain why she was up at the cliff. It might link with the alters bereavement of someone close, that military man Richard Avery, the guy on horseback. It could be a shared pattern of grief, one real and the other conjured to deal with unresolved emotions.'

'You are making progress; we have at least two motives for her attempted suicide, and the disassociation – escape from an abusive relationship, and intense grief resulting from another.'

'She also knows something of this Ryan Williams but just the gentlest of questioning provokes a sudden shutdown. Whatever this guy did to her, her mind is not ready to disclose it. Leigh Anderson is looking in on her every hour tonight and this has to be the final interview until she stabilises.'

Caroline sighed. 'I'll ensure she has the appropriate protections until then, but she's hardly a career criminal by the sound of things, is she? Sounds like she was running away from a world of hurt.'

James sighed at the rhetorical question, scrabbling for a way out of the responsibility. The conversation was not going according to plan and Caroline's stonewalling was second to none.

'Suffice to say,' she continued, 'Emily, or May, or whoever is in charge is staying put at St Jude as a result until I see a comprehensive and robust care plan in place and the police get their answers as well as their act together.'

James rose and clenched his hands in his pockets, searching for a way out. 'What about the refuge rooms in Truro on Weston Road, couldn't she go there?'

'Full,' she said. 'And stop asking me questions you already know the answers to. Besides, if you are telling me she is re-enacting and fantasising about legends of love-struck virgins and lost trinkets, then she's best placed with you to connect and deal with the delusion.'

James grasped at straws, desperate to avoid further involvement. 'I don't agree with keeping her here. The local paper and radio have been running with the story since word got out. It's not a good environment for recovery, and besides, where are we going to place her?'

'The women's refuge opposite the men's hostel. They owe me a favour and it has a room; I've checked.'

'But for how long?' said James. 'It's closing at the end of October without further funding, and they are still uncertain where the residents are going to be housed. They can't all go into bed and breakfasts!'

James looked at his white knuckles wrapped tensely around the phone and relaxed, lowering his voice. 'Sorry, Caroline. I just don't think I can take it on; I'm not ready at the moment, and the way I found her—'

'So, this is about you, rather than anything else you've

been throwing in the way? Don't mess me around, James – do I need to sign you off for post-traumatic stress, here?'

James bit his lip and paced towards the sea wall and back. For a moment, he thought of the easy way out of managing the case, despite the sense he was not clinically suffering from PTSD. There were no flashbacks, insomnia, nightmares, or classic symptoms. Despite the unease and shocking remembrance at the church the preceding week, he concluded the anxiety that had weakened his self-confidence was not linked, but it was wearing out his resistance to halt the pretence of being the dependable, driven Dr James Marshall of several months prior. He longed to tell Karen, curl up in a ball, and doze until the drowsy diazepam took it away for another day.

If I say yes, then they'll strike me off, he thought. *What will you tell Father, and what will you do then?*

'No, just shook me up a bit, that's all; on top of everything else – you know.' He knew the weak sentiment would not stick. His body language silently screamed for support, but she could not see the cry for help, only hearing the breaking of the waves against the mid-water stacks and the jabbering of gulls nearby, clamouring for discarded cod and chips.

Caroline's sigh of relief was audible. 'If, following your care assessment, she needs special care or is a danger to herself, then we can arrange an alternative course of action, but you will remain in charge, and I'll deal with the police. I will not apologise for reminding you of your obligations. I am your line manager, and I can't have you picking and choosing cases, especially where you are eminently qualified in those you are unwilling to take on.'

'Meaning?'

'Until then, she is your problem and not mine.'

'I prefer the term patient, not problem,' he snapped.

'I apologise,' said Caroline, 'and you are thinking straight at least, which is a good sign. Now calm down. You tell me you want your role back and then you seem reluctant to take on a patient that falls squarely in your wheelhouse. I've said my piece, now tell me what's going on?'

James brushed back his hair. 'Tell me this is just between us?'

The hum of the air-con and familiar background hospital sounds receded and her voice became clearer and quieter as though the phone had been removed from hands-free to the closeness of her mouth. 'Of course.'

He looked out towards the sands dotted with late holiday-makers. 'I am worried it will happen again, but this time I'll be taking you down with me. I'm fine with the lesser cases, but I'm lacking confidence and anxious just with the thought of taking on anything with serious consequences. Remember Florence Thompson on the call the other day? It felt like someone else, the person I used to be, was controlling my responses, not the wreck I am standing here. She was far enough down the path to recovery, and I was handing over, so the responsibility for her safety and well-being no longer rested with me. It was a relief. I knew you were there, and I was just about holding it together.'

Caroline raised her voice, unable to disguise the soft clicking of a closing door. 'You did all the work back there on the remote call, I had no part to play. You need to move past this. If you don't, you will be trapped with these feelings of guilt. You need to get back in the driving seat, James, unless you need more time and want me to sign you off?'

James froze, thinking of what it would mean for them both. Gayle and Fellows would be right about his readiness to return. He leaned against the rough, glittering granite of the sea wall, one hand tracing the Braille-raised crystals of quartz. 'No, you are right; I know I have to keep going, but I feel so scared.'

'Welcome to the club,' said Caroline softly. 'I want you to

see Mike Trebarr voluntarily before I pull rank and check the last time you missed your repeat prescription of antidepressants. Don't insult our long friendship by denying it – I know the signs.'

James folded an arm across his chest and grabbed at his opposite shoulder. 'I will. I'm going to need them if you are still adamant about me covering the Q&A next week?'

'I am,' said Caroline, with a hint of amusement. 'I see my favourite alternate personality of yours is back in charge.'

'Don't start,' he said, silently grateful for the banter that had been a consistent foil between them before his breakdown.

'I've missed Mr Witty,' she said, indulging him. 'Or is it Mr Sass? I can never tell them apart.' She returned to a deep and direct tone as he moved out of the way of several e-scooter riders shooting past.

'Stop trying to wriggle out of important academic panels as well as cases; besides, it might help you get your mojo back. We'll take this one step at a time, okay? I still expect your initial assessment at the end of the week. Your confidence and ego has suffered their first major setback and is trying to keep you safe by stopping you moving on. Ignore it, James, or—'

She hesitated, and he turned towards the tolling tenor bell of St Jude, close to a mile away, waiting for her to continue.

'I'll have to let you go.'

CHAPTER 11

'I'm here to see my father, Edward Marshall,' said James to the tanned female receptionist, shielding his eyes from the low, setting sun streaming through the great glass doors to the exclusive residential apartments of Fairhaven Grange.

'If you could just sign here, please,' she replied, offering a stylus and indicating where to sign on the touchscreen. 'We haven't seen you for a while, Dr Marshall.'

James studied her face for any hint of admonition. There was none and he berated himself for thinking the worst, blaming his cynicism on the anxious after-effects of his earlier call.

'I've been a little busy getting back to work but I've moved back to the area and hope to be a little more regular from now on.' He thought suddenly about the number of times he could see the old man before the countdown timer hit zero and deprived him of opportunities.

Fifteen, twelve, less?

'Is he in his apartment or annoying people in the common room?'

She smiled, releasing the electronic lock on the transparent doors to the walled garden. 'He's a sweety, but to answer your question – he has finished entertaining everyone for the day.'

That remains to be seen, thought James, collecting his shoulder bag and bidding the woman goodbye.

The walled garden beyond bloomed with mid-evening colour, and he relaxed into the scent of lavender and night stock as his feet brushed past the fragrant herbs that lined the path to his father's apartment.

The room overlooked the quadrant, and the old man, formally attired, sat at a large table on the shared veranda, musing over a large jigsaw on a rolled-out mat.

His father's white beard contrasted with his dark, spotted skin, and James thought he looked thinner since his last visit three weeks prior. The sombre face momentarily twitched into what might have constituted a smile with the sound of the approaching gravelled footsteps, before dourly refocusing on the seaside-scene puzzle in front of him.

'The prodigal son returns,' he said, rotating a piece to complete the large, colourful beach huts on the cut out cardboard below.

'Father,' said James, neutrally declining to acknowledge any attempt to unsettle him. He dragged a rattan chair and sat down to stare over the colourful borders and central, croquet-hooped area of finely mown lawn.

'Did you bring—?' said Edward, lifting a magnifying glass to study further missing shapes in the puzzle.

James adjusted and unzipped his bag, glancing over his shoulder to the darkened room of his father's lounge. 'Nice to see you, too,' he said, withdrawing a cluster of minibar-sized whisky bottles and a packet of cigars. He placed them on the table.

'If Stephanie finds out I've given these to you, I'll be barred and you'll have some explaining to do.'

Edward put down the glass and hurriedly pocketed the contraband. 'You needn't worry,' he said, returning to the jigsaw, 'she's in the back, making the tea and preparing the pointless pills. How else can I get my supplies when my own son doesn't fulfil his visiting obligations?'

James put down the bag and tugged at his ear. 'You don't need to see me, not when you're calling everybody else to find out what hole I've recently dug for myself.'

'You stopped answering my calls,' said Edward, clasping his liver-spotted hands over the rich and colourful scene below. 'How else can I check on the welfare of my only son?'

'Don't you mean the reputation of the family name?'

Edward glanced away with a huff and dug his hands into his blazer pockets.

'I'm sorry. Let's not fight,' said James. 'It's such a beautiful evening.'

'I agree, seeing as I have so few of them left. Caroline said you got a dressing down from Fellows.'

James drew a long breath and exhaled sharply through his nose. 'Even when I do wrong, you can't let me get away with it, can you? I have to come out winning for the family name every time. Caroline intimated you rustled up the support on my behalf. I didn't expect as much leniency to be honest, and truth be told, I've been avoiding seeing you until I was ready or couldn't care less about the speech that I know you have prepared.' He crossed his arms and looked away. 'Well, let's have it then.'

Edward ignored the latter comment with a tut. 'What you mean is, you hoped I wouldn't interfere, so you could fail on your terms, just to annoy me. I don't want you to throw away your career for one mistake, and I don't want you to compete with me or what I've achieved over the years, either. Didn't that jester of a general practitioner pass on my offer of a truce?'

'Mike is the best GP there is,' said James, turning back and coming to his best man's defence, 'and you know it. Here's me thinking your "interference" was just to see if your shadow still had the influence.' James cocked his head at the old man and was surprised to see his father looking back with an unusually thoughtful face. 'In case you were wondering – it does.'

James rifled in the bag and handed over Harriet's book. 'You'll also be delighted to hear that you have a fan: the new counsellor at St Jude.'

Edward frowned as he looked at the worn dust jacket before smiling with recognition. James reached inside his pocket to retrieve a pen, opening the book to the author's page. The gifted, folded drawing of the grand house lay pinched in the spine, and he put it aside.

'The royalties from this paid for your education,' he said, signing below the photograph. Edward pressed his finger against the grainy image and pointed at the pearl tiepin. James glanced up to see him clasp and look upon at the same decoratively functional item securing the patterned cravat at his neck. 'Your mother gave me this not long after we met.'

A momentary mask of sorrow faded, and he returned to his image on the open page of the book. 'Young fool. My last autograph, and on a first impression, too.'

'How do you know just from seeing this page?' said James, looking down at the shaky spidery letters scratched out on the page.

'It doesn't have my name below the photograph, and I gave the editor an earful until it was sorted. My ego was larger in those days, believe it or not.'

James spun the book to check and stuck out his bottom lip. 'Funny, I dropped this earlier today, and it opened at this page. I was with a new patient and the first thing she said was

"Marshall". I thought she must have read something, but you're right, there's nothing there.'

'Must have been referring to you, then; unless you are accusing me of moonlighting.'

James plucked at his lips, unable to reconcile the facts with the suggestion. 'She said the same when I found her.' He closed the book and placed it into his bag, pointing at the pin in his father's purple paisley cravat. 'You've worn that since before that old photograph was taken.'

Edward glanced across and breathed out. 'It's like carrying a little piece of her, but I think it's time for you to continue the tradition.' He withdrew the pin and handed it to James, barely able to contain his emotions. His voice began to quiver, and he hurriedly continued. 'A peace offering if you like, and to say I'm sorry for lost time, son.'

James took the precious and sentimental object, spinning the brass stem between his fingers and setting off the lustrous, captive pearl in the dying rays of the sun, setting below the high wall of the garden. He punctured the fine tweed thread of his lapel with an approving smile from its donor. Words that James struggled to form were interrupted by the rattle of distant cups and saucers heralding the approach of the carer, and Edward pushed the puzzle mat to the table's edge.

A woman in her early forties, brown-haired and blinking in the low evening sun, bustled across the tiled floor and placed down a tray containing an impromptu early-evening selection of snacks and a porcelain teapot with matching crockery. She greeted James and pointed to the plastic pill box with a well-rehearsed look of matriarchal authority.

'These first, Professor, before you tuck into any of that.'

Both men looked hungrily towards the finger sandwiches and petits fours before Edward leaned forwards to look at the contents of the medicine compartment. A brightly coloured selection of tablets and capsules lay nested in an ice cube type tray. He retrieved a pale amber lozenge and held it up in the low light of the sun. 'What's this?'

'Vitamin D,' she said, crossing her arms and preparing for the skirmish to come.

Edward copied the movement in defiance like a child refusing to eat his greens. 'I'll be dead in weeks, Stephanie,' he said. 'What's the point?'

'Dr Trebarr's orders,' she said, raising an eyebrow at the bulge in his breast pocket, 'and if you don't want me to inform him of the smell of whisky and tobacco on your breath later this evening.'

Edward coughed and looked away like a child caught red-handed as she disappeared back to the apartment. 'Eyes like a hawk,' he whispered, watching James shake his head and pour out the tea, 'with a tongue and beak to match; your mother wouldn't have talked to me like that, though I recall one episode to do with that damn harvest offering the women used to make, where I thoroughly deserved it.'

'The willow maiden?' said James, barely containing his amusement. 'The subject came up in connection with Maiden Point today. Do they still do it?'

'No idea,' he said. 'At least not openly; women take traditions seriously around here and keep secrets closer than they keep their husbands. Your mother used to be involved.'

James put down the pot, eager to hear more.

Edward smiled with a sudden recollection of his wife. 'She was always out in the latter parts of September, and she was a dreadful liar. I thought she was having an affair, so I followed her up to the cliff car park.'

He waited as his father swallowed the assortment of medicines keeping him alert and alive, cleansing his palate with a sip of weak Earl Grey between each pill.

'I was a bit embarrassed to be honest, sneaking around, not trusting what she said.'

'What did she say she was up to?'

'Out with friends, and it was something to do with the harvest. She was out there in the middle of the blessed night making some effigy along with several other women whom I recognised. It was all very innocent, if bizarre for a woman with a sceptical, materialistic worldview. I never thought she would be into pagan tradition or whatever it is, but then I'm an "outsider". I assumed they were going to burn it on the fire until they filled it with stones and tossed it over the cliff. I got a bit too close...' He snorted and blushed.

'You got caught?' said James, brimming with delight at the miscreant.

Edward nodded. 'She turned round, caught sight of me and I ran back to the car like the devil was on my tail. I caught it hot when she got in. No men allowed, apparently. She wouldn't discuss it, saying it was just for the good of the town. I spent the next week eating out of the fish and chip shop and sleeping on the sofa until she calmed down.'

James wiped a comic tear from the corner of his eye, struggling to maintain his dignity. 'If it wasn't for coincidence, I'd have never heard that story from you.'

'Coincidence is a dangerous thing if you don't recognise it early enough,' said Edward sliding a slice of Battenberg onto a side plate. 'Enough about my transgressions – you got away with it, then; you live to practise for another day?'

'Thanks to you it seems,' said James, helping himself to a smoked salmon sandwich. 'Though a demotion to St Jude is hardly getting away with it. She's also put me on the Q&A panel for the upcoming conference at the halls.'

Edward winced. 'Caroline has a nasty streak and a wicked sense of humour; I rather like her.'

James brushed the pin involuntarily on his shoulder. 'I thought perhaps you might like to come with me?'

His father snorted, and James did not press the offer of company.

'We'd probably only end up arguing, I guess,' he said, half to himself. 'Caroline probably told you everything already I'm guessing.'

Edward swallowed a mouthful of cake. 'Not the things that really matter, James.'

'She says I have you to thank for an inferiority complex,' said James, turning to see his father choking a cake-crumbed chuckle. He recovered his composure, but the creased smile remained.

'She's brighter than you are, but not as driven; you have me to thank for that and perhaps one day you will. She also thinks a lot of you, if you haven't noticed.'

James stemmed the thought, and the rising blush, with a sudden necessity to retie a loose shoelace.

'Tell me about this new patient of yours,' said Edward, courteously avoiding his gaze. 'I get so terribly bored with all those fuddy-duddies in the common room.'

James sat back and folded his hands into his lap, rotating his thumbs in meditative concentration.

'It's an attempted suicide, isn't it?' said Edward laying down his plate. 'Or one that is at risk. It has something to do with Caroline's request about the Dene surname, doesn't it?'

'Isn't anything confidential anymore – did she tell you?'

'No, it's because you wouldn't be so reticent about anything else. You obviously tried to get out of it, under the circumstances of the previous six months, and she threw the book at you?'

James twisted, amazed by the old man's pale but alert grey eyes. At seventy-eight, Edward Marshall was proving remarkably astute at cold reading body language, garnered from a lifetime of practical study.

James avoided the temptation to lie under his father's gaze. 'If you must know, I was concerned there would be undue pressure put on us both.'

Edward scoffed and flashed his eyes. 'Rubbish. You mean pressure on you. Caroline Lewisham can take care of herself. It's not inferiority you suffer from, it's imposter syndrome.'

'In all your working life, didn't you ever suffer from self-doubt?'

Edward sat back in his chair and tapped the hollow socket of his cheek. 'If I did, I can't remember now. Sometimes I see their faces – the ones I saved, and the ones I lost. I'm so old now that I cannot remember which. Yes, I rolled the dice occasionally pushing for more than the patient was willing to give me, but I never deviated from procedure or the prevailing theories of the day.'

'That's easy for you to say because most of the time you were expanding the theories.'

Edward flicked away a smattering of sugared grains from his shirt. 'I'll take that as a compliment, shall I?'

'But psychiatry evolves,' said James. 'What do you say now to those you lost whom you might have saved with hindsight?'

Edward leaned forward and peered at the edge of the jigsaw as though searching for an answer among the missing pieces.

'That is a question I have asked myself for nigh on fifty years; as will you when your time comes.' He picked up a piece and offered it to the near corner of the puzzle.

'You said you had completed Mother's side of the family tree?' asked James, nodding towards the journal in his father's lap. 'Any revelations of lost inheritances or treasure that I should know about?'

Edward's eyes lit up, and he abandoned the jigsaw. 'Quite

the opposite,' he said, handing over the book. 'My forefathers are all from London, as you know. You and your mother have been in the area for a long while and her family records go back further than mine – back even before the registration of records began in 1837, thanks to a judicious and foresighted record-keeper at the time, and the patient efforts of the local historian in St Austell to put up with my persistent requests for information. There were a few leads beyond 1801, but that has no useful information – it's essentially just a list of names. You are descended from domestic servants by the name of Cartwright, around the turn of the nineteenth century, who looked after the last surviving member of the Dene family before he fell on hard times.'

James weighed the book in his hand and flicked through the handwritten pages, interspersed with glued snippets of cut-out photocopied clippings. He paused as the page unfolded onto a clipping of a watermarked ink painting, showing the outline of a fine house, strikingly similar in style to the building in Emily's drawing, though more evident in wear and decay. Below the image lay a few lines of beautiful scrolling text:

For sale by private auction to be
determined the estate and chattels of —

James unfolded the sheet on the table and compared the two.

'Remarkably similar,' said Edward, leaning over. 'I didn't know you were interested enough to do your own research—'

'I didn't,' said James. 'This is a drawing given to me by the new case, the woman I found at the church.' He glanced over to the oldest part of the Grange and its mismatch of granite stones, checking back to the foundation stones of Emily's sketch. 'You don't happen to know what Fairhaven Grange was before it became a residential home, do you?'

Edward plucked at his beard. 'It was derelict for decades,

as I recall. It was a field hospital during the First World War—'

'And before then?'

'Some charitable poorhouse and school for disadvantaged mothers and their children, I think. Is it important or another one of your coincidences?'

James shrugged. 'Just a confirmation of something my patient implied.' He stared at the two images, trying to find any discrepancies, but though the aspect was changed, both seemed to have been sketched or painted from broadly the same location. 'It's the same house,' he whispered, 'though this drawing, made a few days ago, shows the building in better condition.'

'The church tower is also different in your sketch,' said Edward, pointing out the difference. The unfamiliar steeple rose from a bank of trees in the drawing, in contrast to the squat tower in the photocopy, just visible behind a taller and thicker belt of trees, that James and the whole community of St Jude knew so well.

'Do you have anything else on this picture, or why you asked for it in the first place?'

'Only that the archivist in Truro found it in the same file having been returned there by the previous person to request the information. I assumed it must be where the servants I spoke of worked before the place was sold off, and this drawing was likely commissioned to sell the place. If you want the whole picture, you'll have to get it yourself. They took so long getting this stuff to me, I'll be dead by the time they get around to it.'

James glanced over with a pinched brow at the suggestion.

'Well, it's the truth, isn't it?' said Edward. 'Why waste time on minutiae?'

'I may be able to get it quicker. I treated his wife, an antiques dealer, for post-natal depression several years ago and he always feels obligated whenever we bump into each other.'

'I wish you'd told me that sooner,' said Edward. 'It would have saved me ringing every few days.'

'What will you do now you've finished?' said James, smoothing over the darkly tanned cover. 'It's kept you occupied for a long time.'

Edward hacked a cough that left him breathless for a short time. James saw the concern of the carer through the window but he shook his head to signal his father was alright. The old man wheezed into a steady breath through a hastily grabbed napkin and grabbed James's hand to steady himself.

'I'm happy with my jigsaws and a copy of The Lancet for now,' he said, dabbing his mouth with the cloth. James noticed faint speckles of blood and Edward scrunched up the linen into his palm to prevent further examination. He held up the napkin-clutching hand to prevent James from interrupting. 'Your mother and I used to clear out the weeds and tidy the older plots in the churchyard and I always meant to carry it on. She was most insistent the Dene graves were kept trimmed but I guess my gardening days are almost done. You can find some interesting inscriptions lower down where the stones have sunk over time – I wonder if she knew about her ancestors' connection; if she did she never said so.'

James clasped the hand and felt it squeeze tightly as Edward spoke again.

'I want you to concentrate on you, not me – I'm fine. I'm not scared of dying, James, but I regret not being a man prone to sharing emotion, especially as a father. I, unfortunately, inherited the trait from my own – a good man, but as cold and unfathomable as one of those stones.' He pointed to the recent drawing and the foundations of the fine house. 'I hope you won't think of me in the same way when I am gone.'

He picked up a piece and offered it to the near corner of the puzzle, humming snatches of a gentle melody.

James pondered the words, listening as the lullaby began clearer and more familiar. 'What is that song?'

'Eh?' said Edward, breaking out of his mindful state.

'The tune you are humming. I heard it yesterday, and the day I found the new patient. It seems to trigger a switch in personality and subdue the host and her anxiety.'

'The naked woman doing the rounds in the papers and TV?'

James nodded. 'She was humming the same tune.'

Edward scratched at his beard. 'Pretty isn't it? Some old folk tune I expect. Something your mother used to sing to you when you were a baby. She said it had been passed down by her grandmother and so forth. It always had a calming effect on you.'

'You don't recall what it is, do you? — it might be important.'

'Not coincidence again.' He paused for a long while, humming snatches of the tune before an accompanying blackbird fluttered to perch and began to warble in a nearby crab apple tree.

'*You shall hear the fond tale of the sweet nightingale,*
As she sings in the valley below...'

The awkwardness of his Father reciting poetry was over-matched by a sudden stillness. The sultry, perfumed air, stirred by a gentle wind, became alive with a chorus of roosting birdsong and James desperately clung to the calming moment. It receded with the tip-tapping approach and stick-raised salutation of an elderly resident from the flagstone path bordering the lower lawn.

Edward returned the gesture and whispered from the corner of his mouth. 'Nice chap but dreadful backgammon player. He owes me thirty pounds, which you should remind him of when I'm gone, speaking of which—

'Your mother kept a music box, passed down through many generations, which plays the same tune if I'm not mistaken,' said Edward closing his eyes to recall the fleeting memory. 'Why don't you come back earlier next time and I'll have Stephanie go through my things.' His open eyes alighted on the pin at James's lapel. 'It's only fitting you have the last remaining item belonging to her.'

Edward offered the journal to James, catching the corner of the drawing of Carmalt. The grand house spun to face him.

'And your family line.'

CHAPTER 12

The sun dipped below the swan neck of the adjacent tennis court wall and Edward put aside the puzzle. 'One more sunset down, my boy.'

James changed the subject, fearing for a melancholic end to a difficult day.

'The patient mentioned a Dr Grayson; does he sound familiar? He's not in any of the databases. One of the social workers in the care team thinks there's a ward named after him further down the coast.'

'There is indeed,' said Edward, relaxing gently back into his chair. 'A historical figure well before the last century, if I recall – promoter of women in medicine – very controversial at the time. Why did she mention him?'

'I'm unsure, at least I am if that is who she is talking about. She's displaying an unusual personality disorder.'

'There's rarely anything usual about personality disorders,' said Edward, leaning towards him with interest. James watched the wizened eyes burst into life, the same look of intense intellect that had made the man a legend in his field. 'Tell me more unless you really don't want to talk about psychiatry. Perhaps we can talk about Tolstoy instead?'

James hurried into the conversation. 'Transient amnesia with a dissociative, dominant historical alter suppressing the trauma of an attempted suicide, or the events leading up to it.'

'Mary Queen of Scots or Anne Boleyn?'

James frowned, seeing his father hold out his open hand.

'Sorry, that was uncalled for,' said Edward. 'Old joke.'

'A woman from the early nineteenth century.'

'It's a popular fantasy, James. Not too distant to be unknowable, but far enough from the madding crowd to be safe and vague from any scrutiny. You'll work it out.'

'She's only got a few days before they move her to the refuge. I'm still not sure I'll be taking it on, long term.'

'You will if you don't want to end up teaching, or worse. I thought the refuge had closed down already; Stephanie used to volunteer there.'

'She still does. At the moment, it's planned to close at the end of October, and they are raising money at the Haldwyn fair at the weekend in Twenty-Acre Field, to keep it going for another few months until they can do the Christmas markets over at Mousehole and Penzance.'

'Your mother used to work at that sad but hopeful place,' said Edward, 'and I'm sad to hear that. They used to call it the battered wife house, which put off many of those to whom it should have helped; for some, the stigma was worse than being brutalised at home. I always knew when Jo had been there that day. She'd be jubilant or in floods of tears; there was never any middle ground.'

Stephanie returned to bring further hot water for the teapot and check his father's pulse. James saw the pretence play out as she checked the emptied pill tray with surety.

'And here is one that knows all about that, isn't that right,

Stephanie? My genealogical assistant and nurse – a strange combination.'

'Anything to keep you quiet and taking those pills, Professor Marshall,' she said with a wry smile, taking away the tray.

James unfolded the sheet to reveal the drawing of the house. 'The patient claims the alternate historical personality drew this and many other period sketches – horses, people and mundane or everyday things, mostly. You can see St Jude Church in the distance before the tower was rebuilt.'

'Assuming it's the same place; don't jump to conclusions.' Edward took out a pair of reading spectacles from his flannel jacket pocket. 'Who is the host, a student of history or period architecture?'

'Apart from a first name and that she's possibly from London, we don't know,' said James, watching as his father put a finger to his mouth and tugged at his bottom lip. 'Do you recognise the house? She calls it Carmalt and says it's fairly local.'

'No, but those lower stones remind me of those old ruins you used to play out in for days on end up in the wooded valley. Why would a woman from London draw a manor house in north Cornwall?'

'She claims she can't draw, not to this level of detail. The other drawings are sublime in detail and style.' James paused. 'Did you ever, in your career, have an alternate personality do anything alien like this where the host denies categorically any skill or aptitude that would account for it?'

Edward frowned. 'Of course not. Why are you suddenly asking undergraduate questions?'

James rolled his eyes. 'It's just I was telling your new fan, Harriet, about Tom Cotter recently, and the story of how he saved me when he claimed he couldn't swim.'

'You shouldn't discuss private matters or become too

familiar with your staff,' said Edward. 'It muddies the water when it's time to review their performance or issue a reprimand.'

James turned his attention to a butterfly fluttering by and twitched his eyebrows. 'Too late for that...'

'Besides,' said Edward. 'That story has been embellished over the years. I think you need a refresher course on Occam's razor – the simplest explanation is usually the right one.'

'Which is?'

'That he could swim and had convinced himself otherwise, like your artist here, or that he since lost the knowledge of it because of post-traumatic stress. I told Fellows the same thing when he was not much older than you.'

'Fellows was curious about Tom Cotter?'

'Among a good many similar things. It led to the beginning of our disagreements, but I am not going there tonight, so don't bother to ask.' He reached over and picked at another slice of cake. 'Tell me more of this woman you are struggling with.'

'I'm not struggling,' he said, watching his father devour the sponge and return to the jigsaw. James gave in after a short silence. 'The personality is caretaking and fronting when the host feels threatened. The police think she's acting to avoid prosecution; they found stolen items at the cliffs in clothing they believe belongs to her.'

'The cliffs up at Maiden Down?'

James nodded. 'Maiden Point, specifically.'

'And what do you think?' asked Edward, studying his face.

'She's not malingering; it's been too long. There's no crack or flaw in her performance if that is what it is. The alter truly believes that she is from the first decades of the nineteenth century.'

'Trauma-induced past-life personality disorder isn't

uncommon as a defence mechanism.'

'I'm aware of that,' said James. 'It's just I've encountered nothing so convincing like this before or one that has emerged suddenly in a fully mature adult. The patient says they have experienced no schizophrenia or personality disorder before coming here.'

'That she knows of, or can recall,' said Edward. 'Don't forget the mind is a most unreliable witness.'

James rubbed at his cheek. 'Did you ever encounter a case where spontaneous emergence of an alternate personality, unrelated to substance abuse or injury, occurred in someone in their thirties?'

'Never as late as that,' said Edward, tapping his feet nervously on the patio deck. 'You may need to re-investigate your diagnosis and the validity of her assertions.'

James frowned. 'You can't be seriously suggesting she's trying to gain attention or that Ganser syndrome might be what I need to consider? I thought you were trying to protect me, not play straight into Gayle and Fellows' hands.'

Edward reached over to rest his hand on James's shoulder. 'I'm not suggesting anything of the sort; just keep an open mind. You must take everything on a case-by-case basis. Just because you were incorrect on one case does not alter the statistical likelihood of the next patient to suffer from it.'

'You know Fellows can access everything I pass to Caroline?'

'I do,' he said, removing his hand and returning it to his lap. 'The question is, do you want to help the patient by forming an alternative diagnosis that might see her removed from your care? You don't have to formalise anything, just keep it to yourself, or tell me, if you want a second opinion.'

James sighed. 'You are something else, you know that? If you want to get back into the saddle one last time, then you'll have to ask Caroline—'

'Or you could,' said Edward, draining the last of his tea. 'Having another eminent and specialist psychiatrist forming the same conclusion, though retired, would bolster your submission. We've never worked on a case together, have we? I don't have the information to make a judgement but your panic at the mere suggestion of a counter-diagnosis means you haven't truly learned from the previous case that caused all this self-doubt. Don't let one incident dictate the rest of your life, James, especially as it is debatable whether you should have been there at all.'

James frowned. 'What do you mean? I was investigated for malpractice; Fellows himself said I incorrectly diagnosed—'

'Fellows has been wrong before,' said Edward. 'Though he and the Board were right, in their report, to reprimand you about the lack of distance between you and the patient, understandable considering your circumstances at the time, but professionally very unwise.'

James shuffled in his seat. 'And how would you know of this unless you had access to confidential documents relating to the case? Not even I could see them.'

Edward tapped a finger to his temple. 'My co-conspirator and I had an agreement.'

'You mean Caroline leaked a sensitive document to you in exchange for information on that historical precedent? She told me you gave her something that would get me off the hook in an emergency, and just for that fleeting moment I thought it may have been just to help me instead of indulging your professional voyeurism or just to get back at Fellows for whatever caused you both to commit to a lifetime of bitterness.'

'If you are finished wallowing in self-pity, I will explain my motivations,' said Edward sternly. 'They have ever been to protect and nurture you. Caroline came to me for guidance about your impending dismissal, for that is what it could have been. I gave her a steer and a "get out of jail free" card in exchange for a heavily redacted copy of his and your diagnosis.' He lowered his voice, waiting for a woman, hobbling along the central path with a small Pekingese, to pass.

'While I cannot rule out obvious bias against my former protege, and fully submit a conflict of interest, I am inclined to agree with your diagnosis based on the evidence you submitted.'

James shook his head, stunned with the revelation. 'But Fellows said Ganser hasn't led to a suicide in my lifetime—'

'Not in yours,' said Edward, softening to a whisper, 'but potentially in his. Caroline told me you had just left the room when I called her. I wasn't interested in the grubby details once I discovered your career was intact, and just wanted to know what my rogue apprentice made of it. I am not a vindictive man, but I would have dearly loved to have been in the room.'

'I think, to all intents and purposes, you were,' said James. 'Gayle did everything she could to twist my words and force Fellows' hand.'

'And by all accounts, you almost succeeded with little effort on their part.'

'What webs you weave,' said James. 'So, what did "Uncle Cameron" do to cause such a rift between you?'

Edward snorted at the use of the name. 'He was genuinely fond of you; I'll give him that. It was a long time ago, and I have no wish on such a fine evening to discuss the painful circumstances that led to our estrangement, along with other regrettable matters for those in our care. He did not see coincidence for what it truly was and I prevented him from pursuing his so-called "evidence" on a similar case to his ruin by clipping his wings and putting him on probation.'

James studied the glint in the sideways glance of his

father's eye. The black pupil at the centre of the milky grey iris twitched as it waited for the penny to drop.

'The historical precedent,' said James, rising and stroking his chin as though his whole being could not restrain itself from the inference. 'You did to Fellows what he did to me?'

'Took you long enough,' said Edward, distracting his amusement with an adjustment of his cravat. 'Caroline worked it out straight away, or at least she thinks she has. I didn't admit it directly.'

James turned and wiped his hands down his cheeks. 'Well, at least the warring factions are even now. Why do I feel as though I am a pawn in all this?'

'I saved your career, James, and his in the long run, but he never saw it that way.'

'You aren't going to expand on the details with Fellows, are you?'

Edward ignored the question and looked over at the drawings. 'This strange land at the edge of the world is full of myth and legends that seep, unaware, into the very fabric of its stones and take root in its superstitious inhabitants. Let it be a warning to you about not seeing coincidences connected with people, place, and personality disorders for what they are, especially here. The beguiling superstition of that woman with her jewellery going over the cliff that you brought up, for example, is both glamorous and dangerous, and there have been many copycat incidents and deaths of that sort, not just here.'

'You think there may be a connection between her and a recollection of the local legend? I hadn't considered she might be a fantasist or sub-consciously acting out the role.'

James studied the thoughtful face and the sudden resolute steadiness in his hand as he reached over to choose a random face-down jigsaw piece.

'There is always a connection and there is nothing more

alluring or that demands sympathy than embellished, romantic nonsense.'

'Now I know why the amorously located hospital garden was as good as Mum got.' James avoided the brief narrowing of his father's eyes and paused, uncertain whether to ask the follow up on his lips. A glance at his father's tapping leg beneath the table suggested his curiosity was barely contained, despite a plain disinterest in anything but the puzzle before him.

'Your hypothesis?'

'An attempted suicide,' said Edward, ready with the answer, 'whose innate personality disassociated at or during the moment of trauma, protecting the host by its own associated stress and shared circumstance. I stake my remaining reputation on it being temporary, which will be good for her, and you.'

The old man's eyebrow twitched as he turned the jigsaw section between his forefinger and thumb and deposited the tiny female figure on a verdant background to its location on the cliff top overlooking the beach scene.

'Well I never,' he whispered, eyes fixed upon the completed top left corner showing the stylised headland with its kites, circling gulls, rock outcrops and solitary figure staring out to sea. 'Be careful with the Dene patient, James, very careful. Listen, but don't encourage it. Keep a rational mind and don't muddle the present with only half-remembered secrets of the past. Coincidence has a seductive habit of creating biases and the need for questions without answers —' Edward's voice softened to a nervous whisper.

James followed his father's wide-eyed stare to the lonely person, back turned, at the edge of the clifftop scene.

'I only hope that you listen where Fellows did not, because dead or alive, my help won't save you a second time.'

CHAPTER 13

The horizon glimmered beneath the light of the harvest moon, gradually broadening as the dark moorland approached its end. James ran, fearful of a future that he was increasingly uncertain of. A single crack of gunfire from the brooding, bible-black wood behind spurred him on though he knew he was out of range, but also increasingly out of ground. From the corners of his eyes, he saw the cliff edge on either side become distinct, no longer a solid black line ahead but a reflecting moonlit face of pale, glittering granite.

I need to slow down and take stock, he thought. *I don't know if I can do this...why am I even here?*

His pace slackened momentarily but his legs recovered, ignoring the sound of the sea and the suggestion in his slumbering mind, racing towards the security of flickering amber light. The salt-laden air became tainted with the acrid smell of burning and he halted by the flames of a well-stacked bonfire, ringed by the figures of gowned women, glad to have convinced his limbs to cease in their terminal insistence to sail over the cliff. One woman broke rank, leaving the others to their making and tending of something in the shadows beyond the burning pyre. She took his hand and guided him within their circle.

Laying him down to rest, James felt the glow of the fire as face after smiling face whispered and sang around him, placing flowers and offerings upon his heaving chest.

I know that song, he thought, trying to recall the past or the present. *I've heard it recently – my mother used to—*'

He turned to see her face, as though saying the word had summoned the woman he never knew, and could not wholly recall. She remained younger than he, humming a gentle lullaby, frozen in age like the treasured photos he kept locked and sacred in an old biscuit tin that had once belonged to her.

He tried to speak, but the words became stuttered and stopped altogether, as though his mouth was locking into an open spasm. 'You used to... sing this to... me...'

She smiled and put a finger to her lips while the other women explored his chest with their fingers, digging them into his flesh and leaving cold stones to weigh him down and prevent him from rising. He panicked and looked down upon what once was a man, but now changed into the lattice and crafted corn work of something humanoid in form but devoid of humanity. He tried to scream, but it was too late. The effigy was complete and nothing but his conscious, terrified spirit remained locked within a carcass of willow, beach cobbles and flowering corn.

Lifted into the air he felt the warmth of the fire diminish, relieved that his fear of being burned alive was receding. Gripped by the strong hands of six Cornish women he watched the stars of heaven sparkle in the chill autumn air, the sound of the sea getting ever closer.

Why are you doing this?

One answered as though hearing his thoughts. 'We do so to remember her. Don't you want her to return?'

With sightless eyes in cavities of spent corncockle and

chamomile, he caught sight of the two closest faces to his own.

'No!' he cried in his mind, struggling without muscle or sinew to break their powerful grasp. The face of Isobel Lee glanced down, a sad, melancholic sympathy in her wide eyes.

'Do not be afraid...' she said, above the crashing waves. The sensation of being carried ceased, and the stars settled into sparkling, sedentary stillness.

James railed and fought to escape realising where he was and what they had planned. The adjacent woman offered a gentle hush to calm his panic, and he strained his eye to see his beloved wife return a look of mournful affection. She raised her free hand to stroke a fine necklace, its silver wire-work dazzling the paleness of her neck setting the three-linked sapphires ablaze in the moon's light as she twisted and turned.

'I have one of my own, now,' she said, joining the others in rocking his frame in time. 'Why did you not bring me one? You promised...'

He gained momentum, rising and falling with greater intensity, and he knew that the end of the cliff and his life approached. A final lurch forward released him into the air and he tumbled, screaming into the rush of night, striking the high tide like glass. The instant cold and dark terrified him, bringing back childhood memories, and he scrabbled, ineffectively, to raise his lifeless limbs and swim upwards, even as the smooth stones in his chest pulled him down to the blood worms of the flooded beach.

Suddenly a bright light, filtering through a colourful, tangled mass of deflating rubber appeared above. The water became clearer, and he felt the cool sting of the summer sea throughout his body, returned to skin and bone. A mighty kick launched himself upward, and he struck out a hand to break the surface.

Instinctively, *he* was there. His strong arms pulling him upwards and into the bay and away from the punctured dinghy. James's head emerged into the air and he spluttered, even as the man beneath him kicked backwards, elbow crooked into his neck, forcing them both into a horizontal float as figures in approaching boats called out wildly.

'Let go...' the man whispered, confident in his strokes as James flailed to remain above water. Close to his ear and against the man's stubbled chin he heard the gasping snatches of the lullaby, soothing and softly washing his fears and doubt away. James relaxed even as the man's grip loosened and slipped away, replaced by the grabbing hands of many others, raising him by his thin T-shirt covered shorts into the swell of sunlight and surf, and into the rescue boat...

James bolted upright, soaked by a chill sweat, kicking away the remaining damp sheets, rippled and rucked by the nightmare. Taking stock of where he was, he panted, feeling the sense of the rocking of the dream boat subside as he clung to the mattress like a life raft. Patting his clammy body as though to ensure its wholeness, he looked through the curtain-less, starlit window and the solid black massif of the distant, silhouetted headland, staring until the faint glimmer of dawn and the loss of feeling in his cramped knees brought him painfully back to his senses.

James turned out of his drive and headed for the town. He breathed deeply, settled his nerves and thought of the day ahead supporting the mental well-being of others while struggling with his own. The empty house was full of memories and each unnecessary room, once visited, now remained firmly locked with whatever joyful or sad remembrance it contained.

The early-morning panic had taken several sedatives and mindfulness techniques to reduce to the level where he felt able to commit to shaving and dressing for the day ahead, all the while knowing that the protective urge to call in sick, lie down and just forget about the decisions and responsibility would have to be conquered again in the early, sleepless hours of the following morning.

He rubbed his eyes and put aside his bruised ego from the perceived demotion back to his hometown. The alternative was intense Truro with a high workload, stress and isolation and he was glad that he finally saw it for what it was; there was no way he would have coped there if gentle St Jude made him panic. Perhaps the return to his former post could no longer happen, even if he was offered it. He wondered whether his confidence would return fully, as it did in small measure during the late afternoon when the world didn't seem so unforgiving and the worries of what might happen did not materialise. No one around him seemed to sense this overwhelming internal change in his otherwise open and professional persona. All of which added to his nervousness, but his decision seemed clear and made; he would see out the winter and consider other, less stressful options within medicine, perhaps even outside of it, and he exhaled slowly with the pleasant thought of it. He would wait until his father was gone – he owed him that much.

The car descended the slope towards the mist-shrouded coast, and he put on the wipers to clear the film of chill water droplets. Up above, the indistinct brightness promised another fine day once the sea fog had burned away. The high pressure looked set to remain and he studied his own taut-skinned, teeth grinding facial response with the irony.

He clicked on the steering wheel to accept the incoming call.

'Is this my early-morning pick-me-up?' he said.

'If you like,' came the voice of Caroline Lewisham through the car's speakers. 'Do you need picking up, after what you said the other day?'

'One day at a time,' said James, yawning.

'Heavy night?'

James snorted with the suggestion. 'Not what you think. I just didn't sleep that well, but today's fairly quiet. I've got consultations from ten o'clock at St Austell and I'm on the interview panel later for replacement members for the care team.'

'You call that quiet?' said Caroline. 'Don't forget you have a meeting to discuss your recovery with Dr Trebarr this afternoon.' She paused. 'I'm just reminding you because you have thus far avoided the discussion—'

'I've been really busy, that's all.'

'Well, you said yourself you are quiet today and I expect it to stay that way. It is non-negotiable, James.'

He sighed. 'Understood.'

'How's Harriet Swanson since you let off steam?'

'Solid,' he replied, turning the car onto the empty coastal road. 'Perceptive and dedicated. She watches me like a hawk but is frustrated by lack of progress occasionally—'

'You mean generally, or regarding a patient?'

'The attempted suicide case, Emily; she's not having the usual initial results from the cognitive behavioural sessions as she is with all of our other patients.'

'It's only been a week,' said Caroline.

'The art therapy is producing results, though only on paper. The subjects are all historical and only provide insight into her active imagination and retentive memory, though the same level of artistry only occurs when May Dene fronts. There's a growing number of contemporary sketches that might be a sign that control is being ceded back to Emily and we've been honest and talked through what she suspects about Maiden Point and the reason for her travel to Cornwall.'

'How did she take it?'

'Calmly, as though it confirmed what she already knew from internal dialogue with the alter. I think she was seeking verification from an outside source, though perhaps it hasn't quite sunk in yet. She knows we aren't keeping things back from her anymore but the subject of the abuser is still too raw. There's still no surname, unfortunately, but we are moving her to the refuge this morning.' He checked the side window for any sight of the sea beyond the narrow beach of high tide. 'She's physically recovered from her ordeal, and I'm popping over later to see how she's settling in.'

'That's very gallant of you?'

'Harriet and I believe that a less clinical situation might encourage her to relax and open up. Asking how she feels in a hospital at every meeting is counter-intuitive. My father's carer, Stephanie, volunteers there.'

'Is your policeman friend relaxed she won't go on the run again?'

'We have an understanding,' said James. 'Off the record, he'll share anything non-sensitive about the case to enable me to better understand what might be going on. I'll reciprocate once I've discussed with you.'

'Sounds a very profitable arrangement, providing you stick to guidelines on patient confidentiality and run everything through me. I don't want you pressured into a course of action that she isn't ready for, friendship or not. Your primary concern is for her well-being, not societal justice.'

'Understood, and the solicitor has clarified that there can be no proceedings until an identity is established, even if she has a connection with a wanted man.'

'I'll leave you to get on with it,' she said. 'I have some

good news – first, your father has stopped ringing me now that you have seen eye to eye.'

James tapped the steering wheel and paused at the lights. 'Small steps. He seems engaged on the Emily Dene case following my initial icebreaker with him. His insights might prove useful if you don't mind me sharing information with a dying man.' He hesitated and looked into the central display showing the call. 'I could heavily redact any of my notes if you like.'

'He told you what I did in exchange for getting you off the hook, then.'

'Yes, and you are in a world of hurt if anyone found out,' said James, turning inland towards the south coast and St Austell.

'Is this blackmail? You share information as I did in exchange for keeping your mouth shut?'

'No,' said James. 'It's about us both sharing the risk. I'm not happy you did this for me.'

'I didn't know you cared,' said Caroline. 'You are still sore that you had to apologise first the other evening before he opened up.' James heard the exasperated sigh as she concluded.

'Men...'

'It was more than that, he seemed genuinely protective of me in a way that I hadn't realised before. I'll admit I was wrong. The opportunity to remind Fellows that he was still breathing and a force to be reckoned with was secondary. The health situation has sharpened his focus on what is important, and I feel I might be seeing his true personality for the first time. On reflection, I went in ready for a fight when I saw him after the disciplinary; I see now he was holding a white flag while I was still pointing a gun.'

'Very well,' she said. 'You could have done this without asking and I would have been unlikely to have found out. I appreciate your honesty, though not strictly the request. I agree providing nothing written is presented, and that it forms an informal and hypothetical discussion on an unnamed patient; is that understood?'

'Agreed, though he knows it's the woman from the media hoo-ha. It might get him to open up about the case that he and Fellows fell out over as well as why Fellows got his hand slapped as I did.'

'You are your father's son,' she said. 'I came to the same conclusion. Make sure that Emily's welfare is your prime motivator.'

James drove over the isolated moorland pass. 'I'm going to lose you in a minute.'

'Well, I might bump into you later; that's the second bit of good news. I'll be over to see the old devil myself with a surprise.'

'You are coming to St Jude, to see me?'

'How self-centred of you,' she said with a hint of amusement. 'I'm visiting an old acquaintance at Fairhaven who looked after my mother for a time. She's recovering from cataract surgery and Fellows has given me some time in lieu. He's also asked me to deliver a letter to your father, along with what sounds like a wrapped jigsaw.' James heard an accompanying shuffling sound as Caroline shook the unseen box. 'Apparently, the traditional postman route has not proved very successful in soliciting a reply.'

'Fellows is trying to reach out and make peace?'

'Yes. That's what I thought, though I was tempted to steam it open to confirm my hypothesis.'

'There's still time,' said James, chuckling. 'You can tell me all about it later.' He gripped the wheel tightly and turned away from the mirror to avoid the timid reflection. 'I look forward to seeing you.'

'As do I,' she replied.

CHAPTER 14

J ames poked his head around the ground floor door. Stephanie greeted him as she unpacked a small, battered suitcase of its meagre, donated belongings.

He entered the small room and pulled up a scratched and threadbare cloth chair at the end of the unmade bed. It was one of the smaller and least attractive refuges, but it was safe, clean, and closing down, so any personal comforts and necessities were simply unaffordable. The charity running the home, housing six women, was out of money, and out of time. He glanced around at the deteriorating décor, scuffed and unchanged for decades. To think that even getting Emily a place to stay here had required all of Caroline Lewisham's persuasion, string-pulling and tenacity.

The wall beside the bed was covered in a ringed patchwork of tacked drawings. James made out the rough, plain style of Emily's hand, juxtaposed against the graceful artistry of another. At the centre lay the original two handsome portraits of May Dene and Richard Avery, facing one another like a homemade cameo. Hints and sketched lines suggested that the self-portrait was as yet incomplete and evolving. The woman's shoulders, capped by the ruffles of her low-cut Empire dress hinted at slender arms yet to be fully realised. Her downward gaze now appeared to be settled upon something forming only a few curved lines about her midriff.

Several new drawings outlined the inside of a once grand house from different perspectives, with several vignettes showing the surprisingly modest, furnished interior rooms like a two-dimensional doll's house. One caught his attention – a heavily laden rowing boat depicted a rescue against the backdrop of a long, curved quay and foreground outcrops of puncturing rocks that James knew all too well. Many arms clutched at a small figure whilst another, nearby on a rising wave, appeared to flounder. From the prow, the arrow of a man in mid-dive shot to his rescue.

'Reminded me of that day you fell in,' said Stephanie, noting his interest.

James closed on the image. 'Did you mention that to Emily?'

'No. That was on the wall before I got here this morning and it's your business.'

'Sounds like I need to remind someone else of that. Where's Emily now?'

Stephanie shoved across a row of clanging wardrobe hangers. 'Washing the smell of hospital out of her hair in the communal bathroom. Ms Swanson let slip that the poor lass has a problem remembering things. She thought it important to tell me without your knowledge, just so I'd be able to understand or support if there was an issue. I hope she won't get into trouble?'

James watched as she bit her lip. 'No. Her intentions were in the right place, but it is important to keep such things confidential. I don't want it leaving the room and getting to the papers or anyone else.'

Stephanie nodded and came closer. 'I wanted to ask a

question,' she said pointing to a drawing of several, faceless women at work on a moonlit cliff top. The skeletal, latticed outline of a body on the open ground peeped through the bell-shaped skirts. James peered at the striking resemblance to his waking dream and shivered.

'Are you alright?'

'Yes, said James. 'Just tired. What was it you wanted to know?'

'How is it that none in St Jude know who she is if she's local?'

'Local?' he said turning to see her suddenly absorbed with sorting socks into pairs. 'It's already been leaked to the public domain that's she's from the south-east. What is it that makes you think otherwise?'

'The daughter of the sea,' said Stephanie. 'She shouldn't know about the making in such detail if she's an outsider.'

James sat down, casting a glance at the partially open door. 'The willow maiden? Is that what these women in the drawing are making, Stephanie?'

She toyed with a bobbled hat and remained silent.

'Father told me it's a sensitive subject with the townswomen, and that my mother used to take part—'

'It's not for outsiders,' she said fixing him intently. 'Only for those girls that grow up and stayed here. We don't share what we do with anyone from outside and I'm only telling you because you were born here. We do it for the good of the town though there are precious few of us left to carry on the old traditions. The menfolk of St Jude know not to pry at Haldwyn time and your mother was an important part of keeping it going as well as keeping it secret. It was...important to her, as well as your...'

James lowered to a whisper, conscious of a dry mouth as he swallowed. 'Was my Karen involved?'

She avoided his gaze, tightening the knitted wool in her

hands. 'Working nights is a good excuse, Dr Marshall. We will miss both of them this year, god bless them, and likely it will be the last time we commemorate—'

'Both?' he said, unwilling to put faith in a simple nightmare for fear of provoking another coincidence. 'Someone else who grew up in St Jude and has since passed away?'

A slammed door across the hall heralded the sound of approaching footsteps.

Emily pushed open the door, towel drying her hair, releasing the tension in the room, and Stephanie into a relieved and sudden, welcoming smile.

'Hello, Dr Marshall – am I talking with you today?' said Emily squeezing past the volunteer and lowering the towel to the defunct and disconnected radiator. She looked out of the window to the warming sun and scratched the receding, itching hairline scabs from her injuries.

James watched for any non-verbal resolution to his unanswered question, but Stephanie remained resolutely focussed upon the folding of clothes. 'Not officially. I was just passing and wanted to see how you were settling in now that you have a place of your own.'

Emily turned from the view overlooking the weeds in the cracked patio of the refuge's rendered walled yard. 'I'm very grateful to be away from the hospital and I understand it's only for the time being – Stephanie says they are closing the place?'

His father's carer and refuge volunteer cleared her throat, pausing in the folding of a bobbled hoodie. 'Sorry, Dr Marshall. Emily overheard the two girls upstairs talking about it and I didn't see any sense in denying it when she asked me.'

'Where will they all go?' said Emily.

'We're all working very hard to find places for everyone here, including you,' said James. 'Until you are well enough, or you discover where you need to be.'

'This is nice,' said Emily, pulling out a soft, Navy coloured, polo necked sweater from a charity bag. 'Why don't you take it, Stephanie? – it would look good on you.'

Stephanie smiled and shook her head. 'It did, but I'd be happier with you wearing it. A woman can only have so many sports tops and sweatshirts. We both share the same dress size and taste by the looks of things.'

Stephanie delved into the suitcase and the remaining clothes to be hung. Her shoulders sagged, and James caught a glance at her pained face in the cupboard mirror. Emily saw it too and put an arm around her.

'Silly me,' Stephanie said, sniffing and wiping back an emerging tear. 'I've been here since your father retired, Dr Marshall, and it doesn't seem right.'

Emily released her and handed over some of the remaining donated clothes. 'It must be hard to know a place for so long and know that it will be gone.' James saw her fleeting glance to the uppermost drawing on the wall, which showed a proud horse, tied to a pillory post in front of the house that James recognised as Carmalt. 'I feel I understand,' she said, looking out of the window towards the higher ground poking over the adjoining seagull-filled rooftops. 'At least part of me does.'

Stephanie composed herself. 'Thank you, Emily; I needed the refuge myself once, a long time ago. I was helped by the doctor in charge after Dr Marshall's mother died. Even if it's only for a short time, I hope it helps you in the same way.

'Your mother died when you were young?' said Emily holding the sweater like a comfort blanket as she sat down on the edge of the bed.

James nodded. 'Shortly after I was born.'

Emily squeezed the side of her head as though wincing from a migraine. James leaned over, but she waved him away. 'Just for a moment, it came back—'

'A memory of someone important in your life?' he asked. 'A parent perhaps?'

Emily lowered her hand and relaxed the muscles in her jaw. 'It's not that. I don't think I have any.'

Stephanie sat down beside her.

'You don't have to talk about this now if you don't want to. Is it a memory or—'

She tapped on the side of her head. 'I think it came from you-know-who, but I felt an overwhelming sense of sadness as though one or both of us recognised or empathised with your situation. When I try to think about who they are, I just get a blankness as though she doesn't know either or there isn't anything to remember; it feels different from when she's trying to keep things under lock and key.'

'Is she present now?' said James, giving the woman next to her a look of reassurance. 'Can she hear me?'

Emily closed her eyes and nodded, accepting a supporting arm from the volunteer. 'She's being cautious, but I don't think the fact that I can't recall my parents has anything to do with my memory loss. I sense she lost her mother at a younger age, but I can only see her silhouetted against a window, I think it's a nursery...it's full of children's things and—' She looked up. 'There's a man, grey-haired with big side-burns, in old clothing like an extra in historical films. She seems comfortable sharing, and with me telling you about them, as though doing so somehow returns them to life.'

'Does he have a name?' said James, reaching into his bag to retrieve the photocopied image of Carmalt.

Stephanie released her. Emily put her hands to her head and rocked forwards, tapping her feet on the floor.

'Thomas,' she whispered, relaxing into a sigh.

James unfolded the image and handed it to her. 'Consider it a moving-in present. Do you recognise it?'

Emily shook her head. 'Wait. Someone has shown this to us before.'

'You or—?'

'It was a long time ago, longer than I can imagine. It must be one of her memories.' Emily stared down at the house. 'How can I know a place I've never seen or heard of?'

'You don't have an interest or job in history that might explain anything? Perhaps you were researching family history, like my father recently?'

'No,' she said. 'I don't think I'm that kind of person— brainy and educated, I mean. I feel I may have spent more time out of school than in it.'

'Me and you both,' said Stephanie. 'Anything else you remember about growing up?'

'I remember lots of moving around and plenty of rooms like this one, some of which I stayed in only briefly.' She plucked at the volunteer's dark green cardigan. 'I remember a door in this colour high up and overlooking lots of houses and other high rises, next to a yellow one.' She pointed to a scene on the wall that showed a modern cityscape from beyond the railings of a high-rise building. 'She drew that from my memories, not hers; I don't know how I feel about her intruding like that when I can't clearly remember it myself.'

'Perhaps she is just trying to jog your memory. Could it be London?' asked James.

She nodded. 'That's where the policeman said I might have driven from. There's a kindly woman at clickety-click—'

'Clickety-click?'

Stephanie interrupted. 'Bingo lingo for sixty-six.'

'Yes,' replied Emily, gripping and twisting her faded pullover into knots as though reeling in the memory before it vanished or was taken away from her. 'She's Jamaican, I think, and plays bingo, but someone keeps turning the last six upside down on the yellow door to wind her up.'

Stephanie blushed, and Emily screwed her face in apology. 'Sorry, my memory is all or nothing. I know I mustn't go back there, that's what the woman in my head, as well as my instinct, is telling me.'

'Is it dangerous or where the person who the police are looking for lives?'

'Not sure. I get a happy feeling about the yellow door and a bad feeling about the green one.' James held out his hand, and she reached over to clasp it momentarily. The gold ring on his wedding finger suddenly felt warm and present. She ran a finger over it. 'I'm glad you have someone,' she said. 'A person who knows you and is there for you.'

James pulled back his hand and buried it within the flap of his jacket, ignoring the startled expression on her face.

Stephanie cleared her throat and stood up, changing the subject. 'I'll need to get over to Fairhaven soon, but you are welcome to use the common room and kitchen, Emily. We've set you up with some necessities in your cupboard, mostly tins, packets and cleaning stuff.' She pointed to the keys hanging in the door. A large disc on the ring displayed a four-digit number. 'The padlock number is on those keys; you will be able to unlock it?'

Emily nodded. 'Providing I'm in control, but if I show May later, she might remember.'

'May?' asked Stephanie, frowning with sudden interest.

'No need to panic,' said James, shaking his head to prevent further questions. 'I'll explain later, with Emily's permission, but there won't be any unauthorised visits or access to the refuge, at least not in the conventional sense.'

Stephanie nodded though her sudden agitated state remained focussed upon the younger woman seated on the bed, biting the ends of her nails.

'There will always be a warden here in the mornings and evenings and you have the care team's number I gave you to call if you need one of us on call urgently,' said James. 'There is a key code on the outside door and you have the keys to your room. The warden has access to a phone and just for the short term, let one of us know when and where you might be going—'

'And when you will be back,' said Stephanie. 'Don't bring back anyone you don't know.'

'That won't be hard,' said Emily. 'I don't know anyone apart from the care team and yourself, Stephanie.'

'It might be better that it stays that way,' said James. 'Until we learn more.'

CHAPTER 15

E mily's stomach growled, and she clutched at her chest in apology.

'Your food bank paperwork is in the cupboard,' said Stephanie. 'You'll have to walk until we get you a pass for the bus and on to income support; we need a surname for that. I'll be off to Fairhaven now, Dr Marshall. Any message for your father?'

'Remind him that Dr Lewisham from Truro will be over later and not to bore her with family history, ancient or modern. Mention I'll be in London at the conference in a few days, so I won't be able to answer a stream of texts. Also, he mentioned a small music box that my mother used to own—'

'We found it,' she said, softening. 'He got emotional when I unwrapped it, but he still wants you to have it.'

James brushed a hand against her arm in thanks. 'See if you can drag him to the Haldwyn fair before then; the change of scene might do him good.'

'I'll see what miracles I can work,' she said fixing him with a smile. 'It will be our little secret, won't it?'

James watched as she looked past him to the drawing on

the wall before returning, waiting for an answer. 'Yes – you have my word.'

She lowered her eyes and collected her shoulder bag.

'Harriet said you are raising money to keep this place open?' asked Emily.

Stephanie unzipped a side pocket and moisturised her dry lips with a chapstick. 'The volunteers and some of the hospital team help at the fair, and again in December if we make it that far.'

Emily pulled on the gifted, soft woollen top over her damp hair. 'I'd like to help. It's not like I'm doing anything at the moment.'

'On the contrary,' said James. 'You are healing, coming to terms with change, but I don't see any reason why not.'

'I feel fine, and I'll avoid the dodgems if that makes you happy.'

James smiled. 'It's not that kind of event, it's much more of a countryside affair: lots of horses, farmers and cider-drinking; a city girl like you might find it boring.'

'Not a fan of horses,' she said, grimacing. 'Or at least I don't think I am, it's hard to tell when you can't remember whose memories are whose. I don't mind giving the other two a try.'

'If you don't mind being chaperoned, perhaps by the social worker, then I have no objection. I'll be there myself to talk to the local media and see if we can't drum up some support.'

'Will the policeman be there?' said Emily, biting on a nail.

'He might be, though he's more likely to be dealing with the traffic that pours into town further down the coastal road where it meets the main road to St Austell. They set up diversions to avoid the centre of town clogging up. If I know Jory Richards, he'll be there later when he's off duty to soak up some of the atmosphere, as well as the scrumpy.'

Stephanie frowned in disapproval.

'You go on,' said James. 'I'll arrange the well-being schedule with the warden on my way out.'

She bid goodbye, leaving the door ajar and James saw her quick casting glance before she buttoned her coat and rotated the handle on the key-coded exit door.

'The policeman is a good man, Emily, and while he has a job to do, he has to have the care team's permission to talk with you.'

'He seems alright,' said Emily, wrapping her arms about her sunken shoulders, 'but it's like there's an alarm bell going off when I see a copper and I don't know what the warning means. What if I discover I'm a bad person and not knowing who I am, or where I came from, might be a good thing?'

James shook his head. 'A bad person doesn't say things like that or offer to help a charity at an event.'

She unfolded her arms and reached into a pad of paper by her side. 'Something came to me that isn't pleasant. I don't know if it will help you or make things worse with the police.'

'Everything you share with me is confidential providing you aren't in any danger,' said James.

'You've all been so kind, Harriet especially, listening to me or the woman in my head ramble and trying to make sense of what is happening to me.'

'She's a caring person and a great counsellor,' said James, pointing to the wall behind. 'Even if she tells you things she shouldn't about me.'

Emily frowned.

'What is it you want to share?'

'I've glimpsed my life behind that green door and it's not pleasant. You must have seen the burn marks on my thigh when you found me?'

James nodded. 'You don't have to—'

'I don't smoke,' she said. 'I can't stand the smell; the marks are not self-inflicted.'

'Someone did this to you, the man who you and May are frightened will find you?'

'Yes. I glimpsed his face and resisted when she tried to take control. I'm not a baby so I pushed back. There were bad things he made me do to prevent it from happening. I can say his name now without May freaking out and putting me to sleep with that song she hums.'

'It's a local tune by all accounts,' said James, leaning back into his chair. 'Are you in the right place to tell me what kind of bad things?'

She glanced away to the window and turned over the pages of the sketch pad, barely glancing at the unfinished or spoiled pieces. 'Illegal things like delivering and collecting stuff that I shouldn't. You are wrong about me; I'm not a good person. The police are right to want to lock me up, but I only do it to stop Ryan from hurting me. He says he loves me, but why would anyone who meant it make me do such things?'

'He was coercing you. It's not your fault; you are a victim.'

'I get the impression May needs to hear that, as well as I do, even if it might take a while to sink in. She knows she can force herself through in an emergency, but I'm able to stop her from taking over more and more, even if it means the snatches of memory I get in between have slowed to a trickle.'

'That's a good sign,' said James. 'Feeling in control often means you are in a better, safer place.'

Emily rubbed at her stomach and pointed to the wall. 'There are times, especially when I'm feeling sick, tired or when I can't be bothered to fight when I let her do her draw-ings and play with the light switch, or whatever fascinates her at the time. It's like she's trying to tell me something without using words, like she needs to have someone like Harriet, or you, know that's she's really there. She's all too real to me, but that is not enough to make her go away.'

'You can tell her I believe she is real and very much part of you.'

Emily shook her head. 'I think you have to try harder, even if you don't mean it, which is why she drew this for you...' Flicking through several of the sheets within the plain paper pad in her lap, she tore out a fine sketch of a car at the end of a narrow, high-hedged track surrounded by trees. The passenger door lay ajar and a solitary female figure, frozen in the act of leaving the scene, walked toward a distant, hinted at gap in the wood. 'It's me, before I trimmed my hair; she's drawn me before I even made it to the cliff where I—'

'You don't have to say it,' said James, looking at the finer details. 'Your memory is recalling itself through these images. Is this car you drove from London?'

'Yes, it's Ryan's. I used to use it to do pickups and stuff.' She pointed to the foundational ruins of a large building beyond a line of tall hedging. Four children, three boys and a girl, were playing amongst the stones, oblivious to the drama taking place thirty yards away on the other side of the wind-blown hawthorn and rowan. 'How can I have drawn something that wasn't visible from my standpoint? This isn't my memory, it's hers before I got to the cliff.'

'I understand it's odd, but you know that isn't possible,' said James reaching over and plucking an image of Carmalt from the wall to lie by its side. The drawings were related, not only in style but in the dimensions and attention to particular blocks and buttresses. 'If these surroundings are accurate, then you probably can't remember the finer details – you were experiencing a traumatic event, and the disassociation could very well have happened much earlier than you realise. Your mind is building on things you may have seen, places you've been but can't recall. The mind is a sponge and it will absorb all manner of things you don't perceive, yet can playback as if you had never encountered them.'

Emily thought about it and relaxed. 'If you say so, but—' She rubbed at the figure heading away from the car. 'We all know what I was about to do here, don't we? You all know, even the damn woman in my head knows. I remember falling from a high cliff, but I don't know if it was me or her.'

'You mustn't dwell on it,' said James. 'You were going through hell and I can see how you might have felt that this was a way out. It wasn't, and it isn't, which is why we are here.'

'But why here, and with no clothes on?' She turned back to the cityscape sketch on the wall. 'Couldn't I just have gone up to the top of wherever that was and—'

James clasped his hands in his lap. 'It's likely random why you chose St Jude though you seem to have some memory or connection to the place. They make plenty of period dramas down at the quay which might explain the subjects in your drawings. When people plan to do something extreme like this, they are looking to escape from everything that the world has thrown at them; that includes discarding material possessions, clothing or jewellery.'

'Like at Beachy Head? I went there once with—' James encouraged her with a gentle nod, waiting for the recollection to emerge, '—the man in the photo the policeman showed me.'

'The blonde-haired man?'

'Yes, but I feel so ashamed that I can't even remember his name. He promised to meet me at the airport, but I haven't seen him since.'

'You were planning to get away?'

'Yes. Back to his home country but Ryan found out and I think something bad happened to him because of me. There's something in the car's boot that Ryan would be desperate to get back, that he was too drunk that night to remove, but I honestly don't know what it is. He'll find it, and me, and then what May Dene says will come true.' She clasped his hands, rubbing her finger across his ring. 'It will be worse than what I planned to do.'

James felt a sudden rush of overwhelming fear and panic. He jerked back his hands even as a lingering image of what Emily had described receded like a dying ember, leaving him cold, clammy and nauseous.

'I'm sorry,' she said. 'I didn't mean to—'

James got up, wiping his brow with his shirt sleeve. 'Sorry, I'm not feeling quite myself.' Breathing steadily, waiting for the sudden sickness to subside, he lowered his arm, catching sight of one of the outer drawings on the wall. In a scruffy, amateur hand, which he guessed to be Emily's, a man in a barely recognisable frock coat and waistcoat leered back in cartoonish mockery of the beautifully drawn cavalryman at its centre. Despite the crudeness of the image, the cruelty of the face could not be hidden, even by the scribbles and defacing lines that attempted to do so.

'She calls him Fallon,' said Emily rising to meet him. 'She doesn't like it but I'm in charge, and until she leaves me alone or at the very least gives me my life back, he stays put to wind her up.'

James regained his composure and sensed the resolute and rising confidence of the woman beside him, even as the sun clouded over, plunging the dingy room into mournful, oppressive shadow.

'I need some air,' he said, rubbing his tired eyes. Emily unhooked a rustling anorak from the back of the door. 'I don't think that's a good idea – there needs to be a chaperone in place, a woman guardian—'

'You're a senior doctor,' she said glancing at the ring on his finger. 'You're also married, and a promenade is a public place. I can make my way back, it's only a quarter of a mile or so.'

Her eyes pleaded like an expectant child desperate for a trip to the park.

'What could possibly go wrong?' she said, grabbing her keys and brushing past him before he could protest.

CHAPTER 16

Open windowed cars with bronzed arms idled past in the queuing, home-time traffic as James and Emily ambled alongside on the wide promenade. The seaweed shifted on the high tide, its supple fingers reaching out to touch the stone-sided sea wall like a swimmer turning to strike out to the six breakwater stones of the bay. James breathed in the brine-scented air, tinged with a sickly-sweet smell of bubblegum.

'Are you enjoying that?' he said, glancing at Emily's masticating jaw.

'No, but it keeps May quiet and forms one of our little bargains. I get some peace, and she gets a sugar rush.'

James turned to the seawall, closing his eyes in the late afternoon sun. He leaned across the waist-high granite defence and checked his phone. Several missed calls from Mike Trebarr were displayed, and he pocketed the phone, wincing with the repercussions of missing his medical appraisal.

'Are you okay?'

'It's nothing; just an appointment I need to reschedule. I

always feel calmer when I can see the sea,' he said. 'What about you – are you still having periods of sickness?'

'It's getting less,' said Emily watching an approaching couple slow to stare. 'But I can't say I feel back to normal, whatever that is.'

The couple were passed by a jogger who checked his pace and returned a similar curious inspection. A group of teenagers on the momentarily stationary school bus leaned against the upstairs windows, phones flashing and clicking as they giggled and pointed, encouraging more faces to appear at the smudged and sticker-covered glass.

James caught the looks and shielded her from further unwanted attention by the local, amateur paparazzi. 'They recognise you from pictures in the papers and the appeal that went out. If you want to go back—'

'I'm not hiding from them.' She bobbed her head sideways and stuck up two fingers in their direction. The top floor faces were struck dumb as the bus moved off in the quay's direction. 'I don't care if they've seen me naked; it's not like anyone knows who I am around here.'

'What would May Dean make of that?'

'I don't think she approves of much, so hopefully it will be an incentive for her to find someone else to bother.' James shook his head as she blew out a large bubble of gum.

'Why do you think May Dene, specifically, is the one that your mind has set on as its protecting alternative influence? said James, turning to lean against the warm stone.

'Isn't that your department?'

'I can only assume you've been immersed in all things Regency in the past. Your drawings, for example, show a local, historical level of detail, but you insist you have never visited before a few weeks ago.'

'You tell me she's not real, and I have to believe that, so

would you prefer I made up someone with a cockney accent to make things less confusing for you?'

James retreated from his chivalrous defence of her person, back to the wall. 'I know you aren't making it up, only that I'm not sure being here isn't reinforcing your mind's belief that the alter it has created belongs here with its own agenda and baggage.'

'You said the amnesia would be temporary. Are you saying that staying here means May Dene won't go away?'

'I don't know,' said James. 'What are your thoughts?'

'She stopped me from doing something rash, but now that things have calmed down, it's as though she empathises with parts of my life that I can recall, even the bad bits. She has unfinished business but won't let me in and she doesn't know why she keeps returning except to help.' Her hands clenched, bouncing against the sharp stone behind. 'I'm telling you the truth when I say I've never been here or that I can't draw.'

'Would you be open to another professional providing an opinion on your condition?' he said, glancing away.

'I thought you said you knew what was wrong with me?'

'I'd like to consider a second opinion to ensure we are on the right track.'

'Okay,' said Emily. 'Is it someone higher up than you?'

James nodded with a smile. 'The man from the picture in the book you saw – my father. And yes, definitely higher up.'

'I don't remember, but if it helps, and it's only talking, then sure.'

'What's it like,' said James, 'when you have someone sharing like that? I've spent my working life telling people why they are feeling the way they do, but I've never experienced it personally.'

Emily wandered from the wall and encouraged him to sit beside her on the opposing bench overlooking the sea. She pulled out the spent, flavourless gum and stuck it beneath the time-worn, sea-silvered slats.

'It confuses and frightens me especially when I sense her begin to take control, but when she does, it's like going over the top of a rollercoaster hill and falling into the most over-whelming and calming experience I have ever felt.' She winked. 'Better than anything under or over the counter, that's for sure.'

James picked at his nails and looked down between the spread of his legs to the gum-stained lichens on the asphalt in the seat's shade. 'Can you describe it?'

'It's like my memories and hers suddenly recognise each other. When she comes out, it's just a powerful sense of protection and solidarity, even if it's somehow tinged with sadness. It's like I've been adopted, warts and all.'

'Then that cannot be a bad thing, said James, rubbing his hands and rotating the golden band upon his third finger. 'What I wouldn't give for a few moments like that.'

A scooter-mounted toddler zoomed ahead of her pushchair-laden mother. She gave James an eyeball rolling look of resigned weariness as she passed, outpaced by the purple glitter and sea-rust encrusted speedster.

'Do you and your wife have kids?' asked Emily, folding her arms and watching the pair disappear beyond the distant begonia bedded public conveniences.

James shook his head, ready to nip the conversation and reminder in the bud but finding himself revealing more to the stranger than he expected. 'My wife died earlier this year from leukaemia; I haven't fully let her go yet. It helps when things get a bit much, just to know that she was once here, though I deserve to wear it as a penance for not being there for her.'

'I'm sorry,' said Emily, clutching at her cheeks and lightly placing a palm upon his hand, gripping the edge of the bench tightly. 'I'm such an idiot for mentioning it.'

'No reason to apologise, I just wanted to be honest with you, and myself.'

'Do you want to talk about it?'

He smiled and looked down at the innocence of her touch but did not withdraw from its comforting presence. 'I thought I was the one administering care, not the other way around,' he said.

'I'm just here to listen,' said Emily. 'Consider it payback for all my nonsense you have had to endure.'

James fought against the descending calm and insistence that everything would be alright if only he unburdened his grief. A wall appeared in his mind to block out the image of his wife, but he felt a gentle shimmer in its foundations like sand had been released from beneath the blocks of stone. The reticence to continue dissolved as the linked memories of his wife and Isobel Lee revealed themselves from the rubble.

'I became heavily involved with a patient, not in any unprofessional way as far as I was concerned, but as an antidote to the late discovery that my wife was dying. Karen only revealed it to me in the final few weeks, knowing how important it was for me to save another, whose future was not as pre-determined as her own. It was at the cost of time that she should have had with me, and I could only possibly save one of them.' James felt the run of a tear streak down his face. 'I let her down; I let them both down.'

'The patient died?'

He nodded. 'I did everything I could, but it wasn't enough.'

'Is that why you are so worried about me and the others you look after, in case the same happens again?'

He wiped down his face with his free hand. 'Maybe. I

can't get over that I might be wrong about lots of things, myself included.'

She squeezed his hand. 'I don't believe that a man who saves a naked wreck in a graveyard made a mistake in my case.'

He leaned back, releasing himself from her tender grasp, and pointed to the engraved plaque on the back of the bench, its brass patina scoured by saltwater spray.

The past is a foreign country: They do things differently there. L. P. Hartley.

'He had it right,' said James pointing down the wide stretch of gum-pocked tarmac. 'The council engraved famous quotes from novels on all the benches around twenty years ago, and Karen and I used the quotes to let each other know where to meet.' She followed his hand to the quay, curving round a seaward arm of granite to protect the bobbing boats within its igneous embrace. 'See that far bench with the gulls pecking at the chip packets?'

Emily put a hand to shield her eyes and nodded.

'It reads: "...when pain is over, the remembrance of it often becomes a pleasure." It's—'

'Jane Austen,' interrupted Emily, turning to face him. 'How did I know that?'

'Long term memory; you must have been at least a fan of the period. It's from *Persuasion*.' His phone buzzed inside his pocket and he frowned with the distraction.

'Hello?'

'Dr Marshall, it's Harriet. Where are you? Dr Trebarr's been trying to get in touch but he says if you come now he can see you.'

James rose and turned away, placing a hand against his opposite ear to block out a departing car, pulling out of the lay-by behind.

'It's not a great time,' he said, chastising himself for being late. 'I'm down at the seafront. If you can ask him to rearrange—'

'He said it was important.'

'Just tell him I'll sort out a more convenient time when I get back later on.' He paced, oblivious to all but a sudden need to put down the phone.

'He's leaving early, and he wanted me to let you know,' said Harriet. 'Do you want me to get him to call you now?'

'No,' said James. A raucous gull landed nearby setting off a screeching squawk and scattering a smattering of sparrows.

'Get away you noisy devil,' said Emily. 'Dr Marshall is on the phone.'

'Is that Emily?' said Harriet. 'Have the care team been informed about this because I have nothing down for this afternoon? – she's supposed to have a female chaperone—'

'It's alright,' he said, hearing snatches of talk from the bench behind. 'It was just for a moment and I'll make sure she gets back to the refuge. We needed some air.'

'You've been to the refuge? I don't mean to rock the boat, Dr Marshall, but isn't that, and what you are doing now, against procedure?'

James ground his teeth. 'We are on our way back.' He disconnected the call and rose, turning to see Emily engaged in murmured conversation with a much older man, downbeat and ragged in appearance. His lined and tanned leathery face, heavily stubbled chin and loose-fitting trousers, several sizes too large, were enough to hint at his name. The smell of alcohol on his breath was obvious, but his initial request for cigarettes died on his lips as he became passive, no longer listing to each side to maintain his balance. His aged, tattoo-bled hand was entwined with Emily's but was being held, submissive and willingly.

'Tom?' said James. 'I hope you aren't bothering...'

Tom Cotter remained transfixed upon his young captive,

ceasing in his attempt to woo, beg or bother the easy-looking mark. His worn face softened into a relaxed calm.

'Tom,' said James, loudly, trying to gain his attention. The man looked up, broken from his reverie, as the woman's hand was withdrawn slowly until only the tips of their touching fingers remained.

'She's come back,' he whispered, breaking the bond and backing away with a broadening smile. 'My sweet nightingale has come back!'

'What did you say to him?' said James, sitting back down to watch the old man caper and waltz down the promenade, repeating the insistence to locals, attempting a wide berth to avoid any entanglement. 'What's got into him?'

Emily's dilated eyes glanced meekly back. 'It has been a long time since he had hope, and joy,' she said in a gentle Cornish lilt. Sitting upright on the edge of the bench, toying with her hair, she watched several couples walk past with sudden sideways glances of recognition. 'Do men and women now walk together without the need for chaperones?'

'Emily?' said James in a whisper.

She shook her head, observing the commonplace scene with interest. A car pulled into the lay-by behind unsettling her for a moment with its sudden noisy appearance.

'So many people; the world is busy beyond my reckoning.'

'I think we should get back to the refuge,' said James, silencing a further call from the counsellor. 'I'm in enough trouble as it is.'

'You miss her greatly,' she said. 'The one whose golden band binds your heart beyond death's dark door.'

James narrowed his eyes, sensing the switch. 'I told you, she died. Now let's—'

'I once heard tell of a sailor from Penzance who cut off his ringed finger to lie eternally within the closed hand of his deceased lover. It was more than grief; he felt such remorse for being away on the sea during her agony that he spent the rest of his life looking down upon his guilt. The gap in his hand mirrored the chasm in his life. I sense that there is more than simple grief that you bear.'

She reached out to touch the ring on his finger and he felt a rising anxiety melt away.

James stared into the enlarged pupils ringed with a penumbra of bright blue fire. Her mouth moved, but he heard the words in his mind. 'Death does not end your relationship with either of them, but you are continuing to pay a debt that has already been settled by what their lives meant to you. We are not so different.'

'What are you doing?' he said, feeling the clasp of her hand against his own.

'You asked Emily what it was like,' she said. 'To feel another so closely, so intimately. Don't be afraid...'

There was a sudden disorientating sense of falling and James fell back onto the bench blinking at the fading promenade.

A sudden rush of dizziness made him clutch his chest with his free hand. Closing his eyes to block out conflicting sensory signals, a sudden sound of gunshot caused him to panic and he opened his eyes to see the promenade removed. In its place, a dark wooded area approached by a narrow hedge-lined track appeared. He blinked and tried to move his legs but they remained elusive, out of view and out of action. A sensation of floating in the sea-salted, resinous void caused him to focus on the approaching headlights of a car below. The car rolled to a quiet stop among taller grass at the end of the track and the dark silhouette of a woman got out, illuminated by the interior lights. She slammed the car door behind her, and it bounced back from the seat belt draped against the sill to lie open. She walked away in the pre-dawn light oblivious, and he tried to call out even as she melted into the margins of the trees.

'Emily...?'

The sun burst, high and blistering upon a different day and he raised his arm to shield the sting and wipe the painful reactive tears from his dark-adapted eyes. His eyes adjusted to look beyond a tall hedge, where children played with toy figures and raced around the stinging nettled stones of a long-forgotten building.

'The drawing,' said James to himself. 'I know this place...'

Two boys emerged from hiding to ambush one other who was in the awkward and amorous clutches of a young girl.

'Karen?' he murmured as the scene darkened to a memory from which James struggled to escape.

Pursued by someone unknown, he felt himself tripping and falling among great mounds of headland heather, desperate to reach the end of the headland. Picking himself up and reaching the edge of the cliff, he glanced down through the eyes of another upon the crashing waves at its base. He clutched at his stomach, stone laden within a lattice of worked willow and flowers and fell forward into the form-less, rushing air, silently free-falling toward the green foaming water below. Instinctively, he held up his left arm as the promenade and the sights of the ordinary and commonplace returned. Panting with the fearful and familiar final memory, he lowered his arm, conscious that his right hand was still being braced against the bench.

'What the—?' he murmured trying to make sense of the waking dream. Emily's dilated eyes receded to a pin prick as she gained control, grabbing a hold of his free hand to steady herself. 'I don't know,' she gasped. 'It's May...'

The ringing of his phone startled him back into rush hour reality as he released a hand and answered the call.

'Tell me straight,' said Caroline Lewisham in a guarded tone. 'Where are you now and who are you with?'

James cleared his head. 'Harriet's called you?'

'Answer the damn question!'

'I'm at the sea wall down at the promenade with Emily.'

Caroline lowered her voice. 'At least you are telling me the truth.'

From the lay-by came the startling sound of a car's horn. James twisted round to see the woman on the end of the line, staring at the pair of them, stone-faced in disbelief from her parked car. James released his other hand from Emily as though he had been stung.

'How long have you been there?' he asked, still conversing with the phone. He heard the echo of his reply in the car's hands-free as she wound down the window.

'Long enough,' she said. 'Now get in the car, both of you.'

CHAPTER 17

Caroline returned to the car, parked on the double-yellow lines outside the refuge.

James sat, pensive, readying himself for the ride and hiding of his life as she got in, calmly put on her seatbelt, and started the car.

She pulled into the side street and James glanced over, wondering whether to ask where they were going to ascertain how long he would have to endure whatever was brewing.

'It's not what you think,' he said, eager to release the pressure valve among the frightening and deafening silence.

Caroline dragged her teeth across her bottom lip, baring her white front incisors.

It was worse than he realised.

'What do I think?' she whispered, like a parent admonishing a child for some gross indiscretion at school.

'That I wasn't observing client–patient distance, and you'd be right, but it's not—'

'Not like Isobel Lee?' she said, indicating right and checking the main road to hide her face.

James winced, suddenly aware that she was going to be frank and brutal; exactly the qualities that had gotten her this far career-wise. 'No. I told Harriet it was only to grab some air. She didn't have to call you like some sneak. I had little choice in the matter; Emily insisted.'

'You always have a choice, James,' said Caroline briefly catching his eye before grinding the gear knob into a grumbling higher gear. 'Harriet didn't call me. I was on my way to see you before your father, or had you forgotten?'

'Tell me you are just pissed about me being stupidly unprofessional and this is not something else. I told you, it's not—'

Caroline shook her head. 'You are something else and it's you that needs your head looking at if you think I'm bothered by that suggestion.' She swept back her hair, glancing over to catch his response. James shrugged and remained obstinate in his silence as she continued with a snort of unrequited annoyance. 'There were countless people on that seafront, snapping their merry camera phones like there was no tomorrow. Some of those images of you holding hands are going to be on social media already, not to mention the papers tomorrow. The only defence Emily has is anonymity – you have no such luxury.'

James placed his head in his hands and rubbed at his face, turning away from her stare as the car stood at a junction.

'You bloody fool,' she said.

James nodded. 'I'm sorry. Drop me back at the hospital, I'm supposed to see Mike.'

'He's left for the day and has an evening planned, which is why he was trying to reach you about your medical appraisal. What excuse is it this time?'

'I'll go after I get back from the panel in London and I mean it this time; I don't feel right.'

'You look worse,' she said, sighing and winding down the

window to release the warm air and emotional heat from the car. 'What's wrong with you?'

'I don't know,' said James. 'I felt like I was having a panic attack or some hallucination back at the seafront.'

'Same here,' she said sarcastically. 'I thought you were just tired when you slumped onto the bench.'

'It was more than that,' he said, watching the kite-flying kids atop the dunes as the car sped by on the coastal road. 'Bad dreams and crazy palpitations, like I'm coming off something.'

'And are you?'

He jerked his head across. 'No. Only the anti-depressants which you already know I stopped taking, and the sleeping tablets that didn't agree with me, but I would have thought any side-effects would have worked their way through my system by now.'

Caroline turned the car inland. 'I think I should sign you off.'

'No!' said James. 'I just need to get checked out. Give it until Mike sees me in a few days; you can trust him to be impartial. There is no risk to any of my patients, or to myself, it's just lack of sleep or something. Besides, you aren't thinking of the consequences for both of us.' He tugged on his seatbelt for comfort. 'You in particular. I don't want you suffering for backing a lame horse.'

She shook her head in resignation, and a hint of red flushed her cheeks. 'Just concentrate on getting out the starting gate for now, okay? I can deal with the hurdles.'

James nodded. 'What did you say to Emily?'

'That your father was waiting for you and that in future she's to let the team know if she is going on any extended trips into town.'

'We are going to Fairhaven Grange – now?'

The car turned off the coastal road and sped on between meadows of baled hay and furrowed fields.

'I have a delivery for your father, or had you forgotten? Under the circumstances, I think he is exactly the person you need to see right now and who should be looking after you, not to mention Emily. I need a few private moments with him before you arrive, and that's non-negotiable.'

'You are going to give him leave to assess her?'

'No. Fellows is.'

'What?' he choked. 'How would he know about our arrangement unless you told him?'

'I didn't tell him,' she said defensively. 'He came to the same conclusion after reviewing your progress.'

'He was in the room when I called the other day, wasn't he?'

James saw her knuckles whiten on the wheel.

'I'm fed up with being in the middle of something that I'm not aware of, Caroline.'

James watched her sullen, reflected gaze on the navigation screen. 'That makes two of us.'

She turned on the radio, drowning out his attempts to engage in further questions as the car meandered its way over the approaching rise and turned into the private, privet-hedged drive to the care home.

From his vantage point, lurking among the seeding cascades of the laburnum arch, James could see Caroline and his father engaged in debate upon the terrace. Banished like a child, he waited for them to conclude their business, eager to discover what Edward Marshall had made of the letter and approval to practice one last time. To what end and why this was so important that would cause such bitter rivals to co-operate outweighed James's feeling of inadequacy and lack of control. The latter appeared to be slipping away, but he was unsure whether it had to do with the former or something as yet unrevealed.

She's had her ten minutes, he thought, as he emerged from his second perambulation around the quadrant and made his way up the hand-railed steps from the sunken, herbaceous bordered croquet lawn. Caroline caught his approach and hurriedly dropped something, clinking, from her bag and into Edward's unsuspecting lap. She coughed to alert his father who removed the smuggled goods to his tweed sports jacket.

'Not you as well,' he said, shaking his head as one of the small mini bar-sized bottles missed its mark and came to rest with a thud on top of a cardboard box beside his chair. Caroline collected the whisky with a guilty glance back at the dark windows of the apartment and handed it into Edward's cupped, shaking palm.

'Payment for services to be rendered,' said Edward, flitting between the two guests, sensing the friction. 'No fighting, children.' He tore open the wrapped gift on the table and withdrew a jigsaw puzzle. The cover of the box pictured the painting of a middle eastern man in orange robes, perplexed head in hand and hiding from a rabble of ruffians and Roman soldiers on their way to Christ's imminent crucifixion.

'Remorso de Judas,' said Edward, casting the box upon the table. 'The remorse of a traitor as his teacher is taken away from the world at his very hands; Fellows hasn't lost his sense of humour, or hubris.'

Caroline pointed to the open letter, which Edward returned to its envelope. 'Any message by way of reply, apart from your agreement on a limited and single-case consultation with the patient alongside James and a member of the care team?'

Edward glanced up. 'Only what you and I have agreed, no more, and despite the outcome.'

'I'll see you when I see you, then.' She bent down to kiss him on the side of his sunken cheek. 'I'll be back in an hour, James, after I've seen old Margaret unless you want Stephanie to drop you back?'

'Thank you,' he said, even as she was halfway down the steps to the lawn and the linked annexe of the lower apartments. 'Perhaps we can talk later, say at the house?'

She paused, mulling the offer but did not look round.

'What have you done to upset her this time?' said Edward, watching her disappear beyond the laburnum-covered archway.

James sat down on the vacant seat opposite and plucked at his lips. 'If she didn't tell you, then let's just say it's a private matter.'

'As bad as that?'

James gave his father a look of feigned injury. 'I missed an appointment to see Mike Trebarr for a check-up today, that's all.'

'You mean medical assessment.'

'I see Caroline has already shared her frustrations.' James joined his hands and rotated his thumbs, staring at the opened letter on the table.

'It's a common interest we share,' joked Edward. 'She is extremely fond of you but concerned about your wellbeing.' He removed the missive from James's attention and buried it in his inside pocket. 'So am I, which is why I've agreed to help you.'

'With certain conditions, I understand.' James folded his arms and cocked his head across. 'What exactly are you getting out of this?'

The gentle drone of a light aircraft circling the coast caught the old man's attention. 'Nothing but peace of mind,' he said returning to earth as the plane wobbled in the offshore breeze and glided out of view. 'It's you and Caroline that stand to benefit.'

'You are helping me assess Emily, then – Fellow asked for your help, and you agreed?'

'Yes. Not help, more of a second opinion and the closing of an argument between us, long-held. What that is does not and will not concern you – I have made certain of that.'

'You won't tell me the particulars of why the two of you are settling scores while I sit around like a spectator on my own case?'

Edward plucked at his lips, imitating James's former gesture. 'If Caroline didn't tell you, then let's just say it's a private matter…'. Edward prodded at the jigsaw box with derision. 'Have you discovered any more coincidences or the whereabouts of that place your ancestors may or may not have worked at – the Dene's house?'

'I'm seeing the archivist tomorrow when I get off work; he's offered to connect a few dots and dig out the originals that got clipped in the copies he sent to you.'

James stretched out his legs, knocking against the cardboard box alongside.

'What's this?' he said.

'That heirloom of your mother's you were asking about, along with some other knick-knacks I found. I thought you could take the smaller items to the fair for the white elephant stall. She used to run it.'

'You never talked about her much when I was growing up, even though I was desperate to ask.'

Edward bit his lip and nodded. 'Even after all these years such selfish comfort sustains me and deprives those who would have benefited from knowing more of her. You'll hope-fully forgive me for my reticence in sharing my treasure box of memories having gone through the same thing yourself with Karen.' He leaned over his chair and opened the lid of the box, thrusting an arm inside.

'I always felt guilty,' said James. 'As though somehow, I was responsible for her death shortly after she gave birth like somehow I broke her. That maybe you blamed me...'

Edward retrieved a smaller cardboard box and swung upright to place it on the table. He extended his arms, entreating James to join him in an unusual display of intimacy. James clasped the bony hands and buried his face into the joining like a penitent sinner receiving absolution from a priest.

'My dear boy, you did nothing of the sort. Nature gave and took away in equal measure.' Edward placed a hand on top of his head, kneading the soft curls. 'The fault is all mine. I should not have let you feel this way but had the sense to see how my grief would impact yours. I've been blind to your true needs and wants, but I want you to know that I am still protecting you, and will protect you for as long as I have left.' James lifted his head and retreated into his chair, releasing his hands to pinch his eyes lest further watery emotion reveal itself.

'I think I needed to hear that,' said James, 'though I thought I had got over it. Whatever Stephanie is putting in your tea, or Mike is prescribing to make you so genial and open, I hope it's patented.'

His father clasped his hands and studied a warbling black-bird on the finial of a clematis-covered obelisk rising from the herbaceous border. 'It's called life, and it becomes more potent the less you have of it. I've been wanting to talk about her for so long.' He bowed his head and placed his hand across his eyes. 'And to explain how I feel because I let your mother down at her greatest time of need. I buried myself in work and I wasn't there for her.'

'Then we have something in common that doesn't revolve

around psychiatry,' said James. 'I feel the same thing with Karen; unable to share, at least to those that matter or knew her.'

'You should try talking to a stranger about it.'

James tapped his cheek, recalling the release of feeling on the promenade. 'Perhaps.'

'Then we both understand each other, finally,' said Edward, breathing in the scent of the fading night phlox wafting from the adjacent border. After a moment, he lifted the cardboard box and placed it into James's hands. 'I share her with you now, and the final treasure from her side of the family; it has absorbed and comforted me these past few days.'

James placed the box between his legs and opened the flap to discover a tissue-wrapped object, roughly rectangular, ten inches in length and height, and eight inches in width. The creased paper revealed the dark patina and intricate marquetry of a smooth antique box. James looked up in amazement and joy.

'I remember this as a child of five or six,' he said, marvelling at the beautiful stained wooden pieces that encircled the polished exterior. 'You said it was valuable and used to stop me from playing with it.'

His father smiled and reached out to pat his hand on the box. 'It is precious, at least to me, and belonged to your mother and grandmother before her. She thought she'd have a girl but—'

'Does it still play?' asked James, ignoring the unintended slur on his gender.

Edward caressed the smooth wood until his forefinger located a small keyhole in the box's side. He pulled back his hand and reached inside his top pocket to hand over an intricately worked brass key with a short stem. 'You already have all the important things: the house, my long overdue apology

as an inadequate parent, my forgiveness, my research notes—'
He retrieved a leather-bound journal stuffed between his left
leg and the comfy outdoor chair and placed it into his lap
then returned to smile at the box. 'Now you have my heart.'

James inserted the key carefully and wound the clockwork
mechanism. He rotated the key twice and opened the lock-
less lid to see the soft blue velvet cushion, threadbare in
patches where jewellery had been pinned or stored over
countless years. A rich battened margin of dark wood,
roughly one inch wide, surrounded the depository, hiding a
secret. On the hinged side, a delicate brass lever caught his
attention, and he remembered.

'Go on,' said Edward, and James tapped the bar to the left
with his thumb. The beautiful and haunting melody of the
lullaby suddenly chimed from the concealed rotating cylinder
rolling over individual spring tines of a metal comb hidden
within the frame.

'It's even more resonant closed,' said Edward, his face now
brimming with joyful tears.

James closed the lid bearing a central diamond bisected by
eight lines, each intricately lined with mother-of-pearl, to
hear the familiar melodiously musical tones increased in rich-
ness and depth.

'This is like the carving on the Dene cross at the churchyard, where I found Emily.'

'The one I'm helping you with?'

James nodded, thankful for his father's involvement. 'She
was humming the same tune as the box. I knew I had heard it
before.' The tune began to repeat, and he opened the lid to
stab the point of the pearl tiepin from his lapel into the
sumptuous cloth. 'What a coincidence to find the woman
clinging to a memorial belonging to the same family that once
owned this. How did Mother's side of the family come by it?'

'Your distant grandparents, four times removed, worked

for the family, right until the line died out. It may have been a parting gift or payment in lieu from the last Dene, who died without an heir or a fortune. She maintained the custom that it once held an object of great value, but what it was she could not say, only that your mother's family, the Cartwrights, always considered it a loan and that one day a Dene would reclaim it.'

James rubbed lovingly at the sides. 'Well, you said they were extant, so there's no danger of that happening.'

'Which is just as well,' said Edward. 'The box itself is pretty but not overly valuable, though there are collectors for this kind of thing. It's undoubtedly worth more as a family heirloom. Who knows what treasures it once contained?'

'Would you mind if I showed it to the archivist, and maybe his wife? She might be able to shed some interesting insights into it?'

Edward shrugged. 'You do as you please with your things, my boy.'

He swivelled to look back at the apartment. 'Stephanie's on her break; put away the box and grab my wheelchair. We've got twenty minutes head start on her, and I'd like to see Caroline before she leaves.'

'Why?' said James, opening his bag. 'Where are we going?'

'To find a new and undiscovered place to smoke and drink these—' he said, jabbing a finger behind him at the dark window and tapping the bottles in the breast of his tweed jacket. 'Somewhere that my surveillance officer doesn't know about.' He held out his shaking hand and James helped him to rise. For a moment, the space between them closed and James looked into the old man's tired and withered face, trying to fill his memory to the brim for the time when death would remove the option entirely. As though in imitation, Edward gripped him by the shoulders and pressed his forehead against his own, taking stock to prepare for an eternity apart.

'But more importantly,' he whispered, 'so you can ask me all the questions about your mother that you never got answers to.'

CHAPTER 18

J ames completed the signing-in book, shouldered his bag, and was ushered through the modern county library extension to the older section of the building housing the county archives.

A jovial, curly-haired man tipped down his reading spectacles and rose from a nearby computer terminal to greet him. 'James, good to see you.'

'You too, George. How's Frances?'

'All well,' he said. 'Coping better with every day as it comes thanks to the support group you put her in touch with. I was happy to help with your request for information on the manor house document, considering what you did for her; for us both, really.'

'I'm glad,' said James. 'Send her my best.'

The archivist pointed to a large table next to the monitor. Several large sheets were laid out. 'Sorry about clipping the previous copy for your father,' said George, glancing towards a young man leaning against a distant bookshelf and checking his phone. 'Got a new intern, and he's not what you might call "precise".'

James put down his bag on the table and saw the enlarged version of the house auction document. The archive print displayed the house and estate of Thomas Algernon Dene, by public auction in August 1823.

'The last surviving member of the family was named Thomas?' said James.

'Yes, I understand we have helped you with a connection of your own?'

'My ancestors used to work for the family, probably at this house, assuming this is the place. It's somewhere I'm inter-ested in locating, for several reasons, if anything remains, of course. Thomas Dene died without passing on his inheritance to an heir?'

'I assume so unless his issue died before his death. I understand there wasn't a great deal to pass on, sadly. Winners and losers with the Napoleonic War, I'm afraid, hence the sale of the estate to pay off his creditors.'

James unfolded Emily's sketch from the journal in his bag and placed it next to the auction drawing. 'What do you make of this?'

George glanced down, murmuring over the similarities. 'Looks like a sketch of the same house but from a different angle. I see the old church steeple is still up; you don't see many drawings of that.'

'Have you seen this before? Could it have been copied from something in the archives?'

'Not from this vantage point so I'd have to say no,' said George, tugging at his chin. 'I was pretty thorough finding everything that related locally that he wanted.'

'Do you know when and why the tower was changed, to establish a rough before and after date on these two drawings?'

'There was a bicentenary about eight years ago,' said George, staring into the dark ether of the high ceiling, several floors above. 'The original spire was struck by lightning in 1811 but its replacement was abandoned partway through for want of specialist masons and carpenters who were all building forts or ships during the war. The squat, non-steepled tower you see today, and in the auction drawing, would have been patched up around the year 1813.'

'Do you have any maps that might show where the house once stood, considering the perspective and rough distance to the church?'

George held up a finger as though waiting for further lightning, or memory, to strike. He pushed back his glasses and strode over to pull out a sheet from a low, wide drawer. Checking with a notepad from his pocket he rifled through the numbered sheets before pulling out an old regional map.

He returned to lay out the faded sheet and hovered a finger over certain features that James recognised.

'This is the earliest remaining hand-drawn map of this part of Cornwall, with any accuracy. It's thirty years after the house sale, so things might have changed a bit.' George carefully raised and turned the buckled and brittle edge to match the perspective of the two drawings. 'I'd say about four miles, give or take...' he said half to himself as he dragged a finger back from the church, checking on the scale and slowing his movement as he approached the approximate location.

'It's near the moorland and the cliff,' said James, anticipating the area marked with stands of trees, dykes, and walled enclosures. George circled his finger and tapped a small circle of smudged dots, with the words 'Ruin – Calm Holt', several miles south of St Jude and about a mile from the coast.

James pinched his brow and double-checked against the fine ink drawing. 'The woman who drew this said the house was called Carmalt; could it be the same place?'

'Fits the description and the reverse perspective; words evolve so it could be,' said George, dragging his finger in a straight line back towards St Jude Church and the hill beyond as if to confirm. 'The only way to know would be to visit the site; it's almost certain to be less wooded than what's presented here.' He wandered over to his desk and rifled through another slim drawer to pull out and unfold a modern copy of an ordnance survey map. The two men compared side by side, but it was James that first caught sight of the dashed worm-like symbol for earthworks. 'It's still there.' His finger wandered across the smooth paper to the headland and the words Maiden Point.

'Well, I never,' said George, pointing at the same location on the older map. 'Looks as though the cliff name evolved too. I've never made that connection before.'

George passed him a magnifier as he glanced across at the archivist's finger on the map.

... *Dene Point formerly Myrgh an Mor*

'It's definitely Dene Point, but there's a preceding word that's blurred.'

George borrowed the glass and studied the smudged word. 'It's short and there's an "M" and possibly an "A"; could be "Maid" given the present usage – I can see how it got shortened to "Maiden" It must have been important to rename a place or the result of something tragic in these parts. Could just as easily be the name of a boat that wrecked, or something more personal to the family – the Denes were here a long time before they died out.'

'What was the meaning behind the previous name it replaced in 1843?' he said.

'Almost certainly earlier than that. Maps weren't updated regularly, so it could date back to any point when the Denes were still around. 'George got out his phone and typed into a Cornish dictionary app. He turned the screen to show the revealed translation.

'"Myrgh an Mor" means "Daughter of the Sea" or close

enough.'

'Curious,' said James. 'A colleague mentioned that phrase yesterday, someone who has an involvement with the making of the willow maiden of St Jude.'

George widened his eyes. 'Folklore, eh? I'm assuming she's female and born in the town because if you are after specifics, then asking men won't lead anywhere. A few years ago, Frances was approached by one of them to join their diminishing group; it's tough to keep traditions alive when the younger ones aren't interested.'

'She didn't take part though?'

George shook his head. 'A bit too macabre, commemorating a suicide all those years ago. I thought it was some pagan ritual to give thanks for the harvest until she put me straight, though they seem happiest to let folk think so, especially outsiders that get wind of it. Besides, she's not into funny handshakes and said her chilblains wouldn't stand being out in the cold despite the closeness of an outdoor fire.'

'I thought it was a woman that fell after trying to hide or escape from the duty-men with jewels and gemstones – isn't that what the treasure hunters come for?'

George tapped at the map and drawings below. 'Legends get embellished and evolve to fit the times just the same as old documents and place names. I have to say I prefer your interpretation, and I'm sure the tourist board would agree with me. I hear the place has an unsavoury reputation for the latter especially recently if the papers are anything to go by?'

James wondered if the question had been rhetorical. The shrewd guesses of the archivist were disconcerting in their accuracy, but his jovial demeanour betrayed no further signs of interest.

'Is it common knowledge that it's connected to a historical suicide? It's the first I've heard of it and my father thought it was pre-Christian, too.'

'Unless you have some close link to the town, and are female, then I'd say it was a fairly well-kept secret, though I'm not saying it doesn't go back a long time – traditions change, too, and can be overwritten sometimes; take Saturnalia or Yule, and Christmas, for example.' George raised his arms to the roof in mock supplication to the distant, dimly made out ceiling fan. 'I've probably brought down a curse upon the town for mentioning it, even to a St Judian like yourself.'

Despite his sceptical nature, James felt uncomfortable with the lightness of the man's words; George was an outsider and local differences still separated small communities only a few miles apart. 'The person I'm helping appears to know about this and the area but claims never to have visited before. Is this available online?'

George frowned. 'This is Cornwall, James. We don't have any of these digitised. We are still getting around to births, deaths and marriages, which is why it took so long to get the information your father wanted. You are welcome to take some pictures if you like, but I can't photocopy the maps as they can be adversely affected by the lamps in the machine.'

'So, someone would have had to visit you personally to find these?' said James, taking out his phone to capture the images. He turned at the sound of a scraping chair against the worn tiled floor to see the young man return sluggishly to his desk to begin work.

'Of course,' said George, rolling his eyes sarcastically. 'We are the thirteenth most visited public attraction in St Austell; who could resist a visit on holiday?'

'There are twelve others?' said James, enjoying settling a score with the townsman, born and bred. George pushed back his glasses and grinned with self-deprecating humour.

'Do you keep a record of who comes to access the

archives once they have been through the library?' asked James.

'Only on a document-by-document basis so we can manage the fragility of the assets.'

'Can you find out if anyone has accessed this map or the other items you've found for me today?'

He nodded and took a note of several catalogue numbers attached to the maps and documents. From within a series of long, brass-handled boxes, arranged in numbered order, he flicked through several index cards before removing one.

He stuck out his bottom lip. 'Seems the map hasn't been requested since 1986, and a doctor at that, but the Dene stuff was requested around three weeks ago.'

'By whom?'

George frowned and looked down in annoyance. 'Hugo,' he shouted towards the man slouched at the far desk. 'How many times must I tell you to fill in the names? It's no use putting in a date and then leaving it anonymous.'

The man turned round. 'Why do you think it's me?'

'Because it's your handwriting and I have Wednesdays off. Perhaps it's the same pixies that don't put things back in the right place, hmm?' George folded his arms on his waist like an angry schoolteacher. 'Well, come on, surely you can remember something about who anonymous was. We don't get more than a dozen people a month back here.'

'It was a woman. I told her to fill out the card, but she just left.'

'Can you describe her?' asked James.

Hugo shrugged. 'I remember the photocopier was playing up, and she was in a hurry. Dark, long hair, older than me, but not really old. She had a tattoo on her arm. Tank top. Sorry, I don't take much notice of faces.'

'Or procedure,' whispered George, returning to the desk, card in hand. 'Sorry, James. Is it important?'

'Maybe. It would explain a great deal if we are talking about the same woman I am helping. Can you let me know if you find anything on the word next to Dene Point or if Thomas Dene had any children? Also, anything on a man named Richard Avery or Henry Fallon; there might be a connection.'

'I'm interested myself, to be honest, so I'll be happy to share; I'm pally with the parish historian who keeps the records – we play skittles together.'

'I know you aren't supposed to divulge sensitive data about who might have accessed requests for information like this, but if your friend or you come across anything, would you mind letting me know if the woman that your assistant described fits the bill? It's important.'

'Does this have to do with that woman they found wandering about a few weeks ago? There was a picture of her on the seafront with you—'

'Yes,' said James eager to deflect the conversation. 'I'm helping her like I helped Frances but I need you to keep that to yourself, albeit it seems everyone is already aware, otherwise...' He pointed at the ceiling and watched as George puzzled at the end of his finger before looking up.

'One curse is enough,' said George. 'Understood.'

He turned the index card over in his hand. 'Strange coincidence that two doctors, thirty-odd years apart are interested in the same map,' he said, reading the faded fountain pen signature. 'I guess that tells you about the poor state of historical education and interest these days.'

'Who was the doctor?' said James, offhand and immersed in taking more photographs.

'Dr Cameron Fellows – do you know him, assuming he's still alive?'

James grabbed the card and confirmed the signature, the same that had appeared on his release to St Jude.

'Yes,' said James, dropping the card down on the map. It landed squarely beneath the forgotten name of the popular suicide point, underlining the blurred word. 'Only too well.'

'Is there anything else I can help you with?'

James opened his bag and withdrew the cardboard box containing the music box. George wiggled his fingers in anticipation.

'What do we have here?' he said as James handed him the dark, polished box.

'It belonged to my mother. I'm wondering if you or Frances can verify its age or anything about it?'

George ran his fingers lightly over the inlaid diamond on the lid. 'This is the Dene family motif, and it occurs in pieces of furniture that Frances has had through the antiques shop in the past; likely enough from the same house sale.'

George opened the lid and widened his eyes at the brass lever and the key on the velvet cushion. 'A musical box?'

James nodded. 'Are we all right to—?'

George scoffed and tripped the brass lever triggering the mechanism. The music filled the air, resonating among the box and book-lined shelves. 'There's only you, me and Mr Personality in today.' The young man looked up for a moment, searching for the sound of the hammered chimes. He shrugged his shoulders with disinterest and returned to his hand-held screen.

George closed his eyes and eccentrically waved his finger before him like a conductor.

'Do you think that my ancestors would have been able to afford to buy a musical jewellery box like this, or do you think it was given as a gift, maybe as a pay-off given Thomas Dene's financial situation?'

He opened his eyes. 'It would have fallen out of fashion at the time, so they may have picked it up for a song, but it's almost certainly not a jewellery box originally; it's a tea caddy – bespoke, made in Central Asia possibly, and late eighteenth or early nineteenth century by the style and the choice of wood inlays.' He clicked back the lever, and the song ceased. 'The interior modification to a jewellery box is probably Victorian, though the musical mechanism might be early Regency. I could ask Frances if you want to leave it with me. She's running things at the Cennen shop full-time while I indulge my love of history here in a public-oriented capacity for most of the week.'

James nodded as George replaced the box with its wrappings. 'I was hoping she might look at it to restore or recommend someone, as there's a corner that's cracking. Some of the small wooden pieces are coming loose along the lower part of the side, too.'

'It will be our pleasure and I'll have her call you.'

'I think the lullaby may be a local tune,' said James.

'It's no lullaby,' said George clearing his throat, and only briefly made eye contact in his sudden bashfulness. 'It's a saucy little song about a man trying to woo a young woman back to his house; I've never heard this arrangement of it before. Fishermen and women used to sing songs like these as they worked while doing menial tasks, like mending nets; it's a work song if you will. It repeats like *Row, Row, Row Your Boat* until someone wearies of it and they start on something else.'

'Does it have a name?' said James.

George nodded. Its official title is "Down in the Valley", but it's more commonly known as "Sweet Nightingale".'

***

The drive back along the moorland road gave James time to digest the insights of the past few hours. He was more than sure Emily must have visited the dry and dusty archive weeks earlier, though to what end was unknown. Was it possible she had immersed herself in some academic capacity or was there some other motive, like his father, that might account for her interest in the area's history? The revelation of the tune's heritage and name created even more questions.

The car descended towards the north coast, and the cracks in the parched fields opened their mouths wide to receive the welcome light rain from the south that began to fall. James glanced at his watch and then at the ordnance survey map on his knee. At the first crossroads, he took the longer route towards Maiden Point, and away from the seaside town of his birth, still basking in the golden glow of late afternoon.

With frequent glances at the map and through the wipers to the narrowing myriad of lanes, he reached a lonely passing place and pulled over to check his location regarding the ruins. A silvered oak, stripped of all green life, stood sentry over a narrow grass rutted path, potholed and pummelled by time. Even as he left the car to put on his waterproof and change into his boots, he knew he had been here before.

Vivid came the memories of long-forgotten summers. With tired legs and rusting bicycles, all four of them had escaped, as children, to the ruins to play among the mossy stones, before sharing the cakes, crisps, and crab paste sandwiches washed down with purloined bottles of cider, to laugh and sleep away another school holiday before the sun dipped and the racing rush of the downhill miles brought them sunkissed and sleepy to St Jude and home.

James glanced at the wild place, trying to place his fallible memory to fit what he knew to be the right location. He climbed the tumble of a dry-stone wall to check on the carvings in the tree for final confirmation. All four names, along with many others were there. Gouged with penknives, the inscriptions now calloused, and he rubbed a hand lovingly across the heart that separated his name and that of his wife.

Pulling up his hood, he followed the field boundary alongside the track until a low place in the wall allowed him to follow the parallel lines to the woodland ahead. He glanced down at the worn tyre marks in the mud, all but obscured by weeks of sea-blown dust. No other footprints were visible, so far off the beaten track to even the most gorse battle-hardened rambler, but he knew the track didn't lead anywhere except Camelot, the Death Star, or whatever choice of venue had been assigned for the day's play thirty-odd years ago.

The resinous pines towered mournfully over the high hedged and narrow track as he clambered round a recent rockfall from an outcrop of granite. Black marks scoured the largest boulder, matched by similar lines on the stones of the opposing rubble wall, but he took little notice and pushed through a thorny gap in the hawthorn to an overgrown clearing of brash, willow herb and nettles scraping an existence in the thin, acidic soils. He trod forwards, folding the softer stems before him until he emerged, arms raised to avoid the barbs of bramble, into the foundations of stone. The thinner ground and remnants of walls and rotting beams of oak delineated the reclamation of nature and he jumped onto a higher section to survey the surrounds at Calm Holt.

He unfolded the drawing briefly as the spots of rain bled into the ink, threatening to turn the sketch into a watercolour. The outer walls were there, the opening that once held a large archway and the hint of cobblestones leading to the pillory post, socketed and empty like a toothless gum. The photocopy from the auction hinted at the detail, though to a much lesser degree, preferring to highlight the more saleable facade, rather than the barns, outhouses, and stables visible in Emily's detailed sketch. A thicket of pioneer fir and stunted birch suggested on the drawing as a small outhouse kitchen, completed the tour of the once large house.

'Carmalt,' he whispered, suddenly fearful as an equally surprised buzzard flitted from a tall pine to cry mournfully above the remnants of fortune. The clouds thickened as the rain became heavier, darkening the sky and making the surrounding wood ominous and unwelcoming. From the vantage point, his attention was suddenly focussed upon a dim spot of light a hundred yards into the trees. It wavered and blinked, as though feeble, among the swaying branches that lay between, and James headed towards the source to investigate.

Gaining the track, he strode forwards as his eyes adjusted to the low light. The light became steady but feeble, gaining clarity as he turned the corner at the end of the track and saw the abandoned black, side scraped Volkswagen, the door slightly ajar allowing the weak interior light to bleed through with the last remaining charge from the battery. He peered in through the driver's window to see the key fob in the cup holder and a half-opened bottle of water, lying upon a map. A fluorescent pink felt line traced the journey from London to St Jude, ending in a large question mark at the end of a crude arrow. It pointed to Maiden Point, a mile or so in a straight line through the trees.

James felt his heart race as he fumbled with his phone beneath a fallen fir. From above, the buzzard cried out as the wind picked up and peppered his face with fresh rain.

'Be quick,' said Jory. 'I'm up to my ears in permits and diversions for the fair tomorrow.'

'I found the car,' said James, watching the circling bird

among the wind and rain. 'The one Emily drove. It's up at Calm Holt.'

'Where's that?' said Jory.

'The place we used to call Camelot,' said James, recalling Emily's words. 'But it's just a ruinous pile of stones now...'

CHAPTER 19

'Sorry about the other day,' said James, walking the steep lane to the church. 'I should have called you last night, but I spent most of it with the police.'

'We can reschedule,' said Caroline, alongside him. 'I've heard some excuses in my time but finding a stolen car to avoid spending the evening apologising to me, with a bottle of Merlot and a takeaway, is the best one yet.'

'It was after midnight when I got in, and the plus side is I slept through. How long will you be stopping at the fair?'

'Not long,' she said. 'Just to show my face and appreciation. I won't come into the churchyard with you; it feels inappropriate if you know what I mean.'

James turned to see her bouncing ponytail and flushed face.

'I understand, and thanks for coming just this far with me.'

'Did they question Emily about the car?' she said, hopping over the gurgling brook that cut across the road. The early-morning rain had ceased, and the new coffee-coloured waters were flooding from the hard, parched farmland on either side.

'They were with her this morning, and the assigned solicitor. Harriet insisted on being there and she called when I was out getting milk. Emily has nothing to offer beyond what she has told them already – that the car belongs to Ryan Williams, and she stole it to escape from him and wherever she lived.'

'You think it's selective amnesia, or is she telling the truth?'

'You sound like Jory,' said James. 'He still thinks she's not telling the whole story.'

'Then I'd agree with him to a point, albeit it's currently out of her control.'

James tugged her arm to his side, pulling her closer to the soggy grass verge to allow a vehicle to pass.

'What did Fellows say about my father's reaction and acceptance to help when I get back from London?'

Caroline dragged in a large breath between her clenched teeth. 'He pretended to be ambivalent, but I knew he was eager to know every nuanced gesture and breath.'

'You tease,' said James. 'Where are we holding the observation and assessment?'

'At the Grange, in the medical room; Fellows has arranged it with the site manager considering your father's health.'

'If the General Medical Council find out, there will be questions asked,' said James.

'Fortunate then that Fellows and your father are taking full responsibility. Edward is still within the five-year window for re-validation, so he's able to practise within the Trust, providing Fellows says so.'

'How convenient. One of them is retiring in six months, and the other...'

Caroline paused in the ascent and leaned against a mile marker to retie her shoelace. 'I'll be needing you back at Truro at that stage.'

James watched her absorbed in the meticulous and time-wasting exercise, trying to catch her eye and intention. 'You got the job?'

She rose and looked him squarely in the face. 'I've been asked to act as the interim, and Deborah Gayle and I are having to co-operate for the time being. If the board offers me the position over her, then my role will become vacant for someone suitably qualified that I can depend upon. You catch my drift?'

James raised a hand to several local fair goers coming up from behind, waiting for their bouncing backpacks to recede out of earshot. 'Was this part of what my father arranged for his involvement in Emily's case – my reinstatement and your investiture?'

'The former,' she said, picking at a spent seed head of cow parsley in the hedged bank. 'Subject to a final medical review. I have insisted the latter be handled by the book – I'm not taking a job I haven't earned.'

'And neither am I,' said James returning to the climb, 'or a promotion I don't deserve.'

After a short rise, the road levelled off and James halted to look up into the brittle, brown-streaked leaves of a shedding chestnut.

'You don't have to decide straight away,' said Caroline, eager to broach the contemplative silence. 'Nothing's been decided, but it would mean leaving St Jude and this case behind, as well as taking a back seat on face-to-face consultations.' James studied the high cirrus in the azure sky, heralding change, and acutely aware of her gaze.

'It's time to move up, James, and I think a move away from deep-dive work to a more strategic role would be good for you and your career.'

'You sound like my father. Did he put you up to this?'

'Yes and no. It's my assessment based on what I'm

seeing. If you aren't making progress and she's stable, then there are several options for maintenance – I don't want you obsessed by something that's causing you sleepless nights or whatever it was you were suffering from at the seafront the other day. Your other patients aren't having this effect on you, just her.'

James stuffed his hands into his back pockets. 'I'll freely admit I didn't want to take this on, but considering the mystery surrounding who she is and the alter's apparent interest in affairs close to my family history, I am the right person to be dealing with this right now but...'

'What?' said Caroline.

'It feels like I am trying to help someone that is being pulled apart by things outside my control. Every time I get closer something drags her away, which is why I'll take my father's input on this; but it's my call and I need to find out what is going on, and quickly.'

'What do you have in mind?'

'Hypnosis, under observation, to regress Emily to the point of trauma and beyond, possibly to recall the weeks before her appearance in St Jude. We need to know who she is, and why she's here, and if I have to connect or regress with May Dene and local history, to find some connection in their experiences, then so be it.'

'Isn't that a little "hocus-pocus"?' said Caroline, discarding the stalk and moving on. 'I thought past-life regression went the way of ouija boards as a therapeutic technique.'

'It's just called age regression, as well you know, and my father is skilled at it. I'm planning to use it alongside hypnotherapy to help Emily return briefly to painful periods in her life. Once there, we can help her overcome the trauma and find healing.'

'And how does the alternate personality feel about this, won't it just try to shut her down?'

James dabbed his trouser pocket to confirm his phone was there; it contained the recorded sound of the music box.

'We may have a safe way of bypassing or accessing the shared memories that involves music as part of the therapy. Emily subconsciously retreats using a tune that closely matches the sound of a music box belonging to my mother.'

'The humming?'

'Yes. Not always, but the alter often presents following its emergence. We need to let May Dene know we can be trusted to look after Emily and having some connection through the folk tune and my family history might build enough trust to release the host's memories.'

'I don't want Emily pushed beyond anything she isn't ready for, and I don't want you assuming or discounting other inputs. You understand we have to avoid you going down that path again.'

'Agreed. My father wants us to keep an open mind and we share a belief that Emily may be projecting her trauma through the lens of a historical suicide from two hundred years ago. I suspect she has visited the archives before coming here and has subdued memories surrounding the information she gathered. My father also wants to discount something—' James hesitated, considering whether to bring up the conflicting conjecture.

'The old man has a counter-diagnosis?'

'He has pointed out the overwhelming desire to behave dramatically to get attention with all the hallmarks of what might be Ganser: the nudity, the threat of suicide, and the theft of a car belonging to a criminal.'

'Please tell me you are kidding me, and this isn't some twisted joke of his to stick it to Fellows before he pops his clogs. Are you sure he is in his right mind, let alone you? I thought he was trying to protect you, not deliver you on a plate to Deborah Gayle.'

'I don't believe this,' said James. 'But I'm keeping the option open, and you can get as many opinions as you like before you submit the final report.'

They reached the churchyard gate and paused.

'Don't you worry,' said Caroline. 'I will be doing just that, and you know that I'll relieve you if I find this is going in the wrong direction?'

'I understand,' said James, watching her retreat to the centre of the road.

'This is dangerous, James, for all three of you; but only you and Emily are likely to suffer the long-term consequences if you get this wrong.'

'I spoke with Father yesterday,' said James, staring down at the black marble book of his mother's memorial. 'Same as usual to begin with, but it's heading in the right direction for as long as the journey still has to run.' He stooped and wiped a finger on the blank and waiting page to form a diamond bisected by eight lines in the dew. 'I have your box, and it's been a great comfort. I'm getting it mended and I thought about making it a box for your photos.' He plucked at the longer grass surrounding his mother's gravestone, as the clock struck for ten o'clock.

The distant crackle of the tannoy loudspeaker in Twenty-Acre Field cut through the silence. The rook in the great yew above cocked an ear to the feedback and mindless babble from the festival grounds before flying off to perch on the hard stone of the church tower.

Down in the bay, the sea mist lingered, condensing from the higher ground of the headland and rolling in to the seafront far below. The chilly air and clearing sky above promised much for the afternoon as the warm lingering hold of summer squeezed into September's slumbering slot. A distant bonfire smouldered, sending up a smudge of sooty wood smoke.

'Got to go,' he said, rising to his feet to sniff at the air. 'I'm helping at the charity stall and tombola for the hostel up at Twenty-Acre; the Haldwyn fair is celebrating its two hundred and fiftieth anniversary this year, so it should be busy.'

Turning to go, he glanced over at the opening to the older part of the churchyard. The moment of finding Emily came flooding back, and he gingerly approached the opening and peered through the gap in the hedge to a changed scene. The grass was flattened and trimmed in many places to allow the weathered stones to appear like twisted, worn teeth from a green, turfed gum. Following revelations in the papers, the site had become something of a minor tourist attraction, and whether by orders or embarrassment of the condition of the area, the parish council had done a rough-and-ready job of tidying up the oldest plot.

The cross lay central, surrounded by nearby recumbent stones. A path had been cleared, and the ground surrounding the Dene memorial was level and smooth. A naked doll sat on the protruding base with legs and arms akimbo, but whether in reverence or mockery James could not tell. Alongside was propped a small corn dolly, akin to the one at his wife's grave though fresh and recently placed. Woven stems of wheat imprisoned a solitary, sea-polished stone of veined quartz and at its stubby feet lay a torn bunch of freshly gathered wildflowers, though shedding and spent. He looked around at the amphitheatre of untended brambles and long grass, picking out the footfalls of the person who had purposefully sought the remaining flowers as a tribute. The dark-wooded spinney next to the churchyard encircled the mournful and, until recently, forgotten place.

James sought for remaining wildflowers, pulling them to form a bunch, and setting off the fluffy ashes of seeding fireweed. After dividing the bouquet into two and placing his tribute alongside those already present, he left the area and tramped down the recently mown path, avoiding the rolled clods of grass dumped in the wake of the flail mower. Laying down the flowers and righting the fallen toy figure, he placed a hand against the engraved image of his wife.

He rose and froze at the sight of a woman in her early fifties standing next to the white stone of the grave of Isobel Lee. The fresh flowers she placed were bright and exuberant, just like the spirit and personality of the woman who lay beneath. She turned away on catching sight of him but stopped suddenly and made her way across. Coming closer, he remembered her distraught face from the hospital, six months prior.

'I'm not here to make a scene, Dr Marshall,' she said, holding out her empty hands. 'Just looking for some peace and closure. I think we've all suffered enough.'

James stuck his hands behind his back and glanced up to meet her tired eyes. 'Mrs Lee, I didn't see you arrive, and I'll leave if my presence upsets you.'

'You have the same right to be here as I do.' She glanced down at the dark marble, streaked with tears of dew in the warming air. 'I'm sorry for your loss, though I've not had the strength to say so to your face until now, only to your wife when I paid my respects not so long back.'

'It was you who placed the flowers recently and the—?'

'It was. An intermediary step to dealing with my grief. I knew Karen. She was a good person, and after all I hear about what you did and are still doing, for that poor girl you found over there, I know you to be the same.'

'I don't know what to say,' said James, hanging his head. 'I never expected you to forgive—'

'Forgive is a strong word and the guilt that comes before such action is a strong teacher to those needing it. I'm not there yet, but I want you to know that we can't go around avoiding each other in graveyards and grocers till we seal ourselves up in God's good granite beneath us where no chance of it being said, or listened, to can happen.'

'I understand,' he said, wiping his sweaty palms down the side of his trousers. 'You are aware I'm back at St Jude – I understood you asked for action to be taken?'

'Jim and I asked for no such thing, only that those responsible for Isobel's care learned from it to stop it from happening again. I only found out when Stephanie Carter told me last week and it caused me a lot of anxiety, I can tell you, till she helped me see sense. You being here won't change what happened and I don't blame you for everything, considering you lost yours on the same day I lost mine.' She reached over and tapped the black headstone reverently.

'Stephanie's a good woman,' said James, exhaling a deep steamy breath into the chill autumn air, 'and I can't thank her enough for whatever she has done or said that has enabled you to get to this point with me.'

She nodded and walked away, pausing at the path to turn back.

'You promise me you'll save this woman, the one they call the maiden, from whatever comes her way, lest the past comes back to haunt us all?'

'I do, and I will,' he said, watching her click shut the gate and head towards the rising half-mile entrance to the festival field.

CHAPTER 20

The stubbled, unploughed field stretched out like a great colourful tablecloth littered with bright craft tents and marquees positioned around a central show area dotted with bales of straw. Many cars were already being parked by brightly vested stewards, and James hurried beneath the directional bunting to avoid many more queuing for entry through the nearby hedged gate. The scent of sweet, sugary confections mixed with the fragrance of fried burgers and fish. A distant banjo band, playing from the trailer of a lorry, began a country reel, lost against the backdrop of the clay pigeon shooting, steam-powered pipe organ and small fairground rides all clamouring for attention and paying visitors.

People strolled across the sticky, hard earth with eager, boisterous children and barking dogs for the day ahead, just as they had done for over two centuries. James acknowledged several local acquaintances and made his way past a busy burger van to reach the quieter corner of the field overlooking the showring currently occupied by a falconry display team. The charity pop-ups huddled together, and he spotted the waving arms of Harriet and Stephanie, momentarily putting down boxes still to be unpacked for the appeals display.

'Morning all,' he said. 'Guess you couldn't stay away from the highlight of the St Jude social calendar, Harriet?'

'Something like that,' she said with a grin, brushing past him, to offer a leaflet to a woman in a waxed jacket-wearing wisteria-coloured Wellingtons. The woman took the informative pamphlet and got out some spare change for the collecting tin.

'You said it was one of the oldest continuous fairs in the south-west,' said Harriet, returning to his side. 'Plus, the social worker had trouble with her car on the way over from Penzance, so she called me to see if I could cover.'

'Well, I'm ready to clock in and man the stall unless you need me to help finish setting up?'

Stephanie pointed behind the open boot of the off-road vehicle. 'Give Emily a hand, she's getting more boxes.'

'Emily's here?'

'Kind of,' said Harriet, flashing her eyes. 'She got agitated when I said I didn't think it was a good idea with all the locals staring and taking pictures, which they have been doing all morning. Even that film crew were here and started talking with her before I shooed them away; I wouldn't bother talking with them later, they weren't interested in the refuge, only her story – apparently, it's in "the public interest" following her unorthodox arrival, and the discovery of the abandoned car yesterday.'

'Did she tell them anything?' said James, concerned.

'Let's hope not; she wasn't herself if you know what I mean, but Emily is back in control or was once we'd threatened to take away the bubblegum we bought her.'

'She's not a child, Harriet.'

'Anyway, she said you told her it was fine to come, and as I am officially the chaperone today, I couldn't be here and monitor her at the same time.' Harriet pulled him to one side. 'I hope you understand that what I said on the phone the other day was for Emily's benefit, as well as yours. I'm still new here, so if I stepped out of—'

James nodded, conscious of a rising blush response. 'I wasn't feeling well or thinking straight; you did the right thing.'

Harriet breathed a sigh of relief. 'I guess there was no harm done.'

James cleared his throat and nodded. 'How is Emily today?'

'May Dene fronted earlier during our trip past the church and says she was here during the first years of the festival's existence. Following your notes about familiar places and confirmation biases, I thought it might be a useful place for her to reconcile or expand on her memories, even if they are just delusions. It might encourage recovery, especially in light of this being a safe environment.'

'Sounds like you've been at my father's book again – chapter eighteen, "The Path to Recovery: Rescuing the Subdued Subconscious" – am I right?'

'Actually,' she said, 'it was from a paper you delivered a few years ago in Plymouth.'

'I'm flattered,' said James, suddenly recalling the weekend and the emotional fallout of the evening with Caroline.

'It was what encouraged me to transition from counselling and work towards a psychologically focussed role.'

James presumptuously wondered if something else was in play. He looked into the young face, gentle and caring, to detect any other motive for her flattery. His mind reeled with sudden and unexpected outcomes.

'Didn't Mike say he'd be along this morning?' she said, turning to Stephanie with a brief look of disappointment on her face. She snatched a glance at her watch. 'He's late.'

Stephanie nodded, winking covertly behind her back as Harriet returned to look into James's relieved face.

'I have a confession to make,' she said, 'though I think nothing negative has happened, in fact, quite the opposite.'

'What do you mean?'

'We had a good walk from the refuge, and she insisted on visiting the church on the way up. It was all I could do to keep up with her; we should have driven, but she wasn't happy with the "horseless carriage", as she put it.'

'She laid flowers at the cross, didn't she?'

Harriet pinched her brow and cocked her head in surprise. 'Yes, and I think it helped with some kind of closure. She hasn't shut up about the past until I distracted her with a candy floss twenty minutes ago.'

'How did she handle the visit to the Dene grave?'

'It was strange. She said she never got the chance to say goodbye to her father; that they parted on poor terms and that "the absence of everyone and everything she loved was an eternity of homesickness for her".'

'Poignant stuff,' said James, shuffling his feet and glancing down at the showring now inhabited by a shepherd whistling to his dog herding geese through wooden gates.

'I'll go check on her; thanks for keeping me up to date with the police situation this morning.'

Harriet nodded and returned to the stall.

James turned and clambered over the taut guide ropes of the marquee to see Emily standing thoughtfully, chewing gum and blowing a bubble to bursting as she overlooked the rising downs and wooded valleys towards Maiden Point.

'How's the gum?' he whispered so as not to disturb her thoughts.

'Disgusting,' said Emily. 'But it keeps you-know-who happy and quiet. I had to intervene with a song of my own to stop her from swallowing it; apparently spitting it out is very unladylike.'

'You can control her appearance using the same humming technique as she does?'

'To a degree, if we are both calm. My musical tastes, and my singing voice, I have discovered, are somewhat embarrassing, so I can usually do it without letting everyone hear my renditions from a certain Britpop-era girl band.'

An involuntary shake of her head did not break her study of the dramatic landscape as though searching for some familiar signs. James approached, hands in pockets, and stood beside her.

'Is she conscious of us, here and now?'

She nodded. 'She's been here before.' James followed a pointed finger towards a distant plantation of trees, several miles away in the direction of the moorland cliffs. 'It was you who found the car, wasn't it?'

'Yes,' said James. 'You don't have to talk about it; I know you've had a busy morning.'

'She was right. Carmalt is somewhere over there, isn't it?' she said, biting her lip in a struggle to be certain.

'It's a series of foundation walls, but yes; it's still there. Its last known name was Calm Holt.'

She sighed. 'Strong foundations endure a long time.' Emily turned to look excitedly into his face. 'The soldier from the drawing once rode the distance to the house between the striking of the hourly church bell, and the quarter-hour chime.'

'The one she calls Richard?' he said. 'That is a fair distance in fifteen minutes, even in a straight line across rough ground, bog and field.'

'Richard Avery,' she said, holding a hand above her eyes to

filter out the rising sun. 'She thinks about him all the time and was very much in love with him, but she was promised to another in order to save her father and the line. Yet he accomplished it, and so did she with his instruction, though it nearly killed her and the horse.'

She blew out another bubble, bursting it with her fingers. 'She calls it "pointing" and it's a reckless sport fraught with pitfalls and danger. The one she was promised to, the Fallon man, tried and failed to do it. He grew angry with both of them and—'

James watched as she put a hand to her temple and shook her head. 'Is this a film or book I've read?' she said, clutching her arms closely and rubbing her sides. 'The images and memories are so vivid – it's like I've been there and seen it, but how can this be true when it's all made up; not real?'

'It's real to you, and will make sense in its own good time, like recalling things you picked up from a visit to an archive, perhaps, or your visit to the church earlier.'

'I couldn't do very much about it. She took over and, in a way, I was safe from the feelings of my own that came back.' She blushed. 'I'm sorry about the condition you found me in; it must have been quite a shock.'

James shrugged. 'I did what any other caring human being would have done. What did May make of the churchyard?'

Emily turned to look into the boxes of donated goods for the white elephant stall. 'It was like someone saying goodbye and coming to terms after waiting an interminably long time.' She grabbed a box and ducked beneath the boot lid. 'We cried.'

James lifted the final box into the crook of his arm and shut the lid. 'Well, today, you are here to enjoy yourself, relax and help us raise funds.'

'I hope I didn't get you into trouble the other day,' she said. 'Your boss seems pretty fierce.'

James shook his head. 'It was my fault if any existed. I wasn't well or thinking straight for most of the day, especially after the seafront. I thought I'd feel better until—'

'I hope whatever May said or did, didn't cause it. It was like that for me till I got used to it.'

'Got used to what?'

Emily stopped chewing. 'Falling.'

James frowned at the inference. 'I'm more interested in what you said to the old man, Tom Cotter? I was on the phone.'

'He just wanted a cigarette,' said Emily 'and that's the last thing I remember until May took charge like a bull in a china shop. It was as though she recognised him, but how can that be? Is he okay?'

'Yes, he's fine, just…different, calmer, less erratic. What do you mean about recognised—?'

She glanced over his shoulder through the slit in the marquee wall. 'Look, Dr Trebarr's arrived.'

Emily watched as Harriet rushed to meet him. 'The handsome doctor appears to be in trouble.'

James nodded. 'I think you may be right. About Tom—'

Emily disappeared into the boot of the estate car and dragged several carrier bags of bric-a-brac, to the tailgate. 'Will the authorities close the refuge if we don't raise the money this afternoon?'

James shook his head. 'No, not just this afternoon, but soon. There isn't the money to support it.'

'If I had anything to give, I would.' She dug her hands into her pocket to reveal several blue globes of wrapped gum and her door key. 'May believes there is always hope, though I don't know what she means by that.'

James took and unwrapped a sweet with his free hand and began to chew on the mouthful of hard gum. Emily laughed as he grimaced with the sweet and sickly taste.

'I have to agree with her on hope,' he said lifting several of the bags ready to return to the stall. 'But I side with you on the gum. It's disgusting.'

CHAPTER 21

The morning wore on, warm and heady with the sounds and smells of the country fair beckoning people from far and wide. The visitors cheered and clapped the programme of entertainments heralded and described from tinny loudspeakers that echoed around the showground. A busy crowd milled among the stalls and around the central arena like a slowly turning wheel of humanity.

'Might be sixty quid in shrapnel,' said Harriet, sorting the legal tender from the foreign coins in one of the charity tins. 'Not bad, but hard for a morning's work.'

'Would antique jewellery be valuable enough to keep the refuge going?' asked Emily, dabbing her neck with the communal sun cream, and smoothing the moisturising beads into her pale skin.

'It depends on the age, intrinsic value and fashion,' replied Harriet. 'Then you'd have to find someone wealthy and kind enough to donate it. We've tried all the local philanthropists already.'

'What would something that cost eight hundred guineas in 1789 be worth now?'

James rose from tapping in a wayward guide rope pin. 'A lot. We need to go buy ourselves a metal detector and hunt around those cliffs.'

'Why?' said Emily.

'There's supposed to be treasure or such that went over—' He paused. 'Just a local legend, that's all.'

Mike borrowed the mallet and stared down at the mountain of copper and silver. 'You know, we should put all this on a horse or something; get a dead cert on a 50-1.'

'You've no eye for a winner, Mike,' said James, playfully punching his shoulder.

'That is a despicable pastime that leads to a debtor's jail,' said Emily, shaking and momentarily clutching at her head. The rest of the voluntary team stopped in their tracks with the sudden archaic admonishment.

James tapped the side of his nose at the GP as she regained her composure.

Mike winked and regained the attention. 'Not if you win.'

The loudspeaker sprang to static-charged life, announcing the start of the terrier racing. 'Care to put that to the test?' said Harriet, joining in the distraction. 'Using your own money?'

Emily clutched at James's arm. 'The Cartwrights used to run a dog.'

'The Cartwrights?' he said, extricating her arm from his and calming down the sudden impulsive outburst. The mention of his ancestors unsettled him.

'The servants who look after my father following the death of my mother. They have a dog called Badger. It won two years in a row—' Emily hung her head. 'It's not true, is it? I've never been here before; I'm sorry.'

Harriet put an arm around her. 'Do you want to sit down for a bit? It's been a hectic morning.'

Emily shook her head. 'She comes and goes so quickly like

the barriers between us are weakening. I'll be fine, just don't let me, or her, spoil your day.'

'You won't and you haven't. It's been hot, and you've worked like a trouper. I think it's time you took a break.'

'What do you say about coming to watch my good friend lose some money on a dog?' said Mike, lightening the mood, encouraged by Harriet's hand in his own and her face brightening with the idea of a change of scene. 'Even as children, he couldn't pick a winner.'

James protested with mock offence and accepted the challenge even as Emily closed her eyes. Snatches of a familiar kitsch tune broke through her attempts to keep the humming as silent as possible. James watched as she sought mastery over the alter within, to calm and subdue the personality desperate to front. She breathed out and opened her eyes to the bemused care team and volunteers. 'I'm ready now.'

The four of them left the stall in the capable hands of Stephanie and the other volunteers. Mike led them meandering through the crowd to the corner of the showring where the makeshift bookmaker explained the rules in play while five dogs were shown around the ring.

'Place a bet, Harriet,' said Mike, getting out a ten-pound note. 'Pick a fast dog, maybe that younger, fitter one in tow.'

Harriet nodded. 'Number four, then.'

The bookkeeper took the money and handed Mike a betting slip. 'Good luck to you both, it's a fine-looking dog. Got a lot of money going on him, so the payout will be shared among those that win. We've got a tote system in place today.'

'How about it?' said James as Emily scrutinised the remaining terriers. 'We'll both agree to put whatever we win into the refuge collecting tin; do you think that will be okay with both of you?'

Emily nodded. 'It's for a good cause and I can sense her

excitement. The end justifies the means in this case.' She pointed towards a younger dog, then frowned and switched back to a brown, stockier creature walking passively at the rear around the ring, chewing at the makeshift bailer twine that bound him to his moleskin trousered master.

'That one,' said Emily. 'She wants that older terrier.'

James looked at the creature, aged by any dog's standards, and not just for racing. His heart sank as he caught the smirk of his best friend, tall above the growing crowd at the edge of the rope-lined arena. Friendly rivalry overcame his better judgement.

'Number five,' he said to the bookkeeper, handing him his bet. The man returned the slip, giving Emily a courteous smile.

'It's the taking part that counts,' he said, scratching his head. 'Enjoy the race all the same.'

They pushed their way through the scrum to find a less-crowded spot to overlook the race ring with its several bales of straw strategically placed to hinder and increase the length of the dogs' path towards the finish line. A young girl pulled out a rabbit-furred pelt tied to a strong line, let out from a winding wheel manned by a strong young man. He waited as the dogs were loaded into the starter pens.

The starter teased the dogs in the cages with the line-attached furred skin, driving them into a frenzy. The terriers hurled themselves against the steel mesh of their temporary prison trying to chew through the bars holding back their instinct to chase, run-down, and rip apart the already deceased quarry. A steward held up a megaphone and called over to the man at the finish line to start his winding.

The furry antagonist dropped from the starter's hand and into the grass of the central showring, scurrying away on its unbreakable line from the incandescent, yapping dogs. The steward studied the rapidly moving lure, gauging the distance to prevent the initial surge of the dogs from ending the race prematurely. He raised his arm and waited no longer. The starter saw the arm thrown towards the ground and pulled back the lever, releasing the front of the restraining mesh. The dogs launched into the air to a great tumultuous cheer from the crowd. Harriet clenched her fists and jumped with excitement as Mike called out encouragement, clutching at his sure-fire winning ticket.

The youngest dog reached the first hay bale and sailed over it. Two black-and-white Jack Russell terriers, closely behind, hesitated and ran round the obstruction, on opposite sides, meeting each other before turning and spinning in wild abandon. They chased each other around the bale to the dismay of a section of the crowd and their respective owners, and gambolled away, leaving space for the fourth dog to sprint past, now intent on chasing down the dog in the lead with the lure rapidly retreating out of view. The wiry-haired border terrier, on which James's hopes lay, loped in pursuit at a steady but unremarkable pace. He looked down at his tote slip and shook his head at Emily, who looked unfazed, chewing a fresh batch of bubblegum.

'Come on Badger—' Her voice was drowned out by the enthusiastic cries of the GP and the counsellor as their lead dog approached the first corner. James felt a friendly slap on his shoulder, and he hung his head and placed a hand over his eyes in mock shame as the GP lowered his arm around Harriet's waist.

The man at the winder increased his speed, seeing the young dog close on the furry lure. With several sudden rapid turns, the line pulled the mock rabbit ninety degrees around the shiny inner recess of a tractor hub. The dog behind lunged out but narrowly missed in his bite, leaving no time to react to the prey's unexpected change in direction. It over-shot the turning point, wondering where the object had vanished to, tracking back and forth unable to find the trail, before giving up and retiring, heavily panting and cocking a leg to urinate at the mysterious metal portal that had consumed and taken away its prey and purpose. A portion of the crowd roared with laughter, while other more serious dog-fanciers ripped up their slips and turned from the arena to find other diversions.

The remaining two dogs behind caught sight of the hastily retreating lure and cut across in renewed pursuit. James swung around to see the lead dog join the other two frolicking terriers in a triad of mayhem and saliva. He glanced back to see Mike and Harriet open-mouthed as their dog, and race favourite, left the arena, distracted by the allure of littered, half-eaten hot dogs.

James's dog plodded along and sensed the approaching deception, whether through experience or some innate intelligence; it veered to the left as the other dog ran on to the next tractor hub, following its predicted path but unable to track the sudden change in direction of the mock rabbit. The animal slowed and left the ring, misinterpreting several of the protesting and cheering crowd as an encouragement to run over and be rewarded with a lick of ice cream from several kneeling and non-compliant children.

It was James's turn to look across to see Mike shaking his head in disbelief as the aged terrier sauntered around a final and inconveniently obstructive hay bale, putting on a final sprint as the furry lure slowed against the winding machine. With a final pounce, the old dog bit into his prize and threw the ragged skin back and forth to break its worthless, missing neck. The steward announced the winner and marked his card as the crowd clapped and cheered for the end of the entertainment. James turned to find Emily already looking up smugly.

'How did you know the older dog would win?' he said.

'Someone helped in that department,' she said. 'I'm as surprised as you are, though you said it had been run here for hundreds of years. I've seen this before, but not through these eyes; how can that be possible?'

James did not answer as he was congratulated by his team and ushered towards the bookmaker. The man retrieved his calculator and handed over the eighty pounds with a puzzled look at Emily. 'Tortoise and the hare, isn't that right, miss? You've got a good eye for dogs.'

The group meandered back through a group of restless and rein-tugging horses, being led by a young woman intent on coaxing the beasts into the ring for a display of jumping and horsemanship. James looked across at the dismantling of the bales and dog-racing equipment as the central arena was rapidly turned around to accommodate the poles and jumps. The heavily dressed horses displayed brass and leather thongs, several of which dragged along the ground in unguarded loops. Children raced alongside, some patting the hind quarters while others looked in envy at the solitary young boy perched and helmeted atop the end horse. He looked uncomfortable and wrapped his wrists around the reins before gripping the pommel of the overly large saddle. Emily pressed herself into James's side, unsure and uncomfortable with the closeness of the skittish steeds.

'It's okay,' said James, putting his arm protectively around her. 'The horses are just as nervous about the crowds as that small boy is of being up there.'

The sound of an unscheduled shotgun blast overhead, dispatching a wayward clay pigeon, followed by a rear of the horses and a piercing scream, caused Harriet and many others to spin in alarm. James caught the look of horror on her face. She clenched one hand to her mouth as Mike sprinted back and past her. James felt Emily pull away from him and turn towards the sound of the dreadful cry to see waves of people part and the horses, now free of any restraint from the handler on her back in the dry stubble, twist and spin with sudden panic at the falling pieces from the sky and the repeated firing of the shotguns, behind the craft stalls away to their left.

A solitary horse, carrying the slumped and bouncing boy, parted the crowd like the bow of a racing boat and raced away in terror. The boy slipped over to the side, tethered to the side of the saddle by his trapped foot in the stirrup, to the repeated cries of a woman who chased after him. Several brave souls stood their ground trying to wave the horse from its intended course, before covering their heads and flinging themselves to the ground. James saw the film crew from the corner of his eye hastily set up and begin to shoot the impending disaster. The boy screeched as he slipped to within inches of the ground, thrown in limp uncontrollable lurches like the rabbit in the terrier's mouth. The horse jumped a low display of bric-a-brac and headed down the slope towards a funnelled and roped area displaying agricultural implements and vintage metalwork.

He looked for Emily as he saw Mike rushing for the St John ambulance across the arena to prepare for the worst. Even as his friend passed him, James saw the horse veer to the right to avoid the impenetrable pipe organ, and race toward the sharp tines of ploughs, harrows, and grass rotator rakes in the field ahead.

His attention was rapidly diverted closer to hand as the shocked crowd returned to fill the space, some reaching for mobile phones with panting breath to capture on film what they could not affect or help with.

All except one.

She raced over to pull at the reins of a stallion, spinning him around to distract and confound the great horse before placing a foot high into the stirrup and pulling herself up with a great effort to clutch at the mane. The stallion lurched and spun, unaccustomed to the person clambering to gain purchase on its back, narrowly missing the kneeling and impotent figure of its trainer, who struggled to rise, clutching at what James could see was a dislocated shoulder. The horse reared, and the rider swung a leg over the wide back, throwing a hand high against the neck to grasp and pull herself up and into the saddle. She gripped the reins and pulled, calling out to clear the way and stared momentarily at James with dilated blue eyes and purposeful intent.

In a second, Emily spurred the horse forwards with skilful and reckless speed across the intervening distance in pursuit of the grey horse, and the approaching lines of static machinery.

CHAPTER 22

The loose grey horse threw up great clods of caked clay as it galloped across the obstacle-strewn field, desperate in its desire to discard the screaming jetsam jutting from the side of its saddle.

Emily weaved the stallion in pursuit between guy ropes and fairground revellers, cantering with sharp turns to gain the direct route ahead of and trim the distance needed to reach the wayward mount. She pushed herself forwards, shortening the reins like a point-to-point jockey jostling in a race towards an unseen finishing line. With a final and unsuccessful attempt to raise its head, the horse gave in to her commands and its necessity to run, burning up and consuming the restless energy acquired while standing idly in the horse trailer from the journey to the fair.

The scattered crowds split and gave way before the black steed. James hurried across, keeping sight of the chase as Emily vaulted a stall table stuffed with raffle items. Mike had reached the voluntary ambulance crew and they bumped their way across the stubble to follow the grey horse at a safe enough distance to avoid spooking the horse any further. The

GP ran ahead, clearing a path like a furious funeral director ahead of a speeding cortège.

James heard Harriet close behind, calling out, 'What the hell is she doing?'

He saw the stallion approaching a four-high stack of baled hay for use around the showground. The horse tensed, about to pull up as the rider lifted herself up and forwards from the saddle committing both to the jump. It shook its head in a final act of defiance before surrendering to the skill and will of the rider. Emily dug her heels into the horse's midriff and pressed forward over the beast's neck, readying for the leap. The stallion stuttered in its stride, gauging the launching point and sprung from its hind quarters, raising its forelegs high into the air. It stretched out and flew over the hedge of hay and straw, landing in stride, and raced on. Someone in the nearby crowd screamed as Emily slipped over to her left before correcting herself from the impact of the return to hard ground.

'Has she lost her mind?' cried Harriet, breathlessly overtaking him.

She halted at the opposite side of the arena circumference rope, lifting it for James to duck beneath, and set off across the arena in the straightest line that now existed between them and the grey horse. The ambulance veered alongside, sped off and away from them.

'I don't think it's Emily, in control,' he said, keeping pace with the younger woman.

The grey horse was still attempting to shake off the unaccustomed baggage but was being pulled by the weight of the child on the right rein into an unavoidable route towards the approaching minefield of metal and machinery. Several men ran through the auction and display equipment, ripping off their hats and waving to force the horse away from the danger, but the steed was still in the grip of panic, longing to escape and cast aside the child. Emily spurred the stallion on, gaining ground until she was within a length of the animal. A sudden appearance of a farmer on a four-wheeled all-terrain vehicle spooked the stallion momentarily, causing it to twist and almost throw her even as she lunged out her left hand for the taut right rein of the child-carrying horse. Emily drew alongside as the grey horse nudged into her leg and pulled ahead towards the farm implements, oblivious to all danger.

Shielded by the black horse, James could not see the child, but he saw Emily look up at the approaching and unavoidable mass of steel like a doubtful captain of a doomed cavalry, tasked with charging headlong into a wall of pikes and spears. He saw her consider the jump from her saddle to the other, but she pulled back as the grey horse sensed her plan and altered its stride to avoid the sudden mounting. Emily tugged up on her reins and spun around on the other side as the ATV shot past, distracting the wayward horse momentarily. Finally, the grey steed saw no way out ahead and no way to avoid being corralled into a jump across the back of a vicious and rusting harrow.

Even if the tiring horse could make it over, the child below would be impaled, bringing down the beast to an unknown fate among the rusting barbs.

With a final flick of the reins from side to side across the stallion's broad neck, she reached out, even as the horse began its stuttering measured pace to ready for the jump. Emily threw out her right hand and grabbed at the grey horse's bridle, pulling the weight of the heavier horse beneath her towards the lighter grey and forcing a deviation in their path. Her hands buried themselves between the sweat-lathered leather and cheek of the wild horse. Harriet cried out ahead as James watched the final, fateful few seconds unfold.

Emily clung on, pulling the stallion into a sharp lurch to the left. Over the sound of the showground and the distance of over two hundred yards, James heard the grey horse's whinny with the command to veer left. It twisted round and would have been pulled over except for the proximity of Emily's horse, counterbalancing with a sudden change of direction and forcing the horses to swing over as one. With metres to spare, the grey horse gave up on the attempted jump to freedom and was dragged sideways from the harrow, throwing out the child in a centrifugal action towards the sharp metal points. Emily threw herself back into the saddle as the distance between the steeds closed and pulled the combined horses into a final rotating canter. The child bounced away from the grey horse and reconnected with its belly, inches away from the machinery as the horses thundered past.

Emily fought to control both horses and slow their speed until a sparse crowd of hardy farmers surrounded them in a ring of outstretched arms. The ambulance crew, already parked and assisted by Mike, rushed over to help in freeing the terrified and delirious child. The grey horse quivered and snorted even as Emily removed her bloodied and grazed hand from its bridle, releasing the animal to several strong men.

She sagged in the saddle, exhausted, as the stallion paced back and forth, unwilling to be tamed by the reaching of hands. For a moment, she lifted her head with a defiant and masterful look of piercing blue into a myriad of camera phone flashes. James and Harriet, out of breath, joined the swelling crowd seeking to remove the swaying rider from the sweat-lathered saddle before she fell. The stallion steamed, trembled and spun, finally dislodging Emily in a sliding, sprawling fall, broken in part by the impromptu crash mat of an enormous farm labourer. He fell backwards to the ground and Emily rolled from his chest and onto the grass, coming to rest beneath the prancing legs of the black stallion.

James pushed through the ring, clattering into a camera,

hastily mounted on one of the film crew's shoulders, and struggled through the mass of people. Harriet raced between the horses to drag her clear and onto her back. The child was freed and carried screaming, bruised and battered, by one of the ambulance crew to the waiting vehicle and Mike spun round, arms outstretched, to move everyone back as he assessed the next highest priority like a battlefield medic. The crowd inched back as James broke through to see Emily's chest heaving with exertion, her eyes shut and her arms fitfully flailing like a spent marathon runner beyond the end of a race and their limits.

She struggled to lift her head. 'The child...'

'Almost certainly a broken wrist and dislocated ankle,' said Mike, forcing her back to a sedentary position and peering between the legs of the onlookers at the ugly metal-tractor-pulled pre-war harrow. 'But alive. Now lie down; you took a nasty tumble.'

James removed his jacket and rolled it beneath her head, but she fought them off with remarkable strength, and sat up, leaning to one side on her blood-blistered fingers, gasping for breath.

'Are you crazy?' he said.

She shook her head and opened her eyes. James saw the deep blue, dilated eyes piercing and present as though staring through him, trying to reach him with a glance with what words could not express.

'Intervention required haste... do not blame her for being... a vessel to my folly.' Her injured hand clung to his own and James felt the same rush of nausea and falling return with such vehemence and severity, he briefly clasped his eyes shut to avoid toppling over. When he opened them, the sensation was replaced by something else.

He looked down to find a woman's delicate hand in place

of his own, clutching onto the reins of a great horse, racing across the rushing grass beneath a sun-soaked sky.

'I'm going to fall—' James felt himself recede to an observer within the waking vision, reliving as though it were his own.

'I hear the first bell, Richard,' said a woman's voice in his stead. She turned to the man on horseback who galloped alongside. 'I'm not going to make it.'

'Faster, if you are so resolved,' the man shouted, spurring on her horse with a strike of his crop across its flank. 'Look to the weight in your stirrups; the final hurdle approaches.'

Even as he knelt among the grass consumed by the hallucination, James leaned forward, sensing the woman's weight pressing forward as the beast stamped its hind legs into the ground. The horse launched into the air, sailing above the high hedge, coming to ground with a sudden lurch to the left. James placed his hand down on the grass he knew to be there to steady his fall, but the woman regained her balance and thundered through an open field gate on approach to a grand country house surrounded by stables. A distant bell tower tolled and ceased in its wide pealing echo. The woman whooped with delight, turning to see her male companion slow and retreat from her victory.

'Now finally I may have some peace,' said the man spiralling his tired horse, 'and enjoy my Sundays with you in more gentile pastimes as befits a lady. I will retire – your father approaches and your games with his strongest horse may cost you your freedom for now.'

'I love you!' she cried as he broke into a canter and disappeared down the narrow carriage track.

A well-dressed, whiskered gentleman called out in blasphemous words as the male rider receded and approached the mounted woman in hobbled strides brandishing a walking stick in fury. A ring of stable hands and farmworkers surrounded the lathered horse, trying to cool the blood boiling in its veins with words and water thrown from leather buckets. The woman was dragged from the saddle by the irate, fatherly figure, and the hand she clutched dropped away from the saddle and James's own. The bond was broken, and he returned to the encircling ring of fair goers.

Harriet frowned at the confusion in his face and glanced around as a ripple of cheers, clapping, and relief broke out. James watched as Emily's bright, wide eyes softened with a contraction of her pupils as the confident and heroic alter vanished as suddenly as they had appeared. The personality switched, panic and potential calamity averted, leaving behind a terrified and shaking young woman as though under the effects of withdrawal from an addictive substance. Emily sweated, shuddered and lolled in dizziness, falling forward into his arms.

'What... is happening?' she breathed, clutching at her head with both hands and lifting her eyes to stare fully into the crowd.

Harriet grabbed her hand, pulling it down to grasp at it. 'Something you did, Emily. You saved a boy.'

Emily released herself from the clutch and gripped James tightly as though steadying herself from the fear. She glanced up with desperation in her quivering mouth. Pulling herself close to him in a pinning, painful embrace, she gagged and shuddered out the words.

'Make her go away, Marshall.'

'She's going into shock, James,' said Mike urgently. 'We need to get her back to St Jude at once.'

James felt the tremble in her tensed arms, mirroring the spasms of the horse's sweat-lathered hind leg only metres away. He nodded, trying to calm her with any action that would take away one person's pain, suffering that he was eminently qualified to deal with, but powerless to prevent or impotent to cure. He gripped her upper arms as one of the St John crew returned with a stretcher, shuffling her round and laying her down onto the canvas-covered aluminium frame.

Inches apart and face to face she released him with a departing look into his eyes and pleaded with him.

'Stop us from falling.'

James paced outside the recovery room.

'She's all right,' said Harriet, moving out of the way to allow a nurse to pass by in the busy corridor. 'Mike said so on the way over; just bruised, battered, and confused. I wish you'd let him examine you – you don't look well.'

'It's okay, probably a sugar rush from that damn gum combined with the shock of what happened. You saw what she did?' he said, thrusting his hands in his pockets. 'An inner-city woman from what sounds like a deprived background, frightened of horses, doing something that Olympic three-day eventers would struggle with.'

Harriet swiped at her phone and held up the local news website. 'Shortly, everyone is going to see. The film crew that you spoke with earlier in the day have uploaded most of it, interlaced with countless other phone footage being put up online; it's going to make the local TV from the level of engagement.'

James watched the shaky replays from many perspectives showing the distant chase between the two horses, blurring in and out of focus as the phone camera sought to track the rider. His own experience briefly resurfaced, and he exhaled, unwilling to allow it space to brood. Worried members of the public, powerless to intervene, provided an anxious commentary and James caught glimpses of himself and those around him as they raced to an uncertain outcome. Emily launched over the various obstacles to gasps and fearful cries before closing on the horse and preventing a disastrous outcome for the child, now en route to Truro for a wrist cast. Incredibly, the chase and rescue appeared even more hazardous and close run than his memory could recount. A final static image of her atop the great sweating steed, blue eyes dilated and aflame with a hand and fingers stained with dark brooding blood blisters, burned into his mind. The headline read:

Maiden of Maiden Point saves child.

'Are they still outside, waiting for a scoop?' he said, kicking at the skirting boards. 'I should have prevented her going; Caroline will have my head for this.'

'In which case,' said Harriet, putting things into perspective, 'the child she saved would be on the way to the mortuary.' She lowered the phone. 'She's not a prisoner and if anyone is to blame, then I was the care officer on the day.'

James puffed out his cheek and leaned against the wall. 'I'm not worrying about the consequences for either of us, Harriet, but for Emily. They've just broadcast to the south-west and the world that someone who is running or hiding, for good reason, is here.'

'You think someone bad might recognise her?'

'Yes,' he said, seeing the approach of a policeman. 'That is what I'm afraid of.'

Jory Richards bustled down the corridor looking flustered and ill at ease. 'I've told them she's gone to Truro in the ambulance with the kiddie, but they'll be back when they discover I've sent them on a wild goose chase.' He twitched his head to the closed door opposite. 'How is Calamity Jane doing?'

'Remarkably good but confused. Mike's in there with a triage nurse.'

'She still thinks she is from two hundred years ago?'

James frowned. 'No, she does not. The personality that

takes control has emerged with that belief, but Emily is remembering things about her life; speaking of which – anything on that car?'

Jory nodded. 'Considering the man they are after, we went through the vehicle, stripping it, sniffer dogs and everything. I'm not privy to much but I know they found cling-filmed wrapped bundles of cash hidden in the spare wheel; around fifty-thousand by what I saw.'

'Drug money?'

'Up there it's all one thing,' said the policeman, shuffling his feet and lowering his voice. 'Gangs, drugs, robberies – you name it. Count ourselves lucky we only have weed-smokers and those gangly scooter youths annoying the church group to worry about.'

James wiped his face with his hands. 'You saw or heard what she just did up at Twenty-Acre, Jory. You can't be seriously wanting to question her again; she stole a car. If she'd known about a small fortune, do you think she'd have left it there, or used a stolen credit card for £8?'

'How'd you know about the amount?' he said, shaking his head with the realisation. 'Thick as thieves you lot.'

'And friends, as well as blood, are thicker than water,' said James. 'Don't have a go at Caroline, it was a slip of the tongue that I found out; it won't go any further.'

'Just a few questions when she's calmed down,' said the policeman, raising an eyebrow, 'under supervision and once Mike's patched her up – deal?'

James wrinkled his nose and nodded, pulling him to one side, out of earshot. 'I need your help with her safety. Your little discovery is likely to be headline news locally before long if I know the leaks at the station.'

Jory gave him a hurt look. 'No more than the colander you have here.'

'My point is, Jory, this guy is likely the main reason for her attempted suicide. She stole his car that has his money in the boot. If he sees the footage of her this afternoon, he'll know she's in this area and come looking for it and her.'

'Well, we've got it now, but I take your point if he's the vindictive type.'

'He's the abusive type and you know what that means.'

'Well, let's hope we find him first. Her little wild-west stunt this afternoon has caused a stir. It's all over the radio and—'

His walkie-talkie burst noisily into life.

'What is it?' said Jory, cocking a shoulder to click on the receiver.

'Positive ID on the stolen credit card suspect, gaffer. Just been confirmed by a call put through from a riding stable outside Bermondsey, London. They've confirmed the woman as Emily Dunn, no other information except she's local to that area.'

James felt a tap on his shoulder. 'There's only one stable near Bermondsey,' said Harriet, meekly. 'It's called "Fresh Fields", a mile or so from St Guy's. It's a sanctuary and riding school for kids with disabilities – you can see it from the hospital roof.'

The door opened on the opposite side of the corridor and Mike came out. 'She's okay, and I've given her a sedative. Considering the situation and the public interest and her fragile mental state, I'm recommending she stay here tonight.'

'Agreed,' said James. 'We've got an ID on her second name. It's Dunn, Emily Dunn, and she's from Bermondsey.'

Mike nodded and wrung his hands in front of him. 'If you are going in, then don't overload her with information at the moment, because I need her to stay for another reason. I'm recommending just Harriet at the moment; she'll be comfortable with her and Nurse Anderson.'

'I'll need to speak with her, Mike,' said Jory. 'My hands are tied.'

'Later,' he said sternly, 'considering developments.'

'What developments?' said James, moving across to peer through the open door. Emily sat dazed, rubbing her stomach and staring at the nurse relaying information and words of assurance.

Mike closed the door behind him quietly. 'When Truro sent her back to us they didn't include the usual urine test results because of severe dehydration. She's been suffering from nausea and fatigue as well as more private physiological changes which I won't go into here. I need her to see the sonographer.'

'I thought you said she was okay?' said Jory.

'Let's hope they both are,' said Mike. 'She's pregnant.'

CHAPTER 23

James peered through the dashing wipers of the windscreen to the line of brake lights and smoking exhausts. An early-morning start in darkness, and the journey of five hours, had given him time to think about the events and revelations of the previous day. Not that he was any closer to explaining things to himself. The nagging worry, in the sleepless hours, that his mental health was being compromised only added to the stress forming an endless quest for answers and fears of reaching out. In desperation, he had opened the medicine cabinet and re-read the known side-effects of the sleeping tablets, desperate to avoid making the situation worse. With shaking hands, he slammed the mirrored door shut and returned to his phone to prescribe the only holistic solution that provided relief.

In the absence of the music box, he tapped on the repeat function of the recorded audio and let it play until he gave himself up to the welcome serenity of the sound and to the memory of the comfort it had instilled. Brief thoughts of Tom Cotter, and Emily, faded as he drifted off to dream fitfully of coincidence, crooked churchyard crosses and cliff tops overlooking a calm, cloudless sea.

According to Harriet, Emily Dunn had taken the news of her surname with relief and as though reclaiming a valuable part of her identity, though any knowledge of a riding stable or home location in London remained unresolved. It was like a missing jigsaw piece revealing a greater part of the picture, and under the familiar surroundings and effects of the painkillers, she had relaxed as the care team discussed her impending motherhood.

The positive ultrasound scan came as a confirmation of something she had suspected, rather than as a surprise. Who the father was, she would not say, and Harriet's opinion was that this was unrelated to amnesia but a reluctance to discuss the subject for her safety, or perhaps his. It triggered a series of memories surrounding someone she appeared to care for very much but was no longer part of her life. When pressed, Emily began to retreat into the soft hum of the old folk tune, and Mike called a halt to any more discussion.

James pondered the heroics of horsemanship now endlessly being discussed on local radio and shown on TV. Emily had asserted that she had been a mere passenger, watching as something or someone took control. She had likened it to the feeling of being on a ride that she could not get off, forced to watch and experience what she could not affect. The saving of the child was small comfort to her, and she refused to talk about it or answer any further questions relating to the car. Mike forced them all out, leaving Harriet with her until she fell into a troubled sleep aided by a mutually agreed sedative.

It had triggered an enormous outpouring of praise, and donations appeared soon after at the hospital as well as the refuge when it was understood the accidental hero was still among them, recovering from fatigue and the rigours of her earlier naked appearance. James put aside the coincidence of Emily's delusional remembrances of riding now that he was certain the horsemanship was not suddenly acquired, like the skill in drawing, but learned, somewhere in North London. He gladly dismissed the alleged and unexplained cases where people suddenly spoke in languages or accomplished feats beyond their normal capabilities. They were mostly anecdotal, these everyday superheroes, and often felt the same sense of confusion in a lack of rational explanation.

Tom Cotter, who had swum out from the harbour to save him without allegedly knowing how to swim, had never properly come to terms with the experience, while he himself had very little memory of the occasion. There were fleeting thoughts of being surrounded by people on the quay, shivering and covered with a blanket that smelled of wet dogs. He remembered the punishment meted out by his father and the locked bedroom that imprisoned him from the summer sands, woods, and his friends. He recalled them trading bubblegum cards and playing with toy figures on the edge of the garden wall, waiting for his sentence to be concluded and debt to society to be repaid. James found his anxiety rising and, without thought, began to hum the sweet and comforting tune of his mother's music box.

For a moment, he gave in to the memory of being safe, clasped by someone he could not remember, but desperate to be hugged by someone he could. James glanced at his wedding ring and across at the empty passenger seat. This was the first time he had travelled out of Cornwall since Karen had passed away.

The car in front came to a sudden halt, and he slammed on the brakes. The vehicle behind beeped their horn to wake him from his thoughts and he held up a hand in silhouetted apology. Over the sound of busy skies above and the horns of frustrated motorists, he watched the rivulets of water streaming down the exterior glass, cast aside by the flip-flak of the wipers, and thought of the tedious and tiring day ahead, locked away in a lecture theatre, peer-reviewing papers and answering questions from prospective post-graduates on a panel with far less enthusiastic colleagues. Despite his reduced caseload, James's mind had rarely felt so full.

The flashing lights of an ambulance, followed by several police vehicles, suggested an accident ahead. Looking down at his watch, with the distance to go, he knew it would be tight. A call left on the event halls' answerphone had yet to be acknowledged and he tried again without success. After a few minutes, the cars in front began to indicate over to the left, and he followed a hastily arranged diversionary route past the blocked main road to the halls.

Several confusing and contradictory turns later, he realised he was taking a long and laborious route through north London but heading south. The diverted traffic stop-started every few minutes, and he realised he would miss the keynote address, and the start of the panel shortly after. He looked about him as the rain eased, unfamiliar with the new high rises and warehouses.

Lights ahead flashed to indicate Tower Bridge was closed, and he took a longer route west to cross the Thames at Rotherhithe. He emerged from the tunnel as his phone buzzed with a text from Caroline:

Have a great day in London. Chill out. Make us look good :)

James cast the phone onto the passenger seat, turning out of the side window to see growing crowds of placard-holding protesters milling around the cars ahead and slowing the traffic. The taxi in front dodged into a side street and James instinctively followed, hoping that the driver's extensive knowledge included shortcuts in the area. He zipped into the side street, trying to keep up with the confident city driver, before seeing the adjoining road ahead was crammed with stationary cars. He called a final time to the halls to leave a third message and briefly entertained phoning Caroline, but he looked at the time, realising the conference was now underway without him.

The car approached a sign for Bermondsey Beach and James gathered his bearings. As he was about to pull over, he saw the battered and flaking sign for 'Green Fields Stables'. With no way to get to the halls, save an indeterminately long walk or Tube ride, he turned into the estate to follow the hand-painted signs to a loose gravel cul-de-sac surrounded by wooden flake-painted outbuildings and stable sheds. Several horses meandered across a sandy manège surrounded by post and rail fencing. Pulling on his jacket, he fought his way out of the car in the buffeting wind.

'We're closed today,' said a stocky, older woman in stained camel jodhpurs, brandishing a large stable broom in her hand. 'Climate protesters mean we can't get the riding instructors in or the staff – the buses can't get in. We've had to cancel all the kids' hacks today, too. Hope you're not asking to park here and walk to work; I need the room to turn the trailers and I've already sent a few packing.' She jabbed the end of the broom up in the air as though to demonstrate the threat.

'Are you the owner?'

'And the only one in, so tell me what you want because I'm busy.' She stabbed a finger behind her at the hot, condensing breaths curling from the livery building as though dragons were stabled within. 'These lot are hungry, and so am I.'

James pulled his thin coat around his jacket and walked towards the gate in the squall. A larger paddock of muddy divot-pocked grass overlooked the brown river and the tall office buildings near St Katherine's wharf. He looked down the rows of steaming horses' heads protruding from many top-opened stable doors. They kicked and whinnied to be let out as the woman planted her feet and the broom beneath, before folding her arms around it like a doorman barring the way to her tack room and the animals beyond.

'I'm looking to speak to someone who might have called in about Emily Dunn?'

The woman widened her eyes and wiped her matted ginger hair away from her rain-splattered face.

'You a journalist?'

'No,' said James, opening the side of his jacket to reveal his suit and damp shirt. He pointed to the lapel badge giving his name and title. 'I'm a psychiatrist.'

'You don't say...' she said, looking him up and down. 'When I rang in yesterday after seeing her heroics, I said I didn't want anyone coming round.'

James nodded, looking up into the steady falling stair rods of rain. 'I understand, but I'm the lead clinician in her case and the one that found her. I need your help.'

The woman sharply inclined a nod, imitating the horses behind. 'Article said she was poorly, lost her memory. Said she was found wandering about in Cornwall or some god-forsaken place. You speak funny – where you from then, Mr Psychiatrist?'

'Cornwall,' he said, seeing her close her eyes and shake her head with the faux pas. 'And it's James, James Marshall.'

'You came all the way from down there to ask me questions you could have done on the phone?'

'Not exactly. The same protesters have stopped me getting to a conference up at the halls near Herne Hill, but I figure that you probably would have put the phone down; I share your concern for her well-being, especially now that she's become an unlooked-for celebrity. Where did you see her – on the TV?'

'Difficult not to,' she said, closing the distance between them. She stood studying his wet leather shoes and sodden frame. 'Are you here because you care what happens to her, and trying to help as I did?'

James nodded, sending droplets of rain cascading down his cheeks.

'You look harmless enough,' she said, swinging back the clasp and inviting him in. 'You can have ten minutes while I have my bait; I apologise for being grumpy but I'm like that when I'm hungry and overworked, which, as the girls will tell you, is most of the time.'

'My wife was like that,' said James. 'I always kept Jaffa Cakes in the car as a precaution.'

'Smart man,' she said, swinging the gate shut and inviting him into the cosy, but cramped, tack room. Helmets and harnesses adorned the walls, and the glowing smokeless fuel stove in the corner warmed the air, heavy with the horse-laden smell of leather and wax. Supplementary feed sacks and empty white molasses buckets lay stacked behind a heavy wooden table and mismatched chairs.

'I'd still be with mine if she'd bought me so much as a custard cream over the years.' She held out a clammy, strong hand and James gripped it, surprised at its muscular grip. 'Name's Joyce, I've run this place for over twenty years, giving those less fortunate in mind or body an escape and the confidence to do other things in life.'

'Like Emily?'

'Kind of,' she said, following him into the dimly lit space. 'She needed a place to get away from the crap going on in her life. She helped with the kids, mostly.'

Joyce opened a Tupperware box and bit into a thick bacon sandwich.

'Tea?' she mumbled.

James declined with a glance inside the tannin-stained and chipped mugs hanging from hooks secured into the warped wooden panelling. He shook off his coat and sat down.

Joyce leaned back in her threadbare wicker chair, throwing her phone from her back pocket onto the table. James looked at the cracked screen with its fractured image of herself as a younger, slimmer woman beside a dapple-grey horse festooned with winning blue rosettes. He looked over at a white board framed with the same fading frilly silk blooms, dusty with age, and glanced out at the rain through the door to the poles and makeshift jump supports in the training area.

'You recognised her straight away then?' said James, rubbing heat back into his cold hands.

Joyce pointed to a photograph snapped from an enlargement. 'That's our Emily all right unless she's got a twin.' She pursed her lips. 'Except for the wild look in her eyes. She was rather timid, taken advantage of if you get my drift. What is she doing in Cornwall?'

James shifted and put his cold hands between his legs. 'I can't say too much for fear of breaking patient confidentiality, but I think she'd reached an impasse in her life if you get *my* drift.'

Joyce sighed and nodded. 'Tried to top herself, is that it?'

'Kind of,' said James. 'It's a bit more complicated than that.'

'Article says you found her naked and unable to remember who she is?'

James nodded. 'I was hoping you might be able to shed some background while I try to contact family or her doctor.'

'I don't think she has either,' said Joyce. 'She told me she never knew her father, and likely enough, neither did the mother for very long, but she died in a nuthouse—'

James shifted uncomfortably, and she held up her hand in apology.

'Don't mind me, I'm old-fashioned and call a spade a spade. One of the market girls said her mother was from your neck of the woods by all accounts, so I guess she went back to find her roots or something.'

James sighed with relief and stretched out his hands, glancing at the splintered picture on her phone. 'That would explain many coincidences. Did she live nearby?'

'About a quarter of a mile back down the road towards the tunnel. I dropped her back once and even with my tidy hands —' she clenched her fist like a boxer and bit into the sandwich dripping with brown sauce in the other '—halfway up Sunnyside tower block isn't a place you want to find yourself on your own. She came pretty regularly, to begin with, a year ago last March and I could see from the heavy eye-shadow she was looking for a place to be away from whoever was doing the bruising.'

'I'm a bit surprised she learned to ride at all because she gave me the impression, before the expertise she showed yesterday, that horses made her nervous.'

'They did that all right,' said Joyce. 'We had to force her up on top and she was as rigid as a pole till she fell off. After that, she just helped to look after the kids or getting them suited and booted; it can take a long while to get a less-mobile person ready to go.'

Joyce puckered her nose and folded her hands. 'Truth be told, I didn't think she'd stay long when the new fella turned up.'

'The one that was abusing her?'

She shook her head. 'No. She wasn't in a proper relationship, as far as I know, with him; he just used to turn up for a few days, take what he wanted, including her social money, and then send her out to do deliveries and pick up stuff. When she refused, he used to knock her about; I found her sleeping in the foaling stable once. The bloke I'm on about came later, an east European fella and nice enough. They used to meet up, and he'd walk her home until it wasn't safe to be in sight of the tower block in case the bruiser or his nasty mates were doing the rounds of the manor.'

James thought of the missing blonde-haired man in the photograph found in her clothing. 'So, Emily met a guy and kept their relationship secret?'

Joyce screwed her face. 'Went away they did, somewhere down on the south coast for a few nights. The bruiser came round here swinging his weight around having caught wind of it, but he didn't hear it from any of the girls or me.' She turned down her lip. 'Possessive type, you know what I mean?'

James nodded and sighed. 'All too well, I'm afraid.'

'After that, I never saw her until she popped up on the TV. I thought she might have run away or maybe he'd finally caught up with her. I couldn't have done any more for her.'

She lowered her voice and shuddered. 'The bloke's a monster, James; I would have told him anything if I'd known where she was, just to get him off the premises. Trust me, you don't want any of that, or you'll end up with concrete boots at the bottom of the Thames. Word is, he owes money to some Russian geezer and has bit off more than he can chew. He'll be on the run from more than just the Old Bill and if he has any sense, he'll give himself up. If you know what's best for her, tell her to stay away or get herself gone someplace else when she's better.' The woman covered her eyes as though shielding from a difficult follow-on.

'I'm a tough cookie, James, but I don't like to see any of them suffer, and I've seen a few in my time, like you I expect?'

He nodded and gave a smile of encouragement. 'I think we understand each other.'

'Just say that Joyce hopes she'll be okay and that I hope she finds a better life with someone that will take care of her.'

'I will,' he said. He glanced across at the rosettes and Joyce followed his gaze towards the trophies with a tinge of pride. 'I'm sure she'll appreciate hearing from the woman that taught her to ride like that. I wouldn't broadcast that information though, for her safety, even if it would be good for business.'

'I didn't teach her to ride,' she said, reaching for an accident book. 'She only took a gentle accompanied walk around the manège twice before she panicked and fell off. That was three months ago.'

James twisted to look at the entry. 'She came to work here eighteen months ago, but it took most of that time to get her up there?'

She pointed to the cracked screen. 'Only time on a horse that I was aware of until I saw that yesterday.'

'So where did she learn to ride like that?' said James, flipping it and handing the phone back to her.

'Not from me or from here.'

James rose and looked out into the clearing sky. 'She mentioned a kindly neighbour; do you think she might be able to shed more light on Emily's background?'

Joyce looked him up and down and got up to unhook a dark green, faded wax jacket. James caught it as she threw it over. 'Take this,' she said. 'You look like a housing or tax inspector in that clobber and that will make folk nervous.'

James avoided the temptation to sniff at the coat and was about to remove his own when he caught sight of the nametag within.

'Yes,' said Joyce. 'It's hers. Oversized admittedly, but the only one we had to spare. It'll fit you in the meantime if you will give it back with my blessings.'

She glanced at the exposed pearl tie pin. 'Hide that for the time being, if you want to keep it, and the rest of your teeth.'

'I will,' he said, pulling out the gift that his mother had made to his father, 'and thank you for the information.'

Joyce rubbed at the side of her head. 'The Emily I knew had a tattoo on her right arm.'

'Yes, the Emily that I know has the same; it's not a twin,' said James, glancing back from the doorway. 'So, what are the chances of her or anyone being able to do something like this in three months when someone's life was at stake?'

'Try nil,' she said, clicking to replay the video. 'She should be on that hard unploughed field with broken bones or worse.' James watched as she looked down to her phone and shook her head incredulously at the speck of the rider racing through and over the obstacles to pull the horse into a final and sudden twisting stop.

'I've been eventing and riding all my life, and even I couldn't do what she did.'

CHAPTER 24

J ames tossed the tie pin into the concealed recess in the
passenger-side dashboard and checked for phone
messages as he waited at the clogged junction. Protests
in London were causing havoc with attendees, and a panic-
stricken conference organiser had finally left a voicemail
advising him that the keynote speaker had yet to arrive. A
delay of several hours meant the panel was cancelled, and
one-to-one sessions later that afternoon with a heavily
reduced attendance had been hastily convened. James relaxed
as he was mercifully flashed into the left turn by a generous
city driver. There was no way he was going to arrive early and
have to sit through talks just to swell the numbers in the
lecture theatre. There was one place he had more than
enough time to visit.

He drove past the tunnel and aimed for a solitary high rise
on the left. The traffic thinned as he pulled into the side
street and headed through the estate. Boarded up or abandoned houses lined one side of the litter-lined lane leading to
a row of grimy and graffiti-scrawled garages. Several truant
children kicked a ball against a bonfire-blasted brick building,

setting off a rattling as their skilled, curling shots slammed into the meshed window protectors.

The 1960s tower block loomed ahead like a concrete cathedral among the prefabricated post-war dwellings, still congregating in memory of a promise of brighter days that had been all too brief before the communities decayed and were abandoned.

Avoiding several burned-out cars, James parked between two council vans, hoping for some aura of protection. He got out and looked up at Sunnyside Tower, outliving the optimism of its name and clouded by decades of inequality and poverty.

He turned to see a powerful black Audi on the opposite side of the threadbare and fire-blighted grass that might once have been called a green. A puff of vaped cigarette smoke curled from the top inch of the car's darkened glass windows. James put up his hand to shield his eyes from a brief appearance of the sun. The sun backlit the passenger window and the merest silhouette of a driver could be seen staring back, mirrored by the looming tower behind.

James locked the car and strode as confidently as he could through the broken bottle glass before the front doors of the tenement block. With a final, furtive glance at the parked car, he turned and squeaked open the entrance door and stepped into the lobby. He entered the stainless steel sarcophagus of the lift, stinking of urine and stale takeaways, and clicked the button for the sixth floor. The doors shuddered shut, and he rose in the building's belly to emerge high up and overlooking a long connecting corridor, which led out and around to the open sky.

He stepped onto a high balcony overlooking the plaza and glanced down to see his vehicle, safe for the present. The black car wound up its window and reversed out of sight, but not before he caught the flash of reflected binocular glass from within. Telling himself it was likely nothing more than a bailiff, he followed the peeling numbered sign for flats numbered between sixty-five and seventy, looking for a yellow door.

The brisk, chill air whistled down the exposed walkway and his footsteps echoed as he came upon a green door boarded and barricaded with sheets of ply, peppered with painted scrawls of obscenity and filth. A cracked ceiling light flickered against the signs of scorched paint framing the boarded door. He glimpsed movement in the netted curtains of the adjacent window and, next to it, the sight of a canary-yellow coloured door.

His phone rang, and he moved back to the shelter of a concrete column along the windy balcony.

'Where the bloody hell are you?' said Caroline Lewisham. 'At sea?'

'I'm on my way to the halls still,' lied James, covering his ear to hear and staring down at several discarded needles. 'The traffic's murder here.'

'Well, get your arse back to St Jude, pronto. I've cleared it with the organiser. Most of it's been cancelled anyway.'

'Why?' he said, seeing the curtains opposite twitch. 'Is Emily all right? You heard about what happened?' A brief glimpse beyond the lace revealed a many-ringed hand with brightly rainbow-painted nails at the end of a wrist of many bangles.

'I heard and saw, along with everyone else,' continued Caroline. 'Someone has blabbed about her pregnancy to the press.'

James winced and spun to see the momentary sun glance off the glittering brown ribbon of the Thames. He leaned over, straining to the right to see the black car just in view, silent and shining a hundred feet below.

'What are they saying?'

'That the maiden of Maiden Point is no maiden,' she said. 'That enough for you at present or shall I continue?'

'I should not have let you talk me into taking this case, even if it meant my career,' said James.

'Then I suppose that child at the fair would be dead now,' said Caroline.

'That's what Harriet said when—'

'She offered her resignation? Harriet's already apologised for a mess that neither of you could have foreseen. It was very noble of her but uncalled for; I'm not looking for scapegoats, I'm looking for safety and security plus assurances that we are getting somewhere with Emily Dunn. Our media bod is out crowd controlling the situation so you can do your job and make sense of it all. As soon as we hear from anyone that has her on the books, I'll send her back to London. Fellows is not happy with the media circus, and neither is the hospital at St Jude.'

James pinched his brow. 'I don't think that's a good idea.' He looked around at the squalor and into a pair of large brown eyes from beyond the window. 'Emily isn't safe here, Caroline.'

'Something you wish to share, James?'

'The police are after someone who has gone missing and could be desperately searching for her. They found a large amount of money hidden in the boot, money which he might owe to someone far worse. I can't say any more lest Jory clams up and our little arrangement works against us. Sending her back here could have devastating consequences.'

Caroline paused. 'Monitor her and sort out what's going on. Your father is expecting her tomorrow after you've spoken with Mike Trebarr about your health. Just make sure you explore all avenues so we can hand over when the time comes; it's what you wanted all along, isn't it?'

'Wouldn't that be proving everyone right, including myself – that I'm not capable anymore?'

'This may be beyond any of us to sort in the time and tools we have to work with; it's about her welfare, as much as yours.'

James caught sight of the woman listening intently. 'Everything I'm doing is for Emily's well-being; I even promised Isobel's mother I would take care of her.'

'You spoke to Christine Lee? You've got some balls.'

'Actually, she spoke to me. I'm not forgiven, but there was a truce, so to speak. Investigate the truth that Gayle was pressured by the parents to suspend me because she said the pair of them knew nothing about it.'

'Gayle lied?' said Caroline, brightening. 'That might be worth looking into; I'm sure Fellows wouldn't be thrilled to hear he was misled.'

'The family were upset I was back, to begin with, but Christine Lee was gracious and courageous enough to confront me. I was pretty stoked; I can tell you.'

'Just get yourself back and do what you have to do with the team and your father. Ring me in the evening.' The call disconnected and James rubbed at his face, hearing several latches click and unlock behind the yellow door. The rattle of a chain pulled taut as the door opened to reveal the face of a large, incandescently dressed woman, probably of Caribbean descent. Her bright red lipstick parted to reveal a set of white teeth with a conspicuous gold incisor.

'She's not here, and neither is he,' she said in a thick Jamaican accent. 'We don't want any trouble here.'

James shook his head and opened his jacket, revealing his badge. 'I'm not with the police. I'm a psychiatrist who is looking after the woman who may have lived next door.'

The woman's eyes widened to the size of billiard balls.

'You don't look much like a head doctor in that.'

He plucked at the coat and pointed towards the tidal stretch of Bermondsey Beach, just visible beyond the buildings and warehouses. 'I think that was the point. Joyce down at the stables gave me this and told me Emily Dunn used to live here.'

'Not anymore,' she said, closing the door.

James rushed forwards to line up with the disappearing face. 'Clickety-click!' he said hurriedly, pointing to the brass numerals above. The door remained partially open and James caught the heavy scent of jasmine and joss sticks from beyond the myriad of foliage and interior pot plants. The glimpse through the slit of the flat seemed to be the exact opposite of what the concrete jungle exterior cried out to be.

'Emily said you were kind to her, that you looked out for her when bad things were going on.' He spun the second brass six on the door to its lower position from the sixty-nine of moments ago. 'She said the kids do this to upset you.'

'They aren't Christian,' she said. 'Neither was she, but that girl had a heart of gold. I heard you on the phone talking; sounds like you are in trouble with another woman.'

James blushed, rubbed at his eyes and stretched his tired face. She burst into full-bellied laughter.

'It's Emily that's really in need of help, but she can't remember things that would help me and the medical team find her way back to recovery.'

A door further down the row opened and an old man poked his head out.

'Go back inside, Albert,' she called between the widened chain-set door. The woman looked into James's desperate face. 'He's not come for either of us.' The man retreated and slammed his door.

She closed her own momentarily, and James heard a rattle as she unhooked the safety chain. The door opened wider to reveal a large, exuberant, and charismatic woman of pensionable age. 'I can't ask you in,' she said. 'Too many prying eyes.'

James looked up and down the walkway to see various timid and curious faces appear at windows.

'I tried to help her and get her away, but she always came back,' she said. 'Sometimes when it got too bad, I would let her stay over on the settee when Ryan Williams had something for her to do or he just wanted to hurt someone that wouldn't fight back. The sounds through the wall at night were heartbreaking.'

'Was she the tenant of the flat?' he asked, wondering if the abusive behaviour was connected to the security of her home.

'While the rent was paid,' she said. 'But she couldn't eat and stay warm if she did. He kept her hungry and frightened, poor lamb, till she had no choice. She was a good girl, despite what he tried to get her to do when he came. Even though she owed him money, to begin with, it was paid back in so many ways, several times over.' She looked at him sternly. 'Women can't fight back against the evil that the devil has put into men's hearts and loins.'

'Did she ever go to the police about him?' asked James.

The woman pushed her head back into her rubbery neck and put her hands on her wide hips. 'You're not from around here, Mr Head Doctor Man. You don't go to the authorities for men like Ryan Williams or the wicked devil he works for; the police don't come here, not unless there's been a stabbing or worse.' She glanced behind him to the partially derelict estate.

'I've been here with my plants for forty years and now look at the place. Not the land of milk and honey, but there are one or two god-fearing souls still fighting for the place, and the Lord.'

'Joyce says Emily wasn't involved with him, but someone else?'

The lady sighed. 'His name was Florin and for a while, she had some hope until Williams found out about them. She came round to tell me the boy was going to take her back to Romania or someplace safe where that pig couldn't find her. I disapproved because they weren't married but it was a darn sight better than staying with that pig.' She poked her head through the opening to look at the dereliction next door. 'He was supposed to meet her some place secret, but he never turned up, and when she came back in tears, Williams was waiting for her, drunk and full of rage; he knocked her around and to my shame I sat against the sitting room wall and cried. I didn't dare to ring the police for fear he'd know it was me that called.'

James nodded. 'Don't blame yourself. If it is any comfort, then I think you couldn't do anything to help her at that point; you could have been hurt yourself.'

She glanced up with a film of tears on her wide eyes. 'The last time, she didn't make a sound, almost as though she had given in, looking for him to finish it there and then. He had his way with her, battered and bruised – I heard the whole thing.' She screwed her face in sorrow, letting free a single accumulated tear.

James reached inside his interior jacket and offered her a handkerchief, but she declined, composing herself.

'He started crying like a kitten. I thought he'd killed her, but I heard her get up and turn on the bath as though nothing had happened.' She passed a hand over her eyes. 'It had. The last time I saw her, it was still the middle of the night. He was still inside, and she crept out and I thought she was dropping off drugs or picking up bad money until I heard her snap her key in the lock and throw the end skittering down the row. She took his car, the one he used to do "business" in. I'll never forget her face as she glanced back under that flickering light. There was no emotion or recognition as she caught me in the window, like—'

James listened as she sought for the words pulled from the uncomfortable memory.

'Like she wasn't there inside, or something had broken. I tell you, Mr Head Doctor Man, I thought I was seeing a ghost. He left later and found his car missing, thinking it was the gang from the next estate. He came back later that night in a shaking fit; I'd almost say he was scared but he couldn't get in because of the obstruction in the lock; she must have had the door on the catch and he was unaware he'd not be able to gain entry when he slammed it on the way out earlier. He broke into the flat and trashed the place and when she didn't come back the day after, tried to get in here. Several of the younger men who go to my church forced him off. I was terrified. When the council boarded it up he finally stopped coming.'

'Did Emily ever mention suffering from mental health issues besides the abuse? Perhaps an imaginary friend, or a different personality?'

'No. She told me her mother died in an asylum but that she only found out about it a few years ago; until then she thought she was an orphan.'

'How did she find out?'

'Some men came round to apologise for mistakes in paperwork and being unable to match her records from all the places she stayed after the social services let her go. She said she couldn't feel heartbroken when there was nothing to grieve for.' The woman looked behind her. 'They left Emily some of her things. When neither of them came back, the flat was ransacked and bad people tried to do evil things inside. I called the council, and they sent men to board up the place, but not before I saw the mess and picked up a few of her things. Everything was spoiled, burned, or just taken, though she had nothing of value. It was wrong to see her things lying in there with no one to care for them. I put them in a box in case she ever came back.'

'What things?' asked James.

'Give me your right hand first.'

James frowned and offered his hand. She gently twisted his hand to face palm upwards and stroked the lines as she read the criss-cross of creases.

'My grandmother back in Kingston taught me to read people's hearts and fortunes.' She made the sign of the cross with her other hand and gazed to the ceiling. 'Forgive me, Lord, but sometimes I need to use the old ways to find the truth of things.'

She glanced back into his eyes. 'You are an honest man, but your fate is bound with that of hers. Save her, and you save yourself. If you don't then you won't get a second chance and it will eat you up inside.'

James frowned, and retrieved his palm, feeling uncomfortable with the unconventional personality assessment. 'Wait here,' she said, closing the door.

In a moment, the door reopened, and the woman handed over a small cardboard box. 'Not much for a lifetime, is it?' she said. 'You see she gets the things and tell her Amancia says she is praying for her.'

James collected the box and peered in through the open flaps. Several smudged T-shirts encircled several books, a soft toy rabbit and some personal items including partially burned photos of Emily smiling, face pressed against the cheek of the blonde-haired man she had briefly known. A threadbare baby blanket was bundled, wrapped around some object within, but it was a file containing a series of sheets, jammed down one side that caught his attention.

James lowered the box and knelt to pull off the stretchy

band securing several drawings in the same detailed style. 'So, she can draw after all,' he whispered. He flicked through several scenes of a house, recognising Carmalt. Further detailed images of a period doctor attending to a priest, stable hands exercising magnificent horses, several of St Jude Church, with the older tower, and several of the handsome rider from Emily's wall back at the refuge. An image of a newborn in the arms of a woman whose face was hidden caught his eye. The infant reached a tiny hand out towards the three-stoned necklace that adorned the neck of the self-portrait, evidently of May Dene. He stopped at one showing extreme and scrawled violence, as though the image had been drawn under duress of a hurried need to purge or expel the image to paper. A man, dressed in a similar period costume to the handsome rider, stared maliciously back, a scar on his left cheek. A thicket of vicious ink streaks like an unholy halo gave the military collared figure an ominous and ill look. Across the bottom was scrawled the word 'never' in a modern hand.

James held up the unpleasant portrait as Amancia crossed herself. 'The devil or I'm no Christian.'

'He's not real, or at least not alive anymore,' he said, closing the file and collecting the box. He rose to meet the eyes of the next-door guardian angel. 'I'll give them to her, I promise.'

Amancia nodded and opened her clenched fist to reveal a set of painted rosary beads threaded with a silvered metal chain, fused in an unbroken circle. 'For protection against the evil one in that life' – she turned to look at the boarded flat next door – 'and this.'

James followed her gaze even as the beads were deposited into his jacket pocket. He turned after a moment to see the door closing and he stood alone on the bleak and lonely walkway. He left for the lift to take him down and back to the car.

There was no sign of the black Audi as he took off the waxed coat and deposited the box in the passenger seat before getting into the car.

Glad to be away from the danger and depression of the block, he thrust his hands through his hair, then programmed the satnav for the return journey, switching on the local radio for details of the protests and further diversions. He looked mournfully at the travel time of six hours and reversed, leaving the estate. After several miles, he found his way back through the tunnel to the north side of the Thames and the hustle and bustle of slow-moving traffic. A glance in the rearview mirror showed a black Audi, several cars behind, but he told himself that it was only a coincidence. London was full of such cars. He called to cancel his hotel room and glanced down at the box in the passenger seat as the call connected but he hung up, suddenly in need of an emergency stop, sending the box flying into the dashboard and spilling its contents back onto the seat as it came to rest in the footwell. A woman glared from the zebra crossing, and he felt a rush of adrenalin, shamed but relieved that his lack of concentration had caused nothing more serious than a wake-up call to concentrate on the road.

As he waited for the crossing to clear, he fumbled blindly to clear some of the smaller items from the central console. His hand dragged away the thin blanket, tossing its cargo into his lap. Grabbing at the object he retracted sharply as though pricked by the sharpness of its dried and brittle stems. A car horn sounded from behind, urging him to move, but his focus remained upon the small corn dolly in his lap, pregnant like the others back in St Jude, with a bead of weathered sea-glass.

CHAPTER 25

The warden knocked on Emily's door. 'I'll need you to keep the door ajar, Dr Marshall. It's protocol and you are unaccompanied.'

James shifted the box and wax coat beneath his arm. 'I understand.'

Emily opened the door with a look of surprise.

'I'll be just down the hall if either of you need me,' said the warden, turning to return to his office overlooking the front door.

'Don't tell me you've discovered it's my birthday,' she said allowing him in. 'At least you can sign my card with a second name now. I'm not sure whether I like Dunn any better than Dene, but at least it's mine.'

'You want to talk about it?'

'Not really. I had a full day yesterday with the social worker.' She rubbed at her belly. 'I guess this explains the morning sickness, and I'd rather concentrate on more pressing matters than my ability to ride like a lunatic.'

James gave her a moment, discounting the Freudian slip. 'Don't you mean like a hero?'

Emily blushed. 'We both know I can't take credit for that. I keep telling everyone I was a passive, terrified observer, but they think I'm just being humble.' She cleared a seat for him, scattering unfinished drawings of horses, and images of country gatherings attended by people in period dress.

'Is drawing making things easier for you as part of the therapy or making things more complicated?'

'Both.' Emily rubbed at her wrist. May hasn't stopped with it and I can barely feel my wrist anymore. I think it triggered some passion of hers and now all I get are bloody racehorses, her soldier boyfriend, and fairs.' She cast a glance at the shrine-like cameos on the wall beside him.

It was covered with sheets, most with the flowing, artistic style showing historic subjects and landscapes. On the wall opposite, next to the small mirror and table, were plastered a growing array of her own, crude imitations depicting fragments and recollections from more recent memory. James sat between two opposing sides like a neutral observer at a sporting event wondering which team would ultimately gain the upper hand by sheer weight of numbers. Many drawings were now only peeping through, crowded out by more recent images. Despite the uncertain future of the refuge, one thing was clear.

Emily was rapidly running out of space to continue the conflict.

'Still, I'm glad the kiddy is going to be okay,' she said, glancing at the box and coat. 'What you got there?'

James lifted the jacket, opening it to reveal her name.

'This used to be mine...' she said, frowning as she rubbed at the coarse, waxed cotton. Putting it to her nose she breathed in the odour releasing it with a shake of her head. 'Horses? The person at the stables sent it – the woman there, her name was Jules—'

'Joyce,' said James. 'Not quite – I made a little unscheduled diversion, just between us. She wanted to know you were all right, just like the other person who gave me this—'

Digging into his jacket pocket he handed her the rosary beads from her erstwhile neighbour.

'Clickety-click?'

'Amancia,' he said, pointing to the box. 'She saved these for you.'

Emily stole a momentary glance at the image of the tower block on the wall. Putting down the coat she rifled through the items, shaking her head as though they were still unfamiliar. She paused at a burned and blistered image of herself and the young blonde man.

James leaned over. 'Amancia said his name is Florin.'

Unsure whether to repeat the name, she stood all but motionless, her freehand with the lightest of touches on her stomach. 'Yes, I remember. Is there any news – did either of them say if he'd been back?'

He shook his head. 'The place is boarded up.'

'No. He is gone, and I'll never be able to tell him.' James looked at the slimmest of curves through her tight-fitting sweater and she put down the image and turned back to the box, as though conscious of his guesses.

'What are these?' Emily opened the file and shook her head, discarding the drawings across the bed in resignation.

James picked up an image of women, long-skirted, huddled around a fire on a moonlit moor. 'Proof you can really draw or that your disassociation began long before coming here. Do you know what this is or represents?'

Emily screwed up her face and glanced across at the similar scenes on the wall. 'No, but it's important, I can feel it. May just comes out with it when she feels lonely or when I'm trying to forget her.'

'Stephanie or Harriet mentioned nothing to you?' He rose to point at the uncomfortable scene of the small boy being dragged into the boat, undeniably himself. 'Particularly this one—'

She shook her head. 'I don't like it; it's some kiddy that's drowning and that other bloke in the water looks like he's going under. The man jumping into the water is going to be too late to save him.'

'I don't think so,' he said. 'Quite the opposite. No one has talked about this or said who the boy or man is?'

'No.' She hesitated, tapping on a tall man, suited and out of place among the casually dressed onlookers, desperately observing the rescue. His gaunt, short-bearded face was more detailed than his companions, singling him out among the worried crowd. Hints of tweed and tie, held in place by a single pen stroke suggested a tiepin.

James studied the man, the scene, and the recollections of countless individuals who had embellished the tale over the years. 'Do you know who this is or why you or May have drawn any of this?'

She folded her arms and twitched her nose. 'No. Looks miserable like a school teacher or academic. Who is he?'

James snorted in amusement. 'Two out of three, if I'm right. This is a scene showing a rescue of me when I was around six years old, out in the bay. My dinghy got snagged and there was a rip-tide pulling me out.' He tapped on the drowning man. 'That's Tom Cotter, the man you talked to on the promenade. He saved my life, almost at the expense of his own. The tall man on the quay looks very much like my father, and the one you are seeing later when Harriet arrives.'

'It's an asylum, isn't it? You are taking me away, aren't you?'

'No. It's a care home - my father is terminally ill.'

She relaxed. 'I thought you were trying to sweeten things. I don't want to end up like my mother...'

'Your memory is coming back,' said James. 'Sometimes

familiar objects, smells, or feelings can trigger them. Take your time.'

'There's nothing there, just the knowledge she died before I found out. Could what she had be hereditary?'

'It's highly unlikely because what you are suffering from is non-physiological. Your formative years in care and lack of a strong family unit could have played some part in triggering what you are re-experiencing from a long time ago – the need for a protector. Couple that with some prior knowledge of the area and we are getting somewhere, Emily.' James retrieved the corn dolly from the baby blanket.

'I feel like I'm going backwards. The thought that May Dene has been part of my life for a long time is not comforting in the slightest.' She glanced down at the faceless untidy doll.

James offered it up. 'Does this trigger any memories?'

She turned over the shabby, split weaving, spinning the glass bead within her nail. 'I think it was in the small box that belonged to my mother. Some men came round, asked to see some ID and told me she died in hospital a long time ago. Said she was from around here. They didn't stay long.'

'Can you remember her name?'

She shook her head and threw the doll against the wall, striking the self-portrait of May Dene. 'I don't have a picture or anything to remind me of her. Just someone else's loved ones filling up my head and my room.'

'A woman fitting your description asked for local information on St Jude a few weeks before the event. I think this is perhaps where you are getting these from, some recollection of what you discovered.'

The door wavered in its open position, unsettled by a breeze blowing in from the front entrance. A short knock revealed the face of Harriet Swanson.

'James? You're early. I thought we agreed half-past?'

'It's okay, the warden allowed me in and the door was left open.' He rose to join her in the corridor outside.

'You are supposed to have a female chaperone,' she whispered. 'I can't believe you are doing it again. Dr Lewisham will do her nut.'

'There's no need to keep mentioning every minor misdemeanour in a complex case to Dr Lewisham,' he said. 'I'm doing my best to understand what's going on and help her. I know where she might be getting these memories from now. It's stuff she's read and absorbed on a prior visit to the area. She's reliving her own experiences through the lens of a historic suicide that's connected to Maiden Point.'

'The end doesn't justify the means, Dr Marshall. These interactions should be in a controlled environment with the appropriate measures in place for everyone's safety and security. Home visits and personal contact are a no-no and you know that.' She glanced into the room at Emily, picking through the box. 'Professional or otherwise.'

'What do you mean by that?' said James, thrusting his hands in his pockets.

Harriet pursed her lips. 'Dr Trebarr told me about what happened before with the patient that caused you to be sent back here.'

'He did what!'

The warden briefly glanced over and returned to his paperwork. James looked away eager to remove himself from further condemnation, conscious that a row born primarily in defence of his pride would be ill-advised. From the glazed wire-meshed safety glass of the entrance door, he caught sight of a black car parked against the kerb on the opposite wide of the road. The tinted windows, partially opened by several inches, billowed in great steaming clouds from the vaping smoker within.

'I asked him for the truth about it because I was getting conflicting—'

'Shush,' said James sternly as Harriet was interrupted again, much to her annoyance. He stepped out of the light streaming through the paned door glass. 'Tell me what you see outside.'

Harriet walked closer to the glass.

'No! Get back, someone is watching the refuge.'

She froze. 'It's just a black car, but there's no one in it. You are getting paranoid. Mike said—'

James peered from the side to see the Audi, windows now closed. 'Damn what Mike said, right at this moment. I've seen that car before. I think it might be someone after Emily.'

She stepped out of the corridor, clicking the door shut to her room. 'And how would you know that?'

The polished car remained passive, reflecting the front elevation of the pebble-dashed grey building. The dark glass held its secrets as James struggled to see any movements within.

'I was in London, at Emily's place. Someone was watching the tower block when I picked up her things.' He feigned a smile. 'You can tell Mike if you like, seeing as you too are sharing now.'

'You went to her flat?' said Harriet, ignoring the childish behaviour and assertions. She grabbed the attention of the warden. 'And now you've brought someone back here? I'm calling the police.'

The man left his cubby hole, bolted the door and made for the stairs. 'I'll go check on the register to see who's in. Everyone needs to stay in their rooms till the police arrive.'

James watched the car, oblivious to Harriet's conversation, but mindful of his folly.

I've led him straight here…

Harriet put down the phone. 'They are on their way. They've told us to stay put.'

'He's not in there,' said James. 'I'm pretty certain—'

A sudden scream from Emily's room caused them both to spin round, clutching at the auto-locked door.

James tugged and twisted the handle, throwing his weight against the shuddering door. 'Emily!'

The warden came flying down the stairs, vaulting the lower handrail, keys jingling at his belt. Harriet banged on the door as James was pushed away. The man thrust in his skeleton key, releasing the mechanism, and the door flew open, knocking Emily forward from her braced, defensive retreat against its inner side.

A man, thickset, and bald with an annoyed look of discovery retreated a muscled, tattoo-ed arm from the partially open window. Briefly assessing the three newcomers to the room he glanced at Emily and downwards at her protective hands, clasped around her unborn child, and slammed a signet ringed hand against the glass in frustration.

The warden stepped forward, and the man turned, sprinting to the partially trellised wall and threw his combat trousered leg over. With a final glance back, he slipped from view.

Harriet clasped Emily who pushed away. 'He frightened me and said it wasn't safe here, that he was coming...'

'It's alright,' said the counsellor. 'The police are on their way.' The warden closed the window, dulling the distant sound of an approaching police siren.

Not knowing if it was folly or bravery, James raced into the corridor in time to see the man returning to his car. Removing the bolts, he threw open the door determined to catch the number plate. The man stood resolute, assessing whether there was time to escape. James raced forward to distract him, long enough for the flashing lights of the police car to emerge at the top of the street. Sensing the man's options were receding James turned, frantic to get back inside and lock the door. The man raced around the bonnet and towards the wide-open refuge. James got inside, but the man grabbed at his back, spinning him round. An overpowering smell of aftershave and vaped liquorice assaulted his nostrils as the man grabbed hold of his jacket and pushed him back into the hall.

'Emily,' said the man. 'I must protect the child, take her away or bad things will happen to her, maybe to you. Do you understand?'

James shook his head, preparing for some terrible act of violence. He thought to cry out but the man released his clothing, pointing to the door behind.

'I saw you at the flat and I saw your picture with her in the newspapers. I know you are involved.'

From the doorway, Jory Richards and his police partner raised their batons calling for him to stand down. The man complied, raised his arms to the back of his head, and stared into James's eyes as though pleading for his final words to resonate.

'You or the police can't protect her, do you understand?'

'What do you want?' said James. 'She doesn't have the money—leave her be. She wants nothing to do with you anymore.'

The man shook his head, even as his arms were dragged to the cuffs at his back. 'Revenge,' he said. 'For my brother and his unborn child. He is already here in your town – I have seen him.'

'Williams?' called James as the man was dragged away.

'He will find her,' said the man struggling to resist, 'and when he discovers the money he owes Mostoff is gone, he will kill them both.'

CHAPTER 26

From the passenger seat of the police car, James watched Emily and Harriet stroll away along the lavender lined path to be met at the glass doors of Fairhaven Grange by the resident nurse. He picked at the open lid of the cardboard box between his feet. Emily's things, only recently acquired, were now part of a police investigation.

'I made an innocent mistake, Jory. I only went to the stables and flat to learn more about Emily's background.'

The policeman sat alongside, arms folded. A burst of radio chatter from the control centre broke through the silence.

'Overstepping your authority, boundaries, and playing detective could land you in serious trouble with your boss, not to mention mine. You could both get the sack for this.'

'I know, and what started as an innocent attempt to discover more insights into Emily Dunn's past has put her at greater risk.'

'Go on.'

'I hadn't planned to go there but there was a demonstration which took me to the stable woman from the call you took in the hospital corridor. From there, she gave me directions to where Emily used to live; it's a tower block on the way to the exhibition halls.'

'You did what? That constitutes a breach of data protection. I never authorised you to act on it.'

'I know, but the place was right there as I was passing. There was nothing to see at her flat but graffiti scrawled boarding put up by the council. It's rough, Jory, a real tough place to grow up. A neighbour told me there was nothing for Emily to come back to and to stay away. She gave me some of her things rescued after the place got ransacked. Ryan Williams had been back the night before and trashed the place before disappearing.'

'That's a City of London Police issue, not mine, and certainly not yours.'

James shook his head. 'It is now. The guy you arrested followed me back to St Jude. The car outside the refuge was the same parked outside the tower block. Why didn't he run or drive off when he had the chance?'

'You tell me,' said Jory. 'I've got your statement, but he doesn't fit the profile of what I expected from Ryan Williams, or what he implied as we dragged him to the car.'

'It's not him, is it?'

Jory shifted his wide girth in the cramped bucket seat. 'We won't know until the checks are done. The number plate is foreign, so it might take a while. If it's not, and we can trust what this bloke says, then at least we know Williams is not far away. So, Inspector Poirot, what did you learn at the stables?'

'That there's no way she could have learned to ride like that from her time there.'

'Then she learned it some place else, didn't she? She's playing you, James, and the police, to avoid prosecution while her scum-bag of a boyfriend gets away with murder.'

'What do you mean by that?'

Jory backtracked and rubbed his mouth and chin. 'I meant proverbially.'

'I'm being honest with you, Jory. I need to know if what the neighbour said is true about her missing boyfriend, proverbially. We are both on the same side here.'

'You breaking rules doesn't mean I can do the same. Lives are at risk, remember?'

'Exactly,' said James. 'Emily's in particular. I don't give a damn about mine under the circumstances. Whether she's guilty or innocent of anything, she deserves to be kept safe until due medical and judicial processes can take place.'

'No more secrets or sharing after this,' said Jory. 'Even for you; now you first.'

James nodded.

'Emily was seeing some other guy, possibly the father of her unborn child. He went missing several weeks ago and may have been the trigger for Emily's breakdown and decision to come here. The neighbour suspects Williams found out, and that it was only a matter of time for both of them.'

James lifted the box from between his legs revealing the pathetic possessions of a young life.

'This is what the woman gave me. Not much, is it?'

Jory scanned through the items as James sifted through. 'You've shown these things to Emily?'

'Yes, but she has little recollection of them. I hoped the familiar things might trigger some response to enable us to move forward.'

James rummaged inside, past the hurriedly stuffed drawings, letters and faded Polaroids. He lifted out the partially burned photograph of the blonde-haired man.

'His name is Florin. She was upset but tried to hide it.'

'It might just as easily be Ryan Williams,' said Jory, glancing away and shuffling his feet on the pedals.

'But it's not, is it? It's the same guy you found in the photos from the cliff top. There was only grief, not fear when she saw the photo, and she would have freaked out if Williams had appeared at the window, never mind about her switching into a defensive state. Emily screamed from the shock of seeing someone suddenly appear she said she's never met, nothing more. I would have expected the alter to have taken control if her abuser had shown up. Now it's your turn.'

Jory puckered his lips and clicked off the internal recording camera above the sun flap.

'The body of a guy, East European by all accounts and matching this blonde guy's appearance, was found shot in a place called Wapping Woods. It's around 2 miles from Bermondsey. This information could make Emily Dunn a suspect, James. You can see why I was trying to avoid having this discussion at the refuge. I'm not in control of the investigation, but I am obliged by law to reveal any pertinent information to the City boys. It has put us all in a difficult position.'

'She's no murderer, Jory.'

'She intended to kill herself. What better motive than remorse?'

'I agree that she genuinely intended to kill herself, but someone or something stopped her.'

'Not a two-hundred-year-old suicide, James.'

'I know that, it's not what I think, it's what she does. Even with the obvious conclusions of her having visited here before, maybe to search for information on her mother, there is something I'm missing and it's personal and related to me. It's why we are here this afternoon to unravel what's going on. My father's going to give his opinion this afternoon so I can submit my care assessment to Fellows and Lewisham up at Truro. They want me reinstated even though it might mean giving up the case.'

'What do you mean?' said Jory twisting with an injured look on his face. 'I thought you were staying on here. Don't you want to?'

James rubbed his hand across his face. 'Politics at the top might mean I need to move back, but I'm not the man I once was. I won't say anymore.'

'Now you are being coy?' said Jory. 'You come back, work all hours, avoid going out with me and Mike, create a mess for us all to deal with and then swan off back to Truro, is that it?' The policeman folded his arms in an exaggerated display of personal annoyance. 'Is this for her or you? Remember what happened the last time you got too involved, trying to solve something at the expense of everything and everyone else? It's not Emily I'm thinking of now, James, it's you. She's a woman running away from an abusive and criminal partner, and suspected murderer, who came down here to end it all and then had a meltdown or change of heart and now can't find a way out. You are overthinking it and getting in too deep.'

'That's your medical assessment, is it?'

'It's my honest assessment. You've heard of Occam's Razor, right?'

'The simplest explanation is usually the right one. I'm surprised you have.'

Jory frowned. 'That's unkind; I can read you know. I'm professionally acquainted with Conan Doyle's greatest detective, too – "When you have eliminated all which is impossible, then whatever remains, however improbable, must be the truth." Spirits of expert horse-riding women from the 1800s are impossible.'

'I don't believe in that nonsense either, Jory. Emily has to be suffering from a personality disorder brought on by emotional stress and a traumatic childhood, either that or she's suffering from Ganser—'

Jory shook his head. 'That's what you said about Isobel Lee, wasn't it?'

James took in a deep breath. 'I'm seeking context and background to unlock the path to help her, and you.'

Jory flicked through the social media channels on his phone. 'Look, the information about where she lived is out there now, so I can cover that part of your indiscretion. I'll need to take the box and have the dogs and team go over it considering we have this Ryan Williams in custody or prowling around. If there is anything on it, I'll have to ask you to come in and explain it to the London boys. Do you understand?'

He lifted out a battered and watermarked copy of *Sense and Sensibility*. 'Well, here's your answer to the old-fashioned talking and period stuff; she's a fan of Austen.'

'Emily says she's never read it, and the personality presenting as May Dene says she's never heard of her. It was one of the first discussions the counsellor had when offering the same hypothesis, but it is consistent with the alter's hints that she died before Austen's first novel was published.'

'It wasn't Austen's first novel.'

'Excuse me?' said James, assuming the information came from his friend's domination at the local pub quiz.

'*Pride and Prejudice* was her first completed novel; it was originally called *First Impressions* and published after the success of *Sense and Sensibility*. She is correct in one thing – Austen wasn't credited as the author at the time of publication, so yes, she wouldn't have heard of her. That doesn't make her past-life regression, or whatever it is, more likely; it's a common mistake.'

James frowned and narrowed his eyes.

Jory shrugged. 'So I'm a fan, too. Arrest me.' He flicked through the drawings, pausing at a scene of many labourers bundling hay stooks and baling great forked sheathes into wide and high-sided, horse-drawn trailers. 'Looks like Twenty-Acre Field.

'Why didn't you trust me enough to tell me? She's been involved, knowingly or otherwise, with a notorious and wanted criminal.'

'I'm sorry,' said James, unbuckling his seatbelt and handing over the box. 'I went too far. Thanks for following us here. I'll be fine dropping them back in my car. Until we know if this guy is Williams or not, I'd rather not spook Emily into believing he's still out there. Who was this Mostoff he mentioned?'

'Some Russian gangster, apparently. When I asked the same question of the Inspector from the City, he went pale. If we don't have him already or find him soon, then those fellas will find the same trail of breadcrumbs. I'm resourced to smack hands and keep people from knocking hell's bells out of each other after closing time, not the middleman in a war against Moscow Mafiosi.'

James swallowed, trying to lubricate his dry mouth. The repercussions of his naivety had become all too clear.

'Don't panic, James. We've got this. I'll be over in Cennen later – you'll have to go that way yourself because they are shutting the route back to the coast for a burst water main.'

'Thanks for the tip. I've been meaning to pick up something of my mother's from the antiques shop in the high street; I'll see if the others don't mind a brief stopover.'

'Well, keep your wits about you, okay? I've got some "non-explaining" to do on your behalf back at the station, but I'll talk to the gaffer about setting up some close protection support.' He turned with a genuine look of concern, tinged with apprehension that James had rarely seen.

'No more secrets,' said Jory. 'I don't want you getting hurt. I give a damn about you, mate. Leave the detective work to me in the future, okay?'

James nodded and got out of the car. He turned to bid farewell as Jory leaned over to catch his eye.

'And don't tell Mike about me liking Austen. It was your Karen that got me into it, and it's all I have left of her.'

'You've been through my notes, then?' said James, wheeling his father into the homely and holistic medical room. Large, glazed doors, one of which was slid open, gently let in the noon's autumnal warmth from the lawn-edged patio beyond.

'Your preliminary assessment,' Edward tapped at the folder, softly resting on the tartan rug around the old man's knees. 'As well as the unofficial personal interpretations you will be keeping out if you don't want me to come back and haunt you.'

'I thought they might provide context?'

Edward shook his head. 'Connections are fine but it would be pertinent, given your history, to remove any sense that you are somehow connected to the patient, even if it's only by historical concoctions and coincidence.'

'But Emily is feeding on a catalogue of local knowledge and historical fact.' James glanced out of the window to see Emily and Harriet taking a break from their initial meeting. Emily reached out to drag a hand across the smooth granite blocks of the older manor, oblivious to the counsellors' attempts at shepherding back to the cool, flag-stoned medical room. 'She said the stones were from Carmalt...'

Edward slapped the folder against James's thigh. 'She says a lot of things that have resulted from being immersed in local history and her interests in all things Georgian if you and the archivist are correct about her visiting the area before her breakdown.'

James rubbed at the mild sting. 'How do you explain all

the images of the cliff top ceremony, the house and me being pulled from the sea, not to mention her extreme equestrianism if no one has spoken to her?'

Edward wheeled to gain a glass of water. 'Simple. She has and can't recall. You told my young superfan out there on your first meeting about your rescue, not to mention your homecoming would have sparked off the last great point of interest until Emily Dunn arrived and took over in that department. You've indicated that Stephanie is involved with that willow woman nonsense and it's no secret at this time of year. As to her horsemanship, I have no opinion, other than your conclusion that extraordinary events can trigger extraordinary responses. Hell, at her age I might have risked the same thing.'

'You didn't see it as I did. Even the woman in London said it was impossible.'

Edward rubbed his eyes. 'Improbable, not impossible, James. Coincidence and bias are clouding your judgement. I don't wonder if St Jude is getting to you, and you should move back to Truro...'

James turned, uncertain of his meaning and conscious of Caroline's potential offer. The old man's hand shook more than it had done before noon as he replaced the empty glass on a nearby table.

'You look tired,' said James. 'Are you sure you are well enough to continue?'

Edward rubbed at his eyes. 'Yes, but I could be asking the same question of you. The power of suggestion, titbits here and there, her own research, all linking into one glamorous fantasy that she's being protected by a two-hundred-year-old suicide who is empathetic to those facing their own dangerous tendencies, not to mention this barbarian that the police have in custody.'

'At the fair, she said mum's ancestors used to look after the

Denes; you only made that connection recently. I need to know how and why she knows things that are so closely related to my own story.'

'We assessed Emily this morning and came up with nothing but confirmation bias and sad revelations of her childhood experiences. The drawings you keep alluding to show nothing specific to testify they have any basis in fact.'

'What about Carmalt?'

'Ignoring that it could be somewhere unrelated, you said that Emily parked her car there. Picture a Georgian house in your mind, James; a two-storied block of a house with sash windows — am I right? Throw in some horses from an interest she already held, and a few bodice-ripping rivals, and you have the basis for most Regency romances. She had access to the same auction drawings I did.'

James folded his arms. 'Regressing her through hypnosis and asking the alter directly might be more insightful. You have expertise in that field—'

'That would also put her in a suggestive state, open to any input we might inadvertently provide and further complicating things. We are here to ascertain the depth and nature of the self-delusion, and you can't force this May Dene to appear. I hope you aren't suggesting the host is put under some form of stress to initiate the switch?'

'Leave that to me,' said James, shaking his head and getting out his phone. 'There may be a safe way to encourage dialogue without being unethical.'

Edward sighed and stared at his manicured fingernails, bright and polished in contrast to the dark lesions developing on his withered hands. 'It's finally come down to it, then.'

'What has?' said James.

'I suspect something else is at play here. Fellows is more invested in this than any of us realise. He is sticking out his neck, as well as his hand, in allowing this to happen. Beware of becoming a pawn in a game where you don't know the rules and only one of you knows how to win. Luckily I do.'

'Why is Fellows overly interested in a case with a historical alter? I thought he would be trying to do everything in his power to make me fail, just to get back at you.'

'On the contrary. He wants to see you succeed to get back at me. Fellows seeks to open old wounds and the answer to a question that will end our dispute, sending me to my grave knowing he was right.'

'What question?'

'That something connects these copycat suicides and bizarre customs down through the centuries, and not just here. A ridiculous notion he held that even suspension and a lifetime of reflection can obviously not purge. Very well, let us indulge him and see just how accurate Emily's delusion is, without judgement, and if she can answer it. There is always a flaw in every performance.'

'Why do I guess you already know the answer?' said James.

Edward adjusted his cuffs and brushed down the arms of his jacket. 'Because I'm the only one who can know. If I do this, you must go back to Truro when the opportunity arises and forget this case and have nothing more to do with Cameron Fellows. I also insist you include nothing that transpires this afternoon into your submission unless I tell you to.'

'Why not?'

'Because if I'm wrong,' said Edward rolling forward to greet the two women approaching the open door,'what nearly ended his career, will certainly end yours.'

CHAPTER 27

E mily lay quiet, breathing slowly in and out to the sounds of Edward's soft, measured instructions from a chair beside. The vertical blinds were drawn, shattering the early afternoon sun into shards across the finely polished stones of the private medical room. The beige strips tapped together like a nylon wind chime, set in motion by ventilating air from a solitary side window. James sat in his chair at the far end of the reclining couch alongside Harriet, uncomfortably reminded of the same sounds that had preceded his disciplinary. He studied the soles of Emily's socked feet upon the couch, scrunching and relaxing with the gentle relaxation pathway to stillness, softness, and answers.

'I'm not overly comfortable with this,' whispered Harriet, almost to a breath. 'Surely encouraging May Dene will only entrench things further?'

James put a finger to his lips. 'We need to convince her that Emily is safe with us, now that we have a man in custody. My father and I need to ask a few questions about her experiences, that's all.'

Edward studied his watch. 'Open your eyes now, Emily. How do you feel?'

Emily blinked and studied the swirls of textured Artex above. 'Relaxed – like I'm floating. The ceiling reminds me of the sea.'

Edward gently creaked forward from his chair. 'That's good. Imagine yourself floating upon it, calming your mind. Do you like the sea?'

'I'm not sure,' she said hesitantly. 'I think so, but it's cold, wild and wrathful.'

'It's Cornwall. Have you been here before this September?'

Emily gently shifted her head. 'No, but May has; she used to live here.'

'Will she tell me about Cornwall?'

Emily's face twitched as though an inner monologue was in silent concourse.

'She says you didn't believe her the last time.'

Edward frowned, and James heard his heart beating in his head as his father continued, sidetracked for a moment.

'What last time?'

Emily shut her eyes and James noticed the twitching in her upturned palm, yellowing from the blue bruise it had received when crushed under the wild horse's bridle. 'The time before me. You were there with someone else, but you sent him away and...'

Edward gripped his left thigh, suddenly aware of the trembling caused by the unconscious tapping of his foot against the hard floor. He leaned back into the chair to compose himself, waiting for her to finish.

Emily sighed and gently cast her eyes upon his neck. 'Did you lose your pearl pin?'

A brief spasm twitched across the old man's cheek before

a look of controlled resolve resurfaced on his father's face, snuffing out some other emotion beneath. A pinch of his brows preceded the lie.

'I never owned a pearl tie pin. Perhaps it is someone else you are confusing me with.'

Emily returned to stare at the ceiling. 'Why am I here?'

'We want you to know that you are safe and that the person who makes you say and do things can be confident that we will look after you.'

Emily tilted her head towards the end of the bed. 'I just want my life back so I can take care of myself.'

James had looked into the same innocent eyes, desperate for help at their first meeting. How one person could endure being a victim on so many levels caused him to glance away in guilt for his own seemingly inconsequential trauma.

So do I...

'Can you tell us why the other person might want to keep things back from you,' said Edward, 'now that you are safe?'

Emily writhed across the squeaking mock leather lounger. Harriet rose to intercede but James held her back. 'She's trying to gain control of the alter's memories but it's not working.'

Edward gripped the end of his chair and signalled to James, already pulling out his phone.

'I think we should stop this now,' said Harriet, being encouraged back into her chair. 'We should go back to the refuge.'

James tapped the play button on his recording of the music box, releasing the melody. The sound settled his nerves and had an immediate effect on the woman lying before him. Relaxed and released from the tension in her limbs she sat upright, hands in her lap, searching for the source of the beautiful, resonant chimes within the enclosed room.

'Mother's box,' she said, reaching out her hand towards him. 'Did you find it, Marshall?'

Edward raised a shaking hand to regain the initiative, but James cut him off, seeing the switch and the return of the gentle Cornish in her speech.

'What box do you mean, May – can you describe it?'

She smiled with the mention of her name, in contrast to the melancholic sadness mirrored in her welling, dilated eyes.

'Father brought it from India.' Realising the box was not present she lowered her hand, setting them apart to demonstrate the dimensions. James ignored his father's intercession and held up his hand for silence as she closed her eyes and traced out with a finger onto the black faux leather of the lounger. Even before he thought of it, Harriet was ready, handing over her pad and paper.

Emily's hand felt for the pen and began to sketch the box that James had recently inherited. After a moment, she split the outlined lozenged crest of a diamond into eight equal segments.

'James, showing her this was unwise,' said Edward with a croak. 'It's your mother's box—'

'My mother's box,' she said possessively. 'Before father gave it to the Cartwrights and sent them away, but he didn't know what I had hidden within, safe from his lecherous pawnbroker.'

'What was inside, May?' asked James.

She put down the pen and raised a hand to caress her neck. 'Mother's jewelled necklace, the last thing of value that we had before ruin beset us. Even after all our beloved horses and the furniture were sold, it remained as hope for better times. I couldn't bear him to sell it. Is it still hidden, Marshall, or is it lost?'

'There's nothing inside, May,' said James. 'Not anymore.'

Edward rose, unsteady on his feet. Harriet leaned across and instinctively offered her arm. 'Stop filling her head with nonsense, my boy. You are giving her what she needs to fuel the delusion. Enough—'

Emily twisted to her knees, under the influence of another, and fixed him with such a stare that he sank back into his chair, aided by the counsellor.

'I did not conceal it inside,' said Emily stroking a finger against the fine lines on the page. 'Not in that sense. From the upstairs window, I watched as father dismissed them. They carried away something more valuable than they realised, as well my shame and loss.' She rubbed at her swelling belly. 'I am no longer ashamed, not now this one shares my predicament.'

'Your father sent them away to protect your reputation?' said James.

She sighed. 'And to bury the day-old child born of the love between Richard and I, far away, so that no-one, not even Henry Fallon would know when he returned from the war with France. They only let me hold her for a moment after I gave birth...father said she was too weak and died in the night. The Cartwrights took her away, and I grieved with such rage that not even the tempests of the autumn sea could rival. She had no grave, and neither would I; they took her from me.' Clasping her arms around her midriff she clenched her fists giving Edward a sideways glance. 'Just like before, Marshall.'

'Where have you heard this?' said Edward, bringing out his handkerchief to stifle the worst of a bout of coughing. 'This isn't a story local to St Jude.'

'There are some who remember it, even now,' she said. 'Locked away in my room before my body began to swell and openly dishonour the Denes, I failed to get word to Richard in France. Fallon returned from the war after I gave birth, and there was no longer any delay in the union my father had arranged between our families. My child was forgotten, and so was I.'

'I'm sorry,' said Edward. 'But Thomas Dene didn't have an heir, my dear. I should know.'

'No, he did not. Even now I consider what might have been if only I had consented to marry the vile creature.

'When Richard finally got word via my confidant, the doctor, Fallon had already challenged his rival for my affections. All the horses were gone, so I raced to the wood to stop the duel and I heard the shot. The rooks emerged from the old yews that used to grow there and flew away to the cliff top. The silence before my scream told me that things had gone ill for Richard; there was no returned shot. I remember the call of the sea from the headland of Myrgh an Mor and the sound of the bells far away. I turned only once to see him pursuing me, but I got to the edge first...'

Harriet came close and sat at the side of the bed. 'It's just bad thoughts. Just because you have them doesn't mean you have to act upon them, or that they are real.'

Edward shook his head. 'This is leading nowhere, James, not to mention feeding the delusion. Your diagnosis stands.'

'Please, May,' said James, ignoring his father. 'It's important to me. Tell me where Emily discovered what you know. Tell me about the time before she tried to jump. Was it the archive, or a library perhaps?'

'She came to the cliff, and I perceived her intent. I reached out to her as I had done so many times before. This place was new and unfamiliar to her, and so much had changed, all but the church. She knew nothing of my life prior to our meeting.'

'And why are you here now?' asked Edward, steadying

himself against the side of the chair from a further fit of coughing. He drew back the blood speckled cloth as James put down his phone and filled a cup of water from the cooler in the corner.

'I ruined my father,' she said turning with tears in her eyes. 'There was nothing left for him with me gone, his final asset, and now I make amends by protecting all those who let me in, those who cannot fight back and have no hope. That's why I am here, Marshall. That's why I come back; I told you this before.'

Harriet grabbed at the phone beside her, muting the looped musical accompaniment. 'Enough of this, can't you see she's upset?'

'How many more questions?' she said to her right as Edward raised his head from his hands, pale and clammy. 'If you wouldn't believe me before, then why do you persist, Marshall? I do not blame you for your scepticism – I both pity and forgive you.'

'No more questions,' said James offering the water. Edward's hand shook as he gulped from the cup, spilling the liquid across his lap. 'I agree with Harriet; bring her back. We need to call the doctor; you are unwell—'

Edward held up his hand in rejection and took out a clean handkerchief to mop his brow.

'You say that you knew me in a time before Emily?' said Edward, 'and that I didn't believe you then.'

She nodded.

'Then you will know the answer to my final question.' Gripping the damp monographed cotton, he leaned forward, twisting his ear in her direction.

'What two words?' he murmured.

She swivelled and gently cradled hands around his head, leaning in as though to kiss his jaundiced cheek. She cupped her hands about his ear and breathed into the void, falling back onto the couch aided by the timely reactions of the counsellor.

Edward shook his head, recoiling to strike the headrest of the high-backed chair. James took one look at his father's blood drained face and raced for the blinds to slide back the glass door, letting in a refreshing breath of air.

The old man recovered himself and sat upright, breathing in deeply to regain composure. Colour began to return to his face, and he reached for the file, ignoring James's attempts to check on his condition. 'Stop fussing, boy. I felt nauseous for a moment, nothing more.'

'She's coming round,' said Harriet. 'Her eyes are no longer dilated.'

James leaned over the couch, trying to gain Emily's attention. 'Get her out into the air and call for the nurse. I need her to see my father, too.'

Emily got up groggily and slipped on her shoes. Supported by the counsellor, she shuffled out into the sunshine clutching at her stomach.

'What was all that about?' said James kneeling before his father.

'A flaw in the performance. She gave me the wrong answer, do you understand?' he said, grasping tightly onto James's hand and repeating it to a whisper.

'Alright,' said James, putting his arms around him. 'Whatever it was between you and Fellows, it's over.' To his surprise, Edward dropped the file and joined him in a firm embrace. From within the hug, James heard the wheezing of his father's rapid breath.

'Promise me you will submit only the report with my supporting statement, nothing more. We were both right, but you must drop this, my boy. It's torn apart too many lives.'

James nodded as he receded from the huddle. 'As soon as she's safe, dad.'

Edward turned to stare at the black leather couch, unable to remove his eyes from the deep impressions of Emily's hands and knees rebounding from the stiff foam underlay as though a ghostly and unseen figure was rising.

'And when you see Fellows,' he said, averting his eyes, 'tell him I'll see him in hell.'

CHAPTER 28

'Well, that could have gone better,' said Harriet, striding ahead to open the passenger car door. 'Considering it wasn't anything remotely connected with her welfare or your father's.'

James threw her a pensive glance. 'Dr Lewisham and the director approved my father's involvement—'

'Can I sit in the front?' piped Emily. 'I get travel sick and I still feel a bit woozy despite what the nurse gave me half an hour ago.' Harriet shrugged and opened the rear door. 'Plus, I feel that I'm already in the back seat, being talked about, and in the dark about what's going on.'

'You and me both,' said Harriet assisting Emily into the car and handing her the seat belt clip.

James got in and saw Harriet slide across the back seat to force another look of annoyance upon him. 'What chapter was that in your father's book, hmm?'

'Did I do something wrong in there?' said Emily. 'It feels like there's a row coming. Your father got upset with me.'

'He wasn't upset,' said James, pulling out of the car park and heading for the drive. 'He's just exhausted now, because of his illness. The last question my father asked you; what did you answer?'

'I don't remember. It was May—'

Harriet leaned forward into the space between the two of them. 'I think we've had quite enough for one day, Dr Marshall, if you want my continued support. This is not a therapeutic environment, and neither was that.'

James turned left, inland and overtook a slow-moving tractor. 'I'm sorry if you were upset by anything back there, Emily.' Harriet retreated to the back seat, arms folded.

She remained steadfastly staring at the fading leaves of the sporadic and stunted moorland trees lining the minor road. 'I prefer to tackle May on my own. What you did back there with that music let her in and made me feel powerless.'

James nodded. 'It won't happen again, I promise.'

'Why are we going this way?' asked Harriet. 'St Jude is behind us.'

'Road's closed,' said James, checking the rear-view mirror to see a single solitary car overtake the tractor behind. 'We have to go via Cennen Bridge, but it's only twenty minutes difference.'

Emily turned to examine the pearl tipped, brass tie pin rolling in the dashboard cubby. 'Is this yours?'

'Yes, but it once belonged to my father.'

'Why did he lie about not having one?'

'How did you know he did?'

Harriet appeared between the front seats. 'I mean what I said, both of you.'

Emily threw a guilty grin across at James who turned to the side window to avoid his own from plunging him deeper into trouble with the back seat driver.

Naughty kids usually sit in the back, he thought.

Emily distracted herself by running a hand across the dashboard, over the airbag warning sign. 'Do these things go off before or after you hit something? May doesn't understand what they do.'

'Hopefully before,' said James, winking across. 'But don't worry, you can tell her I'm a safe driver, and neither of you have anything to worry about.'

The road wound through the upland moor and the uneven grasslands gave way to gorse tussocks and hardy sheep. Light rain speckled the windscreen setting off the wipers, much to Emily's alarm, until she regained a sense of control, telling herself out loud that the strange mechanical devices were functional and no threat. She raised and lowered the passenger window like an intrigued child until Harriet, rain-splattered and in no mood for further blasts of autumnal ventilation, requested an immediate cessation in the play with a curt tone of teacher-like authority.

After several miles, the car forded a narrow, single-lane bridge and rose to meet the outskirts of the small town among the craggy outcropped granite tors. Emily grabbed at her bloated stomach.

'I could use the bathroom and some air.'

James glanced in the mirror to see Harriet nod in agreement.

'There's a car park not far ahead and a public convenience in Cennen halfway down the high street opposite the memorial gardens. Mike brought me here on Monday night. There's a great Italian...'

James raised an eyebrow, and the conversation ceased abruptly as he pulled into the car park, allowing the only car behind to pass and pull in to a double yellow line not far ahead.

'They'll get caught pretty soon if they park there,' said James, pulling to a stop. 'The wardens in Cennen are notorious.' He flashed his eyes, teasing his passenger as they both released their seat belts. 'They are descended from head-hunting Celts, you know.'

'We'll only be twenty minutes,' said Harriet getting out of the car. 'It's not that far.'

James emerged from beneath the roof. 'Under the circumstances, I'm happier coming with you, and there is something I need to pick up pretty much opposite.'

Checking the allowed free parking time, James escorted them through the shopping centre portico and onto the grey, stone-clad, cobbled high street beyond. Almost at once, the newcomers to the bustling street were aware of them, and Emily in particular. Some stopped and stared, others pointed.

'Ignore them,' said James. 'It appears your exploits are more widely known than just St Jude.'

After a few minutes, a small group of disciples formed behind the trio attracting further interest. James turned to see the growing swathe of shoppers, many with phones raised eager to catch the local celebrity for posterity. Shopkeepers alerted to the suddenness of distracted passing trade stuck out their heads from bell ringing doorways to see the disorganised march pass by.

James offered his arm. 'We might need to be quick—'

Emily glanced behind and froze, almost becoming entangled and overwhelmed by the phone flashing mob. James and the counsellor spun round to collect her, but she remained rigid, her face masked by an overwhelming thousand-yard stare of dread.

'What is it?' said James, urging her on.

She raised a hand, quivering toward a man, less than a hundred yards away, who turned and ambled away in stark contrast to the growing crowd around them.

'He's...here.'

'Who?' said Harriet, lifting herself upon the tips of her toes to scan the location.

'Emily?' said James, gently grasping her shoulder and feeling the shaking of her body with all-consuming terror.

She began to hum, even as the figure disappeared with a final, furtive glance behind the entrance to the shopping arcade. James felt her relax as the gentle bars of *Sweet Nightingale* took hold and her wide blue eyes met his own.

'He's here, Marshall. Ryan Williams is here.'

'You're sure?' he said, getting out his phone and connecting to the police station.

'We both are,' she said. 'I have seen him now in the flesh where once was only dreadful memory. Fetch for the beadle and I will make sure she is kept calm.'

'It's the alter that's presenting,' said Harriet stealing a look into her eyes. 'What do we do?'

James brushed aside people with his free hand as Harriet grabbed Emily to follow closely behind. 'There's a shop up ahead, I know the owners. We'll be safe there until the police arrive but until then, we need to make sure there are plenty of people around.'

The phone connected as they raced to the antique dealer's door, pushing themselves in as though the accompanying hoard of smartphone zombies were the main threat.

'What is it, James?' said Jory.

'We are in Cennen,' he replied. 'Harriet, Emily and I are in Tucker's Antiques on the High Street. Williams is here, in the town, near to the shopping centre. Emily just got eyeballs on him and I saw someone, a nasty-looking fella. There's a big crowd in front of the shop after pictures—'

'Stay put, we are on our way. Don't leave the shop and bar the door – front and back if it has one.'

James put down the phone and turned to meet the confused owner, a plain-faced, brown-haired woman in navy dungarees emerging from behind a series of display cabinets housing small items of silver.

'Dr Marshall?'

'Frances, we need your help. I don't want to worry you, but there's someone outside that the police are looking for. They are on their way, but we need you to lock the door and not let anyone in. He's after someone in my care.'

She glanced at the two accompanying women, huddled close and staring out of the large bay window across a sea of faces like frightened rabbits. 'Then he won't get in here. Is it the man that's wanted on the posters recently put up?' She retreated to the desk and retrieved a sharp-tipped letter opener from beside the till.

James nodded at the stonewashed denim warrior, brandishing the stainless steel weapon. 'You need to lock the back if you have one.'

'George!' she cried to the back room, summoning the archivist. 'Lock the yard door.'

He appeared, throwing a look of confusion at his wife, throwing the bars across the front door and across in surprise at seeing James and the two women. He gawked at Emily in recognition. 'The rider. What's going on?'

'Dr Marshall says that wanted man is in the street. The police are coming, now lock the back door, you fool.'

James made certain Harriet and Emily were somewhat out of view from the mob, peering in through condensed breaths on the paned glass, and turned to follow him through to the room beyond.

'Make sure he locks the window,' called Frances from behind. 'He's had his head in books and papers all morning. I'll watch the front.'

George was already drawing the bolts and sliding across the safety chain as he entered the box stacked storeroom. A large table of books, charts and curios lay to one side, as part of George's bookish man cave.

'You can see why I work at the archive, can't you?' he said

rolling his eyes and locking the window. Mind you, this is exciting.'

'That's one way to describe it,' said James, peering out at the dustbins against the low back wall to the side street. 'We need to keep an eye out from here.'

'Is he after you or the one that saved the child at Haldwyn, the one they call the maiden?'

James felt he owed some sort of explanation for putting the man and former patient at risk. 'He's after Emily. She's with Harriet, her counsellor, and we only stopped to catch some air before heading back to St Jude. I was going to pop in and catch up, maybe have a word with Frances to see what she found out about the music box. I'm sorry if this puts either of you in a dangerous situation, but I don't think he'll try to break in. It's more likely he was just following us and waiting for an opportunity when there are far fewer people around.'

George grabbed his arm and swung him round to the table. 'Glad to be of help, James. As you are here, I found out plenty to keep us occupied till the police arrive.'

'What do you mean?' said James watching the man plough through a leaf of maps and photocopies, finally wrestling a large sea chart onto the top of the pile and securing it with several flat sea cobbles. He pointed to a spot in the upper right.

'It's a Spanish naval chart from 1835,' he beamed proudly. 'It took some locating but I have a contact in militaria antiques who was happy to exchange for a few bits of Portmeirion.' He pulled his jaw. 'Don't tell Frances, will you? She thinks I've just had them sent out for approval, but this chart is worth more considering it has local interest.'

'Your secret's safe with—' James stopped, stunned by the name preceding Dene Point.

'Maria?'

George twitched his nose. 'It's Mary. The chart ordinates from a merchant shipping fleet out of Almeria. What's more, it connects nicely with what my skittle playing parish clerk discovered. He was as intrigued as I was to discover the link. He wants to write a book on it.'

'On what?' said James. 'What link?'

'You asked if Thomas Dene had any heir and you were right, he didn't.'

'Yes, I know. He had to sell to clear debts or through some calamity around the time of the Napoleonic wars. He was a merchant.'

'But he had issue, a daughter.' George flicked open a journal, scribbled and stuffed with post-it notes and taped photocopies. James peered down at what appeared to be a historical register and list of accounts.

'I don't see—?'

George collected his reading glasses from atop one box and began to read:

'"For the installation of a stone cross in memoriam of my beloved daughter Mary-Anne, whose body lies with the sea. Eighteen pounds and six shillings." It wasn't a ship that foundered out on the rocks in front of the cliff, it was renamed after his daughter.'

'Mary-Anne Point...' whispered James, staring at the entry in the old ledger. 'May Dene Point...'

'Maiden Point,' said George smugly. 'God, I love historical detective work almost as much as etymology. Frances thinks it's not worthy of my time but it's priceless compared to the knick-knacks out front.'

'The cross is still there, but it's worn. Thomas Dene had enough money to commemorate his daughter, then?'

'Barely by the looks of things,' said George highlighting an earlier entry. 'The money for the new steeple was struck out. It's why it never got completed after the storm.'

James returned to the window deep in thought.

'It's a memorial cross, you say?'

'Probably, though there's nothing to say he wasn't buried nearby or even underneath at a later stage. It sounds as though she was lost at sea, not unheard of in those days. We have more wrecks than anywhere in the UK.'

'Anything on Richard Avery or Henry Fallon?' said James.

'Nothing on the former though he may be an outsider. The Fallons bought up some of the estate though their line appears to have faltered not long after they began stripping the place to build what would become a Grange further inland.'

'Fairhaven Grange?'

'Possibly.' George folded his arms and looked up at the ceiling. 'Perhaps another curse descended on the family; that or war, hard times, typhus or smallpox. Take your pick.'

Frances's voice came booming through from the shop. 'Anything back there, or are you asleep?'

George rolled his eyes. 'Queen Mab summons. I think she might actually enjoy sticking someone with that letter opener.'

They re-entered the shop, keeping the door ajar. George stood in between rooms, monitoring the unkempt access yard and rear of the building. Frances held the small, mock dagger behind her back, peering out among the crowd. She turned the sign in the window to "closed", ignoring the trials at the handle and taps on the glazed windows from those outside eager to gain entry.

'Go away,' she mouthed. 'We're closed.'

'Everything alright?' said James, coming over to see Harriet stroking the arm of a vacant Emily, chewing gum and examining the valuable items in the cases as though familiar but commonplace.

'All calm now thanks to the switch and the diversion,'

she said, moving away to whisper. 'She said one candlestick over there used to belong to her father, or one very much like it.'

'What's this fella look like?' said Frances. 'I paid little attention to the news the other day.'

James came to stand beside her and scanned the street. 'Well-built, black combat jacket, close-cropped hair—'

'I know,' said a voice, softly.

'Maybe it's better if we all just remain calm and leave things to the police,' said Harriet, moving to intercept Emily, reaching for a pen.

'Are you sure you want to do this?' asked James, requesting a nod of approval from the shop owner to hand over a coloured advertisement flyer, blank on one side.

'I think we have little option considering our present predicament,' she said.

Frances came to join them at the counter, watching as a face began to appear on the sheet beside Emily's rapidly working hand.

'The papers said she was from London?' whispered Frances. 'Her accent's local enough.'

'It's...complicated,' said James. 'Emily has different aspects to her personality. We are witnessing the one that takes charge when she is under stress.'

The face took shape and James twisted his head in amazement at the likeness of the man taking shape, briefly and distantly glanced in the street. 'It's the guy I saw.'

Her hand slowed and stopped as she placed her other on the counter to steady herself. Wet splashes appeared on the page, blurring the ink as Frances turned her head to the ceiling instinctively, searching for leaks.

James glanced up only to see Emily's dilated eyes spilling with tears, her mouth and face otherwise engaged with the calm aspect of one enjoying a day out shopping with friends.

She blew out a bubble of gum and it popped, mopping the streaks streaming down her face.

'I'm sorry,' said James. 'You can stop now – I don't want you to be upset.'

'I'm not,' she said. 'It's Emily that's crying. It's hopeless, isn't it? Wherever we go, he will find us.' Harriet handed her a tissue and she wiped her eyes, humming the opening bars of *Sweet Nightingale*.

'That reminds me,' said Frances, laying down the letter opener. 'I had your musical caddy back from the conservator. Wait there.' She disappeared into the back and returned after several minutes of settling boxes in the other room. She reappeared with the wrapped object, placing it upon the counter and opening the uppermost sheets of thin foam. The dark, patina of the wooden box emerged, its segmented diamond inlaid lid glittered beneath the high-intensity jewellery lights from a lamp nearby.

'The good news is they can find the exotic woods to fabricate the small tiles that are damaged, but it's going to cost more than the piece could be worth.' She opened the lid, setting off the musical chimes, repeating alongside the low humming of Emily's voice. 'They are recommending a natural conservation resin to stabilise—'

Unbidden, and with a swift action Emily grabbed at the box, holding it tight and refusing to let go as Frances instinctively tried to retrieve it.

'It's my mother's!' said Emily. 'Even if it belonged to the Cartwright's for a time. They are long gone, childless, and doubtless they sold the box. Tell her, Marshall.'

James held up his hand to defuse the situation. 'It's okay, Frances – let her have it for now.'

'I thought you said you were descended from the Cartwright's?' said George. 'They couldn't have been child—'

'Not now, George!' said Frances.

Emily scanned the interior, frowning and picking at the worn jewellery cushion.

'Please don't damage it,' said Harriet. 'Just be gentle.'

Emily closed the lid and smoothed her hands over the lid. Turning and twisting the box like an antique Rubik's cube she finally slammed it down upon the counter, dislodging several of the small tiles. Before James intervened, she grabbed the letter opener by the hilt and began to jab at a small void, working and prising until several pieces were flung into the air, rebounding against the glass cabinets near the window like shot from a blunderbuss. Splintered amber fragments of some resinous origin lay scattered as she dug into the precious wood, scoring along a letter-boxed size marquetry outline like a possessed vandal.

'Stop!' cried James. 'Emily—'

'Leave me be,' she said, brandishing the sharp stiletto in warning at James's approaching hands. 'I have to know...'

The bang of a heavy fist struck the glass door behind. James turned to see the face of his friend and saviour for the second time that day, backed up by other plain-clothed officers he took to be from the City of London police. Frances made for the door.

Harriet gave a startled gasp, and he turned back to see Emily in the final act of extricating a small and previously hidden drawer.

'It's a spoon housing...' said George, placing a hand over his mouth as she prised something altogether more remarkable from its bound, resin security. 'Beneath the main compartment – it was there all along.'

James heard the unlocking of the door and the sound of many voices in the street, some trying to gain access, others urging them to disperse. He felt Jory at his side, glancing down at the image of the man sketched out on the paper. 'It's Williams alright. You all okay, mate?'

James nodded fixated on Emily as she raised the fine, but tarnished chain and three stoned, blue-stoned necklace among a filigree of fine silver from its reliquary and clasped it about her neck. In a moment he recognised it from the drawing, miles away on a wall in a rundown refuge – the first drawing he had seen from this unremarkable patient suffering from a textbook alternate personality disorder.

'James,' said Jory shaking him before his attention became focussed on the bright flashes of cameras from the outside window and those that had barged their way in past the policemen.

Hidden for centuries, Emily adjusted the glittering jewels to face forward, glancing with her matching eyes. For an instant, James caught a reflection of the Georgian woman before her pupils sharpened to a pinpoint, and she relinquished control.

'Mary Dene?' whispered James, as she cast the letter opener to the floor and teetered back into the arms of the counsellor in a swoon, one hand clasped at the priceless jewels at her throat.

'Father calls me…May.'

CHAPTER 29

J ames woke suddenly in the darkness, desperate to purge
the sensation of falling. He fumbled for the light,
knocking over the empty bottle of rum, blaming it for
the sudden bout of nausea, and clicked on the side lamp to
wipe his sweating brow. His blurred vision stabilised to reveal
the time on his watch. The period of alcohol-induced sleep
had been all too brief, and he sidled to the sideboard, opening
the sunglasses case that now contained something of
infinitely greater value than his upended Ray-Bans atop the
carcass of the music box.

The bedside lamp buzzed and the bulb went out, plunging
the room into curtain-veiled moonlight. He swore and pulled
open the drapes to reveal the silhouettes of garden trees,
background hedgerows and distant rocky outcrops. The first
frost of autumn glistened on the lawn and adjoining fields
mirroring the specks of fire in the firmament above. One
bright star on the horizon glowed red, flickering like an angry
glede trying to stem the onset of winter, mourning for the
loss of the seemingly endless summer. He cleared the blur of
sleep from his eyes and blinked to recognise the unmistakable

pinpoint of fire replacing his initial premise. Far away, against the blackness, and blocking out the glow of the vertical belt of the milky way, something was alight on Maiden Point.

He squeezed at the necklace, cutting the facets of the precious stones into his hands. A kaleidoscope of sapphire-blue fractured against the far wall as he revealed the jewels to their first moon in two hundred years.

Indian sapphires at the end of an Indian summer...

A flicker of light from a car at the far corner of the street caught his attention and he moved back into the shade of the curtain, watchful until his eyes accustomed to the dark and the moonlit monotone of a police car released his anxiety into a long-drawn-out sigh. He reached for his phone and dialled from his recent calls screen.

'I thought stakeouts only happened in films,' said James, smiling as the large frame of the policeman suddenly shifted in surprise within the driver's seat. 'Or is it just a chance to eat doughnuts like your American counterparts?'

James watched the penny drop as Jory's head pressed against the car window, searching the house opposite. He finally caught sight of his moonlit, t-shirt and boxer-clad friend from the first-floor window, and raised a salutatory, single-fingered greeting. He raised something bundled in paper.

'It's chips, actually. What you doing up so late, or early?'

'What are you doing outside my house, Jory? Stalking me or watching out for someone you've yet to apprehend? Either way, I'm not sure I approve.'

'It's my night shift and Gotham's quiet tonight.'

James glanced back to the fire burning on the headland. 'There's something ablaze on the Point.'

'I know,' mumbled Jory with a mouthful of food. 'Local ladies doing their willow woman thing. They let the fire brigade know and we don't interfere as long as they tidy up.

Christine Lee's husband is on call tonight to make sure his missus doesn't set the whole headland alight.'

'Christine Lee is part of the willow maiden thing?'

'Runs it, or what's left of it. The old sergeant let me know who was in charge if there was any funny business. I don't think they are planning anymore after tonight. Box sets and on-demand *Scandinavian noir* is preferable to making Mrs Guy Fawkes or whatever they get up to. Most likely they just get pissed like the rest of us. Part of me is a little sad – it's yet another thing that will get lost to modernity.'

James turned back to the car.

'Anything on Williams?'

'Nah. Disappeared like a bad fart and Cennen doesn't have CCTV, but all your testimonies check out. We'll get him – St Jude is a small enough place.'

'It took us over a week to find the car, remember?' said James, running his fingers through his clammy hair. 'You think he could come here, to the house?'

Jory paused. 'Dunno. You have that piece of old tat with you still?'

'Yes, and Frances Tucker said it could be worth upward of a hundred grand.'

'Should be in a safe or the bank, not unguarded in an isolated old two up and two down at the end of Carog lane.'

'Thanks,' said James. 'You make me feel so much safer. While I appreciate the sentiment, wouldn't you be better keeping an eye on the refuge?'

'The plain-clothed coppers are over there now. Might even be some up here for all I know. It's gone a bit "need to know" at the station.'

'Did you find anything out about the fella you arrested yesterday morning?

'Only that he's definitely not Williams.' Jory tossed the empty chip packet into the rear and wiped his hands down his black stab jacket. James heard the fizz of a drink can being opened before he continued. 'You remember I told you about Emily's boyfriend turning up dead? Turns out he was telling the truth.'

'He's related?'

'Yep,' said Jory taking a gasping breath after a long swig from the can. 'He's the brother and clean, apart from over-staying his visa by several weeks and owning an illegal, modi-fied handgun replica with several rounds. When the City boys put him under pressure, Mr Pavel suddenly lost the ability to understand English and clammed up.'

'He said he wanted to look after Emily's child – his nephew if it's true.'

'My thoughts exactly. These Romanians are super child orientated. They also get very upset if you mess with any of their family. I think our little vigilante was waiting for an opportunity to kill two birds with one stone – save his broth-er's pregnant girlfriend and child, and cut out the police middlemen regarding justice. Sounds like they'll end up just deporting him.'

'He doesn't work for that Mostoff you mentioned?'

'Doubt it, but as I said, what Pavel failed to do might end up in someone else's wheelhouse.' A break of static and station control voices signalled the end of the call.

'Go to go,' said Jory. 'Pot heads at the boat shed.'

'Thanks, Jory. I mean it.'

Jory wound down the window and stuck out his head to raise a thumb. 'Just be careful of that necklace. It could pay for a lot of good things if you decide to sell it if it doesn't end up killing you.'

The churchyard lay blanketed with early morning dew. Strands of silken cobwebs, bedecked by rime, netted the gravestones like the rigging of old sailing ships, connecting the nearby dead as they had been in life.

James knelt by his wife's grave and blew on his hands with a steaming breath of moist warm air, counteracting the onshore sea mist that brewed in the bay. He checked his watch – time enough before his patients for the day streamed in; a welcome distraction from the raging questions without sensible answers that filled his waking mind and silenced the desperate plea for sleep. His care proposal had been finalised and emailed to Truro, following the events at Fairhaven Grange, but doubt gnawed at his decision following the discovery of the hidden treasure and the revelations from the charts and the archivist. Everything neatly presented itself to a conclusion that he could not accept.

Several shots of rum had dulled his surprise as he flicked through his father's genealogical journal. Emily had insisted that May Dene's child was dead within hours of giving birth, but something was amiss and he was unsure if it comforted or drew him deeper into questions he knew he had no right to ask a patient, struggling to remove herself from one who held the answers. According to the first census, the Cartwrights had ended up in Bristol to continue working for a small family, along with their daughter, Mary, from whom James was descended. Emily had described them as old, and child-less. If the dates of Thomas Dene's death and Mary Cartwright's return to the area, twenty years later were to align, aged only twenty-two, her parents had adopted or fostered in their early sixties before moving from St Jude but following the suicide of Mary-Anne Dene.

'Occam's razor,' he whispered several times, but the mantra held less power out here in the cold and wild than it had done in the presence of his father.

She gave me the wrong answer... you must drop this, my boy. It's torn apart too many lives.

Wiping at the dew on the etched, smiling face of his wife, he clicked open the glasses case and removed the jewelled necklace.

'I fulfil a promise made when I was a boy, Karen,' he said, securing the chain around the raised profile of the cameo. The kiss was cold and long overdue. He retreated to see the moisture develop around her beautiful face, condensing into a single, tear-like bead that splashed upon the sapphires at her stony neck.

His phone buzzed against his chest, an unwelcome and startling intrusion. Instinctively, he recovered the necklace and answered the call.

'You're up early,' said Caroline.

James rose and stamped his feet to remove the stiffness from his knees. 'It's late. I've barely slept.'

'I don't think many of us have considering yesterday's evening news. What possessed you to take her shopping, for God's sake?'

'I didn't. The road back to St Jude was closed. She needed to use the bathroom; she's pregnant remember?'

'And being hunted by a murderer. It's official, they are tying Williams to the death of a guy in London. Enough is enough, James.'

The cry of a gull far above hovered on the breeze. 'What do you mean?'

'Don't you think the time has come for you to let go? What better time to hand over as principal care leader for her sake, and yours?'

'Not yet,' he said. 'There may be a link between me and Thomas' Dene's daughter or possibly granddaughter; there's more at stake here than just a personality disorder.'

'Your assessment, now in front of Fellows, contradicts this. What are you talking about?'

'Something is happening that is connecting me, my family and Emily, to the influence of May Dene.'

'You mean the alternate personality. Influence has far too many connotations, and that makes me nervous as well as others that are concerned about your welfare.'

'I see Jory was right, my care team are as leaky as a colander. Well, until Fellows removes me, I'm staying put.'

'Fellows is signing off on your reinstatement this afternoon after he gets over the disappointment of whatever your father didn't find. His gamble obviously didn't pay off.'

'It was something that settled an old score. I'm not to blame for that, you can't pin any extra-curricular questioning of the patient on me.'

'No, but I can question your standards of ethics in subduing the host against her will, leading her on a merry dance in Cennen, and providing reinforcement bias that could well have extended her recovery and chance at a normal life away from fables and fantasies.'

James switched ears and dug his cold hand into his trouser pocket. 'It doesn't account for her extraordinary feat at the fair and the discovery of this necklace that she had previous knowledge of. Not to mention my experiences—'

'What experiences? You mean you've had further hallucinations like the ones that you described to me after your little seafront tryst?'

'I've already explained and apologised for that, but yes.'

'Mike Trebarr prescribed nothing? – you've been to see him as I requested, right?'

James hesitated and glanced up, realising he had wandered unknowingly towards the older plots and even now stood at the gap in the hedge staring at the Dene cross. The grave offerings had grown substantially, but beyond the stubs and blobs of candle-waxed votives, he glimpsed a larger, fresh corn doll, holding court on its prominent upper ledge.

'I'm asking you to give this up,' said Caroline, bringing him back to the here and now. 'You are becoming obsessive and it's impacting your health, the welfare of the patient, and putting a strain on relationships around you. Can't you see?'

'She's not safe yet,' said James. 'Given that Williams is running around, and Emily is growing more and more despondent, she could relapse at any moment. She's carrying a dead man's child, and a dead woman in her head, Caroline. I'm not even sure if she'd listen a second time if she took off to Maiden Point.'

'That's not your responsibility. We are beginning with therapy according to your and your father's assessment and I'm more than happy to include anti-depressants and further cognitive therapies. You've done your job now let me do mine.'

'You can't medicate against insecurity or the belief she has. She's using Occam's razor for the same reasons we are. The simplest explanation to her is that May Dene is real – can you blame her? It's getting worse, not better, and I have to change this somehow. I don't want to lose her.'

'That is a risk we all face when we signed up for this career, but I'm more concerned about you. I know what's been happening outside of the reports. Your judgement is being compromised, and you have failed on multiple occasions to submit yourself for medical assessment. Now you tell me you are having delusions. It's time to get off the horse, James, so come back to Truro in readiness to take over my role and do what your father asks; leave it be. Don't make me force you.'

'You got the nod from Fellows and a call from my father? My God, Caroline, you are playing the field. I can't, I'm sorry. Not even for you.'

'I made a promise to your father that you'd be off this case as soon as possible, and I've given you every chance to do so voluntarily...'

'Just say it, Caroline,' said James, walking forward and planting his hand on the cross. 'We've both run out of road.'

'Finish up with the patients you have this morning and clear your desk. As a duty of care, I expect you at Truro, first thing in the morning, for an independent medical assessment, otherwise consider yourself suspended with immediate effect.'

CHAPTER 30

Outside of James's office window, the mature cordyline tree bent and bowed with the bluster and sea-blown mizzle of the first named storm of the season. The squall squandered the last of summer's goodwill and savaged the shrubbery and spindle trees, putting the back bordered bench of the hospital garden at the centre of a flurried snow globe of autumnal leaves.

James turned from the glass and snapped shut the second of his briefcases, burgeoned with files, facsimiles, and papers. Rifling through the ink-stained, veneered drawers he opened the folded drawing of the house at Carmalt, placing it on the cleared table. The racehorses gambolled in the field about the stable block, serving staff milled around a hand pump drawing water and an estate worker fixed a low and damaged hurdle in the perimeter hedge. He glanced at the lane to which Richard Avery, in James's hallucination, had ridden away, conscious of his lover's impending punishment for the rash and dangerous ride from the church.

She calls it "pointing" and it's a reckless sport fraught with pitfalls and danger...

'That is a fair distance in fifteen minutes, even in a straight line,' whispered James, circling the steeple.

'What is?' said Harriet, knocking and poking her head around the door.

James scrunched the sheet and tossed it into the corner with the overflowing wastepaper basket. 'Nothing.'

The counsellor frowned, coming in to stand among boxes and the spartan surroundings, devoid of any personal items except the necessary clerical and medical items.

'You're moving office?' she said. 'Only I thought we had a catch up in twenty minutes to go over the Mallory case before setting him up on—'

'Speak to Dr Lewisham. She'll let you know who may be taking responsibility and what will be going on. I have to head back to Truro.'

'Truro?' Harriet forced herself into his eye-line. 'Won't you tell me, after everything I've tried to do for you and your patients? Did I do something wrong that's landed you—'

James ceased in his fiddling with the catch on his case. 'How about letting my superior know about my missed appointments with my GP, which is none of your business, my misdemeanours and management of a patient under my care?'

Harriet shook her head in denial. 'I've done no such thing.'

James scoffed and continued his packing, grabbing at a flimsy cardboard box. 'How about filling Emily Dunn's head with my being pulled from the bay as a child or sensitive information about Tom Cotter and what happened to him?

'You know he has become someone I barely recognise now since Emily spoke with him on the promenade?'

Harriet looked him squarely in the face. 'Mike said he's calmed down and is happier in himself, but it's none of my doing.'

'Well, there you go. Now it's Mike sharing sensitive information and breaking client confidentiality. Tom Cotter is not one of your patients.' He watched her stiffen and look away. 'I hope Mike and you will be thrilled in whatever arrangement you have with each other.' Even as he threw the box on the floor, he regretted the words. Had he and Caroline not done the same, not to mention one of his best friends down at the police station?

'It's my fault,' he offered turning to see her striding to the door. 'I shouldn't have trusted someone I barely knew with personal information.'

Harriet almost collided with the door as it opened revealing the gentle face of his best friend, GP, and ten-thirty catch-up. James's phone buzzed, and he silenced the screen without a glance at the caller.

'Hello, what's this?'

Harriet flung herself into the doctor's chest, raising her fists to squeeze back any sign of visible upset.

'James is leaving for Truro and he's accused me of leaking personal information relating to his childhood to Emily.'

'What information?' said Mike, squishing his eyebrows at the signs of departure in the room.

James stuffed his arms into his pockets. 'The day I almost drowned. Emily has a drawing of it on her wall at the refuge and couldn't have got the level of detail from just hearsay.'

'I'd all but forgotten about it,' said Harriet turning, defiantly. 'The last time I called Dr Lewisham was after the incident at the fair to offer my resignation, to protect you, and now you accuse me of ratting. I said nothing to either of them.' She sidled past the tall GP and left the doorway.

The phone in his pocket called out like a hungry chick for attention. Taking it out James threw it, buzzing, into the wastepaper basket.

'You need to calm down,' said Mike holding up a hand. 'Right now.'

James clasped his hands, turning the knuckles white. 'I should be grateful to her, sending me back to my old life and away from this backwater.'

'That's unkind,' said Mike. 'Even from someone like you.' His pager went off and he glanced down briefly at the device. 'An external call; it can wait.'

'Well, at least I won't be blamed for any more failures, thanks to Caroline's little sneak. I can see now why she was so keen to have her on board.'

'Harriet didn't call Caroline to tell her what's been going on with Emily Dunn. She divulged it to me during our recent evenings together, to reach out to someone she knew you'd listen to. She's as worried about you as I am.'

James folded his arms and kicked at the loose, scrunched balls around the basket. From within, the phone buzzed once more. 'Well, if it wasn't her, then who was it?'

'Me.'

James bounced a knuckle against his mouth. 'Et tu, Brute? I knew my father wanted me off this case, but never did I think someone like you would go behind my back to encourage Caroline's decision.'

Mike cast his head to the side to avoid eye contact. 'You've consistently avoided your medical assessment and any opportunity with me to discuss your mental health. Caroline said you were having some visual hallucinations and I've seen you slide further and further away from who you are or were. I had to get you off this case, whatever the cost to our relationship; it's killing you—'

The door behind flew open and Harriet barged past, bleary-eyed with a phone pressed to her ear.

'I'm here now, Stephanie. I'll pass you over.'

James took the phone from her shaking hands, and she

retreated into the arms of the GP, murmuring words that were being repeated from the carer.

'What is it?' said James. 'Is it Emily—?'

'It's your father, James. He's had a major heart attack or stroke, I... don't know what they said...the paramedics.'

'Slow down,' he said, pacing to the window. 'Tell me where he is now.'

'On his way to The Royal Cornwall. I've been trying to reach you for ten minutes and I've tried everyone on his critical call list...'

'What happened?' He fished out his phone to see several missed calls and a text from Caroline.

Urgent. Where are you? It's Edward. On way to Royal...

'He's been upset with himself since you came yesterday,' she said hurriedly. 'The nurse said he was okay but not to overexert himself. He was fine one minute when I left him in front of the TV, then when I came back in with his meds, he was gasping for breath on his knees clawing at the footage of Emily on screen in a shop...he just kept mouthing "no!" till he started having a fit.'

'It's my father,' said James glancing up. Mike relinquished his hold of the counsellor and studied his pager.

'External call! Stephanie tried to get hold of me, too. I'll sort out everything here, James. Go!'

'I'm on my way, Stephanie,' said James shaking with panic.

'I'm so sorry, Dr Marshall. I was watching the channel before he came in. If only he hadn't seen her, then he might not have had the seizure – it's all my fault...'

James leaned forward across the hospital bed to grasp at the old man's hand, conscious of the two women opposite, clasping each other. Edward lolled his head to one side, eyes flickering with semi-conscious awareness in a silence broken only by the slow, metronomic beep of the electrocardiogram. The weak beat signalled the damage done to the heart, now barely able to keep the blood pumping around the old man's body and only a timely emergency intervention by the on-site team at Fairhaven Grange had saved him, for a few more hours.

Caroline fished in her bag for a tissue and offered it to the tearful carer alongside.

'It's all my fault...' whispered Stephanie.

James broke from his blank, overloaded stare. 'Without you, he'd have been gone long ago. I can't thank you enough for giving me the chance to say goodbye.'

'Fellows,' wheezed Edward from the slackness of his open mouth.

'He's not here.' James dragged himself closer to hear his father's whispers. 'Lie still till the cardiologist from Bristol gets here. It's not everyone that can call in a favour like that, you old dog.'

Edward opened an eye and imperceptibly shook his head. James saw the realisation that it would be a wasted journey but felt the spasmodic grip within his own hand, revealing in tactile trembling what he did not have the strength to say in words.

'Dene...'

James's lips trembled and pressed together. 'She's safe and so am I. I'm coming back here, father, just as you wanted.'

Edward's face creased into a visage of terror as he struggled for breath and shook his head.

'Alright, Professor,' said the attending nurse, clicking at the in-line pain device on the delivery drip. 'Just stay calm.'

Edward continued to fight and screwed his eyes in frustration.

'It's more than pain,' said James. 'What is it, father?'

'Lie...lies. Fellows...I lied...Emily.'

'I don't understand,' he said trying to calm down the man whose grip on life was as tenuous as the grip on James's hand.

'Two words...truth...Dene. I lied...protect you...career'

Edward began to hyperventilate and his back arching laboured breaths became erratic, echoed by the heart monitor to his side. He glanced across at Caroline. 'Fellows...right.'

A final desperate look of agony coincided with his terminal breath. 'Son...' he said, turning wide-eyed as his heart gave out.

'Must forgive...save them...save them both...'

CHAPTER 31

J ames was numb.

The late October cold bit into his lightweight, black gloves trying to elicit an emotional response as he stood motionless, listening to the priest at the open grave.

Ashes to ashes, dust to dust...

The words barely registered, but he was conscious of the many eyes upon him and of the ready arm, should he need it, of Caroline Lewisham at his side. She stood resolute with grief, pausing occasionally to wipe her eyes, and exhaled great steaming breaths that joined the miasma of those that surrounded the lowered coffin like dry ice.

He caught his reflection in the black memorial marble page and distracted his pain by running through the minutiae of what to instruct the monumental mason to inscribe. A wave of loss broke over him and he nuzzled his hand against Caroline's heavy parka. She responded with a generous grasp of her gloved fingers. He thought of the day that his Father must have stood in this exact spot while his infancy had spared him the trauma, with no one apart from colleagues to console him. He saw those that still lived: distinguished doctors, psychiatrists and hospital alumni bent with age, bowed and hooded like a wizened murder of crows. Many of them he knew, a dominant portion of which had added their names to the list of advocates at his disciplinary. James resisted the urge to scoff at the irony; the list of addresses only recently collated for that purpose had been refashioned into a mailing list for his father's funeral.

One stood apart beneath the great yew as though respectful in his distance. Younger and more upright than the others, he remained rigid, his close-bearded face a graven image of grief and unrequited forgiveness.

Fellows stood as still as the lichen-covered angels on the memorials nearby, eyes resolute and unwavering on the artificial grass edged grave of his mentor and onetime friend. He blinked into life and into James's eye-line delivering the unspoken comfort of one who does not know what to say to another at such a time of crisis except "I'm sorry".

James looked down to relieve both of them and shuffled his feet in the damp, tufted grass. The priest continued his recital of Tennyson's classic poem, *Crossing the Bar*, a favourite of his father's and which had been meticulously laid out in his preparations.

> 'Twilight and evening bell,
> And after that the dark!
> And may there be no sadness of farewell,
> When I embark...'

The mention of ships drew his gaze across the treetops to the still, reflecting calm of the sea out in the bay. One other was focussed on the tranquil scene: the tall, once dependable figure of Mike Trebarr, arms wrapped around the back of the blonde, bleary-eyed counsellor. Beyond, head bowed, shuffled Jory, policeman's cap held across his tabard, barely able to contain his sadness on behalf of a friend.

> 'For tho' from out our bourne of Time and
>   Place
> The flood may bear me far,
> I hope to see my Pilot face to face
> When I have crost the bar.'

The service concluded and James stood back and shook hands until he felt that all emotion had been dissolved to the mourners from within him, their kind words of comfort acting to dilute and mitigate his sadness.

'What's she doing here?' asked Caroline, as the crowd dispersed, leaving behind a few close friends to cast soil upon the casket.

From the hedged opening, Emily stood in borrowed black, clutching a small bunch of flowering heather. Her pregnancy had advanced in the previous three weeks to be noticeable, and she lingered close to the Dene cross, a spot still vivid in his mind. Chaperoned by the similar build and style of his father's former carer, she sought his gaze for permission to approach, but it was Stephanie that broke ranks and reached them first.

'I'm sorry, James, but I told her it might not be appropriate, after what happened and all, but she insisted. She'd have come without me in any case, but wearing what, I hate to think. I had to sort her out some of my clothes; hopefully I didn't cause any offence?'

No,' said James, watching as Emily bent down at the graveside. 'It's alright. She has a right just the same as everyone else. How has she been coping and how is the baby?'

'Both well. Things have calmed down a bit and Dr Roscoe thinks it may be down to the distraction and influence of the unborn child. I'll see she gets back to the hostel, so forgive me if I don't come to the wake.'

'I understand, Stephanie, and thank you for all you did for him.'

She offered a hug and beckoned to Emily, retreating to the hedge to allow her to pass.

James whispered to his side. 'You put Roscoe in charge of her?'

Caroline cleared her throat. 'In your absence, yes. Things have calmed down dramatically.'

'Not permanently, then?' He glanced over to see Harriet lean an offering against the marble headstone. She rose and linked hands with the GP who glanced over, nodding with a fleeting acknowledgement, before awkwardly turning away and joining the sombre, red-faced policeman.

'That remains to be seen,' said Caroline. 'I haven't officially reprimanded or relieved you, under the circumstances, though it was your father's final wish you leave this behind and return to Truro.'

'All the relationships I hold dear are unravelling, Caroline; I feel like I am losing the people around me and I have only myself to blame. Everyone is leaving, eventually.'

'Not all,' she said, exhaling a deep cloud of breath.

'I thought they were trying to undermine me, prevent me from doing my job, and now I feel as alone as she does.'

Emily side-stepped several departing mourners and offered her condolences.

'I was very glad to have met him,' she said. 'We liked his smile.'

James listened, ignoring the interchange of pronouns. She fidgeted with the sprig of heather. 'I feel guilty if either of us had anything—'

'No,' said James curtly, before releasing into a sigh and softening his reply. 'He was very ill and confused at the end.

Nothing you did caused what happened. It wasn't your fault, Emily, it was his heart.'

'I'm sorry.'

'I know, and thank you.' He indicated toward Stephanie who stood by the grave, beckoning as she walked away.

'They could be sisters if it weren't for the distance and where they grew up,' said Caroline. 'Maybe it's the Cornish in Emily's past, perhaps?'

James ignored the suggestion, focussing on the solitary figure of Fellows. The director broke free from his reserved stillness and weaved his way over.

Caroline turned to go. 'I'll leave you two alone and see you at the house for the wake.' She hesitated and whispered in his ear. 'He doesn't know about our little conversation.'

'He still thinks I'm clinical lead?'

'Who is on compassionate leave, remember.' Caroline laid a hand on his arm. 'No work talk, James. I'm done feeding him information, and I didn't do it for any commendation; you should know that. I've been upfront about what your father wanted, too. He can read any updated report when it's ready, which means when you are good and ready, understand?'

James met her hazel eyes, and for a moment he wished they were alone so he could take greater comfort in a solitary embrace, enabling the flood of tears to be released from a dam of pent up emotion.

'I'm nailing my flag to your post, Dr Marshall, whichever way the wind blows, so don't let me down.'

She gave him a final squeeze of her hand and departed as Fellows closed and removed his own from his long, wool coat and extended it in condolence.

James shook it. 'Thank you for coming; I wasn't sure if you would.'

Fellows humbly cast his eyes on the trampled grass. 'I

hope this comes out right, but I feel I've lost a second father, for the second time.'

James waited for him to compose himself. 'I understand, and while you weren't fully reconciled, I want you to know he never truly cut you out during his last few weeks. I think he only had the strength to apologise to one of us while he lived, but I think he regretted the issue between you to his dying breath.'

The grey eyes remained fixed as his brow furrowed, searching to comprehend.

'His last words included something for you, information and an apology that only you will understand. I'm damned if I do.'

Fellows moved closer. 'Does it relate to our estrangement? If it does, then I have much to discuss that he may have kept from you.'

'It relates to—'

'Emily!' called Stephanie from the path leading to the church. 'We must go now, please.'

Fellows turned, even as she brushed past, looking her full in the face.

'She knows you,' she said. 'You were with Marshall all those years ago. You tried to help, but Edward sent her away.'

'What's this, James?' he said stepping back as though stung. 'You brought a patient to Edward's funeral?'

'No, I didn't know she—'

'I'm not a patient today, I'm Emily Dunn and she says she knows you.'

Fellows raised an eyebrow at the name and stabbed a finger. 'Are you losing your perspective, James?'

'You didn't believe her either,' continued Emily, 'not until it was too late, and she died.'

Fellows scoffed and flashed his eyes at James. 'We've never

met, young lady, and this is in bad taste. I don't know who you are referring to—"

'Don't patronise us, Fellows,' said Emily. 'She says for you to tell the truth, and maybe this Marshall will understand. He suspects, as have you all your long life, but he may have the courage or conviction to act.'

'Who tells you—what are you talking about, woman?'

'May Dene,' said Emily advancing towards him. Fellows backed away, shooting James a look of consternation and confusion.

'This is some final sick joke of your father's,' he said, raising his hands as though to ward off her outreaching arms. 'My God, man, have you no forgiveness?'

James stepped between them, calling out for Harriet to avoid any physical restraint. In an instant she was over, aided by the rapid return of Stephanie, but Fellows was gone, with a last, shocked glance back to the scrum.

'What the hell was all that about?' he said, twisting to see Emily twitch only once. She became passive and silent except for the gentle hum upon her pale lips. Her pupils flashed into sudden dilation, retreating to pinpoints as she was turned from his gaze. It was a look of defiance, tinged with a hint of satisfaction, despite the inappropriateness of the occasion.

'Let's get you back and in the warm,' said Harriet, one arm linked and accompanied by an apologetic look from Stephanie.

Left briefly by the graveside alone, James was joined by his two closest companions. Silently they greeted each other, putting aside any differences and linked arms in an unspoken bond of friendship. For a while they stood, easy in each other's company, as they had done earlier that spring for another of their own.

James released them and lifted the first impression of the book leaning against the marbled page. Harriet had bookmarked a chapter towards its end, though he wondered if there was any relevance to highlighting the final chapter. He knew its title without turning the page.

Self-diagnosis and the power of forgiveness.

'Harriet wanted you or Edward to have it because it meant a lot to her, and she felt obliged after divulging information to me. If there's any fault, it's mine, James.'

James rolled his lip and shook his head. 'She did the right thing, you both did. I'm glad you are here, so I can say thank you, if not directly to Harriet.'

'I'll let her know.'

James was about to toss the book onto the polished pine coffin lid, four feet below, but he hesitated and turned to look upon the foxed image of his father, one last time. The scratching quill-like dedication fluttered on a stiff, chilling sea breeze.

'Dear Ms Swanson,

There are always more questions than answers. Go with your gut.

Best Wishes, Edward John Marshall.'

'We'll see about that,' he said handing back the book into Mike's keeping and strode through the sodden grass setting the settled rooks to flight like a threat of thunder.

CHAPTER 32

J ames lifted the brass handle and rapped on the townhouse knocker plate.

A moment later, it was answered by Cameron Fellows.

'You had better come in,' he said retreating into the dark hallway. 'I thought you'd come eventually, and I apologise for my sharp words to you last week; Caroline told me you had no part in it and it was inappropriate of me to chastise one of your patients.'

James wiped his feet and closed the door behind him, following the penitent director into his home study.

'Can I get you anything?' he asked. 'Tea, perhaps?'

James accepted the offer and browsed among the books, files, and quiet tick-tocking of a carriage clock on the picture frame laden mantelpiece. He put down his bag and wandered over to look through the old images, several of which contained his father. Hidden behind several more recent pictures was one of a much younger man cradling a newborn baby. James lifted the silver-filigree framed photograph. It was the first time that he could recall Fellows ever smiling, and from the size of the tie and the lapels, he guessed the image to have been taken somewhere in the early to mid-eighties.

'Yes,' said Fellows from behind, startling him. 'It's you.'

James hurriedly placed the image back on the mantelpiece, knocking over several other frames.

'Why do you have a photo of me and my father in your house, especially considering your estrangement?'

Fellows offered him a seat and put down the tray containing the teapot, cups, and saucers. Several napkins emerged from his pocket, and he shuffled a pack of Garibaldi biscuits onto a side plate.

'Because you're my godson,' he said falling stiffly into his worn, burgundy, leather-buttoned armchair. 'Even when he revoked every other aspect of our relationship, he couldn't remove that privilege. Unless I'm mistaken, a Godfather can't be divorced, annulled or whatever the phrase may be, but I still take that honour seriously in memory of one I once called friend.'

James glimpsed the rising disappointment on his face.

'He never told you?'

James shook his head, taking the offered seat beside the small coffee table. He unbuttoned his jacket knocking an elbow into a pole-mounted medical skeleton at his left-hand side. Fellows opened the teapot lid to stir the dark, malty Assam leaves with a spoon. The released steam billowed and swirled around the suspended nylon bones of the macabre, gently swaying, uninvited guest.

'Your father gave me that for my thirtieth,' he said, pouring out the tea into a hovered strainer. 'I used to think he was keeping tabs on me through those bony eye sockets, making sure I didn't step out of line.'

'I see we shared the same anxiety.' James held out his cup as Fellows lifted the plain brown teapot and began to pour. 'As a child, I buried all my teddy bears for the same reason.'

Fellows twitched, splashing the black liquid across the tray.

'Too much information, sorry,' said James, wiping the spill with a napkin. 'He should have told me about you.'

'No one ever told your father what he should do.' Fellows refilled the cup and glanced up at the skull between them. '*When a man masters the art of persuasion, he ceases to be persuaded, except by himself.*'

'Voltaire?'

Fellows switched to a smile and covered the teapot with a knitted mauve cosy, the only splash of colour within the otherwise drab room. 'No. Your father. It was one of the most arrogant and self-assured things I ever heard him say, and one of the last before we parted ways.'

James sipped the strong black tea from the delicate porcelain cup, uniquely feminine in contrast to the bachelor's otherwise plain ornaments dotted around the book-lined study. 'I'm confused why you were so very hard on me during my training and yet here you are, holding onto a memory of something or someone clearly important to you. Did I end up disappointing you, too?'

Fellows stuck out his bottom lip and shook his head. 'I owe you an apology, and yes, in the beginning I selfishly took whatever petty revenge I could against him by forcing you through additional checks and intolerances that my other students did not encounter.'

'And later?'

'When I saw that reconciliation with your father was beyond hope I honoured my obligations to make you a better man than him. You may have bent like a tree beneath a great weight of its branches, James, but you did not break.'

'Making me a better psychiatrist didn't exactly go to plan, did it?' James replaced the cup on the table and prodded the skeleton gently into clinking movement.

The mantelpiece clock chimed, and Fellows waited for the echo to recede. 'On the contrary, it succeeded though not through any direct intervention of mine. I said better man, not better doctor; neither of us could aspire to that. You accept fallibility and consequence; your father could or would not. Flaws are there to test you and strengthen you. Your father had few, but they were deep, and none of them could teach him anything.'

'Are you going to tell me why you fell out so dramatically with him?'

Fellows crossed his legs and sighed. 'I have a feeling it's why you are here now, James. Whatever your father said to you before he died that concerned me must have been very important indeed; time is a precious commodity to those with very little.'

'He said to tell you he was sorry, and that he was wrong about something significant; I'm guessing it's a case that caused the rift between you, which has something to do with Emily Dunn's outburst three days ago.'

'It was,' he said, rubbing his cheek and returning his attention to the skeleton, 'and it does. You should have seen him in his prime, James. Edward Marshall was beyond any teacher or mentor I had ever, or have ever, met. Your father was more like an older brother or father to me following the death of my parents, which is why he sought to protect me from what he described as "pseudo-science". In doing so, he robbed me of an alternate path though my reputation was my own to do with as I pleased, even if it led to the oblivion he feared; he was trying to do the same to you it seems. Protection is a noble thing until it is declined and then enforced despite you. Emily Dunn would, perhaps, agree.' Fellows held out a hand to still the swaying, bony arm at his side.

'I approved your father's request to meddle one last time; he regressed her, didn't he?'

James fidgeted with his fingers to avoid the gaze. 'Yes. It was an attempt to learn more about the historical alter that's caretaking and who emerged at the moment of her suicide attempt. I initially tried to bargain with her for access to Emily's long-term memories, but she had other plans. There were revelations about a former life two hundred years ago that accurately represent the history of my family as researched by my father, convincing details that no-one else could know, and—'

'Coincidences?' said Fellows, leaning back into his chair and bridging his hands beneath his chin. 'Your father used hypnotherapy and past-life regression techniques to help you understand the fragile woman's predicament when traditional talking therapies weren't leading anywhere – am I right?'

James nodded. 'I'm only interested in the patient's welfare and answers to these strange, unlearned behaviours that arise out of nowhere. I know it was risky and you can have my hide if that's what you want, but be honest with me – whoever was fronting at the funeral said they knew you, and my father. Everything either of them has told me has turned out to be true. She's not lying about you, is she?'

Fellows exhaled a mighty breath and relaxed into his chair for a long while, tapping his fingers against the worn leather arm.

'The simple answer is no. I've been keeping a close eye on every case that comes out of St Jude where an alternate personality conflict arises. While I bear some regret that this episode may have strained whatever relationship you have with Caroline and others, I did it with the best of intentions. It appears, however, that the well of communication with my potential interim replacement has now dried up, so I must be frank with you, and I hope you will do the same.' He buried his chin into his chest and stared down into the hands resting in his lap as though unsure where to begin. 'If you haven't already guessed or discovered it, I was the historic precedent your ally, Caroline Lewisham, brought up at your hearing.'

'Father told me, but not the reason behind it. He wouldn't reveal it, though whether it was professional courtesy or to do with protecting you or me I don't know.'

Fellows pursed his lips and glanced at the skeleton. 'That was very noble of him. I know how Caroline learned of this; she's a smart woman and will go far, even if her loyalties and ability to keep confidential information are dictated by an overactive, internal moral compass prone to deviation. You'll almost certainly be aware that she agreed to be my interme-diary in patching things up.' He held up a hand as James sought to interrupt. 'Let me finish this time, James. You don't need to defend her constantly and I said the same to her, about you.

'We share a common curiosity in that we go where the evidence or coincidence leads us.' He rose and took down a file from a shelf nearby. 'Your father did not, and that became the issue between us. He had more to lose than I did, you see.'

He handed over the bound document, indicating for James to open it.

'We also shared a father figure that was such a dominating influence in our lives as to stifle any independent action contrary to his perceived wisdom. I only hope that with his passing that you can do so, finally. I could never explore avenues that might have advanced psychiatry or the search for truth.'

James opened the cover and flicked through the loosely bound pages. Several case notes, medical files, and redacted sheets of text unfurled. 'What truth are you talking about?'

'The same you are searching for and which has brought you to me. Tell me, in a mature adult with no previous history, how many cases of disassociation, schizophrenia or any other personality disorders, unrelated to physiological change, trauma or drug use have you seen where an alter spontaneously manifests to protect the host at a time of critical need?'

James answered quickly. 'None and neither has Caroline. Father was adamant—'

'And prior to recent events, how many cases where a patient has conclusively been proven to have acted with unexplained and unlearned behaviours, say professional portraiture or extreme displays of equestrianism, for example?'

'None.'

Fellows glanced at the file on James's lap. 'Then wouldn't you say the chances of the two occurring concurrently would be tiny indeed, not to mention knowledge of and a sudden discovery of an extremely valuable heirloom that has lain hidden in plain sight for two hundred years?'

'Almost nil.' James flicked through the pages. 'If you discount coincidence.'

'But not nil,' said Fellows, reaching behind from the lowest shelf to toss a copy of his father's book onto the table. 'I do discount it, despite what chapter seven in his bible says. What was it that Emily Dunn said that prompted your father to lie to you?'

James glanced up to see the eager look on the man's face and the tightly clasped hands.

'She whispered something in answer to his final question, but I didn't hear—'

'He asked her for two words, didn't he, and then lied to you when he discovered she had answered correctly?'

James frowned. 'He reacted sharply when she gave him the words, but I thought it was his illness. How do you know all this if Caroline is being honest with me about keeping my off-the-record conversations confidential?'

Fellows opened the teapot and poured in a flask of hot water.

'Because,' said Fellows, replacing the lid and briefly pointing to the skeleton with a trembling hand, 'I can read people almost as well as his majesty did.'

'What was so important about what she whispered in his ear that caused my father to react so badly? I can't recall an instance where he lied to me or anyone; he looked like he'd seen a ghost.'

Fellows leaned forward, wide-eyed and amused by the idiom. 'In one sense he had. The same caretaking alter claiming to be the suicide of an early nineteenth-century woman protecting another woman in similar unhappy circumstances was given the same words thirty-four years ago by your father.'

'Why?' said James, glancing down at his father's book, its page open on the author's picture.

'In case she should return.'

CHAPTER 33

James folded his arms and shook his head in disbelief as Fellows continued from the confines of his armchair.

'I was there when he whispered those words to a patient claiming to be under the same protective influence. He said they were words that no other could guess within the realm of probability and did so at my pleading and great cost to our relationship. I discovered that the personality has a precedent in the area, but he refused to listen to "urban myth" and "impressionable legend".'

'You went to the archives, didn't you? There are records of you visiting.'

Fellows looked across the library on his wall. 'Yes, and I see curiosity is still a trait in you that hasn't been dimmed by time. Your father was unconvinced by the coincidences of repeat historical occurrences, putting them down to local superstition and coincidence. In the darkest days outside of your father's light, I had all but resigned to agree that he was right. I thought the price I paid for my folly was too high until you found her again...'

'That's absurd,' said James, rising to face away from both Fellows and the skeleton.

'Is it? What else did he say before he died?'

James turned and squeezed his jaw with the memory. 'He said that I should save her, save them both, but he was delirious, his brain was undergoing end-of-life trauma—'

He stepped across the room, hands clenched, gathering his thoughts and caught sight of a series of ink drawings on a table overlooking the garden, dew-laden and mossy flagged. He sifted the sheets, revealing the familiar and heavily detailed sketches of horses, nineteenth-century life, wooden sailing ships unloading cargo, dark gowned figures on a headland backlit by bonfire and moonlight, and a sketch of the music box with lid open showing the necklace and other beautiful things within. 'Where did you get these? Shouldn't I have—'

'Being director gives me certain privileges,' said Fellows. 'Legal or not. The answer to your second unfinished question is that these aren't by Emily Dunn – they were sketched by her mother, Angela, in a secure mental hospital in 1984 before she died; look at the date stamp.' James confirmed the assertion and leafed through the sheets. 'This was the case that caused my rift with your father.'

'Angela Dunn was the patient to whom my father gave the two words, like a password in the event of the personality returning?'

Fellows nodded. 'I should be grateful, all things considered, that in a moment of weakness to shut me up he did it all, otherwise we wouldn't be having this conversation now. I believed Angela Dunn, or more correctly, I believed the alter was telling the truth about its existence, while your father, incorrectly but understandably at the time, did not. The question is, James, what do you believe?'

James confirmed the assertion and leafed through the

sheets. 'Consciousness and memory can't be transferred, and it's not hereditary – you can't be suggesting that?'

'No, I'm not.' Fellows tapped the side of his cheek and stared at the file opposite. 'Strange how two people who never met, conversed or were aware of each other could share the same artistic motivations, subjects and identical style of drawing, not to mention a shared history, pattern of speech and memory, don't you think? Even the best forgers would struggle with that; it's the same artist, in one sense, James, or the same influence.'

'My father warned me about not seeing coincidence for what it was, all we need is the connection without resorting to any "pseudo-science" as you put it. Emily's mother must have passed on some information in a letter or picture, to prompt the two-word response, perhaps via the men that dropped off her belongings?'

'The only connection is that both women suffered a life-changing event at or near Maiden Point; Emily an attempted suicide, and her mother a pre-natal depression that advanced into self-harm and addiction. When I tried to discover the truth and bring it to his attention, your father quashed it as fancy, forcing me to diagnose what we originally suspected as Ganser and suspending me when I resisted. By the time I recovered my feet and reputation, he had sent Angela Dunn away, out of reach. In those days she couldn't get access to the child because of her self-harming tendencies, and the care-taking alter realised there was no way out for a mentally ill woman with schizophrenia who claimed to hear voices. It left her, or at least that is my interpretation of what happened.'

James listened and laid out the series of sheets with vignettes depicting church life on the table: A wedding couple in Regency attire, exiting the door surrounded by similarly dressed revellers; a coffin being borne in by Napoleonic-era soldiers, caps placed haphazardly among the simple flowering wreath on the lid; the reconstruction of the church tower with strong masons in shirts and breeches lifting cut pieces of stone high into the air on wooden scaffolds. One photocopied sheet stood out, words scratched furiously into the original notepaper:

Why won't you talk to me? Where have you gone, sweet nightingale?

'What's this?' he said, lifting and turning it to Fellows.

'The last thing she wrote. Her file shows several weeks where the team thought they were making progress with no fronting of any personality but her own, right up to the point where they relaxed their supervision and she hung herself from a curtain rail using a bed sheet. You won't remember, but he dragged you along when he couldn't find a sitter; he was still on the paperwork as the clinician in charge. I rightly berated him for it when he came to me for solace, and that was the last time we spoke. I admit I was angry and unsympathetic, and I confess to you that I regret my words and actions at the time. From what little he offered, it was obvious that in the short period, a dependency on the caretaking personality had developed—'

James threw him a glance, conscious of the words at his hearing and its similar contributory factor in the death of Isobel Lee.

Fellows continued as he looked away, aware of the sensitivity. 'A reliance without which she could not cope once parted.'

'The subject matter of these drawings can be explained,' said James, unconvinced. 'Emily's mother came from these parts, so there is no coincidence there. I know for a fact that a woman in the not-too-distant past has visited the museum archives, so that would explain the similarities. Emily likely visited the place to research her family tree, just like my father. She took the drawings from her mother as inspiration in her own style, perhaps even to the point of them being indistinguishable.' He glanced up to see Fellows watching him intently.

'And yet you don't sound very convinced,' said Fellows. 'In your reports, you note Emily has no affinity or aptitude to explain this; why would she lie? Look to the last page in that folio.'

James dutifully obliged and froze at the sight of his father as a young man, his mother's music box on his lap.

'It's from Angela Dunn's estate,' said Fellows. 'I finally caught up with what little she had on file when your father headed off to teach at Oxford. We both know who sketched them though, or at least claims to, am I right?'

James tore through the rest of the files for some kind of understanding. Names flashed in and out of the text, all with dated stamps, but several names remained constant: Angela Dunn, Edward Marshall, Cameron Fellows...

May Dene.

James studied the dates, handwritten in places, typed in others. 'These files are all from thirty-odd years ago.'

'As are the drawings,' said Fellows rising to turn over the drawing of Edward Marshall.

Marshall, October 1985

'It's not possible,' said James, hesitantly. 'I dropped a book that opened to reveal the author picture of my father, and she recognised him – how can someone who has never met another, remember them or recall two words said to someone long dead?'

'How can someone remember a music box with a secret only she knew,' said Fellows pointing to the object in the drawing, 'or an old folk tune that accompanies it, or the ability to ride like a cavalry officer's pupil?'

'*Sweet Nightingale*,' said James. 'The archivist says it's from the end of the eighteenth century.'

'There are others, such as Thomas Cotter, who recall it, too.' Fellows leaned over and parted several earlier sheets to reveal the old man's name. 'Picture the scenario of a man, local to St Jude, who cannot swim, and a drowning child; need I go on?'

James pinched his eyes, trying to blot out the hazy summer adventure, long ago, that almost cost him his life.

'So Emily is a copycat case or some bizarre, unfathomable—'

'Coincidence?' said Fellows, raising an eyebrow. 'You sound like your father. You know this is not, even though every fibre of your logical, rational mind is telling you otherwise. I was the same before my reputation was "saved" by my suspension and probation. All the while, a heavily pregnant Angela Dunn, at risk of being sectioned, was moved to London out of my reach or knowledge, continuing to believe she was being cared for by the same caretaking alternate personality that her daughter now appears to have inherited.' He continued, whispering as though to himself. 'God knows few others cared for her before it left her, unable to keep them together, and she died.'

'You are hypothesising a hereditary link between schizophrenia and an identical, alternate personality? That's absurd.'

'And yet here we are,' said Fellows. 'But no, I am not, though this is the first instance of this so-called caretaking influence known as May Dene, being involved in a family unit; that is something totally unexpected and possibly the only coincidence in the whole affair.'

'You have non-anecdotal evidence of other cases where an alternate personality has fronted as the same early nineteenth-century suicide?' said James.

'All with the same name,' said Fellows rising two-handed from his seat.

James's hand shook and he put aside the drawing, trying

to make sense of the situation. He glanced down at an earlier entry with another familiar name. 'What has Tom Cotter got to do with all this?'

'It's the very first encounter in my working life, though not if you search back far enough through local stories. Thomas Cotter admitted three years earlier to having been influenced by someone in the saving of a small, drowning boy out in St Jude Bay.'

'Tom Cotter presented as May Dene after he saved my life?' said James.

'No, just the memory of the sudden interventionist encounter, soon over before they pumped drugs into his already turbulent mind and he became so confused that not even he understood what had happened.'

'So, what are you suggesting? said James. 'That we have a supernatural influence, an entity called May Dene that has been constantly looking after people through the ages trying to protect them?'

Fellows frowned and shook his head 'I'm surprised at you,' he said. 'That is neither the most rational explanation nor the simplest. The cases I've collected over the years aren't down to ghosts with time on their hands. The supernatural, by its very nature, cannot be measured; if it could, it wouldn't be supernatural, would it?'

'My father once said that you had an interest in past life regression. Is this where the conversation is leading?'

Fellows stared at the pictures on the mantelpiece. 'Not as a conclusion, but as a starting point to unlocking something that might fundamentally change the way we view the mind.'

He strode across the room and dragged out a heavy box file from the burgeoned bookshelf. Within, he lifted several folios and reeled off a list of curious incidents from their opening pages.

'1850, a young girl, mute, begins to sing and talk, especially provident and timely, as she is about to be hanged for murder close to the crossroads at Maiden Moor. Her sudden testimony incriminates the real murderer, Peter Fields, and upon his hanging, she returns to a life of silence.' Fellows shoved the file into the crook of his arm and opened another. '1864, Jennifer Grey, rows out single-handed in a heavy sea to rescue six men in a damaged lifeboat from a ship, wrecking out between Maiden Point—'

James shook his head. 'People do extraordinary things when under pressure, that much I agree, but it's too far back to be anything but anecdotal.'

Fellows flicked through the file, presenting the newspaper clipping with a photograph of a Victorian period woman in a wheelchair. 'Except that Jennifer Grey was a paraplegic left at the end of the quay that fateful night to watch for storm faring ships bound for Penzance.' Before James interjected, Fellows paced the room, reciting the testimony from the clipping.

'The woman, whose misfortune in life was to be without the use of any purposeful limb, maintains that by the grace of God or divine intervention itself, found herself suddenly able to walk and man the gig to save the drowning souls of the Santa Maria. Upon reaching the men, and bereft of any further need for rescue, the men she saved rowed back to the safety of the shore accompanied and invigorated by her gentle folk tune, *The Sweet Nightingale*, sworn by the men to be strangely heard over the sound of the raging sea.'

'It's coincidence...it has to be...' muttered James, conflicted, and in a struggle to satisfy and ground his reality.

Fellows traced a finger down the page of a newly opened folio that appeared to serve as some kind of index. 'All in all, James, twenty-three instances of a sudden and unexplained or learned, life-preserving behaviour attributed in seventeen of those to a presence by the name of Mary-Anne Dene; all within a six-mile radius of the town.'

'So, what is it about St Jude? You're not telling me some guardian angel is looking after the place?'

'It isn't just St Jude.' said Fellows briskly turning to look at the upper shelves. 'There are other parts of the country and the world where certain locations hold strong legends or traditions that seep into the very fabric of the place and its people.'

'So, are you going to tell me what you think this is?'

'It's something human, global. What if the mind can perform tasks under extreme pressure, and be influenced by nurture as much as nature? External influences, myths and legends, stories and half-remembered truths, all conspiring to affect the mind and unlock its potential.' Fellows crept forward like a hunting cat towards him.

'It wasn't Caroline that wanted a second opinion, was it? It was you, in order to follow this absurd line of reasoning once more.'

'To be certain of any conclusion or scientific method, it is important to remove all biases, the greatest of which is the observer himself.'

'Meaning I observed for you with no prior bias – why didn't you just ask me?'

'Listen to yourself,' said Fellows. 'I've just demoted you in all but name, which was not my doing, my hands were tied, and then I come to you and ask for your help when you discover May Dene has returned once again. With the acrimony still existing between myself and your father, what would you have said then?'

'I would say what I do now,' said James, 'that this borders on obsession, paranoia and parapsychology, not psychiatry. This sounds like some sort of conspiracy theory nonsense. How would you ever even be able to prove this?'

'With two words,' said Fellows. 'The same ones your father took to his grave. We have to be swift, all evidence suggests that once the patient feels in control of their lives and all fear and further trauma are far behind, the influence disappears, unless—' He looked at James with a contorted look of discomfort.

'Unless we continue in these rare cases to keep and study this influence by encouraging and maintaining a sense of jeopardy and fear in the subject...'

James stepped back in horror at the monstrous suggestion.

Fellows, overreaching, backtracked.

'You misunderstand me, James...'

'I see your mind, clearly, Cameron, and I remind you of the Hippocratic Oath you now abandoned. What you propose is grossly unethical and no better than abuse in the name of whatever you are calling this study. I will have no part in it, director or not. I will do no harm, even if everything you say is true.'

Fellows picked up his father's book and beat his hand on the cover. 'Think of the advances and the unlocking of a puzzling aspect of the mind. What if we all had the capacity deep in our subconscious, to perform incredible feats, drawn from instinct but tempered by experience and external factors hitherto dismissed? Consider babies that can swim within moments of being born, people under immense stress that have performed feats of strength or stamina that are impossible. Whatever this is, the subconscious is acting in a way that we cannot compute. This is the first instance of this being hereditary, from Angela Dunn to her daughter Emily. Think of the tremendous opportunities, James, and the advancement of our reputations. We—I could finally reach my full potential with such a discovery! Greater even than your father.'

James lifted his bag and glanced at the mantelpiece picture.

'Out of respect for who you once were, and the love my father once bore you, this conversation never took place Dr Fellows; I will have no part in it.'

'I could have you removed, permanently, and not just from this case.'

James turned, understanding the connotation.

Fellows launched himself to clutch at his jacket. 'You must continue what I have started, my retirement will soon be upon me and I will not have access to patients unlike yourself. I can pave the way for you — there are still people at Oxford not wholly under the influence of your father who would listen to us...'

James shook his arm free. 'I say again what I said in the boardroom several months ago: I have no interest in my reputation or furthering yours, where a patient of mine is at stake.'

James raced through the hallway pursued by the director.

'Wait! If my plan does not commend itself to you, then there are only likely a few days to investigate. The alter does not remain when the patient is safe, or the jeopardy cannot be solved by its intervention. You must act quickly—'

James threw open the door and turned on the threshold to look for the memory of a man he once knew but finding only a pale imitation.

'Yes,' he said, 'I must, and that is the only thing we are agreed upon.'

CHAPTER 34

James sat on the bench at the quay's end, hands in his pockets and neck buried into a scarf, wondering if she would come. He was sure the strength of the prevailing wind wouldn't stop her, assuming she had been the first one to open the curtains to see his note, bubble-gummed to the outside of Emily's window. He knew he could not gain entry to the refuge whilst on compassionate leave, and the plain-clothed policemen that took shifts within would require some reason to visit out of hours or at least a convincing excuse that James had yet to conjure. Taking careful stock of the situation, and the surrounding empty street, he had mounted the wall like a novice cat burglar and grazed an arm dismounting into the small yard. Retreating with all the grace of a forty-year-old psychiatrist climbing a rotting trellis, he had pulled himself, grimy and grazed, back over the wall, disappearing towards the pre-dawn squall of the seafront.

He caught sight of Emily as she rounded the corner of the side street, her donated and unfashionably lurid parka in stark contrast to the grey surroundings that would cloth St Jude until the sunny canopies and spring days returned. She

glanced behind, approaching like a cold war agent suspected of being followed.

'You got my note?' said James, shifting along the seat.

She removed a scrap of colourful paper sticky with pink goo from her pocket and sat down. '*Austen's bench, 8 am, J.M.* – I knew it couldn't be Williams; what you told me about your wife – I'm guessing few others know about, right? I'm guessing this isn't a professional call.'

'You are right on both scores. I'm in danger of being taken off your case when I return from compassionate leave and needed to see you, to ask you honestly a few things that are causing me to question my rationality.'

'You are asking me, a woman that is suffering from delusions, to put your mind at rest? Why do I sense I'm about to be told things aren't as they first seemed and that I've been right all along?'

James pinched at his nose with his gloved hands. 'Just before my father died, he said that the man you gave a tongue lashing to at the funeral had been right, that May Dene had appeared before and to them both, as a protective influence of your mother's.'

Emily sat back and stared at the bell buoy, bobbing and ringing in the swell, just outside the calmer waters of the small harbour. 'It's why those drawings Amancia gave you look the same as the ones on my wall, isn't it?'

'Yes. I'm at a loss to explain to you how this, or your ability to ride like a pro can manifest. I believe you when you say that you have no aptitude or knowledge of learning this. I believe you now. Not to mention—' He withdrew and opened the glasses case to reveal the precious jewellery. '—knowledge of the necklace and box that have been with my family since Thomas Dene died.'

Emily lightly laid a finger over one sapphire, resting her

other across her unborn child. 'It's May's necklace; the one belonging to her mother that she hid.'

'My family always maintained that something of great value was once housed inside and that a Dene would one day return to claim it. They thought it was only a box that would be reclaimed, but I give it to you now to make a new start far away from Bermondsey or north Cornwall.'

He pressed into her hand.

'I can't accept this,' she said. 'It feels like you are paying me off so you have a clear conscience, or that you don't have to come to the same conclusion I have.'

'Whoever you are, or whatever you want,' said James, 'is something bigger than I can deal with right now. My world is falling apart and whether you are telling me the truth or some elaborate story for whatever ends, I need it to stop. My father all but begged me to drop the case and said it had torn apart many lives. I know you likely visited the archives and learned all of this from there.'

'How many times do I have to tell you,' she said, 'I've never been to any archives—'

James raised his voice. 'I want you to be honest, now that you have this – who are you and why are you doing this to me? My father died believing the impossible and you've convinced another man of something similar. I was only trying to help you.'

'We both need to know,' she said, shrinking from his words and gripping at the case. She screwed her eyes as though trying to avoid a sneeze and shuddered with such violence that James wondered if she was having a fit. As he sought to calm her, alongside himself, she opened her eyes and James saw that Emily was no longer there. She held out her hands in rejection to any assistance and rose to a commanding height to match the confident Cornish accent.

'My name is Mary-Anne, daughter of Ariadne and Thomas Dene, born in 1789 and betrothed, against my will, to Henry Fallon at the age of twenty-four. I bore a child out of wedlock that did not survive and ended my life in an act of self-murder on the cliffs of Myrgh an Mor. The daughter of the sea raised my shameful spirit from the deep cold of the bay to atone for my guilt.' She turned over the necklace to point at the initials stamped, almost imperceptibly, around the clasps securing the jewels to the fine silver work surrounding the sapphires.

James squinted to read the fine letters. 'T.D, M.D, A.D.'

'My father and mother beside me, wrought in distant lands in better times when the world was at peace, before she died.' She removed a glove and held onto James's exposed wrist. 'Now tell me whether you truly believe I am who I say I am, for your father did not, even when I recounted our precious, secret words given to me decades ago.'

'It's impossible,' said James. 'Emily visited the archives weeks before coming here. There's a rational explanation. Why are you doing this to Emily, and me? Tell me what else you want from me. I need to understand what is really going on and why Fellows and my father, and the other coincidences, just keep leading down the same irrational path.'

She tightened her grip on his wrist and he glanced down at her painted nails. 'In token payment for the necklace and your noble gesture.'

James shut his eyes as he reeled with the overwhelming sensation of falling, gripping with his free hand at the armrest of the bench. His senses sharpened, and he tasted the salt water through his nose and mouth as though drowning, sinking into the blackness of deep water. He tried to cry out but his mouth was filled with water and he panicked, opening his eyes, struggling to breathe.

The view of the quay was replaced with that of a darkened room. As he tried to combat the lung-bursting lack of breath, he caught sight of a heavily side-whiskered man pacing back and forth in anxious contemplation as a woman in the final painful acts of giving birth, whimpered with her bed-bound exertion. An elderly maid offered words of comfort and hands of deliverance as the mother cried with final, excruciating effort to bring the squealing first sounds of new life into the world amid the blood and blankets of the grand bed.

James struggled to release his hand but he felt her grip, sharpened by her piercing nails, intensify.

I can't breathe!

The scene shifted to a window. Outside, next to a carriage stood the elderly maid and her husband receiving something blanketed and bundled, protected by a hooded wicker basket. The fatherly figure plucked at his long whiskers and opened an ornate box, sparsely filled with silver spoons. He reached into his frock coat pocket and lifted out a golden pocket watch, depositing the personal item to join the meagre treasure. The engraved geometric segments shone with fresh lacquer as he gently lowered the lid and left a lingering palm upon its motif before he encouraged them both to mount the step. The carriage drove away, and the man glanced grimly up at the window, now blurred by the streaming of tears from the woman whose memory James shared.

James felt himself passing out, drowning, a heavy ringing in his ears that dimmed the sounds of the air above. Something moved in the dark water. He raised a feeble, farewell hand to the distant, rippling sky as his wrist was yanked upwards to break the surface. James opened his mouth to release the final bubbling remnants of spent air from his lungs as his head emerged above the water and he spluttered into painful gasping and the lung burning air of a summer's day. With salt-stinging eyes, he forced the water from his lungs in convulsive, coughing wheezes, and saw the rescue boat in the distance as Tom Cotter swam at James's neck-clasped side with deep, steady backstrokes.

'Don't be afraid...' Tom said calmly into his ear, rolling him onto his back.

He felt his wrist slip free from Emily's grip and James tipped onto the promenade as she released him, landing on his knees with hands outstretched. He retched, but found no water in his lungs, trying in vain to subdue the powerful feeling of returning his body to air from near-drowning.

'What was that, and those times before?' he said, panting and clutching at his wrist to find several reddening welts forming from Emily's nail tightened grip.

'My father and the shame that the Cartwrights took away from me.'

'Tom Cotter,' said James. 'My rescue...'

'My memories of the man who listened when I called out to save you.'

James rocked back and clambered upright to stagger to the end of the seawall. 'How?...'

'The "why" is more important than the "how" you said.' She walked forward and James put out a hand to distance himself from her. 'This isn't happening. I'm ill, suffering from my own post-traumatic stress, possibly a delusional...'

'Is it real to you?' she said, halting and snapping the case shut before placing it in her pocket.

'Yes, like I'm there and reliving it.'

'You understand then, finally?' she said. 'Emily needs to be kept safe, but if you will not assist her, and for the sake of the child, I must depart. I cannot countenance the thought of her being imprisoned in an institution, like her mother, because of my interference, not again.' James watched her gentle face soften, as she held out her hand, placing the other on her belly. 'Unless you want me to stay, Marshall. I could be here, with you and bear the child to live a life alongside you – to make you happy. I could ease your grief...'

James retreated from the sudden suggestion and backed away from her. 'No! You are mistaken in my intentions. I only want to see Emily safe and returned to health, nothing more. I came looking for answers, not...'

She lowered her gaze, but he could see the pained look of rejection, just as he had with Isobel Lee. 'Forgive my forthright intentions, Marshall, they were selfish, born out of a desire to have something that does not belong to me. I see that now.' she said. 'I'm going back, where I belong.'

James fled from the encounter, desperate to get out of sight and sound of the sea and into the lonely quiet of the empty house.

The sedatives and music box would do the rest.

James woke two hours later and winced with the memory of his confrontation with Emily. His last cyclical thoughts on falling asleep returned as though a pause button had been reactivated on waking. Isobel Lee and Emily Dunn emerged, his mind replayed the awkwardness and similarities between the two denials for their affection, six months apart. He swung his legs over the bed and rubbed the remnants of fleeting, forgetful sleep from his eyes, recalling the words of Christine Lee.

You promise me you'll save this woman, the one they call the maiden, from whatever comes her way.

He wondered about his future, and what Caroline had planned for him. Summoned to appear the following day, he wondered whether her succinct request bore more than a return-to-work assessment. She had been evasive, and James pondered whether she had decided on his future. Relationships had suffered, even as those around him tried to warn him, but he rued the coolness between them most of all. Would she dare to ask him what he really thought was going on, even when all he knew was that history appeared to be repeating itself and that doctor and patient were heading for a similar outcome to that of Isobel Lee? Telling her what Fellows thought would not improve things, as he had played a part in that diversion.

Any mention of the continued bizarre visions and hallucinations would end the conversation and his career. There was an overwhelming conflict between his reality and what he was experiencing. His father's dying words returned to haunt him.

Save them...save them both...

He lay back on the damp pillow. Caroline had counted on him to pull through, to be the man she thought he was, and he had failed her, himself, and possibly the recovery of Emily Dunn. Not only had he refused her advances, alter or no, but he had denied the existence of her reality to bolster the soft, shaky foundations of his own. He panicked as he realised his folly and the remembrance of her upset and where it might lead; what it might encourage her to do.

I'm going back, where I belong...

She meant Bermondsey, right? he asked himself, his mind speeding through all the other possibilities: London, Carmalt...

...Maiden Point.

He reached for his phone to find it alive and angrily buzzing in his hand. He glanced down and fear gripped him, as it had done six months prior when his best friend had called to inform him of Isobel Lee's whereabouts at the base of the cliff, hours before his wife had died.

Jory Richards Calling.

'Tell me it's good news,' said James.

'You sound rough, Jimbo. Heavy night?' said the

policeman jovially. James absorbed the tone of every word; this was not the sound of a man reporting a suicide. He berated himself for sensing the worst and relaxed momentarily. His best friend at least would have been here in person to deliver that devastating news, almost certainly alongside Mike Trebarr.

'Yes, and no; what is it?'

'Just keeping you in the loop. We've found a stolen car, registered to a London address. It's been abandoned behind the old warehouse units outside of town, but someone's been sleeping rough in it until recently. There's also evidence that they or someone else has been camping out in the spinney behind there, but it's a few days old.'

'You think it's Williams?'

'Could be. There are remnants of tarpaulin and the recent spate of thefts of men's clothing off washing lines and food from the farms and shops without cameras means someone is about, and desperate. Bill at the camping shop says a man fitting William's description shoplifted a sleeping bag and supplies over a week ago before we put out the picture.'

'He's here, and after Emily. I gave her the necklace...'

'You did what?' said Jory with alarm.

'I just wanted her to get out of here, away from everything and everyone. She needed options, and I needed answers.'

'Have you lost your mind? She's out there somewhere, right now, with a hundred grand around her neck with a murderer on the loose that is looking for both. What answers are you talking about?'

'You'll think I'm nuts, but there's something more to her condition than I can explain; she's telling the truth and the only thing stopping my rational brain from falling apart is the knowledge she went to the archives. Even the hospital director and my father have played their part in this. I have told no one, not even Mike, but my father's last words to me urged me to believe in something unbelievable.'

'I think you need a break, mate. A long break while we sort this all out because you are making things worse for all concerned. The refuge warden has just called to say Emily's room has been ransacked; it's a professional job, nice and quiet. Someone came in through the back and must have been watching the place to know which room was the easiest and most accessible to gain entry. There's been an almighty stink about the lack of surveillance and it's tense down here at the station; apparently the handover team didn't appear and no one was covering the inside. The woman in the room above reported hearing something downstairs around 8 am, and they saw Emily go about half an hour before, so they knew it wasn't her. They pressed the panic button, but he was gone before any of our lot could get there. If it was him, then she had a lucky escape. Whoever it was has made a mess but doesn't seem to have taken anything.'

'Has she come back yet?'

'Not while the boys were there getting prints and statements. It was over an hour ago, though. We have a patrol car out looking for her as we speak.'

'I saw her this morning, at the promenade,' said James evasively. 'Have you checked the seafront?'

'Yes,' said Jory. 'Do you mean "saw" or "*saw*"?'

'I spoke with her but I came back after feeling ill.'

'Why do I get the feeling there is more to this than you are telling me? Williams is getting desperate and running out of time. If he finds Emily before we do, then it could be game over.'

'Do you think he'd leave her alone if he got the means to pay off his debt to these Russians?'

'You're the psychologist. You tell me. The question is, will he get what he came for?'

James rose and parted the curtains to see the grey mid-morning mist. 'When you find her, you'll need to move her—'

'Already on it. Your temporary replacement in charge has agreed to move her to the Quaker meeting house at Kerrian Hove – I'm on my way over to check how secure it is. The City of London Police are sending a firearm trained female officer to stay in an adjoining room.'

'Do you think it will come to that?'

'No, we'll get Williams before then. He can't move if he's around St Jude, and Kerrian is too far to walk without getting spotted by someone, even if he finds out where we are taking her. If she returns before we find her, I'll come and pick her up on my way back. When you get back from leave, your team will have to jump through a few hoops to continue with her recovery – if he can steal one car, he can steal another, and we don't want any of them followed. Probably best for them to do things remotely from now on.'

'Agreed. I can help fix things up at the refuge, and if she returns, I need to apologise before you move her.'

'What for?'

'I was unprofessional earlier. I screwed up big time, but the only saving grace from my stupidity is at least she wasn't there when the place was done over.'

CHAPTER 35

The warden opened the locker using the master key with a shaking hand. The visit from the police and the breaking in had unsettled his nerves, and he left to return to his vigilance at the front porch. James looked within at the neatly organised packets and tins, biscuits and bubblegum, hunting around for the necklace. There was no evidence of forced entry or rushed examination, but there was also no sign of the valuable object or the glasses case. Emily had not returned and now had it on her person, wherever she was, in a small town shared with her abuser; a man desperate to get his hands on one precious item and reclaim another.

James returned to step through Emily's door and looked mournfully at the ransacked room. Linen, clothes and emptied, upturned drawers lay strewn upon the soft, boot-printed mattress. The forced latch of the window was mangled and surrounded by hastily driven in screws, securing the damaged frame to the sill. Stephanie stooped to retrieve the scattered drawings creased and water-stained by the trampling prints of large boots.

'Did you find it?' she said.

'No, it's not there. Do you have any idea where Emily could be right now?'

'No idea, poor lamb.'

James banged on the grubby partition wall. 'I was so stupid, lost my patience and tried to get her to see reason. I grew frustrated when she wouldn't accept the evidence that she was deluding herself.'

Stephanie frowned with disappointment, and James looked away in shame. 'That's unlike you, Dr Marshall. What evidence?'

'Several weeks before Emily appeared, a woman requested access to old documents at the county archive in Truro looking for information on the Denes; there has only been one request in the past forty years for the information she copied—'

'What makes you think it was her?' she said scooping up several more sheets and rising to meet him.

'They didn't leave a name and the person who should have recorded it said she left in a hurry. Who else could it be?'

'Around the middle of August?'

'Yes, said James. 'She must have come over, got the information, scouted out the area. I just don't understand why she would have lied to give us the impression that she hadn't.'

He ran his fingers stiffly through his hair and rubbed at his unshaven face.

'She's not told one lie since she's been with us, Dr Marshall,' she said tutting. 'I'm not as learned as you, but we both know that sick people with other personalities aren't lying either and I don't believe her capable of it.'

James felt his cheeks redden, and he slunk his hands into his pockets as she continued. 'It wasn't Emily at the archives, it was me.'

'You?' he said incredulously. 'The young guy said the woman had a tattoo—'

Stephanie rolled up her sleeve to reveal a decorative ink band bearing the name of a man. 'Emily and I both wear the scars of our abusers on our bodies, and the memory of them in our heads.

'I picked up your blessed father's bits of paper and lists for his family research, the papers he left to you. The bus was late, putting me behind, and I remember it was a baking hot day otherwise I'd have had my long sleeves to hide my arms. I didn't know what procedures I was supposed to follow. I've never been in such places or seen the sense in filling out long forms when your father had already requested them. The wet drip of a boy on the counter handed me the papers, and I took them. Your father said I was his "genealogical assistant" when you visited the Grange a few weeks ago, did he not?'

James slumped down on the bed, head in his hands. 'What an idiot...'

Stephanie sat down and placed an arm gently around him. 'That's three lots of Marshall's I've comforted over the years; your father most recently when he thought he'd lost you; your mother in this very room when things got too much for her one day; and now you.'

James sighed and glanced into her gentle, care-lined face. 'I've made a terrible mistake, I thought—'

'Well, you thought wrong, and we need to get her back, don't we? What made you think she was coming all this way from London to study family history for?'

'Her mother was from here – Angela Dunn; have you heard of her?'

Stephanie rolled down her sleeve and laid her hands on the drawings in her lap. 'There was a teenager who used to sell tickets down at the harbour, though Dunn's a common enough name in these parts. I remember a pale-faced girl with dark hair, not dissimilar to our Emily's, but longer. There was gossip about her going about with Tom Cotter after his heroics because he was much older than she was. They were both suffering in their own way, so I guess they made good company despite the age difference and were a "whole from two parts" as they say around here. There was talk of her being poorly upstairs,' she tapped the side of her head, 'despite what your father and the other young man who accompanied him did to help. There was a rumour that she was also with child. I never saw her again, and neither did Tom after she tried to—'

Her face strained with the mention of the word. James heard the thudding of his heart in his head in the utter silence and offered his hypothesis with a glance at her closed mouth. 'She went to Maiden Point, to jump, but something stopped her.'

Stephanie nodded. 'Or someone.' She fidgeted with the pile of drawings in her hand and skimmed through to find the beautiful Regency woman, turning it and clutching the self-portrait of May Dene to her chest. The lower portion of the sketch was now complete, and an almost carbon copy of that drawn by Emily's mother, unseen by her and held within a file in Fellows's possession. The curved lines had developed into arms cradling a newborn child, whose tiny hand reached out toward the necklace.

We both know who sketched them though, or at least claims to...

'You'll think of me as rustic and daft, but women of my generation don't go up there as a rule, not alone at any rate. Call it superstition, but we only go there together to remember her, and countless others, at the Haldwyn when we make the maiden. It serves as a memorial to those whose names we can no longer remember, and the first poor soul that we do. Some things are best forgotten, while others are not.'

She lowered her voice and looked him squarely in the eyes. 'I know you spoke with Christine Lee.'

'She said you had a large part to play in our reconciliation,' said James, 'and her acceptance and ability to live with what happened to Isobel.'

'We look after our own, James.' She shuffled through the drawings of Carmalt, bonfires and headlands, finally coming to pause on the young boy being pulled from the waters of St Jude Bay. 'So does Mary-Anne Dene.'

'You can't believe this is true, that something is watching over St Jude, returning to stop those from repeating something terrible from happening or drowning.'

'We do so to remember her, James, and the child that lived and was sent away. Long before Mary Cartwright, your ancestor, returned to honour her mother and begin the tradition of the making, and long before the cliff was renamed, we are told that the legend of the daughter of the sea still lingered. Ever watchful, and sometimes taking action to save our women and children, the superstition continued to ensure the appeasement of whatever still lives there.'

'Why didn't it save Isobel Lee or May Dene in the first place?'

Stephanie put aside the drawings and dry-rubbed her hands. 'We don't know, but many of the maiden makers have worked alongside the daughter of the sea in places such as this, on an earthly level. We don't question things beyond our ken or understanding. Remembering and honouring is enough. The "why" she is here, is more important than the "how".'

James frowned. 'Emily said the same thing to me this morning, recounting what I said to her at our first contact.'

He looked up to see the carer's thoughtful face. 'Leigh Anderson was there—'

'There are only the three of us makers left, and her return is making everyone nervous.' She glanced around the room. 'Danger is here, and in the town. People are worried and beginning to wake up and ask questions about the long past. We do not know whether what we have done to honour the daughter of the sea has encouraged her return; we fear her as much as love her.'

'Even if I believed this, and that I am somehow related to this Mary-Anne Dene, what am I supposed to do?'

She turned to hear the wind whistling through the gaps in the temporary window repair. The breeze unsettled the drawings at his feet, folding over an image of St Jude Church, a woman in Regency dress standing before a carved cross, cradling a baby of willow and stones.

'Tell her she is not forgotten,' said Stephanie. 'That the child lived, and the line continues – in you. She needs to know the truth and maybe that will finally release her from the guilt and pain. Follow your father's last words, James, but you have to let go, to save them both.'

———

'Emily's been missing for nearly three hours now,' said James to the car's hands-free system. 'She's not at the ruins; I've checked. Mike's been up to the cliffs, but the mist is coming in from the sea and visibility is close to zero. He reckons she couldn't get there on foot in the time. Old Tom stopped me on the promenade to tell me he'd seen her heading north, so I'm pulling into the churchyard as we speak.' He lowered the side window to let in cool, fresh air to clear the rising panic.

'I'm still over at Kerrian for another half hour at least, but the City boys are flooding the town with extra men,' came the voice of the policeman. 'I'll do a sweep of Maiden Moor on my way back. Over and out.'

James pulled into the lay-by alongside two other cars, the boots of which were open and filled with arrangements of flowers. Several women milled around the church entrance before going in and James followed, briefly glimpsing the wedding preparations for the following day. One volunteer came out with the rusting watering can and placed it beneath the dribbling open tap.

'Have you seen a woman, early thirties, dark hair in the churchyard this morning,' said James. 'She may be upset—'

'The woman on the horse that saved that child?' said the florist, indicating behind him. 'Over there by the newer graves.'

James turned round to see Emily, back turned, at the grave of Isobel Lee. Relief overwhelmed him and he exhaled deeply, before clenching his fist at the proximity of the one place he still feared to go.

'We gave her some spare bits we had; they'll only go to waste, and she saved that kiddie, after all.'

'Thank you,' said James turning to walk down the soggy grass path. He called out, and she briefly acknowledged him over her shoulder but remained standing beside the white granite. His steps became heavy as he approached the grave and he looked across at the slick, wet marbled rear of his wife's memorial for comfort and resilience. As if in sympathy, Emily turned to look across as he came to her side.

'She would not want you to be upset,' said Emily, parting a bunch of flowers and handing them to him. 'The woman you told us about, the one that remembered me each year at Haldwyn.'

'Emily, I'm sorry about what I said, and the way I said it—'

She glanced down at the stone. 'I know, and so does the

woman who lies here; we have gone through the same experience. Now I understand the grief that our actions leave behind. Love does not die, and death cannot erase us, even one whose name is now barely remembered.' James looked into the calm seas of her dilated eyes. 'I have no memorial where anyone can leave flowers and live on only as a mere remembrance at a place that now bears my shame; I was no maiden, James Marshall. Even the sweetness of the willow maid offered to the sea every Haldwyn time serves only to remind me of this.'

'I know who you think you are, and I'm here to tell you we didn't forget,' he said, raising to sniff at the fragrant flowers. Some keep the traditions alive, working to save those alongside whatever is happening up at—'

'Myrgh an Mor...'

'They changed its name, and it used to be called Mary Dene Point. People cleared the Dene plot of undergrowth when your actions reminded them of their connection to the past.'

She turned, pupils wide. 'And what of your past? She is done with suffering – is it not time for you to do the same?'

He took a step forward and stared at the inscription below:

The sound ended but the melody lingers on.

He scanned the sky and breathed deeply, trying to stem the tears.

Emily smiled. 'None of us would have you suffer for our actions, sad though they may seem. Do not remember our final page, but the book that was written while we lived.'

James wiped the back of his hand across his face. 'She played the flute and had a mischievous sense of humour. I'm so sorry.'

Emily stepped back, brushing her hand against his tightly bound fist clutching at the flower stems, leaving him alone at the grave side. A profound sense of peace descended, radiating gentle warmth throughout his body. He recognised the experience and gave into its grace, unable to question the feeling's origin or intention. It washed over him as he stooped to place the flowers at the base of the stone, receding to leave a melancholic calm, where once had been extreme and overwhelming anxiety.

'I will remember you, Isobel – your bright spirit, and your melody.'

As if in response, the sound of a familiar song drifted from beyond the yew hedging. He rose and turned, looking for Emily, suddenly realising the reason for his urgency in finding her. Racing back up the slippery slope, he turned through the first opening and past his parent's memorial to reach the oldest part of the graveyard and the source of the *Sweet Nightingale*.

She stood at the Dene cross, holding out the remaining flowers. The song ceased, and she beckoned to him. 'Do not forget me when I depart, for it is best that I do so, for Emily's sake, and yours. I wanted to see it for one last time through these eyes.'

He took the bunch and moved to place the flowers at the base seeing that additional words were inscribed below the family name. The grass and growth had been removed to reveal the hint of further lettering. He scooped the damp earth from the sandstone base and hurriedly smoothed his grubby hand to read the two words:

Amor manet

'Love endures,' she said. 'You have helped me realise I cannot selfishly claim that which does not belong to me, and I give Emily back to you now, into your safe-keeping and back to the world of this time. Take good care of her.'

'These are the two words my father asked you for,' he replied, 'the ones he—'

James glanced, up just in time, to see Emily slump and fall forward. He caught her, inches away from dashing the side of her head against the segmented ray disk in the centre of the cross. His face nestled into her cheek and the strong smell of bubblegum hung on her breath as he propped her back to a standing position. She wavered, clinging one-handed to the cross as though momentarily confused before regaining her balance and staring blankly towards the edge of the clearing.

'What's that?' she said groggily, pointing towards the reflection of sunlight against metal within the encircling spinney. James helped her gain her feet and wandered over, brushing aside the thick growth. Twenty yards in, and all but camouflaged, was a makeshift camp. A narrow porthole of sunlight shone upon a metal stove lukewarm to the touch, while a fleeting scent of cess and sweat suggested that the site was still in occupation. James scanned the area, listening for any sound of passage but hearing nothing but the faint rustle of a dark green nylon, triangular canopy covering a camouflaged bivvy bag.

He raced back to the cross to find Emily fully conscious of her surroundings. Grabbing her shoulders and examining the contracting pupils of her intensely blue eyes he shook her gently, listening for any sound beyond the mass of encircling bramble and untended shrubbery. 'We need to go.'

'What is it?'

James grabbed her arm and pulled her through the opening. 'I need to tell you about what happened at the refuge while you were on your way here, but we need to get to the car.'

They hurried past the open door of the church and the scent of candles and chrysanthemums. James pulled out the car fob and clicked it to discover the car was unlocked. He got out his phone and urged her around the passenger side. Getting in, he leaned over to open the door confused as to the origin of a powerful acrid stench of sweat. Emily got in, sensing his anxiety, suddenly aware of the stowaway emerging from his crouched position in the back seat.

She screamed as the grubby, scarred face of Ryan Williams rose in the rearview mirror.

CHAPTER 36

Williams leaned into the central console and clicked the universal door lock. 'Right, sunshine,' he said, deeply and calmly at James's left ear, 'Drive somewhere quieter than here; I'm not a fan of company especially prim and proper church-folk after I've been camped out for days in this back of beyond.'

He turned to peck Emily roughly on the cheek. 'Hello, babe. What have you been up to making a name for yourself all this way from home? Been having a little holiday without me, have you?'

'Where to?' said James, trying to distract him from pawing at the woman in the passenger seat. He put on his seatbelt, indicating Emily to do the same. She sat rigid, emotionless in shock as James pulled the belt across her. He caught sight of the brass tie pin before glancing back to see a gun in Ryan Williams' hand. The brute smacked him across the cheek. 'Eyes front, Doctor Kildare, or I'll be driving Miss Daisy, alone; understand?'

James put the car into gear, desperate for any of the floral team to poke a head around the church door to see them off. He turned down the hill toward the town.

'Why are you going back down this way?' said Williams. 'That's not what I meant by quiet. No funny business, I've been scouting out your pathetic gaff for days, grubbing for food and watching you hoity-toity Cornish pasties having a right old time at the seaside while I've been cold, hungry and on the run.'

'The road's closed a quarter of a mile further up,' said James. 'Look—'

A council van, laden with cones mounted the verge in the narrow lane to allow them to pass. The sole driver waved a hand and returned to the breakfast bap in his left hand, oblivious to their predicament as they passed.

James caught sight of Williams staring at Emily's hands, clutching protectively around her gently swollen belly.

'Whose baby is it, you whore?' shouted Ryan Williams into the closeness of Emily's right ear.

James caught sight of him in the rearview mirror, sliding across to perch behind the passenger seat. A heavily scarred, tattoo-emblazoned arm thrust through the passenger door side of the headrest. Emily screamed as the thick forearm closed around her throat, its fingers clasping onto the extension of the headrest on the other side. The headlock pinned her rapidly reddening face, and she struggled to free herself from the constricting muscle and iron grip.

'Don't hurt her!' said James, seeing Emily clutch at the powerful arm, scratching until red welts appeared. James thought of the marks on her skin, the thorn scratches and briar raking that she had suffered at their first meeting, naked and alone in the churchyard. Williams tightened his grip, choking the irritating resistance until she relented.

'It was that East European bastard, wasn't it? You bitch.'

Emily shook her head, pleading with him to let go

through gasping thin breaths and fearful, meaningless apologies.

'Well, daddy won't be around to see the little baby grow up,' said Williams, his lined veins popping into pulsing pustules on the side of his head.

'If he ends up growing up at all...'

Emily grimaced and broke into a painful, wheezing sob. Her legs kicked out into the footwell, like an insect on its back, trying to right itself, trying to escape.

'We can have it got rid of, start again – just you and me, babe. I thought we had something special, Emily. Why do you have to spoil it?' Williams's head thrust forward into the space between them and James flinched with the sudden appearance. The back of his neck rippled with creased muscle and skin. James gripped the wheel and returned to the front windscreen to avoid the sudden, checking twist in his direction. The junction of the coast and inland road approached, and he saw the green light transition to amber.

'I love you, Emily,' said Williams, pivoting back to whisper into her ear, straining his face and nudging his nose against her cheek. 'I have to hurt you, so you know that. You've made life very difficult for us and we will have to go away, but I need that trinket you found to pay off the men that are after us. Don't you understand? Why did you steal my car and have the police take our future away? You have caused me a lot of bother, babe.'

Emily burst into tears and leaned forward, trying to grab for the pearl-tipped tiepin rattling in the dashboard's bowl. Williams finally caught sight of the sharp piece of metal and dragged her back into the seat and away from the needle-like weapon.

James turned onto the main street, shuddering with the closeness of the captor's callous caress, his training striving to break through and identify the psychotic condition that was driving the obscene and abusive behaviour. James was too late to slow down, and the car sped through the unseen red light. He shook his mind free of his abductor's motivations and of any attempt at diagnosis, concentrating on the terrifying hostage situation and driving at hand. Talking would not solve the situation here. There was not enough time, and Williams was now too invested in bloodletting and intent on harm, fearing for his life from the gang that would ultimately find him, driving his desperate and violent necessities to harm everyone around him to save himself.

James saw the oncoming vehicle from the right far too late and he swerved to avoid it, driving on with a shot of ice-cold adrenalin in his veins warning him to choose swiftly between fight or flight. A cacophony of car horns blared, communicating the shock and annoyance behind. The reckless driving diverted Williams's attention briefly.

James felt the cold, hard prod from something blunt and metallic against his left temple. He raised his hand instinctively to rub the sudden painful impact and looked in the rearview mirror to see the gun at his head. Williams flicked away the fingers and repeated the hammering on his temple. James winced and cried out in pain, screwing his eyes and clenching his teeth to banish the pain. He controlled the urge to soothe the stinging spot lest the punishment occurred for a third time. When he opened his eyes to blurred, watery vision, the car was close to colliding with the curb.

'Steady, sunshine,' said Williams. 'Baby on board and careless driving costs lives.' His grinning face transformed into a visage of pure malice. 'Slow down and drive normally.'

'Where are we going, and what are you going to do with us?' said James, glancing across at Emily. Her wriggling and murmuring subsided, and she fell silent, slipping into a shockinduced delirium. Her head swayed within the neck brace of her tormentor's violent embrace. The car drove along the promenade, passing the hospital on its way out of the town.

Williams thrust the gun forward, pointing to a junction that James knew led to the higher ground of the headland. 'Up there a bit, somewhere nice and quiet. If you mean, what am I going to do *to you*, then that all rests on you being a good boy. We might do some things together, like go for a nice little walk somewhere. That depends on whether the princess, here, gives up her pretty necklace in compensation for the money she stole from me. Now, where is it? It's not in here – I've checked, and it ain't at the other place either. You got it on you, babe, somewhere nice and private like the little packets you used to deliver for me?'

Emily shuddered, which Williams took in the affirmative. He licked his lips. 'Maybe I could find it for you when we get someplace private, like.'

James thought of the men chasing Ryan Williams and what manner of people they must be to cause such a dangerous man like the one in the space between them to be in such fear of his life.

'Give yourself up. Even if you go to jail, you'll be safe from whoever is after you; it's got to be better than—'

Williams stared back from the rearview mirror in disbelief at the suggestion. 'You really don't know what the bloody hell you are talking out, Mr Clever Clogs. They know where I am in the clink, and besides—' he held up the gun before stabbing them both painfully in the shoulder, 'I've got myself a nice little motor, my two friends here, and a way to pay Mostoff back, haven't I?'

James turned sharply. 'I'll help you with whatever you need if you'll let her go afterwards.'

Williams laughed at the absurd suggestion. 'Right bloody hero, aren't you?' He twisted to study the passive and lolling head within his right arm and nuzzled his crooked nose into the hair on her neck. 'You won't ever leave me, will you, girl?' Emily clenched her eyes tight and shook her head in fright at the thought of returning to a former life of abject misery and violent abuse.

Suddenly James understood, firsthand and in the moment unlike any other case before, how death could be preferable to life for some, and how years of such terror and fear could lead them to places, without hope, like Maiden's Point. All the years of trying to understand the feelings and reasons behind his patient's traumas paled into insignificance with a visceral, practical demonstration of one man's inhumanity to another.

Emily's escape from life had been preferable to survival, and it had been taken away by the sudden intervention of another altogether strange guardian.

James caught sight of a turquoise Toyota tailgating behind, wishing for a moment that Mostoff, whoever he may be, was in pursuit, ready to pull them over. He wondered if there was any humanity or honour among thieves and if they got their man, they might let Emily and himself go. The chance might be worth taking, assuming they knew that both of them were hostages. He looked back and the risky hope vanished with the sight of an older woman unaware of the closeness and danger of a sudden brake-check. Something crooked her head to one side as though in conversation with a phone pinned between her cheek and shoulder. He thought wildly about driving so erratically that she might call the police with news of a drunk driver, but the torment on his temple returned and he snatched an opportunity to rub at the glowing bruise, leaving only one hand on the wheel.

The sudden movement unnerved Williams and he broke away from his one-sided intimacy to look at the road ahead.

'Mirror, signal, manoeuvre, you twat,' said the fugitive, flicking the gun towards the left. James clicked down on the indicator and turned. The vehicle behind disappeared on the road, unaware of the trauma taking place in the car leaving the built-up area.

He had missed an opportunity, and he wondered if there would be another.

James breathed slowly, trying to control the rising panic and the countless scenarios playing out in his mind. He could not overcome the man behind by strength or stealth, and he chastised himself for the cowardly thought of throwing himself from the car at speed and escaping on foot back to the main road leaving Emily to her fate and an imminent, possibly fatal and sudden impact. His anger overcame his survival instinct, and he screamed in his mind, louder than any alternate personality could ever do. The car hit a pothole and jostled the passengers within, setting the pin in the dashboard bowl spinning and careening close to the lip. Emily noticed the pin once more and gently stretched out her hand along her knee to test the distance.

Close, but not close enough. Think you fool!

Fear and frustration grew with every hundred yards now that he had left the main road. The thin metalled surface of the narrow lane became uneven, and the passing places fewer and farther between. He knew the road as a summer shortcut over Maiden Moor; it snaked through an approaching plantation, crowned with mist, that lay between the beaches of St Jude and the headland cliffs. The road ended at a car park linked to a forlorn and disused communication tower whose base was only just visible beneath the mist and cloud. Emily hummed, and the familiar bars of *Sweet Nightingale* momentarily cleared his thoughts.

'Shut Up,' said Williams, clenching his bicep into Emily's

throat. She breathed through her nose in long calm breaths but did not cease in her musical murmuring. In a swift movement, Williams withdrew his arm like a rapidly retreating boa constrictor and jerked back her hair into the headrest with a tug of his large hand, forcing her to exhale suddenly.

'Leave her alone. She's not who you think she is.' James stared back into the shallow eyes in the rearview mirror, no longer afraid of the man behind.

'You don't half believe some bullshit about folks living in other people's heads; It was in the paper,' said Williams. 'I'll also mind you don't tell me to shut up again; no-one tells me what to do with my own property.'

James steadily decreased the speed as he focussed on delay, long enough for the merest hint of a plan to bubble up and make itself known. The car wound along the twisting lane, passing only a single cyclist, before slowing around a bend to be hampered by a wayward sheep. Williams swore at the innocent beast.

'Run the bugger over if you have to and pull over into those trees up ahead.'

James looked over to the many rows of regimented black pencil-trunked larches, their fading yellow needles blurring in and out of the grey sea mist condensing over the higher ground.

James crept the car around the oblivious sheep and heard Emily's gentle hum more clearly now that the hybrid engine was silently returning to electric low-speed use. He twitched a glance to see her sapphire eyes, dilating, but alert and sharp. She stole a look sideways, aware of his gaze and concern. Her nose twitched, imperceptibly and James sensed he was in the presence of her returned protector. Her eyes flashed forward to his father's heart-shaped tiepin. Williams adjusted his grip back to her throat to choke the remaining bars that James knew would herald the appearance and influence of May Dene, if she still lingered.

The car rattled over a cattle grid and climbed towards the brow of the first tree-clad hill. Williams scanned left and right for a place to pull in unobserved, but the stone walls kept the car on its sinuous rail-like track. He looked ahead and stabbed the gun forward.

'Up there,' he barked, pointing to a muddied pull-in area roughly a half of a mile distant. The road beyond snaked out of view approximately the same distance on the other side of the lay-by. James knew he was out of time, and that whatever he had to do, he had to do it now. His mind grasped with anything that might save them both, but the answer presented itself in an approaching, fluorescent marked vehicle.

Beyond the blind corner emerged the hazy but recognisable shape of a police car, approaching at speed over the rough and uneven pot-holed road. The familiar silhouette of the large driver caused overwhelming relief but sudden fear for his best friend's safety.

William stiffened his grip on Emily's throat as he saw the car in the distance. 'Put your foot down, get into that lay-by, nice and casual, like.' He turned and lowered his voice. 'If he stops and you do anything foolish, I'll start shooting, and it will begin with you.'

The hope that rose with the sight of Jory Richards stalled as he recognised the distance to the lay-by was swinging too far against his favour. He saw the police car flash in recognition, unknown to the violent man in the back, and James knew Jory would pull alongside. The dreadful scenario played itself out in his mind – if he pulled over before the police car got to him, both of their lives would be in danger, and the unsuspecting policeman would not realise why they were there or who was in the back before Williams's patience would wear thin and it was too late.

'Did you hear what I said? He's flashing for you to pull in so he can pass. Do it now or your bloody brains will be all over that copper's car bonnet.'

James planted his foot down, and the car increased speed. He could just make out the face of his childhood friend and he hurriedly thought how to warn him from pulling over, or at the very worst, how to communicate the potentially disastrous situation without setting a catastrophic chain of events. He caught Williams watching him from the wing mirror and realised his facial expressions would be visible. All too late, he clicked the folding mirror button as the man behind lowered his profile behind the passenger seat to avoid being seen. The man sensed the ruse and James felt the gun jab against the back of his neck, exposed between the supportive arms of the extended headrest.

'I won't tell you again to behave. Put the bloody mirrors back if you want your brain to remain inside your skull.'

James dutifully returned the mirrors and looked out on the rapidly approaching police patrol car. Desperate to catch the distant man's attention with only limited opportunity, Williams watched his every facial movement. Ahead, the sleeveless right arm of the policeman extended out of the window to give him a customary and friendly middle finger in greeting. James risked flashing the car and Williams jabbed the gun into the top of his spine, causing the car to swerve momentarily.

'I'm letting him know we are moving over, for God's sake,' shouted James. 'Tourists do it all the time.'

'Get a bloody move on!' said Williams, ducking down out of sight like a Punch and Judy professor holding one hand around Emily's throat, and the other gun-toting hand extended towards him.

Whether the erratic driving of James's car or the approaching closeness enabled him to see that something was amiss, James could not tell. Jory removed his arm from the window and put on his blue lights.

In an instant, James knew there was only one thing to do. He glanced across to see Emily's neck, still pinned to the back of the chair. Her eyes flitted between the pin and the seatbelt unseen by the man behind, and she grasped the strap, pulling herself tighter into the back of the chair, tensing for the last encounter that surely approached. James clicked down a gear on the steering wheel, sending the car into a sudden lurch of rev-fuelled acceleration and shoved his foot down hard on the pedal. She gave him a final curt nod, eyes wide with trust and fear in equal measure, sensing what he was about to do.

The lay-by closed to within fifty yards.

'You are going too fast – pull over to the right and wait till he draws alongside,' said Williams close to his ear. James felt the end of the gun's barrel nick his skin as he withdrew it behind the seat to point sideways out of the rear passenger seat window. 'Never done a drive-by shooting before. Now slow down, for Christ's sake.'

James took one furtive glance in the rearview mirror and across to see an outstretched right hand readying the gun at the window for Jory to pull up alongside once they had reached the lay-by. His other hand still clutched around Emily's throat, the thumb stroking the neck in a gruesome and sadistic sense of affection. The car struck a deep hole and James fought for control but did not slow down, engaging in a deadly game of chicken with the flashing lights of the police car two hundred yards away. The lay-by approached and Williams shot a glance out of the front window, sensing the speed and realising that James was not pulling in; they were heading straight on and making for the front of the police car that had nowhere to veer left or right to avoid the collision. In the same instance, James looked from the rising needle of the speed dial passing forty, to see discernible features on Jory's face realising his intention. The policeman waved a hand in alarm, switched on the sirens, and slammed on his brakes. James saw his arms lock onto the steering wheel as he forced the police car into the side of the granite set dry stone wall to slow the car further. James heard the squealing metal collision and saw the shrapnel, clouds of dust, moss and mud fly up and pepper the windscreen as Jory forced a hand down onto the horn.

Williams tried to regain control, but James twitched the wheel suddenly, sending him sprawling. He clung onto Emily's throat to stabilise himself.

James took his foot from the accelerator, judging the remaining sixty yards, and tightened his neck into his shoulders to reduce the whiplash that would come. He hovered his foot over the brake, watching the needle drop into the thirties, and glanced at the green airbag light on the dash. They shot past the lay-by and James did not heed the screams of alarm from their abductor. With only seconds to spare, he saw Emily's hand extend for the pin, inches out of her grasp, and with twenty yards to go, he finally slammed on the brakes. The car shuddered under the effects of the anti-braking system, and the steering wheel became virtually impossible to hold on to. The sudden forward lurch gave Emily the chance to grab at the pin and in one swift movement, fighting against the pre-tensioning seatbelt, she turned the antique metal sting and drove it towards her throat and into Williams's hand. He cried out in agony, releasing his grip at the last moment that James switched pedals and drove his foot once more on the accelerator, flinging the man back like a ragdoll behind the driver's seat.

Emily lurched back as James took one last look at the

impending collision. Jory raised his arms to cover his face in readiness for the impact and James turned to see the wide, dilated eyes of May Dene staring back.

Her hand reached over and gripped his wrist, pulling it back to the closeness of his body.

'Do not be afraid,' she cried above the sound of the squealing tires and hammering of the protesting braking system. 'Let go!'

He clenched his eyes and grabbed at the handbrake, forcing his other foot down on top of the other to pin the brake pedal to the floor.

Instinctively, she pulled at him, and James threw himself across her and buried his head against her neck, hearing the sweet humming begin again.

The cars collided, his mind stilled, safe and secure in the sound of the *Sweet Nightingale*.

CHAPTER 37

J ames came round to the sound of exposed, rushing wind
and Jory's desperate shaking. A soft white and blue light
enveloped him, filtering in through the billowing latex of
the airbag from the static and silent police car. He winced
from a sharp pain in his chest as he clicked out the seatbelt.

'Thank God you're alive, you bloody fool!' came the shaking, shock-laden voice of his friend. 'Driver's door is jammed,
don't move till the ambulance comes.'

'I'm alright, I think.'

He prodded at his ribs to confirm that one of them was
likely cracked but not broken. Removing the last of the
partially deflated balloon and shattered glass from his hair, he
twisted the bent rearview mirror to see his face bruised and
cut in several places. The seat behind was empty, as was the
passenger seat, and he sat back, trying to clear the concussed
fog from his mind. He raised a hand to rub at his aching neck
and looked out on the tangled mess that had once been the
front of the car. Jory's pale face peered in through the twisted
frame of the window. He squeezed at a dislocated finger with
a sharp intake of breath.

'Williams...' said James. 'He was at the church, waiting... where is he, and where's—?'

'After his little flying lesson against the back of your chair and then onwards through the window because of your emergency stop,' said Jory, tugging at the bent driver's door and nodding towards the blood on the crumpled concertina of the bonnet, 'he's gone off after her. He's wounded, and she has a head start.'

James twisted to see the distant running figure of Emily heading cross-country for the safety of the trees, pursued by the loping gait of Ryan Williams, clutching at his thigh but keeping pace four hundred yards behind. His other arm hung low, with a bloodied hand brandishing the gun.

James twisted to push on the door and ground his teeth with a stab of pain from the protesting rib. Jory peeled back the remaining few feet of metal, dislodging the crystal shattered mat of remaining safety glass into sparkling, cascading beads.

James slapped himself on the cheek to clear his grogginess. 'We need to stop him, but he's armed.'

'I know,' said Jory, losing the battle of preventing James from levering himself from the wreck of the car. 'Armed responses are on their way, but they'll take time from Truro, and I've called for the air ambulance; it's over at Plymouth. You didn't bust the radio, thank God, just the sirens and the total front end.'

'I'm so sorry, mate,' said James, clutching at his chest as he stood up. 'He was going to shoot you if you pulled over, then me once he had that necklace and Emily. He wanted the car —' He stared in disbelief at the blinking lights on the dashboard and the hissing tangle of crushed metal and fluids bleeding from both vehicles. The crushed bonnet of the car was so unrecognisable as to be impossible to determine where one car ended and the other started. As if in understanding,

Jory answered, brushing off the glass from James's clothing with his good hand.

'You were doing over twenty when we collided, and I was still moving.' He patted his buckled protective vest. 'Any faster and it might have been curtains, even with this enormous belly.'

'How long was I out, and why didn't he kill either of us?' he said, shivering with the after-effects of shock.

'I came round after Emily was already halfway across the field and saw him get up.' Jory rubbed at James's shoulders to generate warmth, catching the painful rib. James inhaled the cool upland air through his gritted teeth and held out a hand, insisting he was okay. 'Williams didn't blink; just got up like the bleeding terminator clutching his leg and fished out the gun from the back. He took one look over to see I couldn't get out of the car; the doors are shagged, and he must have thought you were dead, as did I.'

'How did you get out?'

Jory raised his eyebrows. 'I pulled myself through the windscreen; not bad for a fat lad.' He raised his damaged middle finger, crooked and erect, as though in a permanent gesture. James examined it roughly, setting off intermittent protestations of pain.

'You'll live, but it's dislocated,' he said, eyes now focussed on the two figures heading away and into the haze. 'And the irony will keep Mike and me in tears for a long time if I ever get to tell him.'

James turned to run, but Jory caught his arm.

'Where the hell are you going?' he said, pointing his damaged middle finger down to the electro-shock weapon on his belt. 'I'm the one with the bloody taser!'

'You've got a damaged trigger finger,' said James, 'and you won't outrun him. Sorry, Jory.' He pulled away, but the big man held him fast.

'This isn't cops and robbers like we used to play; some-one's going to get hurt today, badly, and it will not be you or Emily, alright? Besides, they are slowing.'

James watched as Emily staggered to a standstill and turned, out of breath, back to see her pursuer halt and call out. She turned and fell over something unseen in the heath, climbing back to her feet and hobbling into the trees. Williams walked on, like a well-exercised hound sniffing an injured fox.

'How long till the good guys turn up, Jory?'

'Thirty minutes, maybe longer—'

'Emily hasn't got that long. May Dene is back in control and heading for Maiden Point on the eastern side of the wood. History is repeating itself and she's going to jump; We've got to stop both of them.'

Jory squeezed his arm tighter and peered into his eyes with a genuine and profound look of affection and distrac-tion. 'Stop Williams and maybe we stop Emily.' James barely felt the cold metal of the handcuffs wrap around his chilled wrist and attach themselves to the mangled frame of the side window. Jory released his distracting grip and backed away.

'You tell Mike what I did,' he said, voice and bottom lip quivering. 'You tell him about this so you can both go on laughing all your days if I don't come back.' He held up his damaged middle finger and ran across the lane to mount the damaged dry-stone wall with all the elegance of a short-legged, overweight mountain goat.

James tugged at the restraint and watched as the policeman jogged across the purple, flecked moorland, picking out a sheep path through the thickets of gorse and heather. 'Jory!'

His friend did not look back and pulled out the disarming weapon with his left hand, jogging away at a steady and faster pace towards the felon who approached the edge of the pine wood.

James pulled at the bent metal frame securing him to the spot and slid the cuffs up to a cracked spot in the upper corner. He rocked the twisted upright bar until it became pliable, throwing his weight against the door repeatedly to hammer weakness into the joint from the obstruction of the other cuff and the car chassis. The crack widened.

He knew that the paramedics and police would be too late and even then, they would prevent him from acting on his impulse to save Emily and his best friend. The sudden thought of losing both of them filled him with rage and he flung himself against the door, causing the metal restraint around his hand to twist free through the generated crack, spraining his wrist. He clutched at the cuff and then at his side, making off in painful first strides toward the receding policeman.

She limped from the cool dark of the wood into the hazy moorland sun, sweating with the exertion across the tussock and gorse of the headland heath. Her tormentor's distant cries were nearer now that she had slowed. No hiding place had presented itself in the resinous needle-shedding wood beyond a few obvious fallen log piles and tilted root plates emerging from the thin upland soil like rotten teeth. The sound of the sea battering the rocks led her through the remaining mournful purgatory of the thinning larches but the sprain in her ankle was mercilessly slowing her progress and she wondered if she would make it to the cliff before he caught her.

Seeing the discarded twisted remains of the fallen stock fencing too late, she sprawled forward into a thick covert of thorny gorse. She stifled a painful cry to see her arms scratched and torn, grimy with the damp peat and sweat. History was repeating itself, she thought, and she knew the end all too well.

Fallon, Williams, and whoever came next would always be chasing someone, trying to control and hurt them, but no one would take the final leap away into blessed safety and loneliness from her this time.

From within, a sense of acceptance and grace emerged from the other consciousness. Emily had struggled with her for control following the crash, desperate to help the only man she trusted, fervently shaking him to waking life even as her tormentor rose like a rotting corpse from beyond the steam of the spilling car radiators. There wasn't time and escape back to her previous watchful oblivion was now overwhelmingly desirable to survival.

Infinitely preferable to watching someone like Emily suffer.

She sidled around, cracking and creaking within the temporary shelter of tinder-dry bracken and gorse, catching her face on a sharp thorn to peer back at the wood. Her breath resonated in her heaving chest, and she sought to tame the loud gulping breaths for fear he would hear above the wind and wailing gulls. The depression must at one time have been a grouse butt, for it afforded her a peeping view while her body remained out of sight. The sound of something far above, coming over the moor like the distant and delicate sound of thunder caught her attention as Williams emerged from the mist. Barely three hundred yards away, she saw him return to search the final bleak and empty acres of land for signs of her. He clutched at his left leg, blackened with blood, and wiped the back of his gun-carrying hand across his brow and bleeding lips.

'Emily! Where are you?' he said bellowing like an injured

highland stag. Williams lumbered on for a few paces away from where she lay hid, using the cover of the trees to shield himself from any approach of the strange flying machine, but it was still far off. He cried out in frustration and anguish before listening and softening his voice.

'It's alright, Emily, I am not angry with you, I just need the necklace. I'll get help, and prove I'll be good to you. The money will make things right.'

The shared consciousness of Emily Dunn arose in her mind seeking the truth of the words and an end to anxious flight. May smothered the thoughts.

He's lying. You know he's lying...

She shifted to kneel, leaning on an old branch that snapped, setting off a furiously squawking and flapping pheasant that had taken cover. The bird launched itself into the air several metres away from where it had been sitting. Williams turned sharply in the bird's direction, raising the gun instinctively.

'Come out,' he said with honeyed words. 'I promise I won't hurt you ever again.'

May brushed aside a second attempt by Emily to regain control; the host pleading for the idea to be considered.

If we go to him now, he'll only hurt us a little...

'I need you, Emily. Help me!'

May stared into his eyes flitting back and forth across the scrubby sanctuary and fought against the dizziness and feeling of slipping away, back to the quiet and comforting stillness of Emily's emergence. The sound of the repetitive and annoying tune, a response from Emily to return, began to issue from her unwilling throat. She fought for control, biting down on her finger to sharpen her focus. Emily pressed again, the snatches of the modern song becoming louder, and May did the only thing she could to regain control.

Framed by the coconut-scented blooms of marigold gorse,

she looked upon the monster and began to hum louder with her defiant rebuttal. Emily's consciousness stilled in her mind, with the old folk tune, but did not recede.

Williams' attention shifted to the outcrop of vegetation where snatches of her song were interspersed by large intakes of precious, calming breath. He took a few strides towards the spot before a commanding voice caused him to pivot and look back into the mists of the wood.

'Stay here,' he said. 'I'll deal with the copper and then we can get away together.' He turned and headed back to the margins of thin larch to the repeated sounds of an authoritative voice, scared but professional, as though a long-learned script was coming to mind and speech. It also sounded heavily out of breath. From within the plantation, the unseen voice issued a final demand to put down the gun. Williams entered the mist, dragging his leg, weapon raised.

May pulled herself through the talons and tussocks of the thicket, hearing a distant shout from beyond the southern edge of the trees. It sounded like a cry from someone familiar, repeatedly urging her to halt in her sprained sprint to the edge of the cliffs.

She ignored it, turned, and ran to meet the edge, and end, of the world.

CHAPTER 38

James loped over the mounds of heather in pursuit of the surprising fleetness of the policeman. Every jolting stride stabbed painfully at his damaged rib, and he drew shallow breaths trying to avoid inflating his lungs to make the pain worse. Adrenalin and purpose coursed through his body but James saved his strength and did not call out lest Jory decided to turn and prevent him once again from joining the apprehension of Ryan Williams. He hoped his best friend had a better plan than trying to get within thirty feet of the murderer to fire off the shock weapon before Williams got several bone-shredding rounds off in reply.

The sudden thought of the duel, two hundred years prior, described by May Dene came to mind and he shook his head, trying to remove any lingering coincidences. He thought of his father's words:

Coincidences have a habit of proving otherwise if you do not recognise them...

'History does not repeat,' he said to himself, buckling a knee from a sudden unseen rabbit hole. 'Even if spirits of dead suicides do exist.' He pulled himself up and saw Jory had disappeared into the wood. From the eastern side, he saw the distant limping figure of Emily dragging herself desperately towards the cliffs of Maiden Point. James called out, but she turned behind, back to the wood, to check for something, or someone unseen. The distant sound of the helicopter grew louder as he cut across in her direction. There was no way he could catch up with Jory, or Williams, in time before they met in an endgame that was unpredictable and uncertain. He might cut short the four hundred yards and head off any emergence from the wood, or at least distract him while the policeman got close enough.

He stumbled on for thirty yards and encountered a narrow sheep path, turfed and open. He looked down and followed the direct route to the clifftop sign, barely visible within the morning sea mist pouring above Maiden Point. His ribs rejoiced with the reduction in the painful, jolting impact, and he ran smoothly, pinning his arm to his side to avoid further pain. When he glanced ahead, Emily was nowhere to be seen.

He threw himself behind an erratic granite boulder as Williams exited the wood on the eastern side. Peering from the side he heard the man cry out to the wild and empty scene. Emily had gone to ground.

The hills beyond echoed with the merest murmur of an air ambulance, and Williams scanned the inland horizon. James darted across to another boulder twenty yards away, just off the path. The paramedics might not land on the moor itself or be aware of the figures away to the north and James realised they were on their own. He heard the familiar cry of his friend even as Williams turned and headed back into the wood.

Jory, you bloody fool!

Rising from the rock, James saw the sudden appearance of Emily and he called out. She continued to head towards the cliff, awkwardly stamping across the mounds of thinning heather with immense difficulty. He returned to the path which widened and sought to head her off at a junction of other turf-lined tributaries.

'Emily!' he called again. 'Back to the road; men are coming—'

She looked across and halted, and he saw the relief in her eyes. She shook her head, and he realised it was to see him alive, and not for her own safety. He knew what she planned to do, what she had always intended if all other attempts at saving herself from Williams should fail. Spurred by the anger of one human's cruelty against another, he ran on to cut her off.

'Wait!' he cried.

She made for the junction and paused as if suddenly aware of the grassy ring in which she now stood.

Staring at the ground, she floundered as though acting out or remembering the removing of clothes for which she had no time. She held out a hand as he came to within sight of the ring and he knew she had been here before, naked and ready to jump.

'Stay yourself, James!' she said. 'Your honourable kindness will not prevail upon us to divert our course.'

'Our course?' he replied, seeing the dilation and hearing the voice of May Dene in control. 'What about Emily, don't you think she has a right to choose for herself?'

'She is resolved, as am I to put an end to suffering at the hands of this man. Things do not change, James. Even now, she thinks to return to him, knowing her torment will be even greater in the years that lie ahead. I have stood here for two hundred years, begging each of them to alter their desperate course of action whilst forgetting the reason and honest choice I made for myself. I am no longer ashamed to have died a free woman, and I will do so again for Emily's sake. He will not touch her again.'

James held up his hands and inched closer. 'Even now, my friend is there in the wood to apprehend him, and I am here to help you form a new life away from this place, London or anywhere else you wish to be. There is a man, the uncle of the child, that will take care of you, or at the very least, I will. Do not do this, even just for my sake. I cannot deal with another death that I have played some part in.'

'I know your pain, but how can I save you when I am unsure whether you truly believe in who I really am?'

They both twisted sharply with the sound of a wailing cry of painful anguish from within the wood, tailing off into a thin and mournful scream.

'Go back to the cars, men are coming, good men.' He pointed to the distant sound of the helicopter still many miles away over the inland granite moorland. 'All will be well, trust me.'

'Your father and Fellows said that once to me, long ago.'

'He said a good many things, but right now the only thing that matters is what he said to me as he died.'

She turned to look into his strained face, awaiting the answer.

'Save her,' he said. 'Save them both.' James looked round as a single sudden gunshot from the wood shattered the silence, sending flights of birds squawking into the sky. Emily raised her hands to her mouth and James froze, watching the nebulous shape of a man shift within the mist and emerge into familiar clarity.

'Get behind me,' said James, trying to discern the shape struggling to find its bearings in the wood as though dazed or confused.

He sensed her cower behind his back, shivering and panting. 'Is it the policeman?' she whispered.

James shook his head, uncertain, and called out. 'Jory!'

The shape halted and headed toward his voice. Emily whimpered as Ryan Williams emerged, gun clasped to his chest as though nursing a heavy blow. Fresh pinpricks bled from the wound inflicted from the well-aimed shock weapon and his rigid features on his face sweated profusely from the after-effects of a fifty-thousand-volt pulse– for only as long as someone kept their finger on the trigger. The echo of the gunshot from the granite tor of the distant hills receded and James knew his friend had paid a high price.

Emily turned and fled, falling over an unseen lump of stone, and James moved to shield her knowing that he would at least protect her until the very end. Running for either of them was no longer an option, with only thirty yards of ground before the perilous edge.

'Move aside,' stammered Williams limping towards them.

Emily scrabbled to get up, weak and drained. James bent down and grabbed at a lump of peat-muddied rock, rising to face Williams like a contemporary David readying to bring down the Goliath that approached. He heard the whip-crack of the passing bullet in the air next to his right ear as the gun went off and he ducked, checking to see the unsteady hand wavering to aim a second shot. He turned, terrified to see Emily lying sprawled in the peaty grass. For a moment he thought the worst until he saw her recover and rise to her feet, making off in a second wind, twisting this way and that to escape unharmed. Williams held out the gun in his shaking hand and changed targets. James saw him aim away from his prostrate form and swing across to bring down the woman limping in the cliff's direction. James got to his knees and threw the rock, hitting him squarely in the injured leg. The gun went off wildly, but Emily ran on, unmoved, unnoticed, and uninjured, as James launched himself towards the assailant before he had time to recover his wits or take another shot.

James hurled himself into the bulk of the brute's torso, shielding his cracked rib as much as he could. The gun flew out of his hand and disappeared into the bracken-rich tufts nearby. Both men fell into the deep heather before Williams hammered down an empty fist upon James's back, winding him. James felt him trying to twist him around to put him into an all ending headlock, but he drove his right elbow back into the injured leg causing a momentary release. James rolled over and scrabbled to the bracken but was pulled back by the ankle, bouncing painfully over surface-sleeping stones, to sense another attempt at squeezing the life from his body, this time on his back. His neck constricted and the sudden stoppage of air was pain and terror the like of which James had never experienced. He flailed, trying to escape from the arm, throwing his head back to find little enough distance to have any meaningful impact on the muscled skull inches away. He choked in silence, listening to Williams seethe, taking in sharp breaths, holding and tightening before releasing and trying again. James glanced up to see the blurred outline of Emily running away, knowing they were both going to die this day.

James's arms began to feel limp and the burning need for air overcame his senses. He flailed like a landed frog, swimming against the rough ground. An outstretched right hand knocked against a hard spherical stone, and he scoured the patch trying to relocate it as his vision began to dim and the narrowing tunnel vision of terminal blackout became so severe that he felt he was falling. With a last remaining effort, he splayed his fingers and cast his arm towards the stone. It landed firmly in his palm like a well-caught cricket ball and his fingers closed around it. Whether Williams had his eyes closed with the exertion of throttling him, or whether his head was tilted away from the sudden movement, James did not know or care as he turned his hand and levered back the rock with all the sapped strength he had left. The arm bent at the elbow and struck his assailant on the temple. James fell forward, released and desperate to draw breath like a drowning man rescued from the sea. His windpipe remained locked in spasm, and he rolled over onto his back and tilted back his head to release the airway. The air rushed in as Williams stirred beside him, got to his knees and staggered towards the patch of bracken to find the gun.

James tried to rise but fell backwards. Williams did not look back and gave up the search, making for Emily, she turned and halted to gauge the distance between her pursuer and the cliff edge. He closed despite his injuries, no longer holding onto the leg and surviving on adrenalin. James got to his feet, coughing as Emily ran on, striding stiffly before the rising cramp seized her thighs and she fell forward with the momentum. In a surprising suddenness, Williams was upon her and groping at her top to drag the woman to her feet. She became limp, passive, resigning herself to his dreadful grip as he dragged her slowly towards the cliff edge sign with no way of escape back across the moor.

James rubbed at his rib and stumbled towards the clifftop and the two figures silhouetted against the beams of the sun, breaking through the low cloud. He lurched across the flat-tened bracken as the headland became open and unob-structed. Emily, clutched by the arm of Williams was dragged close to the perilous edge. His bloodied and bruised head peered back over the ledge searching for a way out and down.

James got as close as he could, to within twenty feet, before Williams turned and pulled Emily closer to him.

'Stay back, or I'll do it!'

James held up his hands, thinking to create a sense in Williams's mind that he was still in control, that he still had options. 'Alright, I'm going to do as you say. Just tell me how we all get out of this alive.'

'I just want the bloody necklace,' said Williams.

She winced as he tightened his hold and buried her chin in the arm to look down at the bulge in her tight denim trouser pocket. Williams caught sight and his eyes widened with expectation. 'Give it to me!'

Emily remained calm and nodded, reaching closed fingers into the stitched pouch. She retrieved her clasped hand and Williams looked over lustily at the glasses case.

'Fear not, James,' she gasped between the constricting arm, 'Emily will be safe with me for eternity.'

James rushed forward even as she threw her hand into the air and opened her fingers releasing the case. It arched above, James cried out, too late to prevent Williams from instinctively reaching up. The ground beneath softened as the big man lurched backwards, forgetful for one moment of his closeness to the edge. He teetered as the object sailed over his outstretched arm and the cliff. He fought to regain control, balancing himself against the captive woman in front. James reached out and tugged at her T-shirt as she looked him gently in the eye and kicked her leg up into her captor's groin, forcing him off balance.

Williams wobbled back, beyond the tipping point and struggling with his other arm to hold on to the only other stable thing in his grasp. Emily leaned back, arms at her side preventing James from grabbing hold. James stepped back as the ground gave way beneath Williams's feet and he slid downwards, pulling Emily from James's grasp, over the edge and out of view.

CHAPTER 39

J ames fell to the ground and dived towards the newly carved precipice, throwing himself down on the thin and friable ground at the cliff's edge.

The pain in his ribs did not matter, or the blur in his salt-stinging eyes. He thought of only one thing.

She was gone.

The cascade of falling stones and clods of wildflower turf bounced and skittered upon the mounds of exposed granite, splintering and exploding into dust.

'Emily!' he cried, searching beyond the tops of the stunted rowan below to the foreshore for signs of scarlet among the coarse, white sands of Maiden beach. A squawk of gulls burst from twelve feet below, and he shifted his gaze to see a huddled embrace of bloody-faced bodies precariously balanced on a ledge, lipped and smooth like a soap dish.

Emily lay on her back, out of reach, and within one muscled arm, cushioned from the grazing fall by Williams's body beneath. His chest heaved to show life still clung to his sprawled body even if the deep red gash in his forehead suggested otherwise. His head rolled upon a pillowed nest of pine needles as though in troubled sleep, while a leg, up to his thigh, lolled over the edge of the dangerous cradle.

Emily opened her eyes, realising her predicament. The only way up was a near-vertical wall of thin footholds, inches wide before the reach of James's extended hand could be gained. Halfway between, lay the solitary sentinel of the wild service tree. She glanced back and shook her head, grasping at the cargo jacket of her tormentor and bouncing her weight into a combined cocooned roll from the safety of the ledge.

'No!' whispered James as though fearing to wake the beast from his slumber. 'Don't do this – think of the child.'

She halted, unable to shift the combined weight. 'Even if your prisons can hold him, his malice and influence will haunt her. There will always be more like Henry Fallon and Ryan Williams to fill the void...'

'There will also be more like Richard Avery, too,' he said, pulling himself further forward to extend both arms down in a plea to the memory of her lover and his distant ancestor.

'I cannot save them all, even those who listen and allow me in,' she said. 'We are alike, James, giving away a little of ourselves with every loss, and failure, until what is left of ourselves is no longer worth saving.' She pushed away Williams's flaccid arm from around her waist. 'Emily is in a swoon, let me end what she started. I bid you farewell, Marshall. Let me return to my troubles, and the cliff that now bears my name; at least I have that.' She twisted her head over and into the void.

'It is not your decision to make, Mary-Anne,' said James, watching as she struggled against the writhing body below to lean over the ledge. He appealed to the personality's sensibilities. 'I hear you are very particular about who calls you by that name?'

She shook her head and glanced back. 'Only my father

and my family, and only when it was critical. What does it matter? You believe I am a fantasy—'

'I am family,' cried James, seeing her turn from the sea and glance back to the cliff face. 'Your family. The Cartwrights raised your child, Mary-Anne; yours and Richard's. I believe you, even though I do not understand how this can happen, like Dr Fellows and my father before me.'

'My child died. Father said my baby—'

'He lied, Mary-Anne, to protect you and your honour. He sent the Cartwrights away to protect his granddaughter from the shame and his ruin.'

'I have a daughter?'

'And descendants, many times removed. Your father's name may have died out, but your line continues through them.' He stretched out his fingertips. 'You said on the bench that you did not know why you kept returning. If not to find closure and protect those whom you love, then what else could it be? I am here, now, because of you.'

She rose and splayed her hands against the cliff as though caressing the granite, unsure and on the edge of decision at the lip of the world. James rested his hands against the rocks below and began to hum. From some forgotten place, the words formed in his mind and he opened his mouth to murmur.

> Don't you hear the fond tale
> Of the sweet nightingale,
> As she sings in those valleys below?

From below, her sweet voice sang in reply:

> So be not afraid
> To walk in the shade,
> Nor yet in those valleys below...,

She looked up. 'The music box?'

'Yes. It's what connects us. Sent as a parting gift to devoted servants when circumstance could no longer afford them and for their discretion in raising your baby as their own. Your father was unaware you had hidden your mother's necklace to prevent him from pawning the last item of value. You hid it within the box and began the hope that one day a Dene would return for it. She was right.'

'The Cartwrights raised my daughter?'

'Yes. They left for Bristol where a newborn being raised by grandparents at a time of disease and strife would not be questioned. They never truly left your family's service, and it's where your story ends, and mine begins.'

They both glanced down at the stirring form of Williams as he murmured and fought his way back to painful consciousness.

'Hurry, for Emily's sake,' he said pointing to the tree within her reach.

She inched her way across the cliff-face and, rubbing the sweat and grime from her palm, stretched out to grasp at the smooth iron-solid stem. Forcing her foot upwards and side-ways onto a sliver of protruding rock, she pulled herself up and splayed against the rock face with a shake in her legs.

'It's too slippery,' she said, face buried into the granite. 'We are likely to fall.'

'Trust me,' said James shimmying across to wrap his feet around the leaning cliff-side post holding the warning sign. He leaned over with more confidence as the wooden peg held, reaching down to within a touching distance of her head. Williams opened his eyes and wriggled closer to the wall of rock in sudden awareness of his location and the escape of the only thing that now mattered. He placed one hand on his head to smear the bloodied gash across his face like a savage preparing for a final battle.

'Give me your other hand and use the other to lever yourself up,' said James, hurriedly, and wincing with the sharp pain in his ribs. 'I'll need your help to pull you over.'

Williams got to his knees, shifting soil and stone from the ledge. 'Emily!' he called.

'Don't look down,' said James. 'Keep going. Throw me your hand.'

She paused, breathed in, and pushed against the tree. It bent and bowed causing her to remove her weight and retreat. 'It won't hold.'

'It's just springy,' said James, seeing the root plate rise from the dark crevice and then return. 'The roots are holding; try again. It will only be for a moment till you give me your hand.'

Williams spun around and called out to her, assessing the drop and the narrowest of footholds, watching as she trusted to James's assurance and the time thickened roots buried within the cracks and crannies of the granite blocks. The rowan bent as she threw her other hand, arcing into James's own. Swiftly, he clasped the wrist with both hands and felt pulled forward by the weight as the tree began to bend below. The post slipped through his calves before he clasped his bony ankles around the only thing now preventing them both from falling to their deaths. Emily scrabbled against the cliff face, treading air until her small feet gained purchase and she let go of the tree. The stem rose slightly but did not recover to its full forty-five degrees. It dangled tantalisingly close to Williams who reached out, using it to lever himself to within a grasping distance of Emily's feet. James forced his knees into the unyielding ground struggling to retract into an A-frame and pull her back to safety. At that moment, the roots of the tree emerged, straining under the greater weight of the much heavier man.

'Do you believe who I say I am?' she said, her fingers splayed through the grip of James's hand. 'I must know.'

'I do,' he replied, straining to pull. 'Not ... a good ... time to—'

'Then know us,' she said wrapping her fingers around his wrist. 'Know us all!'

Her eyes dilated further and retracted like a rapidly adjusting camera as James felt a new and conflicting presence in his mind. No longer the gentle grace he had felt at their first contact on the promenade bench; this was raw, unbridled feelings expressed in a rapid montage of powerfully emotive memories, film-like but so overwhelming that James barely made sense of where his own experiences lay among those of the woman, or women, dangling below.

The flashbacks flicked through his mind like a thick catalogue of moving photographs, snapshots of different times and places. He saw through a woman's eyes, blonde hair streaked across the top of her simple linen nightgown, to her father's face, grim and melancholy, witnessing the birth of his grandchild from a fine room devoid of comforts; a plain and kindly serving woman's anxious face, hands clasping the three-stoned necklace protectively until May Dene returned from a tryst with her beloved Richard. He saw and smelled the resinous pine woods of the headland, thicker and more extensive, rising in thick belts from the small fishing village of St Jude with its quay newly under construction. He heard a pistol fire, not the gunshot from earlier but the crack of some earlier ancient and powdered weapon, as the eyes he looked through turned from the murderous soldier breaking from the trees and raced towards the cliff edge. James caught sight of several three-rigged sailing ships in the bay as the ground disappeared leaving only a rush of air and a sudden fearful falling.

He stared back into her eyes, reflecting his astonishment

as he shared the collective experience of all that she had witnessed and experienced over the past two hundred years. The countless souls driven to despair, the reaching out to prevent them from the jump to final and silent oblivion, and her confusion why she still lingered beyond her mortal body. He witnessed her first non-corporeal experiences, the changing of many lonely seasons, the fall and decline of ships and houses, including her own. A horseless carriage appeared one spring day bumping and banging its noisy passengers to the newly admired beauty spot. Time blurred the fleeting moments until high above, he saw the first flying machine and the cries from holidaymakers, emerging from their wooden changing huts wheeled out on the beach. They splashed in their all-in-one swimsuits and pointed excitedly at the fabric winged plane bobbing below the clouds, as a man wound a tripod-mounted camera to capture the scene.

James held on as the image of his father, younger, vigorous, and confused listened intently in a sterile room. He heard heated conversations in a corridor outside and the distinctive booming voice of Cameron Fellows disagreeing with his superior. Pain and confusion enveloped his senses as he left a scene with a midwife and the removal of a child from a raving mother. A nurse bustled past his father, who was dressed unusually in casual clothing and looking haggard, as though being called in to some midnight emergency. He dragged a small child, barely six years old, as he hurried to sign paperwork on a high desk as the boy maintained an iron hold of the toy robot figure in his hand. James recognised the droid and the soiled sci-fi T-shirt he had rarely removed as a child.

'We've met before; briefly,' he said in his mind. 'Emily and I have met before?'

She fixed his gaze and flashed her eyes in recognition.

At that moment, he knew what Emily had been going

through. He knew for certain that his diagnosis was not correct. This was no mental disorder; this was a possession.

James shivered as though suddenly plunged into cold water and he saw the desperate struggle within the mind of a man, struggling against his own mental stress and that of a rough coastal sea. The man took in great gulps of water as he fought his way through to the upended dinghy and the child floundering in the water. He sensed the turmoil until calm descended with the hum of the folk tune in his mind.

'Do not be afraid, sweet nightingale is here. Let go...'

The sea smashed them together, and a middle-aged Tom Cotter dived to retrieve the drowning child. Emerging from the swell, he clung on to the boy in the faded and soiled T-shirt until the boats behind began to emerge from around the end of the quay. The boy spluttered and James looked upon himself, aged six, as though reflected in a mirror.

'You?' said James looking down into the woman's knowing face.

A final image presented itself and the mirage of sailing ships returned to the bay as a feeling of intense vertigo and falling gripped his senses. He saw himself rushing to the broken barrelled beach below, through the last moments of May Dene's mortal life, falling from the same spot he now returned to look down upon as the vision faded. What remained was a sense of such intense loneliness and regret that James felt his heart burst.

'I believe you,' he whispered, recovering his senses and gripping tightly as the woman below released him from her memories.

Williams threw his arm upwards to clasp at Emily's calf even as the tree uprooted like a pulled tooth. He cast it aside, and it fell with a bouncing tumble into the encroaching surf below. She yelped and kicked out, as the gripped foot left the foothold. James held on, pulled forward under tension.

'Get back to the ledge, man!' James said, grimacing with the intense physical exertion. 'You'll pull her off and you with it.'

Williams looked back and gauged the distance. With enough momentum, James realised he could make it until the idea retreated in Williams's face with the distant but approaching sirens of police cars coming up the moorland road. James knew there was no longer any escape for him, and if two would go over the cliffs, why not three? At the very least, he would seek to withhold her as a hostage. Williams tugged at the ankle, no longer using it as an anchor, but trying to dislodge the woman from the cliff and James's grasp.

'You won't take her from me!' said Williams, balancing himself on the slippery foothold and readying for another more vigorous tug.

James's arms burned with the strain, and he felt his grip slipping. He longed to let go momentarily to change position, but it wasn't an option. He pulled her inch by inch until her body became taut like a human tug-of-war. Williams tugged again pulling her lower body away from the cliff edge, and James knew he could no longer hold on to the slick, sweating skin. With one hand, he inched his fingers to grasp at the cuff of her burgundy sweatshirt, even as the fingers slipping through his grasp retreated down through the sleeve of the hooded jacket. From within the cuff, emerged the rosary beads gifted by the high-rise Jamaican woman hundreds of miles away from a similarly high place. James twined his fingers through the silvered wire connecting the painted wooden beads until it bit into her wrist, and the crease between his palm and fingers.

Save her, and you save yourself, came her words from the far away high-rise to this high place.

'Give me your other hand, for God's sake,' he said

clenching the cotton where her wrist and fingers had once been. 'I can't hold on much longer.'

'Then I will release her to you,' she said. 'Let Emily Dunn decide for herself, and I will deal with him.'

James felt the cloth begin to ride up and over as she descended closer to Williams's injured arm. He raised it, limply, as though ready to embrace her and attempt a joint return to the ledge.

'May, wait—' cried James, seeing her other arm droop, becoming out of reach.

'Fare thee well, James. Take good care of her,' she said with a brief backward glance. 'Trust me now.' The groping hand now shunted its way to just below her knee as she turned to face her tormentor with a look of pity. Williams was emboldened by the lengthening stretch of her top and James realised that one more tug might pull her free, as well as himself over the edge.

She hummed and Williams shook his head as though trying to brush off an unseen interaction or thought. James saw the man's confused face relax into one of similar serene acceptance as his mind eased and something else began to take control. Even as James began to lose his grip, Williams loosened his fingers, one by one, causing his thumb and first finger to slip to Emily's ankle. He wobbled with the sudden jerk, his free but injured arm flailing to secure him to the safety of the rock face.

With a final gentle whisper, the remaining spirit of May Dene left the body of Emily Dunn and slipped into the vacant stare of Ryan Williams.

'Don't be afraid,' she said. 'Let go!'

James caught the rapid and all-consuming dilation in the man's eyes, all but removing any presence of white. With a smile, born not from himself but the spirit of the woman now in control, Williams released his grip and fell back and outwards, spread-eagled and sailing for several seconds before striking the sands silently below. The brief stain of scarlet was quickly washed away as his limp and lifeless body lolled like a shipwrecked sailor in the rising reach of the tide.

Emily screamed as she returned to consciousness and dangled as James suddenly felt the removal of the additional weight. Twisting and banging into the wall of granite, James guided her back to the foothold as the sweatshirt beneath rolled up around her neck.

'Throw me your hand!' he called, and she thrust up her bare, tattooed arm. He caught it just above the letters of her name and began to pull her up.

The post between his legs begin to twist and he felt unable to pull himself back in time before it removed itself and he joined Williams on the sands below. He felt the post withdraw from the ground and disappear from his bloodied ankles. He shot forward to be suddenly crushed by an overwhelming weight from above, forcing his ribs and chest into the face of the first few feet of rock. James bent at the waist, his legs trapped by something heavy and shifting. A bloodied arm grabbed onto his own and James saw the twisted and blue-black blister of a dislocated middle finger. The free fingers and thumb clasped around the useless digit and hoisted up the woman along with the rest of James's strength until Emily came over the edge, pulling him into a twisting roll and back from the edge. James heaved and looked up into the bright ball of the sun breaking through the mist. The silhouette of Jory, living but now heavily breathing stared back, clutching at a dark red pool on his left shoulder.

'You damn fool,' he panted, dropping to his knees. James saw the punctured tear of the scuffed tabard and the entry point for the bullet in his bloodied white shirt. Jory's pale face smiled before he swayed back into the encircling arms of the first responder and passed out. James twisted his head to see a race of plain-clothed and uniformed officers in close pursuit of one other paramedic launching herself through the heather with an emergency response bag.

He rolled back, clutching at his ribs even as he felt the warm and comforting embrace of the woman next to him.

'Mm...May?' he whispered into the wet brown locks of her neck.

Emily gently shook her head and buried herself into his arms and shoulder. 'She's gone.'

They lay together, nestled in safe certainty until the distant sound of an air ambulance wiped all notion of the song that, for a moment he had caught drifting up, in his delirium, from the base of the cliffs below.

CHAPTER 40

'How's the shoulder?' said James sitting on the side of the hospital bed.

'Itches like hell,' said Jory, raising his swollen hand to show the bandaged middle finger strapped to the adjacent forefinger. 'This, however, keeps me up all night. Any chance of some of that morphine I had when I was brought in?'

'Not a chance, and it's only been two weeks, mate,' said Mike, professionally curious on his day off. 'Mind you, it makes a nice change from just a single finger. It will be a while before you are sharpening pencils down at the station again.'

The policeman smiled sarcastically and reached out with his undamaged hand to push forward an opened letter. 'When it's knitted back together, they are going to pin a medal on the place the bullet went in; poetic justice, don't you think?'

James lifted the commendation and smiled over at the off-duty doctor. 'We will never hear the end of this, you know.'

'What about Emily Dunn?' asked Jory. 'Is she and her baby alright?'

'Both doing well,' said Mike, glancing over at James and

shuffling his feet. 'She was moved to the Royal Free Hospital this morning before being transferred to the local mental health & social care trust.'

'So soon?' said James.

Mike studied the floor. 'Harriet wanted you to say goodbye this afternoon, but Caroline overruled her when she found out you were here. Seems she wants to avoid any further media speculation about missing treasure and Maiden Point as it relates to a patient still in her care, not to mention your wellbeing.'

'What's that all about?' said Jory, sensing the sadness in James's face.

'Nothing important,' said James, returning to a smile. 'She's right this time, I'm sure.'

The door opened, and a nurse entered to gain their attention. 'Sorry to interrupt, Dr Marshall, but the coun-sellor said you are wanted back at St Jude; a man is asking for you, one of Dr Trebarr's patients I believe, but he's being adamant with the staff that he needs to see you personally.'

James rose and looked blankly at the woman. 'Did she give a name?'

The nurse nodded. 'Says it's an elderly gentleman called Tom Cotter; says he has a secret to tell you.'

Jory rolled his eyes. 'Not another one. What is it this time?'

James shrugged. 'I'll need to sort it out. None of us are there and he can get a little excitable if ignored, despite his recent run of form. Tell her I'll be back as soon as I can and I'll meet him on my mother's bench in the hospital garden to give everyone a little peace.'

The nurse turned to go, and James bid farewell to his companions. He reached into his trouser pocket and placed a worn, brown plastic toy figure on the bed.

'I think Karen and I would like you to have this, seeing as you are the only one never to own it.'

Jory's eyes lit up as he grasped the Star Wars character.

'Just until you get your medal,' joked Mike. 'Then I want it back.'

'I've got a secret,' said Tom, grinning with toothless abandon on the bench.

'I know,' said James, smiling back. 'Your sweet nightingale is back, but—' He looked behind at the new and enlarged plaque on the rail for inspiration and the right words. The brass gleamed with the names of both parents, in stark contrast to the black marble of their shared memorial at the churchyard further up the hill.

'She's left us both again, Tom.'

The old man's face contorted into sadness. 'She said she might and that this time you'd understand more about why I am like I am.'

'I do,' said James. 'I never thanked you for saving my life all those years ago, and for being so brave.' Tom leaned forward and buried his arms between his thighs.

'Tweren't me,' he whispered. ''Twas her. That's the first secret and I ain't told many.'

'I know what you mean, Tom, but the sweet nightingale told me she couldn't have done it without you being good-hearted by nature.'

Tom shifted his shoulders, embarrassed and unused to compliments.

'It was so long ago before I had all me other problems, but just for that moment, and again that time down on the promenade when she came back and stroked my hand, I felt safe and calm again.' He turned to James with a profound

394

expression of thankfulness. 'And to tell you the truth, I still do; it's a marvel. I haven't touched a drop since then.'

'I'm proud of you,' said James watching as Tom returned to look out to the harbour.

'Do you remember a woman called Angela Dunn?'

James saw a small quiver of recollection in his cheek and a developing smile. 'I knew an Angie Dunn, once, but she went away. Folks said I scared her off, but I didn't do anything, not beyond what courting couples are supposed to do when there's no one around.' He glanced over and winked. 'I think I might have been in love with her, but it was so long ago. She had a secret, too, but she never got round to telling me before she went away.' He glanced over. 'Thank you for reminding me of her; I didn't feel so lonely. Why do they all go away and leave me?'

'When the time is right,' said James, I think you'll find her secret may come back one day, soon, and offer you some answers, as well as many more questions.'

Tom looked blankly back before staring thoughtfully at an accompanied child swinging beneath the monkey bars of the climbing frame. James waited to see any sudden change in his demeanour with the unverified suggestion of him being a father, let alone a grandfather next year. His face glowed briefly in comprehension before returning to look at his scuffed tan leather shoes. 'You talk like you are going daft – like me.'

'I'll take that as a compliment.' James smiled and hesitantly put his arm around the old man. 'I wanted to say thank you, Tom, for pulling me out of the water all those years ago, but also to say sorry if I was ever cruel to you as a child. I didn't understand and I deeply regret any teasing or shameful behaviour.'

Tom nodded. 'You're Jimmy, aren't you – the kiddie I saved who turned into a psychic doctor?'

James withdrew his arm and offered his hand. 'Psychiatrist, Tom. Dr James Marshall, alive thanks to you.'

Tom shook it. 'She told me to tell the kiddie I saved about my new secret. She said you'd know where to find it.' He tapped a bony finger against his thin grey hair.

'Find what?'

'No idea,' said Tom cackling, 'but she gave me the secret to tell you, and that's something, ain't it?'

'Yes. I guess she trusted you. What did she say?'

Tom looked around as though expecting the defoliating berberis and buddleias to be harbouring spies from neighbouring Devon.

He lowered his voice to a whisper and James leaned in to hear the words on his tobacco-tainted breath.

'When she said goodbye to me on the promenade the other week, she was in a hurry and going away, but she says I wasn't to be scared no more and that you'd understand it's not my fault who I am.'

'The day she went away?'

Tom frowned. 'I said so, didn't I? She comes rushing past and says she has to go away again, maybe for good this time. It was the day of the Mousehole winter lights going up because all the buses were full of them their tourists. I thought she was going off to see them.'

James thought back to the day when his worldview had been altered. Here he was talking to a man who had shared in such an experience. Who knew if Tom Cotter, least of all himself, had fully come to terms with it? James knew he had to ask himself the same question in the coming weeks and months.

Tom licked his lips as though relishing the captive audience. 'She said that the most valuable jewel is inside here—' He thumped his chest. 'A selfless heart.'

'Very true,' said James. 'It's a shame that we have to keep

things like that a secret. I think the world would be a nicer place if we—'

'That ain't the secret,' said Tom, 'and stop interrupting lest I forget it; it goes in and out like them other people in my head that no-one believes in either.'

'Sorry,' said James, pretending to zip his mouth. 'Please continue.'

Tom turned with a look of joyous epiphany as he came to the end of his missive, like a herald delivering the news across a vast ocean from one distant monarch to another.

'Sweet nightingale says there's something important about a place where "the past is a different country"; she said you'd know where that was.'

James strode along the promenade. He blew into his cold hands now that his head was clear from the day's travels and travails. He felt upset that he had only briefly been allowed to see Emily in the days that followed. His own cracked rib was healing fast though getting in and out of the hire car still reminded him of the day, and of the wide, gentle blue eyes that sometimes appeared in his dreams to wake him feeling refreshed and calm. Despite his gentle probing, and the hints and riddles filtered back from the care team, he concluded that two women had gone up to Maiden Point on that fateful day, but only one had returned. No sign or memory of May Dene was evident. He thought of the empty room at the refuge and its impending closure, wondering what could have been if only the charity had received the funding to help others in similar, but not identical circumstances. The thought of the jewelled necklace in the glasses case came to mind and whether it would return on a tide one day or remain forever lost, swept out to sea.

James leaned on the dressed granite wall overlooking the setting sun, dipping into a rich November layer of honey, hanging above the horizon. He felt a weight lifted from his shoulders, most recently with his conscience and apology to Tom who had suffered the scorn and cruelty of his youth. The thought of Emily Dunn, or May Dene, had passed on something to him, in the foreknowledge, she was being hounded and under threat was courageous. That she had encountered Tom Cotter and stopped at great risk and on her way to the church to impart a parting message felt intimate. With the removal of responsibility came the realisation that something deeply personal was missing, but that he had discovered something about himself and his family that would sustain and guide him for the rest of his days.

'Penny for your thoughts?' said Harriet, startling him from his introspection.

James turned and smiled. 'If I take you up on that offer, you might find yourself quite wealthy by the time I'm finished.'

'Emily Dunn or May Dene?' she said jerking a finger to the bench behind.

James sat down alongside her and crossed his legs. 'Both, in a manner of speaking. I hope you don't think all personality cases are like this?'

Harriet zipped up her fleece and buried her hands into her pockets. 'Is that what you still think this was?'

James pursed his lips and gripped the underside of the bench seat. 'When in doubt use Occam's Razor; it's just I've learned that the simplest explanation might just be one that is staring us in the face all along, providing we dare to include it within our open mind and see where it leads.'

'Coincidences, you mean?'

He shrugged as she continued. 'Thank you for your apology, about my interference by telling Mike, I mean. I hope this didn't play a part in your decision to move on.'

James creased into a smile and turned to the distant cliffs. 'It didn't. Recent events encouraged me to decide. Just like the names of places, I am evolving from psychiatry into whatever comes next. I'm free from any pressure to continue and be more than I need to be, which, at the moment, is better than the feeling of any protective influence. I can sleep easy now and practice what I preach, learning to live with me, rather than who I should be.' He turned back to see her smile.

'I owe you an apology, too. I was truthful about you being formative in my decision to move into counselling from the lecture where we first met, even if you don't remember.' She held up a hand to stop his interruption. 'I thought I was coming to see your father when I booked my ticket.'

James laughed. 'That's very honest of you, and you got to see him in the end. I think wherever he is now that he would be laughing too.'

'Your unorthodox, and borderline methods aside, I am glad to have played some part in Emily's recovery, and yours.' She fidgeted with her hands. 'I know there is more to this story than you can tell either Mike or me at present, but I hope one day you'll be able to share what really happened up there.'

James nodded. 'When I've figured it all out for myself. I hear you and Mike are both official now?'

Harriet blushed. 'Kind of, or at least I think so. He's asked me to move in, to save me the journey time from Penzance.'

James raised his eyebrows. 'How thoughtful of him, and if I can leak my own secret; he's buzzing about it.' He rubbed at his neck. 'If you are coming to St Jude on a long-term basis, I'm wondering if you might be interested in keeping certain traditions alive that some local friends of mine are looking to re-establish?'

'I've already been approached by Stephanie,' she said with a wink. 'Seems the entry bar has just been lowered to allow an outsider into their secret society. I understand it involves crafting and the consumption of wine, both of which I fully endorse. The woman in charge wants to move it from autumn to sometime in the spring; more hopeful – new life, and all that.'

She patted his knuckles clenched around the knee rail and twitched her head towards the dark brooding massif of the distant headland. 'Whatever you did up there, and leading up to it, procedurally sound or not, has resulted in a woman returning to what might be described as miraculous normality.

'I wonder what it must be like to have other personalities sharing in your life.'

James studied her face for any hint of probing, but the young round face simply offered a thoughtful expression to follow her question.

'I think it would be life-changing,' said James cryptically before changing the subject. 'Speaking of which, it was on this very spot I first properly got to know her. He tapped at the engraved quotation. "The past is a different country,"; she seemed to take a special comfort from that—' James clenched the bench and leaned forward sharply, running his fingers beneath the underside of the rail as though playing the keys of an inverted piano.

Harriet twisted and watched the search. 'I'd be careful of what you find beneath there; the school kids sit on it while waiting for the bus.'

James shifted his right hand over several disgustingly soft and thankfully indeterminable items, hard metal nuts bolting the wooden knee rail and general stickiness until, halfway along, his fingers met with something at once cold, hard, and irregular, embedded within a soft, malleable gum. Harriet shifted away as he scrabbled with both hands to grip and prise off the delicate chain-like object from the gelatinous goo that bound it to the underside of the bench. He retrieved his hand and tore away the stretched fortnight old mastic to reveal the three-stoned necklace enveloped in hardened pink, cherry-scented bubblegum.

'Oh, my G—' said Harriet, raising her hands to stifle her mouth. 'It's—'

James's heart thudded with recognition and excitement as he peeled and discarded the soft surroundings to reveal the Dene necklace.

'Coincidence,' he said, completing the sentence for her and tipping a wink. 'And also, a future.'

'For you? You said you were moving on. Planning to move someplace warm?'

James shook his head, looking back to the headland. The first early evening stars glittered above Maiden Point. 'No. A future for every Emily Dunn that's still out there – a refuge, or several of them, that will never close or end so long as there are enough souls with selfless hearts in this world to keep them open.'

EPILOGUE

J ames pulled back his hood and felt the remnants of the spring squall sting his uncovered cheeks. The low sun broke through the backlit, fire-rimmed cloud on the horizon, scattering its welcome warmth upon the churning sea out past the cliff edge of Maiden Point. He removed a glove with his teeth and reached inside the backpack at his feet for the music box.

'One last lullaby,' he said out loud and alone. 'Before the museum puts it on display. For Karen, Isobel and you, if you are, or were, ever really there.'

He turned the key and opened the lid, lifting the box to release the soothing sound.

The melody played, accompanied by an orchestra of wave-crashing percussion. Gulls cried like flutes as they soared above the cliff face to descend, in harmony with the beautiful and haunting motif. The background rustle of the breeze coming off the downs to meet the sea sifted like cymbals through the rattle of spent seed heads and the tips of new grass. As the music ended, he closed the lid, leaving nothing but the coastal sounds of the headland, natural, untamed, and devoid of man's influence once more.

For a moment, he watched the turbulence of the high tide against the base of the cliff. The waves battered against the indomitable headland to little effect, and he thought of his trials from the previous year. He had withstood them all, changed by the previous year of misfortune but tempered by trial and a fresh sense of purpose. James sought for fitting words to mark the solely attended memorial but was interrupted by an approaching figure fighting against the sea-breeze in a rain-splattered waterproof.

'I'm not planning to jump, Caroline,' said James as the approaching woman lowered her hood.

'You'd better not,' she said, handing him a photograph in a plastic sleeve from her breast pocket. 'Not until you've seen this first.'

James gripped the waterproof food bag against the wind and peered through the clear plastic at the Polaroid image of a couple. The smiling face of the man arrested at the refuge sat perched upon a bed wherein lay the happy, but exhausted face of Emily Dunn. A baby lay wrapped in her arms, nestled between the two of them.

'Born four days ago, a little girl – seven and a half pounds; he sent it with her blessing.'

'Did Pavel say what they were going to do?'

'They have decided to go back to Romania, to start again. He's true to his word; he and his family will take good care of them both. She needs to put distance between what happened here and in London, at least for the baby's sake.'

James turned the photograph over and smiled.

Hoping grace has left you far from where it found you. Love MD.

'May Dene?' asked James.

Caroline shook her head, blowing on chapped hands. 'The baby's name is May, but it's May Dunn,'

'No sign of—?'

She looked down at the music box in the crook of James's left arm. 'No resurfacing of May Dene's personality, and it should stay that way, which is why I removed her from St Jude to prevent any relapse or—'

'Recurrence?'

'Following all the circumstantial coincidences surrounding this case, yes.'

James studied the sea-thrift and stonecrop, fluttering their bright bubblegum pink flower heads in the clifftop crevices. 'You did the right thing, even if I was resistant or put out; I just felt personally responsible for her recovery. It would have been selfish and wrong of me to have her relive all those painful memories and the traumatic events that happened here just to satisfy my curiosity or confirm what I believe to be true.'

Caroline leaned over at the grassy narrow ledges and stepped back with a shiver. 'Emily has recollections from her experience and questions that could be answered in time through more conventional talking therapies, but I don't think she needs to know about the more esoteric and unexplainable elements in the report, now heavily redacted, filed at your exit interview with Fellows – wouldn't you agree?'

He raised the lid of the box and placed the bagged photograph upon the faded blue velvet within. 'You wouldn't believe my interpretation, or Fellows's for that matter. Let's just say we have agreed to disagree on certain matters, but in exchange for my hide, and an honourable discharge, I gave him a full account that he cannot act upon in his retirement and will finally close the chapter with my father. If he ever went to his peers, or the public, with my testimony, they would discount my account based on my deteriorating mental health at the time.'

'There was more at play here than coincidence and your

collusion with Fellows. It makes this look as though it was a run-of-the-mill case with a rogue psychiatrist that was in the right place at the right time...'

James shrugged innocently and returned her probing stare with a look of sheer ignorance.

'Which it was not.' she added. 'Both you and my predecessor know it.'

James deflected the subject. 'You got the promotion, then?'

She shrugged and looked out to sea. 'I officially start at the beginning of May, the week after Deborah Gayle leaves for pastures new. Seems the Board took exception to her fabricating the Lee's request to have you removed.' Caroline leaned over and brushed her nose against his ear. 'I could try to wring it from you...' She bit her bottom lip and James saw the vulnerability in her proposal and her face.

'You could try,' he said, smiling and holding out a hand. 'But if this is some ruse about trying to get me to take your old job, then I'm not interested. I feel relieved, you know. Free to follow my own path not laid by my father, Fellows or anyone else.'

She placed her hand in his, feeling her swing it gently back and forth. 'Probably for the best if both of us are not in Truro; you know how tongues wag and all that. Do you still mean to go on with your plan to oversee the new hostel and refuge premises, alongside St Jude's own? Nice touch renaming it after your mother; I approve.'

He indicated toward the wooded valley. 'The planning has been approved to rebuild alongside the ruins, which we hope to turn into a mini walled garden or glass-roofed atrium for horticultural therapy and craft training. The council are on board as well as the charity. They've called it "The Dene"; it has a certain charm as well as relevance, don't you think?'

Caroline squeezed his hand in unspoken agreement. 'I

understand you got over four times the initial estimate for the necklace. Why did you sell through a private auction and keep things secret?'

'Legend has no quantifiable value, but the winning bid yielded a higher price, more than enough to refurbish the existing refuge and build the new one up at Carmalt,' said James. 'The wealthy individual turns out to be distantly related and shares my view that it should remain a belief, whatever the locals may discover, that it went over the edge last November. The museum made me an offer but it would have put an abrupt end to something intangibly part of the fabric of the place – mystery, and a connection to a collective spirit of place. They've agreed to accept the box on loan as a sweetener, and to keep silent.'

'Do you have something personal against metal detectorists? The beach, and the town, are likely to be filled with them this summer looking for treasure that isn't there.'

James smiled, released her hand and crept forward to peer down over the edge at the sun glittered milky spill of sand stretching south to the coastal town. 'Let them come and experience this beautiful place; that's more than enough recompense for time spent hunting for legends. Traditions are healthy; they bind communities and families through time. In the end, what we hold most dear are our memories of those who have gone before us, those that have continued to hand over the past into our hands for us to carry forward to new guardians.'

'You hold more secrets than that box or Fellows's filing cabinet,' said Caroline, glancing around at the empty heath. 'I thought I'd find you up here, and I didn't want you to be alone; not today.'

'A year ago today,' said James, feeling her comforting arm around his waist. 'I've stopped feeling guilty for not thinking about Karen every time I wake up, and there are life-changing events from last year still to process.' A gull soared above them, crying out among the sound of the crashing surf below.

'You missed the townswomen making the willow maiden over earlier; there were a lot of spectators. They have changed the date to allow more people to attend. Given the interest, they felt it appropriate to broaden its appeal as well as its membership.'

'The romantic in you thinks May Dene was watching; am I right?' said Caroline pulling him closer.

'Yes,' replied James, sliding an arm across to fulfil the embrace. 'And the Cornish in me hopes she continues to do so, for us all.'

———

'What is it,' said James, bouncing the toddler on his knee while clamping the phone between cheek and shoulder. I was in the middle of Eddie's—'

'Meet me at the hospital as soon as you can; it's important.' said Caroline, flustered and out of breath. 'I've called Stephanie, and she's on her way to look after our little man.'

'Is everything alright, you're not hurt or—'

'No, it's not anything like that. Harriet called me when she couldn't get hold of you.'

'I was trying to get him to sleep before I headed up to The Dene, but he had other ideas; my phone was on silent, downstairs until a few moments ago. Why does she need me? She's in charge at St Jude now I'm only there twelve hours a week. I don't understand—'

'You will, now hurry and get him ready for Stephanie; she'll be there in—'

James turned to the window to see the temporary babysitter pull into the drive.'

'She's here already.'

'Then what are you still doing on the line you great lump,' James put down the boy and was about to end the call when his wife interjected with a closing line.

'I'm sorry I doubted you over this two years ago,' she said and hung up.

———

James parked and ran into the reception. Caroline was waiting, arms folded and clenching her forearms with her fingers.

'What is it? You're nervous. Is it Mike, Jory—'

She shook her head and dragged him along the corridor to the triage room. 'Jory picked up an attempted suicide case two hours ago, as the beach was clearing. He received reports of a middle-aged woman acting strangely near the cliffs, ready to jump.'

'Not someone we know?'

'Not as such,' said Caroline swinging open the door. 'Another one of your coincidences.'

James walked in to see the back of the sergeant, seated and taking notes in front of a pulled screen. The sounds of a nurse, whispering words of comfort, came from beyond. 'All done,' she said, sliding back the curtain. 'Don't get the dressings wet, okay?'

Caroline closed and leaned with her back to it, rotating a golden ring on the third finger of her left hand. She studied a figure bandaged and bruised who sat on the edge of the raised trolley bed. A woman in her late forties sat hunched and dazed, dirty feet protruding from a hospital gown. Her long blonde hair partially covered a black eye, and she brushed it aside to reveal further defensively gained bruises on her forearm. The nurse collected the stainless tray and pressed past Caroline. 'I'll be back later; the doctor is on his way.'

The policeman turned, face confused and seeking answers for himself and the blank notebook before him. 'She's been asking for you,' said Jory. 'For the past two hours.'

'Marshall,' said the battered woman. Her cut lip quivered as she raised her dilated grey eyes to catch sight of him.

He stooped before her, listening as her quiet hum became louder and more confident. Her legs swung like a child as she accompanied the song.

'Can you give me your name, Ms,' said Jory, 'now that Dr Marshall is here?'

The woman paused as though recalling something from memory on the tip of her tongue. 'Marshall knows,' she said. 'Her name is Paula, but—'

James watched as her face relaxed with a fresh recollection '—father calls me ... May.'

'It's a copycat,' whispered the sergeant, rubbing at his shoulder. 'Tell me we aren't going down that path again.'

James stood and stooped forward, offering his ear close to her cracked lips.

'What two words?' he whispered, flicking his eyes across to his wife, hand raised over her mouth, and leaning against the door.

The woman moved towards a hair's breadth of his lobe and James felt the air gently brush against his ear and cheek with the near-silent sounds of the phrase that no other living could know.

'Shall I call Fellows?' said Caroline, wide-eyed and unmoving.

'No,' he said, recovering from a moment's silent shock. She reached out to brush a finger lightly across the back of his palm. He twisted to catch something familiar in the stranger's dilated eyes and he knew her, and all those that had gone before.

A beautiful smile of recognition ran across her battered face as he stood up and rubbed his hands through his hair in astonishment. 'Get lots of paper, and a pen, and then I want everyone out.'

'So, James,' she said holding up her arms to show the full extent of physical abuse. 'Shall we begin? She needs your help and won't come out until it's safe.'

She cocked her head. 'Would you perchance have any bubble-gum?'

The End

GET EXCLUSIVE CONTENT

Thank you for reading *Maiden Point*.

Building a relationship with my readers is the very best thing about writing. I send monthly newsletters with details on new releases, special offers and other news relating to my books.

Sign up to my readers' group at www.jtcroft.com or by scanning the QR code below, and I'll send you further stories in my collection, *Free Spirits,* exclusive to my reader's group– you can't get this anywhere else.

AFTERWORD

The story behind the novel began with a powerful image of waves breaking against a rugged headland. Something relentless and overpowering in nature and spirit crashing against an equally indomitable force like the toughest of Cornish granite. The emotive words of the writer, Anne Lamott, came to me like a whisper from my own clifftop edge, deep inside. Long ago, grace found me and left me in a different place, and it is no coincidence that my first heroine, Grace Meadows, from my first novel, *A House of Bells*, shares the name and sentiment much like the central characters in *Maiden Point*.

I wanted a story that would envelop the feelings and struggles of those left behind from arguably the most life-changing events I could imagine, with a central character whose counsel to others was difficult to accept on a personal level. The notion that something supernatural, as my readers might expect, was never in doubt and is implicit from the very beginning in both novels. The questions that arose in this case was how would a 'returned' suicide cope with advice and support from one still coming to terms with their own perceived failings? Who, exactly, is helping who, on a pathway to recovery?

My first glimpse of Emily Dunn was sitting alone, overlooking the sea. The sun glinted on the brass plaque of the bench as she warmed her face and removed the spent bubblegum to stick a jewelled object beneath the seat like a generous Jay bird without a nest of trinkets of her own. The giving up of her most valuable possession was miniscule in comparison with the loss for other aspects of life, tasted periodically and enhanced by brief experiences through time, and regretfully abandoned once the saving of a soul was complete or could no longer bear fruit.

May Dene's returns to save those in need, like a supernatural lifeguard or guardian angel, were far from being a punishment for her own remorse and her inability to 'let go', and much more about her innate, all-consuming and caring spirit that could not be dampened even by death. We all have a longing to know that someone, somewhere is looking out for us, whether that be a parent, a friend, a God, or those anonymous angels that are not always in the alcoves of churches. Sometimes we need to look out for them, too.

Kept alive by the memories of others, like May, one never truly dies. That is a great comfort to me even when the pain of losing someone can be difficult to relinquish, like a priceless jewel, as the last connection to what or who we have lost. The inability to make new memories with those no longer present is tempered by time and the back catalogue that must now sustain us.

Be as enduring as granite from whatever the storms of life may hurl against you – erosion is a natural process that often reveals new strength from within. May your spirit and the relationships you have formed endure beyond this life as impenetrable crystal in the minds and memories of those left behind to face new tides.

J. T. Croft
March 2022

ALSO BY J. T. CROFT

Bric-a-Brac

Firelight and Frost

Maiden Point

A House of Bells

High Spirits

Midnight's Treasury

"Dead Brilliant"

"An author whose storytelling really hits the mark"

"Beautifully dark and bittersweet"

ABOUT THE AUTHOR

J. T. Croft is the author of Gothic fiction, supernatural mystery and ghostly short stories.
For more information:
www.jtcroft.com

I hope you enjoyed reading this book as much as I loved writing it. If you did, I'd really appreciate you leaving me a quick review on whichever platform you prefer. Reviews are extremely helpful for any author, and even just a line or two can make a big difference. I'm independently published, so I rely on good folks like you spreading the word!

facebook.com/jtcroftauthor

x.com/jtcroftauthor

instagram.com/jtcroftauthor

Printed in Great Britain
by Amazon

34328000R00243